Interactions

Battling Demons, Volume 8

Kris Morris

Published by Kris Morris, 2018.

INTERACTIONS

First edition. January 12, 2018.

Written by Kris Morris.

This is an unauthorized work of fiction based on a television series. All royalties paid to the author will be donated to TheHorseCourse, a children's charity in Dorset, England.

Thank you to my dear husband for believing in me, my sons for inspiration, and my friends Carole, Shauna, Abby, Janet, Judy, and Anneke for ceaseless encouragement and for tolerating my insecurities.

Special thanks to my dear friends, Abby Bukofzer, Janet Setness, and Shauna Croft, as well as to my husband Tim, for countless hours spent assisting me with proofreading. And to Linda Eichorst, Janet Setness, and Shauna Croft, a special thanks for assisting with marketing. And most of all, to my dear Tim for designing my book covers, tolerating the messy house and all the eating out while I'm in the thick of writing, and for letting me know he's "stinkin' proud" of me. I love you Sweetheart!

I love you all!

Chapter 1

Nautical twilight had begun to shake the village of Portwenn from its slumber as Martin looked out through the frost curtaining their bedroom window. Historically, nautical twilight was the time of day when fishermen were enticed back out to sea, hurrying to set their courses by the stars before they dissolved into the brightening sky.

Nowadays, GPS and radar have replaced the more rudimentary navigational aids of the past, but the rhythm of the village remains unchanged.

The Helen Claire, Ewan and Peder Teague's blue and white craft, bobbed slowly past the harbour walls. Her fishing buoys, like brightly-coloured party balloons, festooned the nets ready to be unfurled at a moment's notice.

It would, no doubt, be a miserable day on the water for the Teague boys, but as proper Cornishmen, they endured the cold and wet with few complaints.

Words Martin hadn't thought of in years ran through his head. *What good is the warmth of summer without the cold of winter to give it sweetness?* As a boy, he had been unable to reconcile the quote from the John Steinbeck novel with his own experiences.

Perhaps there was a time before his earliest rememberings that the dank, dark days of the coldest season left him feeling a bit more sanguine about the impending holidays. But to his recollection, the inverse had been true. The knowledge that the sweetness of summers with Auntie Joan would sharpen the misery of winters at boarding school tempered his enthusiasm for the holidays.

He grunted softly before reaching for his dressing gown, thankful his position as the village GP would keep him inside the warmth of the surgery.

He glanced over to the bed when two small snorts caught in his wife's nose, and he nudged her on to her side.

Louisa had never embraced the breathing strips that could have easily alleviated the problem that required his periodic manual intervention. And his occasional digressions into medical discourse on the consequences of obstructive sleep apnoea were met with cold stares.

He tucked the duvet up around her neck and fastened his sash around him before forcing his feet into his slippers. Then, he headed downstairs to start breakfast.

He had just filled his cup with espresso when the doorbell sounded with a *brring*. "God," he grumbled. Coffee sloshed on to the table as he set it down with a thunk. He yelped, shaking the piping-hot liquid from his hand before lumbering through the lounge.

Pulling the front door open, he was met by their local police constable.

"What is it, Penhale? It's not even seven o'clock."

"Just thought you might appreciate a heads up, Do-*c*. There's been a water main break at the intersection of Back Hill and New Road—pipe froze." Joe's already tight-lipped face grew grimmer, and his leather jacket squeaked as he pulled his arms up, hooking his thumbs over his duty belt. "It came over my scanner about ten minutes ago."

The policeman's pretentious expression might have added an air of gravity to the situation if not for his well-known proclivity towards histrionics.

Martin shook his head. "And?"

"Looks like Old Faithful going off." Joe leaned back against the door frame, his eyes drifting as he stared absently past the doctor. "I've always wanted ta see Old Faithful," he mused. "Mother Nature in all her ... *geyser-ly* glory." His characteristically gormless grin spread across his face. "You ever see it, Doc?"

"No. Is there a point to this, Penhale?"

"Just want to keep you abreast of a potentially problema-*tic* situation. The boys are trying to get sandbags put out to *di*-vert the water, and they've got a crew working on getting it shut off. But there's likely to be some disruption to the village water supply."

"Are you telling me the surgery won't have potable water today?"

"Not sayin' that, Doc. But your water might not be safe to drink. I told Mrs. Clyde down at the market to set aside some gallon jugs for you. They've got rather nice handles on 'em by the way—makes 'em *quite* portable, actually."

The doctor rolled his eyes.

"You want me to collect 'em for you?" Joe asked.

"Mm. Yes, I'd appreciate—erm, that would be helpful."

Given the opportunity to be of assistance to the man he admired, the constable's already broad grin stretched wider. "I'm on it, Doc," he said before pointing a finger at him. "You stay right there—out of the elemen-*ts*. Oh, and Louiser's probably going to want to cancel school today."

"Why?"

Joe wrinkled up his nose. "You know, the whole water thing."

"Well, can't someone get some bottled water over there?"

Joe tipped his head down and peered up at him with a you-should-know-better look on his face. "*That* could be bad for the kiddies."

"Why?" Martin asked before grimacing. "Ohhh, Bert's not peddling his Chateau Sainte Marie again, is he?"

"Chateau Sainte Marie? Sounds French—and potentially dodgy. I'll need to have a friendly conversation with Mr. Large—*re*-fresh his memory about the required VAT and excise duty on said goods."

"You needn't bother, Penhale."

"I have to bother, Doc; it's the law. As a sworn officer of the law, I'm duty-bound to uphold it. And maybe I need to refresh *your* memory as well. The kiddies shouldn't be drinking wine. It could pose a health hazard to their under-developed minds."

Opening his mouth to explain about the portly restaurateur's short-lived side job bottling cryptosporidium-laced water, the doctor thought better of it and snapped his lips together. It was far too early in the morning to relive that ugly, dysenteric episode from his early days as the village GP.

Martin shook his head. "Why do you say bottled water could be bad for the children?"

"Well, think about it, Doc. Those boys and girls sittin' all day—drinkin' bottled water—with *in*-operative toilets and all."

"You mean there's no water at all at the school? I just made coffee; we have water here."

"Don't understand the ins and outs of it. But Sam Boyd, down at the water plant, says parts of the village are out of water completely. But the entire village is under a boil order due to po-*tential* contamination. You'll probably want to apprise Louiser of the situation."

"Yes," Martin said, making a move to swing the door shut.

Joe put his hand out to stop its forward momentum. "Got another little problem we need to discuss. Fore Street's like an ice rink."

"Get barricades up, then, or the village idiots will be ploughing down the hill and into the pub."

"I'm already on top of it."

"Mm ... right."

The constable took a step back and hoisted his duty belt. "You should be prepared for possible casualties—can't guarantee a determined *ju*venile delinquen-*t* or two won't make it past the barriers—go for a joyride down the hill. I'll be back with that bottled water," he said before turning to leave.

Martin latched the door behind him as his wife came down the stairs with James in her arms. "Did I hear Joe Penhale?"

He turned at the sound of her voice, his hand immediately drawn to his son's head. "Mm, yes. It seems there's been a water main break at Back Hill and Fore Street. We're supposed to boil our water before drinking it. Penhale's collecting some bottled water for use here at the surgery."

"Oh, that's nice of him."

Martin winced and grunted as James flopped forward against his chest, pulling at his dressing gown.

"Careful, James. You're getting too big to be doing that to your daddy," Louisa said, shifting him to her opposite hip.

She gave the boy an adoring mother's smile as she toyed with a curl at the end of his lengthening locks. "Well, I guess I better see if Pippa can pick up some bottled water for the kids at the school."

"Mm. There's no water service to the school at all."

"What? Not even to the lavatories?"

"Not according to Penhale. And as I understand it, bottled water is bad for children exposed to inoperative toilets."

She tipped her head and peered up at him quizzically. "Okay. Well, I s'pose we can't risk that. I'll call Stu Mackensie and let him know—tell him to call Caroline at the radio station so she can make the announcement that there won't be school today."

"There won't be no school today? Yippee!" Evan shrieked from the top of the stairs.

A jolt of adrenaline coursed through Martin's veins, and he slapped a hand to his chest. "For God's sake, Evan!"

"Shh. He's just excited, Martin," Louisa said softly, giving him a reproachful look. "It's not often school's cancelled."

"Mm," he grunted. "Evan—there won't be *any* school today."

"I know; I heard. Remember, I gots good—"

"*Yes*, you have good ears," Martin said before huffing out a breath.

The boy flew down the steps, bouncing up and down in front of him. "Ya wanna play with our train in the shed, Dr. Ellig-am? I gots all day now!"

"Well, unfortunately, I don't. I have patients this morning."

Plopping on to the bottom step, the child heaved out a breath. "Then what *am* I gonna do today?"

"Well, first of all, you can go back upstairs and change out of your school uniform," Louisa said, giving a jerk of her head. "Then, come out to the kitchen and you can help me make breakfast."

The boy gave her a grin and clambered up the steps.

"Evan!" Martin called out.

"Yeah?"

"Don't drink the water from the tap. It could be contaminated."

Stopping at the top of the stairs, the seven-year-old screwed up his face. "You mean like your coffee?"

"Con-tam-i-nated, not caffeinated. There could be bacteria in the water, so it needs to be boiled before you can drink it. The heat will kill any bacteria. Mrs. Ellingham or I will get you water if you want it—or Poppy."

The boy hesitated. "I think I'll have milk or apple juice. Drinkin' dead bacteria would be gross," he said before disappearing down the hall.

Aside from the persistent unsolicited briefings from his patients about the water main break at the top of Fore Street, Martin's morning progressed uneventfully.

Lorna Gillett was sat in front of his desk just before half eleven as he wrote in her patient notes.

"So ... how are you doin' now, Doc?" she asked. She let her straw tote drop to the floor and her seashell bracelets clacked together.

The scratching of his pen stopped, and he peered up at her. "I don't believe you came in to inquire about my health. I'll write you a prescription for an ointment that should help clear up that rash of yours, and we'll be done here." He returned his attention to the notes in front of him.

"Sorry." Lorna sighed softly, giving him a small smile. "I can't help myself, Doc. I'm not tryin' to be nosy or anything."

She leaned over and dug around in her bag, extracting a small box wrapped in shiny, gold paper. "I've got something for you. It's nothing big—just my little thank you for taking good care of me."

She set it on the desk and nudged it towards him. "Go on, open it."

Martin's gaze flitted between the box and his patient. "This wasn't necessary. I'm just doing my job."

"Yeah, well ... that Dr. Lippolis was just doing his job, too, and look where that got me. I trust you to do right by me, and I'm grateful for that. So, please ... open it."

Air hissed from Martin's nose before he reached for the small parcel and peeled away the wrapping paper, revealing a worn jewellery box. The hinge on the lid squeaked as he pried it open. What appeared to be two oval cornflower-blue stones in square, silver settings were displayed in the faux velvet holder inside.

"They're the cufflinks I told you I was gonna make," Lorna said. She leaned forward and wagged a finger. "It's sea glass. I wanted to use gold settings but ... well, that's sterling silver."

Aware the woman lived in reduced circumstances, Martin gave her a shake of his head. "Mrs. Gillett, you really shouldn't—"

"Oh, please don't tell me yer not gonna take it, Doc. I made it especially for you. The light blue glass represents health and healing. And blue's associated with expertise, stability, and intelligence—and depth, and trust. I found those two bits over where my sister lives in Dorset—along the Jurassic Coast. There was this castle once, near Lyme Regis, see. Bits of glass and pottery still wash up on the shore there."

"Mrs. Gillett, I appreciate the gesture, but there are ethical considerations."

"Please don't say you can't accept 'em. They just wouldn't be appropriate for anyone else."

His brow furrowed as he looked across the desk at her ruddy, pleading face. Looking down, he kept his eyes fixed on the box in his hand. "Thank you, Mrs. Gillett. They're very nice."

Lorna relaxed into her chair as a smile spread across her face.

Giggles coming from the reception room caused the doctor to scowl and glance towards the door before returning his attention to his medical duties. He scrawled his name on to the signature line on his prescription pad and tore off the top sheet of paper, sliding it across his desk.

"Wash the affected area, and use the ointment twice a day. If the—" A loud thud followed by another round of high pitched giggles, brought the doctor up short.

He got to his feet. "Use the ointment twice a day. If your rash hasn't cleared up in a week, come back and see me."

A loud bang was followed closely by a series of clatters and thumps, topped off by a crash. Martin lumbered across the room, yanking the door open. "What in God's name is going on out here?" he barked, glancing about, taking quick stock of the situation.

Evan stood in the middle of the room, a hand clasped to his mouth, as James Henry turned to look at his father, wide-eyed.

"Uh, oh," the toddler said, pointing a chubby finger at the table that lay on its side and the lamp that had been flung on to the floor. "Ebby do it."

"I didn't!" The seven-year-old sucked in a breath and backed away. "I didn't do it, Dr. Ellig-am!"

"Thank you, Doc. I appreciate it," Lorna said before squeezing past him and towards the front door.

"Mm, yes."

Martin took a step forward and Evan darted under Morwenna's desk.

"What on earth happened here?" the doctor said.

Bert Large and Malcolm Raynor sat in the chairs against the wall. "I didn't do it neither, Doc. Bert knocked the table over and busted your lamp," Malcolm said.

The restaurateur held up a plump hand. "Now, don't yell at me, Doc. I was humourin' the little lads and gettin' a bit of exercise, see. Like you keep tellin' me to. I just got a bit exuberant is all."

"*Exercise?* I didn't mean in my reception room, Bert!"

"See, I knew you were gonna yell. I was just tryin' to entertain the little tykes is all."

Martin limped over to his receptionist's desk and dropped into the empty chair. "Evan, come on out from under there," he said softly. "It's all right. Come on out."

The boy hesitated before emerging, watching his guardian warily. He sat on the floor, his back pressed to the wall with his arms wrapped around his knees. "I didn't mean ta make a problem, Dr. El-lig-am," he said. "I was just tryin' ta help."

Giving his smirking patients a sideways glance, the doctor ducked down behind the desk and spoke softly to the boy. "What do you mean you were trying to help, Evan?"

The child sniffed and wiped at his eyes. "I was exercisin' 'em—so I can get adopted more quicker."

Martin crinkled an eye and cocked his head. "I'm sorry; you've lost me. You were exercising *what?*"

"Your *patients*!" Evan said, slapping his hands to his head. "You said I gots ta do it if I don't want it ta take so long."

The doctor groaned internally, remembering the conversation he'd had with his charge the previous week. "Okay, up you get," he said, giving a tug on his shirt.

James toddled over and latched on to the fixator in his father's arm, pulling at him. "Da-ee, take up."

Grimacing, Martin pried the small fingers loose before swivelling around and hooking his arm under the toddler's bum, pulling him into his lap.

"Evan, we've had a misunderstanding. This isn't, perhaps, the time or place to discuss it, but I'll explain it to you later."

"Are you cross at me, Dr. Ellig-am?" Evan asked.

"No, I'm not cross with you." He turned an angry glare to the two sheepish men in the chairs. "I *am,* however, cross with my patients who can't sit for fifteen minutes without destroying my surgery!

"Bert, clean up that mess. Mr. Raynor, go wait in my consulting room. And"—he craned his neck to look into the lounge—"Morwenna! Jeremy! Get in here!" he bellowed.

Morwenna and Jeremy hurried in from under the stairs.

"You need somethin', Doc?" his doe-eyed receptionist asked.

"Why aren't you at your desk?" he said before wagging a finger at his assistant. "And don't you have patients to screen?"

Jeremy's left eyebrow pulled up. "They've been screened, and Louisa had an emergency in the kitchen."

"What sort of an emergency? Did she hurt herself?" Martin asked, setting James down and starting for the hallway.

Evan got to his feet. "Uh-uh. *Buddy* hurt hisself. But I think he must'a been gettin' all a'barrassed about it 'cause Mrs. Ellig-am told us ta wait out here."

The seven-year-old added in a whisper, "I think it's about his bits."

"His bits?"

"Yeah. So, Mrs. Ellig-am told me and James ta keep entertainin' Mr. Large and that other guy."

Martin blinked his eyes at him before turning and ducking under the doorway, the two little boys trotting along behind.

Hunched over, Louisa glanced up when her husband stepped into the kitchen.

Martin grimaced at the sight of the little terrier, laid out on his back on the kitchen table, his legs splayed. "For heaven's sake, Louisa! That's unhygienic!"

She batted the hair from her eyes. "Would you prefer I use your consulting room, Martin?"

"See, Dr. Ellig-am," Evan said as he climbed up on a chair. "He gots a problem with his bits. Just like I told ya."

Peering over the boy, the doctor curled his lip, and his wife huffed out a breath at him.

"Don't make that face, Martin. Poor Buddy got into burdock somewhere. They're in his feet and stuck all around his ... well, you know."

The seven-year-old jabbed a finger at the dog's belly. "That's called genitals, Mrs. Ellig-am, but Dr. Ellig-am calls 'em bits."

Her lips quivered as she struggled to keep a straight face, and Evan's gaze swung between her and his guardian. "Did I say a word that's not proper?" he asked.

Peering up at him, Louisa gave her husband an impish grin. "What do you think, doctor? Is *bits* a proper word?"

He tugged at an ear. "I believe it gets the point across adequately, yes."

"I know *bits* is a proper word 'cause Dr. Ellig-am says it," the seven-year-old said, reaching out to pull at a burr before quickly jerking his hand back. "Ouch!"

"Oh, oh, oh! Be careful, Evan. Those will stick your fingers," Louisa said.

He shook his hand before sucking at the stinging appendage. "What about genitals? Is it proper 'cause it's like anu—?" The boy glanced over at his head teacher. "Sorry, Mrs. Ellig-am. I keep forgettin' you're a girl, and girls are funny about some words." The cowlick over his forehead flopped back as he tipped his head to look at Martin. "So, is geni—well, you know—is it proper like that *A* word we talked about?"

Martin took hold of the boy's head and turned it side to side. "You need a haircut. And yes, genitals is a proper word *if* used in the proper context."

"Da-ee, take up," James said, pulling at his father's trousers.

Martin looked down, putting his hand on his son's head, sighing. "I can't just now, James."

The terrier whined and began to squirm.

"You have to lie still, Buddy," Louisa said, laying a hand on the dog's chest. "Can you help me here, Martin?"

He pulled up his arm, glancing at his watch before tapping a fingernail against its face. "Louisa, you do realise I have patients who need my attention, don't you?"

"Oh, it's just Bert and Mr. Raynor. And they offered to watch the boys, so they'll be busy anyway."

"Strippedly speaking, they didn't *offer*, Mrs. Ellig-am," Evan said, his palms patting against the table. "Remember, you told 'em you had a situation in the kitchen, and James and me were gonna stay with 'em until you got it sorted. And you expected 'em ta act like 'sponsible adults."

"That was unrealistic," Martin grumbled.

Louisa shot him a dark look before turning a stiff smile to the seven-year-old. "Evan, would you please get a book from the toy basket and take James back out to the reception room. I'm sure if you ask nicely, Mr. Large would be happy to read it to you."

The child slid reluctantly from the chair. "Come on, James," he said, taking the toddler's hand and leading him away.

Louisa waited until the two boys had chosen a book and disappeared past the front door before turning to her husband, tight-lipped. "Martin, I would very much appreciate it if you would help me with the emergency at hand before you return to your patients."

He grimaced. "What do you want me to do?"

"Either hold on to Buddy or start picking out the burrs."

Glancing down the hall, he hissed out a breath. "Can't Evan hold on to him for—"

"I don't want him in here at the moment, Mar-tin. I have a headache."

"What do you mean you have a headache?" He pressed his hand to her forehead. "Describe it. Is it intense—stabbing? Or does it feel as though there's pressure build—"

"Martin, just help me—please!"

"I'm merely trying to work out whether your headache could be related to your AVM, Louisa." He pulled his torch from his pocket and tipped her head back, shining it into her eyes.

"Oh, Martin, stop it!" she said, batting his hand away. "It's just a headache."

The worry on his face softened her taut expression. "It's just a dull ache, but the last thing I need right now is to be answering Evan's questions regarding the whereabouts of Buddy's missing ... parts."

He cocked his head at her and she rolled her eyes. "You *have* noticed he's absent a couple of bits, haven't you?" she said.

Peering closer, he pulled up his bottom lip. "Ah. You mean he's been doctored."

"Yes, he's been doctored. And I'd rather not draw attention to the fact right now. So, please ... can you help me?"

"Mm, I'll get some gloves."

He returned a minute later, his hands now suitably protected, carrying a bandage scissors and forceps. They worked together for the next fifteen minutes, Buddy's shiny eyes fixed on Martin as he snipped each burr from the dog's fur.

The doctor had nearly completed his excision of the painful hitchhikers when Bert Large invited himself into the kitchen, bracing himself in the doorway as air puffed from his chest.

"Oi, Doc. That's not how you wanna go about that."

Martin jumped and whirled around. "What are *you* doing in here?"

"Martin!" Louisa whispered.

"Oh, don't mind me. You go on about your business. I'll just wait until you're done," Bert said.

Martin gave him a scowl. "And that's what the reception room is for. You can wait in there, Bert."

Evan and James darted under the man's arms and Louisa waved her hand. "Come on in, Bert."

"Why, thank you. Don't mind if I do," he said, waddling forward. "You could learn a lesson or two from your lovely wife about the art of hospitality, Doc. I'm surprised you didn't pick a bit of it up, what with your years workin' in *hospitals* and all." The man's jowls shook as he gave his head a vigorous nod. "That's a pretty good one, don't you think, Doc?"

"Gawd," the doctor muttered as he picked away at his patient.

Bert leaned over his shoulder. "You should've told me what the problem was, Doc. I could've saved you a lot of fuss and bother."

"Oh, *really*?"

"Yeah. Yer goin' about it all wrong, see. You wanna rub some butter into the little blighters; then you can just brush 'em right out."

Martin threw his head back before snipping out the last two seed pods, grumbling, "I suppose it would be too much to ask that you share your words of wisdom whilst they could actually prove useful?"

Dropping his instruments on to the table, he pushed himself to his feet, looking down peevishly at his wife. "Now, if you don't mind, I'll go see to the idiot in my consulting room."

She gave him a faint smile. "Thank you, Martin. I appreciate your help. And so does Buddy."

He grunted. "Yes, I'm sure he does."

Chapter 2

The door to the consulting room rattled shut behind him, and Martin pulled Malcolm Raynor's patient notes from his desk, muttering under his breath about having to share his home with a disgusting animal. "I apologise for the delay, Mr. Raynor. Get up on the couch, please," he said, giving a wave of his hand.

Malcolm pushed himself up from the chair. "No need to apologise, Doc. The little missus needed you. You made the right decision there—gettin' her the dog."

"I didn't *get* her the dog. It's not here by choice ... my choice."

"Whose choice was it, then?"

"Our, erm ... foster child sleeps better with the animal in his bed."

"You want a bit of advice from someone with parenting expertise?"

"No, I want you to get up on the couch."

"Trust me, Doc, you don't wanna be givin' in to the little lad's demands. You'll regret it down the road."

"It's none of your business."

"I'm just sayin'; you can't let 'em get the upper hand. You gotta demand his respect now, or he'll end up like one'a them juvenile delinquents throwin' firecrackers at the seagulls down at the harbour."

Martin gave the man's face, weathered by a life working in the harsh summer sun and dank winter winds, a scowl and slapped the notes down on his desk. "As I said, this is *none* of your business."

Malcolm slid himself back on to the exam couch. "Don't mean to be stickin' my nose in where it don't belong."

"Yes, you did. Open your shirt up."

"Look, I know this bein' a father thing's all new to you and all. Just don't wanna see you makin' the same mistakes I did."

"The dog *wasn't* the boy's decision. Now shut up and unbutton your shirt so I can listen to your chest."

"You sayin' it was *her* choice, then?"

Martin gave him a blank stare. "Who?"

"The missus."

"Mm, yes. Now please, open your shirt up!"

"Might not wanna complain about her choices then, Doc. Remember, you're one of 'em," Malcolm said, working the buttons through the buttonholes.

Eyeing him for a moment, the doctor pulled in his chin and grunted. "Did you get rid of those birds?"

"Just like you said to. Your diagnosis was spot on. Can't say I don't miss 'em, but now that my birds are gone, the cough's cleared up. I'm like a new—"

"Stop talking." Martin's brow furrowed in concentration as he moved his stethoscope around on the man's chest. "Take a deep breath in."

Air whistled in and out through his patient's teeth and the doctor grimaced. "Oh, for God's sake! How do you expect me to hear anything with you making all that noise? Breathe through your nose, not your mouth."

"Sorry, Doc. I'm all bunged up."

The doctor took a step back and pulled his stethoscope from his ears. "*Bunged* up?"

"It's my allergies. Can't get any air in through my nose. I can't sleep neither. I wake *myself* up I snore so loud. My cats even have to get up and go sleep in the other room sometimes."

"Cats?" Martin looked back through the man's notes. "There's nothing here about you having cats. How many cats?"

"Just four. I couldn't take the isolation anymore."

"Oh, for goodness' sake. And I presume your rhinitis symptoms began when you invited the microcontaminant-infused clowder into your home?

Malcolm screwed up his craggy face. "Huh?"

"Those disgusting fleabags you've been sharing your bed with! Is there a correlation between their arrival and the onset of your nasal congestion?"

The man's face fell as the penny dropped. "You think I'm allergic to cats?"

"I'm *asking* if your—bunged up nose started when you got the cats." Martin jabbed his stethoscope towards his patient's chest. "You can button up, now."

"Well, I s'pose now that I think about it, yeah." Malcolm looked crestfallen as he stuffed his shirttail into his waistband. "But I'm already attached to 'em, Doc."

"Ohh," Martin groaned softly when he glanced over to see the man's eyes reddening. "All right, just calm down. It's premature to be getting yourself all worked up.

"Your lungs seem to be bearing up under the increased allergen load you've placed on them. I'll write you a prescription for fluticasone. Pick it up from Mrs. Tishell and ask her for a bottle of cetirizine tablets," he said, dropping into his chair.

"So, I might be able to keep 'em?"

"Well, let's wait and see. You need to stop allowing them in your bedroom, though."

"But I get lonely at night." Malcolm slipped from the exam couch and stepped towards the doctor's desk. "It's hard to sleep without a warm body to curl up with."

"Don't tell me you were tucking in with those ghastly pigeons every night!"

"Course not. But ... well, I hadn't had a decent night's sleep since my wife left me—till I got my cats, that is." The man's fingers scratched at the three-day growth of stubble on his chin. "Don't know if I can go back to the lonely, sleepless nights."

"Well, you're going to have to—or find yourself a human companion. You can't be sleeping with those cats. You can keep them for now. We'll see how you do with the fluticasone and antihistamine. But if your symptoms persist or worsen, you'll have to get rid of them."

Martin ripped the top sheet from his prescription pad and slid it across his desk. Malcolm looked over at him, with a pout, before snatching the paper and plodding from the room.

"Next patient!" the doctor called out.

Rapid footsteps could be heard in the hall before Evan sailed around the corner, slipping into the consulting room in front of Bert Large.

"Dr. Ellig-am!" the boy said breathlessly. "Do you want Leicester cheese or Cheddar cheese on your grilled cheese sandwiches?"

Martin's lips pursed as he jabbed his biro towards the child. "Evan, I'm with a patient. And when I'm with a patient you don't interrupt."

"But you're not with him yet, and Mrs. Ellig-am said ta hurry up and ask you before you *are* with him. She gots ta know so she can make your lunch."

"Neither. Grilled cheese sandwiches are full of saturated fat and salt. Tell her I'll make myself a turkey sandwich when I finish up here."

Evan's gaze rolled towards the ceiling and he sighed. "Okay. But she's gonna make her cross face if I tell her that."

"She won't be cross with you; she'll be cross with me."

The boy's shoulders sagged and he kicked his toe against the floor. "I don't like her bein' cross with you, neither."

"Evan ... go back out to the kitchen. Now."

"'Kay." He swung his foot one last time before stomping off.

Martin turned to his patient. "What's the problem, Bert?"

A whoosh of air rushed from the man's lungs as he fell into the chair. "Oh, no problem, no problem. Well, not as such, Doc. I just need a bit of advice."

"Medical advice?"

"Course not. It's like this—after my recent brush with death, it occurred to me that we *may* have been a bit hasty with the whole restaurant business thing."

"We? Wasn't Al in Uganda when you opened your restaurant?"

"Not Al. You and me. I mean, I know you were just tryin' to be helpful and all when you suggested it, but I'm not sure I'm cut out for the hospitality trade. So, I'm thinkin' of making another career change. And seeings how the whole idea was yours in the first place, I wanted to get your advice. What do you think, Doc?"

"It *wasn't* my idea. And I'm a doctor. If you need someone to advise you on your career, hash it out with a career counsellor, Bert. I'm busy." Martin got to his feet and wagged a finger at him. "Get up on the couch; I need to listen to your heart."

The restaurateur hoisted himself from his chair and shuffled across the room. "I don't need you to advise me, per se. It's just—well, you see, I woke up in the middle of the night last night, and I had this feeling. It's got me worried."

"What kind of feeling? In your chest—your arm, you mean?"

"Oh, nothin' like that. A feelin' like something isn't quite right in my life. Like I've missed my chance to make a real difference in the world. Like I need to use my—oh, what's the word I'm searchin' for, Doc? The one that means you're born with it?"

"Congenital?"

"Yeah, yeah, yeah. That's it. I need ta use my congenital abilities. It's been there all the time. I think it just took my recent enlightenment to see it. It hit me like a thunderbolt last night."

Martin threw his head back. "I see. The diva of divinity spoke to you in a dream, did she?"

"Something like that."

"Don't be stupid, Bert. You can barely eke out an existence serving up sub-standard fare to unsuspecting diners. Do you really think you'll be able to support yourself as a self-proclaimed clergyman?"

"You're not gettin' it, Doc. I have a *gift*! I've received a higher calling."

"You're *not* a cleric, Bert."

"No, no, no! Higher than *that*. I got a knack for makin' whiskey, see?"

"Whiskey?"

Bert pulled in his chin. "Don't look at me like that, Doc. I've been perfecting my craft since I was a teenager—when your Auntie Joan was still changin' your nappies. I think I could put Portwenn on the map. Why, I could make this village the whiskey capital of Northwest Cornwall!"

The doctor's eyes rolled to the side, and he wagged another finger. "Open your shirt up."

Bert slipped the buttons through his buttonholes, and Martin positioned his stethoscope on his patient's ample chest.

"So, what do you think, Doc? Should I cut my losses and—"

"Shh!" Martin listened intently for several seconds before pulling his stethoscope from his ears. Then, he reached for his blood pressure cuff, wrapping it around Bert's arm and inflating it.

"Whaddya think, Doc?"

Air hissed from the cuff and Martin ripped the Velcro closure open. "You need to continue to try to bring your weight down—eat smaller meals, make sure you're getting plenty of fruits and vegetables. When's your next appointment with the cardiologist in Truro?"

"In two weeks. But I'm not talkin' about that. Whaddya think about the whiskey?"

"It's nothing but empty calories and will contribute to your weight problem. Not to mention the damage it can do to your liver and neurovascular system."

"But I read one'a them studies that said a couple pints down at the pub now and then isn't gonna do a person any harm. They said it ... let's see, how did they put it? It showed *nominal* benefits."

"Nominal, Bert—*minimal*. That study refuted previous studies suggesting there may be real health benefits to moderate alcohol consumption. And given your recent medical history, my professional recommendation would be to avoid it completely."

"Completely? Why?"

"Because you lack the intestinal fortitude to limit your drinking to a healthy amount. And as I said, you need to lose the weight." Martin dropped into the chair behind his desk and began to jot notes into his patient's file.

"Right you are, Doc. I think I see your point there. But the bein' *around* the whiskey part—what's the problem there?"

"Oh, for heaven's sake, Bert! You can't inhale it or absorb it through your skin. As long as you don't ingest it, there's no way it can adversely affect your health."

The portly man pulled his tie over his head and slipped it under his collar. "It might even be healthy, then? Give me somethin' to look forward to in the morning? Keep me in the social circuitry, so to speak?"

"Social relationships *can* provide health benefits for some people, yes."

"Great! Thanks, Doc!"

Martin shook his head as the door closed behind his patient, and then he slid the notes back into the sleeve.

When he came into the kitchen from under the stairs a few minutes later, Louisa was putting lunch on the table, and the aroma of toasted bread filled the air. He glanced down at the sandwiches on his plate and curled his lip.

"Louisa, you do realise grill—"

"Martin, hush up and sit down. Chris thinks you could stand to put on a few more pounds. And I want you to eat both of those sandwiches."

He pulled out a chair, muttering under his breath. "When did Chris start policing my diet?"

"Chris has been policing your diet and looking out for you from day one of all this, and I'm extremely grateful for it." She jabbed a cooking turner at him. "And you should be, too."

"Mm."

"It gots the turkey on it, Dr. Ellig-am," Evan said, pulling up the top slice of bread to demonstrate.

"Have you washed those hands recently?" Martin asked.

The boy's face contorted as he thought through the question. "I'm almost pretty sure I washed 'em in the bathtub last night. Does that count for recently?"

"No. Go wash."

His chin dropping to his chest, the seven-year-old plodded off under the steps.

The doctor dropped into his chair, stifling a groan. "Where's Poppy?"

"She walked down to Mrs. Tishell's for me; we were out of nappy sacks," Louisa said.

James Henry reached for the bowl of turkey titbits his mother held in her hand. "Mummy! Wan mo!"

"Use your manners, James—say please," she said, raising her eyebrows at him.

The boy tipped his head and gave her his father's half smile. "Peeze."

Her face softening, she set the bowl on the tray and leaned down, kissing his head as her fingers toyed with a golden curl.

Evan came back through under the stairs, wiping his wet hands on his shirt front before climbing back up next to his guardian.

"Can we work on our train in the shed after lunch, Dr. Ellig-am?" he asked.

Martin grimaced at the sandwich crumbs that rained down on to the child's lap. "Keep your head over your plate. And no, I need to drive over to Wadebridge this afternoon."

"But who am I gonna play with, then?"

"Why can't you play with James? Or entertain yourself doing something useful for a change?"

"Or," Louisa said as she slid a sandwich on to her own plate, "you could take Evan with you, Martin."

"Ohhh, the boy doesn't want to sit and watch while I get a haircut."

"I don't mind wa—"

The back door rattled open, pre-empting the seven-year-old's reply, and the Ellingham's childminder stepped into the kitchen.

"Oh, thank you, Poppy. You're a lifesaver," Louisa said, hurrying over to take a bag from the young woman's hand.

"You're welcome. But, Mrs. Ellingham, I think I better go home. I'm not feelin' very well."

"Oh, dear. I'm sorry to hear that."

Martin's head shot up, and he got to his feet, limping over and pressing his fingers to the girl's forehead. "You're hot. What do you mean, you don't feel well? Are you nauseous—stomach ache—headache?"

"Yeah, all of 'em." She took a step back. "And you're not supposed ta be around sick people, so I think I better go home."

Louisa tugged at her husband's sleeve. "That's exactly right, Poppy. Martin, get away from her, and go wash your hands," she said with a snap of her fingers. "Then sit down and eat your lunch. Poppy, we'll see you when you're feeling better." She nudged the childminder out the door and closed it behind her.

Martin hissed a breath through his nose before heading off under the stairs. When he returned a short time later, he gave his wife a peevish look. "I don't think that was necessary, Louisa. Poppy wasn't coughing or sneezing. And I was merely trying to determine the cause of her symptoms so that I could give her the appropriate medical advice."

He sat back down, grimacing at the screech as he pulled his chair back up to the table.

Louisa tipped her head down and eyed him suspiciously for a moment before turning her attention to her lunch. "I'm sorry, Martin. But I will not allow you to take unnecessary chances," she said as she bisected her sandwich with a knife. "I'll call and let Jeremy know she's under the weather. I'm quite sure he won't mind checking up on her." She gave him a coy grin. "I seem to remember you being quite keen to check up on me when I was ill once."

He stared back at her for a moment before his gaze raced to his plate and a flush spread across his cheeks. "Of course, I was *keen*, Louisa. I'm responsible for the health care of this community."

"Hmm. Yes, you are."

Evan reached a buttery hand up and touched his fingers to his guardian's face. "I think you already catched what Poppy gots."

"For goodness' sake, Evan. You're all greasy," Martin said, batting the seven-year-old's hand away.

"Oh, that's just 'cause of my lunch." The child leaned forward and peered up at him. "Your cheeks are all red. And my mum says when my sister gots cheeks like that it's 'cause ... she's ..." He quietened, feigning a sudden, inapt interest in the contents of his sandwich.

Louisa sighed silently as she watched him. "Martin, I think you should take Evan with you to Wadebridge. You mentioned that he needs a haircut, too. *And,* he'd be doing something useful."

"Mm, yes."

Her mobile vibrated against the table next to her, and she glanced at the screen before picking it up. "Hi, Pippa," she said.

Tuning out his wife's conversation, the doctor tapped a finger next to his charge's plate. "You finish your lunch, and we'll stop for ice cream before we go to the barber's."

Evan swiped a hand across his eyes before giving him a small smile. "'Kay."

Louisa rang off and set her phone down. "Well, this is a bit inconvenient. Mr. Townsend, the custodian at the school, wants me over there. They have the water turned back on, but it seems there's a problem with a pipe in the boys' lavatory, now."

"Wouldn't it be more logical to call a properly licensed plumber than to ring up the headmistress to do the job?" Martin asked.

"They don't want me over there to fix up the plumbing, Martin. There's been some water damage, and we need to figure out where to put everyone when classes resume tomorrow."

"Ah. But the hill's apt to be icy. Do you really want to be walking over there with James?"

"No, Martin, I don't. But I'm the head teacher, and there's a problem at the school. I don't have much choice.

"Pippa said one side of the street is clear, so we should be fine." She took a bite of her sandwich and then hesitated, her fingers tapping against her glass of water. "*Although* ... it would be easier without James. Do you think you could take him with you?"

"Oh, I don't know about that."

"I think you could do it. Of course, you wouldn't want to be carrying him unless it was absolutely necessary. But he's getting quite good at climbing in and out of his car seat on his own, so you wouldn't have to be picking him up."

"I'm perfectly capable of picking James up, Louisa. That's not the issue," he said, pulling in his chin and giving her a scowl.

"I'm not saying that. But it wouldn't be a good idea for you to be trying to carry—"

"I said I'm capable!" he snapped.

Pushing himself to his feet, he picked up his dirty dishes and limped to the sink. "I can handle it, Louisa. But I highly doubt a trip to the barbers would be entertaining for an eighteen-month-old."

"I'll put some toys and books in the nappy bag. That'll keep him busy while you two get your hair cut. Then you can do something with him that he *would* find entertaining, hmm?"

"Such as?" His brow furrowed before he screwed up his face. "Ohhh, you don't mean that ghastly happy-clappy story time business at the library, do you?"

"Oh, Martin! Of course not! Just let him do whatever you and Evan do."

She got up from the table and gave him a flick of her ponytail. "Entertain him by doing something *useful* for a change. He'd love it, I'm sure."

Chapter 3

"Anybody home?" Louisa called out when she walked in the kitchen door late that afternoon.

Martin looked up from the accounting book on his desk as his son and young charge scrambled to their feet and dashed out the consulting room door, leaving behind a dappling of blocks and miniature cars and farm animals on the floor.

He groaned as he stood up, and he had just leaned down to reach for a small tow truck when his wife's strident voice cut through the air.

"Martin! What did you do?"

Limping towards the hall, he smacked into her as she came through the doorway.

"Martin Ellingham! How could you?"

A familiar heaviness settled in his chest—the heaviness that accompanied the realisation that he was again clueless as to his latest offence. He swallowed hard and wracked his brain, watching as her eyes filled with tears.

"How could you, Martin? How could you leave me out of something so significant—a milestone in our son's life—his-his-his transition from babyhood? How *could* you?"

His eyes darted up and down the hall as he grasped for an explanation for her agitation. "I, erm ... I'm not really sure what you're referring to."

"His hair, Martin! You cut his hair!"

Martin cocked his head as his mouth opened and closed silently. "Well, to be clear, I didn't cut it; the barber over in Wadebridge cut it."

"Why?"

"What do you mean, why? Because I told him to."

"But you should have asked me first!"

"Did I miss something? You did say to do something useful, didn't you?"

Louisa's hands clenched. "I didn't mean it literally!"

"What *did* you mean, then?"

"I meant for you and Evan to find something to do that James would find entertaining, Mar-tin."

"And that's what we did."

"You thought a toddler would find a haircut entertaining, did you?"

"James seemed interested. And he appeared to enjoy it when the man cut his hair, yes."

He pulled out his handkerchief and handed it to her. "You did say to do something useful. James needed a haircut; a haircut seemed useful."

Reaching into his shirt pocket, he removed a small envelope and held it out. "The man sent this home with me; God knows why."

She took it from his fingers and opened the flap, peering in. "Ohhh, James's curls," she moaned, wiping at the tears on her cheeks.

Martin rubbed a hand over the back of his neck. "Louisa, I gather I may have done something to upset you."

She looked up at him and shook her head. "Martin, a child's first haircut is a big event. And I missed it."

Staring past her for a moment, he sighed before wrapping his arms around her.

"So, you understand now?" she asked, sniffling into his chest.

He grimaced. "Mm, no. I have absolutely no idea why a haircut would be considered a big event. But I know I've upset you, and I'm sorry for that."

He wagged a finger at the envelope. "That's, erm ... that's hair in there—James's hair."

"Yes, Martin. I was able to figure that out for myself. And don't you dare try to bin it; I have plans for it," she said, stepping away from him.

"Plans? What in the world are you going to do with a collection of hair?"

"Oh, I don't know, Martin. Maybe I'll add it to the collection of *your* hair that I have saved away."

"*My* hair?"

"Mm-hmm." She gave him a flick of her ponytail as she turned and headed back towards the kitchen.

Huffing out a breath, he turned back to picking up the toys littering the floor. "Hair? Oh, I don't understand that at all," he grumbled, filling his arms with a hotchpotch of plastic and soft toys. A nasal voice caused him to cringe.

"Sounds like a bit of a problem, eh, Doc?"

He spun around, gravity returning half of the retrieved toys to the floor. "Don't you ever knock, Penhale?"

The officer tipped his head down and narrowed his eyes. "I believe we've covered this already, Do-*c*—not my style."

"What is it, Penhale? You do realise the surgery's closed, don't you?"

"'Course I do. You don't think something as obvious as a locked door would get past me, do you?"

Martin gave him a sneer and a grunt before depositing the toys he had managed to hold on to into a basket on his desk. "How did you get in here?"

"Went to the ba-*ck*. Louiser let me in." The policeman hoisted his duty belt. "Seems there was a bit of a, shall we say, misha-*p* over on Fore Street."

"What sort of mishap?"

"A nine-year-old offender—he was preparing to take his sled down the hill. I went to apprehend said suspect, made a grab for him, lost my footing and lurched forward. We both went hurtling towards the Platt."

"Was someone injured?"

"Injured? *I* haven't received any personal injury reports." Joe took a step forward, eyeing him intensely. "Is there something you're not telling me, Doc?"

"Of course not."

"Perhaps I should remind you of your mandatory reporter status. If there's something you know, you're bound by the law to report it."

"That pertains to incidents of suspected child abuse, not personal injury. I'm trying to work out why you're here. What happened after you and the ... *offender* slid down the hill."

The policeman snapped his fingers. "Gotcha. An unanticipated bump in the road caused me to lose control of the situation. The subject veered one way—*down* the hill. I went the other way."

He put his hands up in front of him. "Not *up* the hill—towards the harbour. Fortunately, a rubbish bin stopped my skid."

"And?"

Joe's eyes blinked in confusion. "And ... what?"

"Where is all this leading, Penhale?"

"Where is *what* leading?"

"This ridiculous story!"

"Oh. I knocked the bin right over. Sent rubbish fly—"

"Penhale! Was there any actual harm done by this comedy of errors?"

"Don't think so, Doc. Why do you ask?"

"Well, I'm assuming, given the fact that you're standing in my consulting room, that someone is in need of medical assistance."

"Can't speak to that. The doctoring is your departmen-*t*. Just wanted to make you aware that Sam Boyd, down at the water plant, is advising everyone in the village to boil all tap water before drinking it."

"Yes, I know that! You told me this morning!" The creases in his forehead deepening, Martin looked at the policeman askance. "Did you receive a blow to your head when you hit that rubbish bin?"

The grin on the constable's face contorted and a snort escaped his nose. "Hit a rubbish bin? Now, why would I be pickin' a fight with a rubbish bin?"

"I didn't say you would! I'm asking you a simple question. Did you, or did you not hit your head when you ran into that rubbish bin?"

Joe drew in a slow breath as he puzzled over the doctor's question. "And ... what rubbish bin is that, exactly?"

"The rubbish bin with which you collided!"

"I don't think I appreciate your tone of voice, Doc. Or the suggestion of collusion ... especially with a rubbish bin."

"Oh, for God's sake! What's your name and date of birth?"

The officer widened his stance and hooked his thumbs over his belt. "I'm not sure that's any of your business. I'm not privy to *your* personal information, am I?"

Martin wagged a finger at him. "Get up on the couch. I need to examine you."

"Why?"

"Because you're exhibiting signs of neurological impairment."

"Ohhh, my god!" Joe groaned. "It's that Huntington-y thing again, isn't it?"

"Of course not. You never had and, in all likelihood, never will have, Huntington's disease," Martin said, regretting for the second time in as many years that he had revealed the remote possibility the affliction could be plaguing the Penhale gene pool. "My guess is that you've hit your head. You may have a concussion."

Joe's eyes widened. "*Really?* How do you think that happened?"

"Just get up on the couch," Martin said, a hiss of air rushing from his nose as he limped across the room, the sharp twinges in his left leg causing him to grimace.

The white couch roll paper crackled as the policeman hoisted himself on to it.

"Does this hurt?" the doctor asked as his fingers palpated a large knot above his patient's right ear.

Joe winced. "Only when you touch it ... and ... a bit when you don't."

"Hmm." Martin put a hand up in front of the officer's face. "How many fingers am I holding up?"

"I'm afraid I'm going to have to exercise my right to silence on that one, Do-*c*."

"Just answer the question!" Martin snapped, his mood careening from mere annoyance to full blown exasperation.

Joe pulled in his chin and squinted his eyes. "Six? Maybe seven?"

Dropping his arm to his side, the doctor sighed heavily. "All right, I'm taking you over to Truro for a neurological workup."

"Oh, that's nice of you, Doc."

"No, it's not. You're my patient, Penhale. And this village can't afford for you, as its sole policeman, to suffer any more damage to your brain than you already have."

"You've got my back, I've got yours—eh, Doc?"

Martin gave him a grunt and started for the door. "I'll get my coat."

By the time Martin left the Royal Cornwall that evening, the wet patches on the road had turned to black ice, making travel treacherous. He pulled into the space next to the surgery and shifted the car into park before flexing his fingers, stiffened by his firm grip on the steering wheel. Then, he forced his weary body into the house.

The rattle of the kitchen door latch woke Louisa where she had drifted off to sleep on the sofa. "Hello," she said through a yawn, grabbing for her novel as it slipped from her lap. "How's Joe?"

"Erm ... fine."

"Fine?"

"Mm. They're keeping him overnight for observation."

"But his odd behaviour? That's temporary?"

"The blow he received to his head today won't rectify his pre-existing condition, if that's what you're wondering."

"Martin," she said, giving him a disapproving look.

"Mm, yes. He should be back to his normal self in a few days. Still a cupcake but—" His wife huffed out a breath, and he averted his gaze, reaching for a glass from the cabinet. "How was your afternoon? Is everything all right at the school?"

Louisa rubbed at her eyes and got to her feet. "A bit wet. Water had been leaking from a burst pipe in the boys' lavatory, and it made its way into one of the classrooms.

"Mr. Townsend and Garrett MacDonald, the year six teacher, moved all the desks out of the way and mopped up the floor—got fans going. Hopefully, it'll be dry in there by morning. How was your drive home?"

"Icy." The tap squeaked off and Martin turned, leaning back against the counter as he drank down his glass of water. "I don't recall such a stretch of cold in the years I've been here."

Louisa walked over and slipped an arm around his waist. "It is cold. I might need you to keep me warm tonight, in fact," she said suggestively as her fingers worked to loosen his tie.

He eyed her bare feet and lightweight, pink eyelet blouse. "I did point out when you were getting dressed this morning that a jumper might be a more practical choice than what you're wearing."

Pulling in a slow breath, she tamped back the knee-jerk defensiveness that her husband's less-than-romantic remark elicited. "Martin, we can either stand here and discuss the wisdom of my wardrobe choice this morning, or you can turn that brain of yours off for … say an hour or so—maybe let another part of your anatomy do the thinking for a while, hmm?"

She pressed up against him and his sharp intake of air assured her the message had been received.

His Adam's apple rose and fell. "I see. Erm, the boys are asleep?"

"Mm-hmm." Grasping on to either end of his tie, she pulled him down, pressing her lips to his. "And I'm still cold, so let's go upstairs." She purred at him between the kisses she trailed down his neck. "You can warm me up—and I can apologise—*properly*—for being so cross with you earlier."

Patting a hand against his cheek, she walked off towards the steps, turning once to give him a coy smile.

"Mm, yes," he mumbled before putting his glass in the dishwasher and following after her.

As they lay in bed a while later, Martin reached out to brush his fingers through his wife's chestnut tresses, now tousled by their passionate activities. He sighed. "I'm sorry about James's hair."

"It's all right, Martin. I can't say that I wasn't disappointed at having missed his first haircut, but I know it was just a misunderstanding."

"Mm." His gaze drifted towards the window for a moment before returning to her. "Why do you keep things, Louisa?"

"What do you mean?"

"Those ghastly pictures of me when I was a child. James's hair. Why do you keep them?"

She propped herself up on an elbow and cocked her head at him. "They're mementos, Martin."

"Yes, but you're not likely to forget James without that envelope of hair, are you?"

"Of course, I won't forget James." Reaching for the cloisonné box her husband had given her for Christmas, she pulled the lid open. "But I might forget what his hair felt like, looked like exactly. I'll have a little piece of our baby forever."

Martin wrinkled up his nose. "It sounds a bit morbid when you put it that way."

"Oh, *Martin,*" she hissed. "Most people would call it sentimental."

He grunted before reaching a hesitant finger into the envelope, lightly stroking a golden curl.

"You want to see yours?" she asked, smiling at him impishly.

His brow furrowed as he stared back at her. "You were serious?"

"Of course, I was." She removed a second envelope from the box and pulled open the flap, revealing its contents to him. "I trimmed off some of your curls while you were asleep in the hospital."

"What on earth for?"

"As a memento."

"Mm. You do realise that hospitals are a breeding ground for any number of virulent pathogens, don't you, Louisa? Technically, that would be considered medical waste and should have—"

"Oh, Martin! Stop it!"

He shook his head. "I would think you'd be keen to put that ugly chapter in your life behind you, not to be reminded of it every time you open that box."

Louisa returned the envelope to its place and the lid closed with a snap. "It wasn't all ugly."

He pushed himself up from the bed with a grunt and reached for his dressing gown. "I need to use the lavatory. Then, I'm going to get something to eat."

"To eat? You worked up an appetite, did you?"

He glanced over before quickly averting his eyes from her mischievous gaze. "I haven't had supper yet."

"Oh, Martin! You should have said; you must be starving!"

"I was ... momentarily distracted."

When he emerged from the bathroom a few minutes later, she got out of the bed and stretched up to kiss him. "I'll be down in a bit to make you some eggs."

"No, no, no, no, no. I'll make a sandwich; you go back to bed."

"I'll be *down* in a minute," she said, giving him a nudge and shooing him away. "Go put the kettle on. I fancy a cup of tea.

"Yes." He gave her a sideways glance. "You should put on your dressing gown and slippers, though," he said, tugging at his ear as he headed out of the room.

When Louisa joined her husband in the kitchen a few minutes later, two steaming mugs had been set out on the table, and he was fishing eggs out of a pot of boiling water.

"I told you *I* would make your eggs! You've had a long day," she said.

He gave his head a half turn, shrugging his shoulders. "Just rationalising time."

Emptying the water from the pan, he gave it a wash and set it in the drying rack. "That man from Children's Services—"

"*Mr. Delaney*. Honestly, Martin."

"Mm, yes. He left a message with Morwenna this morning. Jim Hanley's memorial service will be Thursday afternoon—in Redruth."

"Redruth! Why are they having it all the way down there?"

"It's where the nearest county cemetery is located."

Louisa shoved her hands into her armpits. "Jim Hanley doesn't deserve a memorial service. I would just as soon not remember him."

"You don't have to; I'll go on my own."

"Oh, Martin. I'm not sure I like the idea of you driving that far. Especially not by yourself."

He worked his jaw as air hissed from his nose. "I can manage it, Louisa."

"Yeah. Yeah, I know you can," she said, giving him an uneasy smile. "But is it really necessary?"

"Evan may have questions at some point in time, and I want to be able to answer them."

She gave him a nod. "Hmm, I s'pose. Well, thank you for doing it, Martin."

"You're welcome."

She looked into the cups on the table. "Oh. You made me hot chocolate?"

"Problem?"

"No! No—no problem. It's just that I usually have to twist your arm to get you to make me a cup of hot chocolate."

She pulled out her chair and took a seat before narrowing her eyes at him. "You're not about to give me bad news, are you?"

"Of course not. I thought it might warm you up. Your, erm ... your feet were a bit cold when we were ..." he gave her a surreptitious glance ... "earlier."

"That's very thoughtful, Martin," she said before taking a sip.

The steam drifted up from the cup and swayed past her face, and his chest filled with air. He watched abstractedly until her voice prodded him from his stupor.

"So, the whole time we were ... *earlier,* as you call it, you were thinking about my cold feet?"

"No." His egg cups landed on the table with a sharp clack and he cleared his throat. "Actually, studies have shown that hot drinks can have a *cooling* effect on the body in certain circumstances."

"Oh, really?"

"Mm. It's strange, I know. But thermoreceptors in the tongue send signals to the brain that the body is heating up. If it's a warm day, this triggers the normal cooling mechanisms—sweating and vasodilation."

"Hmm, interesting." She tipped her head down and peered up at him. "Are you going to sit down and eat your eggs?"

He straightened himself and pulled in his chin. "Mm, yes." Chair legs scraped against the slate floor, and he flinched before dropping heavily into it.

Louisa eyed him suspiciously. "Are you having those headaches again, Martin?"

"I'm fine."

"You sure? You did that—that face earlier today."

Air hissed from his nose. "Perhaps a bit. I'm sure they'll clear up." Keeping a wary eye on her as he dabbed at his eggs with a toast soldier, he attempted to change the subject. "I, er ... should remind you that Evan and I have appointments in Truro tomorrow."

"Yes, I did see the reminder on my phone. But thank you for that, Martin. Now, can we discuss your headaches?"

"There's not much to discuss. It's been a bit of a problem but nothing I can't handle."

She leaned back in her chair and folded her arms across her chest. "And when you called Chris and Ed, the consensus was the same—nothing you can't handle?"

"It's not been that much of an issue, Louisa. If it gets any worse, I'll let Jeremy know."

"You haven't even mentioned it to Jeremy? Oh, *Martin*!"

He tipped his head back and wagged his nose in the air. "It's not a question of who should be informed, Louisa. I'm monitoring the situation. If the headaches become any more frequent or severe, I'll discuss it with Jeremy."

They sat silently for several minutes as Martin finished his eggs.

Louisa reached across the table and squeezed his fingers. "I would appreciate it very much, Martin, if you would discuss the headache *situation* with Ed at your appointment tomorrow."

Getting up from the table he set his cup down on the counter with a clank. "If it'll ease your mind, I'll mention it to him."

"Thank you. It *would* ease my mind."

"Dr. Ellig-am," a sleepy voice said. Evan peeked out from behind the door in the lounge. "Can you help me?"

"What is it, Evan?" Martin asked.

"It's ... somethin'."

Glancing over at his wife, he huffed out a breath. "I'll see what this is about."

Louisa got up and carried her cup to the sink, stopping to brush a kiss across his cheek before heading for the stairs. "I'll see you in bed, hmm?"

"Yes."

The seven-year-old pressed his forehead to the doorjamb as his head teacher slipped past him and up the stairs. Then, he watched, dewy-eyed, as his guardian approached.

"You should be in bed. What are you doing up?" Martin asked.

"I can't sleep."

"Did you have a bad dream?"

"No." The boy fidgeted. "I think ... I'm cold."

"Mm, I see. Go back upstairs and I'll get another blanket from the cupboard."

Evan scrambled up the steps, and Martin followed after him, immediately detecting a subtle, urine-like odour wafting from him.

By the time he reached the nursery, the child was nestled in his bed with the covers pulled tightly under his chin. Removing a fresh set of pyjamas from the dresser, the doctor waved a hand. "Okay, up you get. We'll clean you up and get you into dry clothes."

"I'm not wet. I just gots ta have another blanket, I think."

Martin leaned over and slid his hand across the mattress, sighing. "Your bed is wet, Evan. Are you sure you didn't have a nightmare?"

The boy's eyes glinted in the dim light, darting wildly. "I, er ... yeah, I think Buddy had an accident. Maybe 'cause he forgot ta pee before he came to bed."

Fighting back his urge to chastise him for his falsehood, the doctor reached a hand out. "Come on, let's go clean you up. Then we'll get your bed sorted."

Chapter 4

Tuesday ushered in clear blue skies and even colder temperatures. But the sun had thawed the ice from Fore Street by the time Martin headed up the hill towards the school to collect Evan for their trip to Truro.

"Make sure he wears those," Louisa said as her husband picked the seven-year-old's stocking cap and mittens up from her desk.

"Yes, I will." He glanced at her impatiently before passing them to the boy.

"I'm not a baby, Mrs. Ellig-am. I know I gots ta wear 'em; you don't have ta tell me," Evan said as he pulled the hat over his head.

Louisa leaned down and tugged on the child's zip, closing the gap at his throat. "I know you're not a baby. I just don't want you to get sick."

"I'll try not to." Evan grunted as he forced his right hand into a mitten. "Kids are a right pain in the arse when they're sick."

Louisa's gaze darted from the boy to her husband, and the child's shoulders fell. "I said a word that's not proper again, didn't I?"

"No, no, no. Well, yes, arse is not a proper word." The headmistress crouched down in front of him and took hold of his mittened hands. "But, Evan, no one can help getting sick ... or hurt. I don't want you to get sick, because I care about you. Not because you'd be a bother if you were sick." She looked up at Martin. "Isn't that right, Dr. Ellingham?"

"Well, that's not entirely correct. Many of the illnesses I've treated in this village could have been easily avoided if people would just observe the simplest of personal hygiene routines.

"They seem intent on ignoring my instructions, then come into my surgery whinging because they're sick. I certainly find that bothersome.

"And I've treated God knows how many idiots who injure themselves through sheer carelessness, expecting modern medicine to magically—"

"Martin." Louisa's lips tightened and her jaw clenched as she fixed a threatening gaze on him.

He dipped his head. "Mm. No, you won't be a bother, Evan."

Furrowing his brow, the seven-year-old pulled up his bottom lip. "Not even if I puked in my bed?"

Louisa got to her feet and kissed the boy's cheek. "Not even, then."

Giving his head teacher a dubious look, he grasped on to his guardian's wrist.

Louisa took a step towards her husband, and after glancing into the outer office, she stretched up, pressing her lips to his. "Drive carefully," she said, giving him an apprehensive smile before resting a hand on the seven-year-old's head. "And *you* be on your best behaviour."

Martin huffed out a breath. "Yes, I will," he said, heading out the door, his charge in tow.

"I meant Evan, Martin!" she called out after them. She shook her head as an amused smile spread across her face.

Evan trotted alongside the doctor as they crossed the playground to the Lexus, releasing his grip on his wrist when a football skittered across the tarmac in front of them. Scurrying to pick it up, he grunted and heaved it back towards the group of boys to which it belonged.

The ball slipped from his mittened hands before landing a few feet in front of him, and one of the boys broke from the now-snickering group, scooping it up as it rolled slowly to the side.

"You throw like a baby," the boy said as he passed the seven-year-old.

Evan stood for a moment, his hands at his sides, before plodding off after his guardian who was waiting for him beside the car.

"How come I'm the littlest kid in my class, Dr. Ellig-am?" Evan asked as they neared Truro a while later. "Is it 'cause I don't eat my vegetables?"

"Your less than optimal diet may be a factor. But more likely, it's just how your body was meant to develop.

"Children grow at different rates. You could very well hit a growth spurt in your teens and end up being a taller than average adult."

The boy threw his head back and rolled his eyes. "You mean I gots ta wait all the way until I'm a *teenager*?"

"I don't know when you'll hit a growth spurt, Evan. I'm sorry, but your body's going to grow at the rate it was intended to grow. The best thing you can do is to adhere to a healthy diet, and make sure you're getting an adequate amount of sleep."

"But if I eat more vegetables, will my teeth fall out?"

"Of course not. Just the opposite is true. Vegetables provide many vitamins and minerals your body needs to keep your teeth strong and your gums healthy."

Evan rode quietly until they reached the A-30 when his voice broke the silence. "Dr. Ellig-am, how *can* I get my teeth to fall out?"

The Lexus slowed as Martin steered the car through a roundabout. Then, he crinkled an eye and gave a quirk of his head. "Why on earth do you want your teeth to fall out?"

"'Cause they're *baby* teeth, and I'm *not* a baby."

"Ah, I see. Well, I'm afraid there's not much to been done for it. Your baby teeth will fall out when your permanent teeth are ready to come in."

The child's head thudded against the window, and he grew quiet for the remainder of the trip.

Mrs. Teague greeted them warmly as they entered Dr. Peterson's office. "Well, good afternoon, Evan ... Dr. Ellingham! How are my two favourite men today?"

Martin shot her a look that was a bit closer to surprise than annoyance before giving her a grunt.

"My school smells funny," Evan said. "But I didn't hafta go yesterday 'cause of the flood in the loo. So, Dr. Ellig-am and James and me went to Wadebridge. Me and Dr. Ellig-am got haircuts," the seven-year-old said, running his hand over his head. "See?"

The woman put a palm to her cheek and drew in a breath. "Oh, I do! And you look ever so handsome."

"Yeah, I know. Then Dr. Ellig-am got in trouble with Mrs. Ellig-am 'cause he had the man give James a haircut, too, and he wasn't s'posed to."

The receptionist raised her eyebrows at the doctor, and Martin pulled in his chin. "A simple misunderstanding; it's been sorted now. *Not* that it's any of your business."

He put a hand on his charge's back and guided him to the seating area. Leaning his crutch against the wall, he dropped into a chair before Evan scrambled up next to him.

"What do you mean, the school smells funny?" Martin asked.

"It smells like mushrooms." Evan slid down in his seat, stretched his legs out in front of him, and smacked his trainers together. "I'm gettin' pretty good at shoe tyin', dontcha think, Dr. Ellig-am?"

"Mm, yes you are."

Making a mental note to stop at the school to rule out a potential mould situation, Martin rolled his shoulders, attempting to ease the tension in his muscles. *Maybe I should mention the headaches to Jeremy*, he thought.

A door could be heard opening, and a blonde-haired girl, appearing to be a year or two older than Evan, skipped down the hall. She slowed, stopping to hold up a picture.

"Look what I made," she said.

The boy squinted his eyes, peering at it closely. "What is it?"

"It's a church."

Evan screwed up his face. "A church? It looks like a horse. If it's a church it gots ta have a staple."

"It *does*; right—*here*." She tapped a finger impatiently against the paper, before wiping a hand across her nose.

"Oh, I thought that was an ear. Maybe that's how come it looks like a horse."

Martin's brow furrowed as he listened to the conversation, eerily similar to one he'd shared with his wife a few years back.

The girl slapped the paper against her leg and gave her ponytail a flick. "Horses have *two* ears not one, stupid. And it's *not* called a staple. It's called a *steeple*."

Evan folded his arms across his chest as his feet began to swing under him. "I'm *not* stupid. You're just a really bad drawer."

The door down the hall opened again, and the girl glanced to the side before narrowing her eyes at him. "How would you know? *You're* just a baby!" she said, sticking out her tongue and giving another flick of her ponytail for emphasis.

The girl's mother stopped for a moment and looked apologetically at Martin. "I'm sorry, we're working through—"

Her words were drowned out by an enormous sneeze from her daughter. Martin pulled back, wrinkling up his nose, before tugging his handkerchief from his pocket. He wiped at the uncontained spray of saliva on his face.

"For God's sake!" he muttered, turning to dab at the spittle on his young charge's cheek.

The mother caressed her daughter's head. "Poor poppet's had an *awful* cold."

The doctor gave the woman a grunt as a sneer tugged at his lips. "Well, that's all right, then."

Evan glowered at the girl. "I'm *not* a baby, you know."

She jutted her chin out at him. "Yes, you are."

"As I was saying, we're working on some things at the moment," the mother said before taking her daughter's hand and leading her away.

Martin glanced down at his young charge as the psychologist approached, taking note of the seven-year-old's reddened face and teary eyes. Discreetly nudging the boy's leg, he rolled his eyes at the girl, causing a smile to creep on to Evan's face.

"Come on back, Evan; I have something special for us to do today," Abby said, reaching out to take the child's hand.

The boy glanced nervously at Martin. "Don't go anywhere, okay, Dr. Ellig-am?"

"No. No, I'll stay right here."

The therapist gave the doctor a wave before they disappeared down the hall.

Evan was immediately drawn to the rack of miniatures on the wall. He crouched down, examining the bottom row, which had escaped his attention on previous visits.

"Okay, Evan. I think I'm all ready over here," the therapist said, wiggling a finger at the boy."

He gave the toys a final look before joining Dr. Peterson at the table.

"We're going to do some painting today," she said.

The child slid into one of the pint-sized chairs, and a piece of glossy paper was laid down in front of him.

The psychologist took a seat next to him. "I thought a bit of finger painting might be fun."

Huffing out a breath, Evan's shoulders slumped. "How come we gots ta do that? Can't we do the sand table again?"

"We'll play at the sand table after a little while." She set the tubs of coloured paste between them and picked up her own sheet of paper. "I like finger painting. It's a good excuse to be messy, don't you think?"

Evan glanced up at her before poking a finger into the pot of red. "I don't *want* to be messy; babies are messy."

"Yes. They certainly can be. But you know who the messy one in my family is?"

"Do you gots a baby?"

"No. But you don't have to be a baby to be a little messy."

"Mrs. Ellig-am is a little messy. But I still like her 'cause she's nice." The boy's finger snaked across the paper before accentuating the line left behind with a dot at the end. "And she's soft. And she smells good, too."

"Those are excellent qualities for a mum to have, hmm?"

"Yeah. I guess maybe it's just bad when boys are messy."

Evan wiped the remnants of red from his finger on to his trousers before reaching for the pot of blue paint.

Abby laid down a zigzag of yellow, and then she got up and went to the sink, returning with wet paper towels.

Pulling the therapist's artwork over, the child scrutinised it. "Is it you that's the messy one in your family?"

"No." Leaning over, she said surreptitiously, "It's my husband."

"Oh." The boy stared at her quizzically before returning his attention to his painting. "I didn't think girls liked messy husbands."

"Well, I don't mind it too much, because he has so many other qualities I love."

"Dr. Ellig-am doesn't like messy, but he still loves Mrs. Ellig-am." Evan scooped up a dollop of red and a dollop of blue paint and mixed them together on his paper. "Huh, maybe *he* loves her 'cause she's soft and she smells good, too."

"I'm sure those are two qualities that he does find appealing," the therapist said, her eyes crinkling. "And I bet the love she has for you and James—that she's a good mummy—is very important to him as well."

He watched her for a moment before a smile spread across his face. "Is that 'cause he thinks me and James are important?"

"Yes. I'm quite sure that you and James ... and Mrs. Ellingham, of course, are the most important things in Dr. Ellingham's life."

The boy's hand smacked down on to the paper. "Look! It's purple now. Did you know that mixin' red and blue together turns it into purple?"

"I did know that. I like your purple handprint!"

"Yeah, me too. Can I take it home so I can give it to Mrs. Ellig-am?"

"You certainly may. I'm sure it'll make her very happy to know that you like her enough to make it for her."

"My mum doesn't want pictures." Evan picked up the wet towelling and wiped at his hands. "But I bet that's just 'cause she doesn't know I like her enough."

"Hmm. That's quite sad that your mum wasn't able to like your pictures. And sad that she couldn't understand you liked her enough to make her special things.

"But I'm sure your picture will make Mrs. Ellingham very happy. Maybe you can tell me about it next week."

"About if she likes it, you mean?"

"That's right. Have you made things for Mrs. Ellingham before?"

"Yeah. I made her one of those tying-around things for her ponytail for Christmas."

"Did she like it?"

"She liked it a lot. She even weared it!"

"Isn't it wonderful that she could see how special it was?"

Evan screwed up one side of his mouth as he looked over at her. "You mean special 'cause I liked her enough?"

"Yes, that you like her enough to make it for her."

Abby pushed herself away from the table and went to the sink to wash her hands. “Come on over, Evan. We’ll get that paint off, and then we can go over to the sand table.”

The seven-year-old hurriedly added a green heart to his picture before skipping across the room.

“You gots ta use soap, Dr. Peterson,” he said as she rubbed at the paint. “It kills all the mannered bacteria.”

“Oh, I see. Is that important?”

“Bacterias are disgusting. And they make you sick.”

“Yes, some do. So, handwashing is important. I bet you’ve learned all about bacteria from Dr. Ellingham?”

“Uh-huh. He doesn’t like ‘em. Sometimes he boils ‘em and kills ‘em.”

“I see.”

“Buddy gots lots of mannered bacteria, so he gots to have a lot of baths.”

“Who’s Buddy?”

“He’s my new dog. Well, he’s not new. He might be kinda old ‘cause he was Dr. Ellig-am’s aunt’s dog. Not the live one, the dead one. Dr. Ellig-am doesn’t like Buddy. His face gets all wrinkly when Buddy’s around. But he lets him sleep with me anyway.”

“Parents often do things they really don’t want to do. They do it because they love their child, and they know the thing would be good for the child or would make the child happy. It’s very nice of Dr. Ellingham to allow you to have Buddy in your bed.”

“Yeah, I know. But he doesn’t want me gettin’ sick, so that’s why we had to come to a ‘greement about the washin’ him part.”

The therapist turned off the water and pulled several sheets of towelling from the dispenser. “There you go, Evan. Get those hands nice and dry. Then we’ll go and play with the sand.”

It took several minutes for the boy to select his miniatures. They sat at his side, lined up on the floor in an eclectic parade of steel and plastic people, vehicles, and construction machinery.

He gathered them up, stuffing some in his pockets before filling his hands with the remainder. "I'm gonna build a road, and these ones are the workers," he said, dropping the human figures into a pile in the sand. "Do you wanna play, Dr. Peterson?" he asked.

"I'd love to, Evan. That's nice of you to offer."

"I know. Here, you can be the guy that runs the excavator. I'll be the sign-holding guy."

"The flagman? Are you sure you wouldn't rather operate the excavator?"

"Uh-uh. He just gets to dig where another guy tells him to dig. I wanna be the guy that's in charge of all the people driving through. He gets to tell them when they hafta stop and when they can go."

"I see."

The sand play continued for fifteen minutes before the therapist suggested to Evan that his guardian might like to see what they had constructed.

Martin woke with a start when the seven-year-old tugged on his sleeve. "Dr. Ellig-am, you wanna come and see the road me and Dr. Peterson made?"

Abruptly straightening himself, he wiped a hand across his face and cleared his throat. "Mm, yes."

"Take a minute, Dr. Ellingham; there's no rush," Abby said, watching him with what Martin found to be an all-too-understanding look on her face.

He turned his head away. "I'm fine." Pushing himself to his feet, he blinked his eyes and picked up his crutch, following after his young charge as he bounced down the hall.

"See, Dr. Ellig-am! We made the whole road from Portwenn to Truro! And I got ta be the flagman!" the boy said.

Martin looked down through bleary eyes at the channels dug out in the sand, the little cars spaced evenly along them until they clustered at the roundabouts.

"Mm. That's very realistic—very good."

"I know. You wanna try driving a car?"

Looking down at the small chairs and heeding the painful warning from his stiffened limbs, the doctor shook his head. "I think I'd best not, Evan."

"Oh. Is that 'cause you might get stuck down there?"

Martin tugged at an ear as his cheeks warmed. "Mm, yes."

"Evan, here's your finger painting," Dr. Peterson said, leaning over and putting a hand on the boy's back. "Why don't you go out and ask Mrs. Teague if you can have a biscuit. Dr. Ellingham will be out in a few minutes."

"'Kay!" The paper flailing at his side, the child's feet thudded against the carpeted floor as he bolted down the hall.

The therapist closed the door behind him. "Have a seat, Dr. Ellingham," she said, waving a hand towards the sofa.

"Well, Evan seems to be adjusting to his new home quite nicely!" she said, gathering the boy's file from her desk.

"Yes." Martin dropped heavily on to the sofa and rubbed at his neck, attempting to ease the persistent stiffness left by his uncomfortable nap in the waiting area.

"And he mentioned that he has a new pet!"

The doctor wrinkled his nose and grumbled. "It seems to help him sleep at night."

Abby took a seat facing him. "I see. Pets can prove to be very beneficial to children, especially those struggling with the effects of trauma."

"Mm. I, er ... happened to run into Barrett Newell recently. He mentioned that there might be some benefit if the boy were to take the animal to obedience classes. I'd be interested in your opinion on the matter."

"I think it could be a real boost to Evan's self-confidence. I gathered in some of our play today that he's becoming aware that he's seen as different—less mature than his peers, perhaps."

"Yes. We discussed that on the way over today. He's the smallest child in his class."

"And that bothers him?"

"Obviously, it would bother him. He's the smallest boy in his class, so he's probably been the target of every one of the dim-witted boys in that school," Martin grumbled.

"Do you know that to be the case? Has Evan mentioned it?"

"He wouldn't have to. It's the natural course of events in childhood, isn't it?" He huffed out a breath as he rubbed his palms together, the moisture cooling them, and he cleared his throat. "No. He hasn't mentioned it."

"I should caution you, Dr. Ellingham, that though Evan will benefit greatly from the unique understanding you have of his life up to now, you must be careful not to project your own experiences on to him. Take advantage of that unique understanding when it can be of help to him, but remember that you are different people with different personalities. And there will be differences between your experiences as well."

Dr. Peterson's red, neatly-manicured fingernails tapped together, catching Martin's eye. The soft clicking the movement created set him on edge, and he shifted his gaze to the window.

"When Evan was living with his parents," she continued, "his focus was on getting through his days in a tumultuous and unpredictable environment. He's feeling more secure now, and his attention is turning to how he fits in with—compares to his peers."

"And how, exactly, do I—erm, Mrs. Ellingham and I go about helping him to fit in? You know as well as I do that his body will grow and his baby teeth will fall out as nature intended."

"Yes, there's not a lot to be done about his physical maturation. But emotionally and socially, there are things that you and your wife could do to make this transition easier for him.

"Encourage play dates with friends his own age. Social relationships are becoming increasingly important to him at this age.

"And Evan's had a taste of what it's like to play an active part in his life. You and your wife allow him some choices—what clothes he wears, what he orders at a restaurant. Being entrusted with Buddy's training could give him confidence. A confidence that may counter his small size and the developmental lag that his classmates are picking up on."

"Ah," Martin grunted, pulling in his chin.

"Taking Buddy through obedience classes could give him a sense of control," Abby said. "And it could be a wonderful bonding experience for the two of you."

He grimaced. "Yes."

The therapist closed the file and laid it on the coffee table, leaning her elbows on her knees. "I get the feeling this may be something that could prove a bit frustrating for you, Dr. Ellingham?"

"No, it wouldn't prove frustrating. The animal's disgusting."

"Mm, yes. I understand your concerns about Evan and James contracting something from the dog, but it's important to be positive about Buddy. Cleanliness is important, but it's easy to create a fearfulness in the child about germs."

Martin gave the woman a grunt as he dug his thumb into his palm. "If it'll be good for the boy, I'll see to it that he and the dog get to these obedience classes."

"Good," the psychologist said, nodding her head. "Dr. Ellingham, Evan's trying to sort out just what it means to be a family. He's only known a world where he's been unwanted and devalued by his parents.

"I think an opportunity to train his dog with you, the person he admires most in his life, could be invaluable for him. Getting encouragement and validation from you, and through your accomplishments together, could help him to redefine family in much more positive terms."

"Yes." Tugging at his ear, Martin breathed out a heavy sigh. "I, erm—there's an issue—well, I'm not sure if it's an issue."

Abby waited several seconds as the doctor squirmed in his seat, before saying, "Why don't you tell me what it is, and then we can talk about it—determine if it is, indeed, an issue."

"Mm, yes. The boy—well, there are moments, although we do try to monitor our behaviour, w-when the boy's around ..."

The therapist nodded encouragingly. "Yes?"

"Well, sometimes, despite our best efforts ..." He screwed up his face. "Well, there are times when couples display affection for one another."

"That's to be expected in any healthy romantic relationship, Dr. Ellingham."

"Yes, I realise that. But there have been times when, despite our best efforts to be aware of Evan, he—he walks in on us—not in on us in the sense that—I just mean ..."

"Well, it's really quite common for children to, shall we say, surprise their parents. I would suggest you install a lock on your bedroom door if you haven't al—"

"Oh, for God's sake! We're two reasonably intelligent people! We were able to work that one out for ourselves!" he snapped before breathing out a slow breath. "I, erm ... I apologise."

The psychologist gave him a tense smile and smoothed her hand over her skirt. "Dr. Ellingham, what is it that's causing you concern?"

Martin squeezed his eyes shut and rubbed at his temples. "I want to know if the boy's intense interest when my wife and I are—are affectionate should be cause for concern. Could it be an indication of any sort of sexual abuse?"

"By affectionate, I assume you mean kissing and hugging one another."

His jaw tightened as his teeth clenched. "Yes."

"Does Evan seem to be bothered by it—uncomfortable with it?"

"God, no. He seems to take great pleasure in it. I haven't the foggiest idea as to how a normal child reacts to that sort of thing."

"Think back to your own childhood. How did you feel when you saw your parents express their love for one another?"

Giving her a blank stare, he shook his head. "I never—I'm not sure. I don't remember much about that."

"I see," she said, her all-too-understanding smile again forcing his gaze away.

"Evan's a very loving child," she said. "I suspect he takes great pleasure in seeing the two people who are now his sense of security meeting one another's emotional needs.

"It's not likely he saw a lot of affection between his own parents. So, this is novel for him, and he's quite naturally curious. Non-sexual displays of affection between you and your wife almost certainly will strengthen the sense of security that he feels in your home. It's a good thing."

"His leering at us is normal seven-year-old behaviour?"

"I wouldn't say normal. I would say Evan's strong interest is understandable, given his history. I'll watch for any indication of sexual abuse when I'm with him, though. But so far, I've seen no signs of it."

The therapist got to her feet and leaned down to pick up the file. "I would imagine it *is* a bit unsettling to find him staring at you. But try to think of it in positive terms. He's looking for reassurances right now, and each time he sees you and your wife showing the other affection, he feels reassured that his new home is going to be a safe and loving environment."

Grimacing, Martin forced his stiffened body from the sofa. "I, er … the memorial service for Evan's father is on Thursday. None of the surviving family members were willing, or able, to see to his remains, so the county council will be conducting a brief service at the cemetery. What do you recommend—er, regarding Evan being present at the service?"

The therapist rubbed her hands over her arms, and Martin fought his urge to chastise her for her failure to dress appropriately for the weather.

"What do you think would be best for Evan?" she said.

"I can't see that it would benefit the boy in any way to be there. Leastwise, not at this point. He's settling in to our home, rarely has nightmares—or bedwetting incidents, and his attendance at the service could reignite the earlier fears."

"I'm in agreement with you, Dr. Ellingham. Evan feels secure in his new home, and that's exactly what he needs right now—a sense of security."

"I'm disinclined to even bring the matter up with the boy, but I want to be prepared should he have questions in future. How many details should I give him?"

"You have good instincts when it comes to Evan. Trust those instincts—feel your way through it."

"Mm, yes."

It was almost four o'clock when Martin and Evan left Dr. Peterson's office and walked across to the hospital, Evan peppering his guardian with questions as they approached the building's entrance.

"So, *then* what are they gonna do with you?" he asked, trotting along to keep up with the doctor's limited but still-longer stride.

"Mr. Christianson will look at the pictures of my arm and legs and decide if any of the pins can be removed."

"Can I see the pictures?"

"No. I'm going to drop you off at Dr. Parsons office. You can wait for me there."

"I get to play with Old Doc!"

"Mm, yes."

The boy leapt into the beam of the motion detector and the automatic doors hissed open. "Can I go on ahead, Dr. Ellig-am?"

"No, you better sta—erm, yes. I suppose that's all right. But don't go wandering off anywhere else," Martin said warning him with the wag of a finger and an admonishing look.

"I won't! Promise!" Evan bolted down the hallway, dodging a nurse pushing a supply cart before making a sharp left.

By the time Martin reached his friend's office, his young charge was already regaling him with the details of the previous day's flood.

"Hey, Mart."

"Chris. Sorry about our lunch plans. It just wasn't going to work with the schedule."

"No problem. We'll do it next time. Sounds like quite an eventful day in Portwenn yesterday."

"Mm. School had to be cancelled. All's back as it should be today, though." He gave a nod towards the seven-year-old. "You sure you don't mind watching him for a while?"

"Naw. I thought I'd take him to the canteen. Spoil his dinner with a slice of pie or an ice cream cone. If that's okay with you, that is."

"Hey, that's good thinkin', Old Doc!" Evan said as his attention was pulled away from the pendulum on the desktop. "Can I, Dr. Ellig-am?"

"You just had ice cream, Evan."

"Nuh-uh! That wasn't *just*; it was all the way back to yesterday. I can hardly even remember what flavour it was, it's been so long."

Martin glanced at his watch and huffed. "All right. Just one scoop, though. I should be finished in an hour or so," he said to Chris.

"Yep. Good luck, mate. Hope the news is good."

After finishing with the requested blood work, CT scans and x-rays, Martin made his way towards the nearest lift. The occupants already inside stepped back as he entered the cage.

A snort was heard from a fellow passenger and Martin glanced over. He glared at a snickering young man in a white coat before his attention was drawn to the source of the young man's amusement.

Adrian Pitts shifted uncomfortably from one foot to the other, his fingers toying with his tie as the pink flush on his neck spread up to his cheeks and intensified. Martin's lip curled into a reflexive sneer as he mumbled a barely audible, "Arse".

The bell on the lift pinged its arrival at the third floor and some of the passengers exited, trying to hide smirks and stifled sniggers. The altercation between the cocky, womanising Mr. Pitts and the renowned but now-disabled former surgeon had left Mr. Pitt's properly castigated—and with the bottom half of his tie laying on a cafe table. The incident had become hospital legend, it seemed.

The doors rumbled shut again, and Adrian's thin lips drew a tight line across his face. He sneaked another look at Martin, swallowing hard as he pulled absentmindedly at the knot of silk perched at the base of his throat.

When the elevator announced its arrival at the fourth floor, Martin and Adrian stepped forward at once, momentarily wedging themselves in the doorway together.

Adrian attempted to push past him, forcing Martin to reach out with his crutch to maintain his balance. The red-faced young surgeon tripped over it, sending his armload of metal clipboards clattering to the floor before he landed on top of them. Soft, high-pitched giggles emanated from the nurses' station.

Giving him a grunt, Martin stepped around him, stopping momentarily to wag a finger. "You dropped something," he said before continuing down the hall.

Ed Christianson looked up from his paperwork when he heard a knock on the door frame. "Martin! Come on in."

Martin entered the room and Mr. Christianson closed the door behind him. "Bit of a commotion down the hall a minute ago. You didn't upend a dinner trolley that failed to meet nutritional standards, I hope?"

Martin stared at him, expressionless. "Of course not."

"Just joking," the surgeon said. "Have a seat. I just got your pictures; let's have a look at how things are progressing." He swivelled his computer monitor around and sat down on the edge of his desk in front of his patient.

"As you can see, the right leg is looking great—good periosteal callus formation at the fracture lines in the tib/fib fractures. I had a brief conference call with Will Simpson. We both feel the fixators can come off the lower leg. I'd like to pull some of those femoral pins at the same time. What does your schedule look like for Thursday or Friday?"

"I have surgery in the morning, but I could make it Friday afternoon. I have another appointment over here at four o'clock."

"Good. Let's plan on getting this thing done at two o'clock. That gives you a bit of time to sleep off the anaesthesia."

Ed dragged his finger across the computer's touch screen and brought up another series of pictures. "Left leg—we need to talk about that. The fractures themselves are coming along. How has the nerve pain been? Any improvement since your visit to the lads in Wadebridge?"

His eyes drifting shut, Martin breathed out a heavy sigh. "Not really. But I have another appointment tomorrow. Perhaps I'll see some improvement over the course of the next week."

Ed leaned back on his hands and quirked the right side of his mouth. "Could be. Let's give it a few weeks and revisit things then."

"You have doubts?"

"Let's just say I'm not convinced the scar tissue is the problem. Take a look at the pictures we got today." He reached back and tapped the tip of his biro against the screen. "I can't be certain, but the films suggest you may have a fracture callus that's developed around the peroneal nerve.

"Hopefully, the contracting scar tissue is the source of the pain you've been experiencing, but if you don't see improvement with the physiotherapy, and certainly if the pain becomes more severe, Will Simpson may want to go in earlier than planned—have a look-see and release the nerve if necessary. He'd also do some internal fixation."

Martin sat quietly for a few moments before nodding. "All right. What about the arm?"

Ed brought up a new screen. "What we'd expect to see. So, that's good news. I'd like to give it another month before we pull any more pins there, though."

"And how much longer—on both the left leg and the arm?"

"If all continues to progress as it has been, another four to five months with the arm. If the nerve pain resolves in the leg then a bit longer than the arm."

"So, just the right leg on Friday?"

"That's right. Your labs all look good, so still no indication of any permanent damage to your internal organs." Ed got to his feet and returned to his chair. "Any questions or concerns you want to discuss?"

"No." Martin rubbed a thumb into his palm, glancing up at the surgeon. "Well, I should mention that the headaches I was having before ... they may have been a bit of an issue recently."

"A bit of an issue?"

"The triggers are the same, but they haven't been as intense. I just thought I—or Louisa felt it should be addressed."

Ed leaned back in his chair, studying his patient over steepled fingers. "What do you think? Does it need to be addressed?"

"I'll monitor it and let you know if they get more frequent or severe."

"You've discussed this with Portman, I assume?"

"Not as of yet. But as I said—"

"Discuss it with him, Martin, and keep me informed."

The phone on the surgeon's desk chirped and he picked up the receiver. "Tell her I'm with a patient at the moment. I'll call her back in a few minutes," he said before laying the phone back down. "Sorry about that—the wife. How are you and Louisa holding up with all of this, Martin?"

"We're fine. It complicates life for both of us, obviously, but all things considered, we're fine."

"Good."

"Mm. Are we done here?"

"Yes. But I can't let you go without another reminder to take it easy. And use the pain meds."

"Mm, yes." Martin picked up his crutch and got to his feet. "I'll see you on Friday."

Chapter 5

"How come we're stopping at this place?" Evan asked as they pulled into a parking place in front of the Wadebridge Veterinary Surgery.

Martin peered into the rear-view mirror at the boy. "This is the vet's where I've been taking that dog of yours. She mentioned she gives obedience classes."

"What's that?"

"That's training that will, hopefully, make the animal less objectionable to have in the house."

"Don't we want him to be objection-a-full?"

"Objection-a-*ble*. And no, we don't."

"So, what will they do to make him so he's not so objection-a-full?"

A hiss of air rushed from Martin's nose as he shook his head. "Evan, the word is objection-a-*ble.* It means something is unpleasant—nasty—distasteful."

The boy's seatbelt clicked and he boosted himself up to peer out the window. "Oh. Then I think you gots the wrong word, 'cause Buddy's not none of those things you said."

"He's not *any* of those things, Evan."

"*That's* why I think you need a different word."

"Oh, for heaven's sake," Martin grumbled, reaching for the door handle.

As he swung his right leg out of the car, a sudden gust of wind rushed over the top of the hill, pushing the door shut against it. He let out a yelp before hurriedly freeing the now-painful limb.

The seven-year-old peered over the back seat. "Are you okay, Dr. Ellig-am?"

Martin pulled in a deep breath and nodded his head. "I'm fine, Evan."

Stepping from the car, he pulled the back door open and his young charge leapt to the ground. "So, what's the vet gotta do to Buddy?" The boy turned an alarmed face to his guardian. "They don't gotta give him a shot for it, do they?"

"No. You're going to teach him to behave himself … maybe even teach him some tricks."

"*Really?* That's brilliant, Dr. Ellig-am! Can I teach him to get beer from the refrigerator like that dog does on the telly?"

"We don't keep beer in our refrigerator." Martin leaned down and rubbed at his leg.

"How come we don't keep beer in our fridge, Dr. Ellig-am?"

"Because I don't drink beer."

"I know you don't like it, but what about Mrs. Ellig-am? Maybe I could teach Buddy to get it for her."

"As far as I'm aware, she's not a big beer drinker either."

The boy's hands flapped at his sides. "Well, what trick *am* I gonna teach him to do, then?"

"Maybe you could teach him something useful."

"Like what?"

"I don't know. Teach him to wash that contaminant-laden face of his—or wipe his feet before he comes in the house."

Evan's head dropped to the side, and he rolled his eyes at him. "Now you're just being ridiculous, Dr. Ellig-am."

"Mm, yes." Martin wagged a finger at the child. "Come on."

Their feet crunched over the gravel as they crossed the car park, and Evan jogged to the right to swing a foot at a larger stone. It skittered away before banging against a metal wheelie bin.

The smell, unique to veterinary surgeries, greeted them when Martin pulled the door open. He wrinkled his nose at the odour of animal kibble, alcohol, vitamins, and disinfectant.

The acne-faced young woman who was at the desk on his first visit greeted them. "Hello. How can I help you?"

"I need to speak with the vet," he said tersely.

Evan grabbed hold of the edge of the counter and balanced on tiptoe, peering over at the girl. "We wanna take those classes so we can teach our dog some tricks."

A door opened down the hall and heels clicked against the polished tile floor.

"Dr. Ellingham! How are you?" Dr. Brown asked as she approached the desk.

"He just got his leg shut in the car door, so I don't think he's so good," Evan said.

"Oh, dear! Are you all right?"

Martin's cheeks reddened as he avoided the vet's gaze. "It's nothing. It's fine now."

Tessa eyed him dubiously for a moment before turning her attention to the boy. "And what's your name?" she asked, leaning down to talk to him.

"I'm Evan, and Buddy's my dog. We wanna teach him some tricks."

"Oh, I see."

"You, er ... you mentioned obedience classes," Martin said. "How soon can we get started?"

"I actually have a group beginner class starting up next week. You could get to know other dog owners, and Buddy could socialise with the other dogs."

"Oh, gawd," Martin mumbled. "No, definitely not a group class."

"Well, I do have a trainer who uses my facilities for private lessons. Perhaps you know her; she's from Portwenn—Barbara Collingsworth."

"Never heard of her. How do I get in touch with the woman?"

"I can set something up with her if you like."

"Good. The boy will be training the dog, so it would need to be after school—later afternoon. Monday, Wednesday, or Thursday."

"Well, I'll organise something and give you a call."

The throbbing in Martin's leg intensified, bringing on a wave of nausea. The colour drained from his face, and he grimaced before excusing himself to use the lavatory.

When he returned, the vet gestured to the vinyl sofa in the hallway. "Sit down, Dr. Ellingham. You better ice that leg before you head home."

"I said, it's fine."

Tressa tipped her head down and peered up at him. "Your gait would suggest otherwise."

"Oh, it would, would it?" he said with a sneer.

"Yes, it would. My patients can't tell me when or where they hurt. I need to study their behaviour ... their movements. You're walking like you hurt. Now sit down and put your leg up. I'll get some ice."

She turned on her heel and walked down the hall.

Martin took a step towards the door, but the sharp jolt that his weight sent through his leg stopped him, and he dropped on to the sofa.

Evan worried his fingers as he watched him. "You didn't break your leg again, did you, Dr. Ellig-am?"

"No. It'll be fine; I'm sure." He reached out and tugged at the boy's hand. "Try not to do that, Evan. You'll hurt yourself."

Tressa returned with several ice packs. "Okay, let me help you," she said, lifting the doctor's leg on to the sofa before surrounding it with the ice. "There you go."

He wrinkled up his nose. "Those are, no doubt, covered in God-knows-what-kind of pathogens."

"They've be thoroughly disinfected," she said, her hand alighting on his shoulder. "Now, can I get you a cup of tea?"

He turned a furrowed brow to the neatly manicured nails. "Erm, no ... thank you."

"How about you, Evan? Would you like a glass of milk and a biscuit?"

The child's obvious disquietude eased, and he looked to his guardian. "Can I, Dr. Ellig-am?"

"Erm, that would be fine," Martin said, shifting away from the woman's touch. He gave her a nod. "You can go now—get the boy his milk ... and biscuit."

"Okay, come on, Evan. Let's go see what we can find in the kitchen," the vet said, reaching a hand out to him.

Martin tugged at his ear as he watched them disappear into a room off the hall.

His unease with Tressa Brown's attention stayed with him long after they left her surgery. Evan was quiet as they made the twenty-minute drive from Wadebridge to Portwenn. It was only when they passed Trevathan Farm that his voice was heard over the purr of the car's engine.

"Dr. Ellig-am, I wanna give Mrs. Ellig-am a special present."

"What for?"

"'Cause I want her ta know I like her enough. I wanna show her Buddy's new tricks for her present. Like a surprise."

"She'll be aware that you're taking the dog to obedience classes. I'm not sure it'll come as a great surprise."

"Oh ... yeah."

Another minute passed before the boy said, "But she doesn't hafta know. We could tell her that we gotta take him to the vet 'cause he's sick or something."

"That wouldn't be truthful, though, would it?"

"Oh."

Martin peered back at the child's slumped posture and rubbed a hand over his face. "Although, I suppose I might be able to come up with an honest excuse for our weekly trips over to Wadebridge with the dog."

"You mean you're gonna tell her a porky pie?"

"No, of course not. I'll tell her—I'll tell her the animal's condition needs weekly monitoring."

"Oh." The boy scratched at his head. "What's his condition?"

"He's objectionable."

"Oh. So, then I can do my surprise?"

"Yes, you can do your surprise."

"Thanks, Dr. Ellig-am! It's sure a good thing Buddy's objection-a-full, isn't it?"

He grunted. "Mm, yeah. Brilliant." A smile tugged at the left corner of Martin's mouth as he watched his contented charge settle back into his seat.

"Da-ee!" James Henry squealed when his father and Evan came through the kitchen door a few minutes later. His fire engine wailed as it fell to the floor, and he toddled over, latching on to Martin's leg.

"Hello, James," he said, taking his son's hand and leading him to the table. He dropped into a chair before pulling the toddler into his lap.

Louisa gave the soup she was making a final stir and returned the lid to the pot. "Did you have a problem in Truro?" she asked. "It took quite a while."

Evan pulled off his trainers and set them on the rug near the door. "Oh, that's just 'cause we stopped to see Dr. Tressa."

"The vet? What for?"

"'Cause we needed to—"

Martin cleared his throat and wagged a finger under the table.

Giving him an exaggerated nod, the boy's eyes rolled to the side. "We needed to—errrm, I needed a glass of milk and a biscuit! That's it!"

Martin's elbow thunked against the table, and his head dropped into his hand as the seven-year-old gave him a self-satisfied smile.

Louisa eyed the child suspiciously. "You went to the veterinary surgery to get a snack?"

Evan squirmed under her no-nonsense gaze, fumbling for words. "Erm, I had a snack, and Dr. Brown and Dr. Ellig-am were—were just— talkin'. Yeah, they were talkin'."

"Talking? About what, Martin?"

His mouth opened, but his young charge pre-empted his reply. "Oh, just about stuff—the stuff men talk to ladies about. You know, *that* kind of stuff."

Louisa turned a furrowed brow to her husband. "Martin?"

He pulled his son in closer. "It wasn't like *that,* Louisa. I needed to get some appointments scheduled, and it seemed an opportune time."

"*What* appointments?"

"Buddy's appointments," the seven-year-old said. "He gots ta get his commission monitored."

"His commission?" She fixed narrowed eyes on her husband as her fingertips tapped against her elbows.

"He means condition." Martin tugged at his ear and peered up at her. "That *was* our agreement, wasn't it—that I'd run it to the vet whenever necessary?"

"Well, yes. I suppose it was." Cocking her head, she eyed him once more before returning to her dinner preparations.

"Evan flipped his coat over a peg behind the door and jumped down the step into the lounge, settling in with the toys."

"Da-ee, down," James said as he squirmed from his father's arms before toddling off to join the seven-year-old.

"How did your appointment with Ed go? Did you remember to talk to him about the headaches?"

"Yes. I'll monitor it and keep him informed."

"What, that's it? No tests ... scans or anything? He's just going to trust you to keep him informed? That hasn't worked out very well in the past, has it?"

"I'll fill Jeremy in on what's been going on, and he'll help to monitor the situation," Martin said through pursed lips.

She tipped her head down and eyed him suspiciously. "Hmm. What about the fractures? Everything okay?"

Martin grunted, getting up to retrieve a protein shake from the refrigerator. "He wants to pull a few more pins on Friday. And the fixators can come off the lower right leg."

"Oh, that's wonderful news, Martin! Everything looks good, then?"

"Mm, yes—yes it is wonderful news." Air hissed from the can as he popped the top.

Louisa spun around as the soup simmered over the side of the pot, sizzling on to the burner. "Bugger," she grumbled, now distracted by the mess she had to clean up.

Martin grunted and ducked his head. "I have some paperwork to finish up," he said, fleeing the kitchen before his wife could pick up on his half-truth.

The Ellingham's evening progressed in a blissfully banal fashion. Martin was putting the last of the now-washed supper dishes away when Louisa came through the lounge with James Henry, bathed and ready for bed.

Reaching down, she tousled Evan's hair. "Your turn, young man," she said.

The boy flopped back on the floor and huffed out a breath. "But I just started a really good book," he whined.

"And it'll still be a really good book tomorrow. It's late, and you have school in the morning, so scoot." She gave him a snap of her fingers for emphasis.

The seven-year-old slapped his book shut and shoved it to the side before plodding off towards the stairs.

"And don't forget to brush your teeth!" Louisa called out after him.

A gust of wind rattled the windows on the front of the house, causing the lights to flicker. "I'm beginning to think this winter will never end," she said as she stepped up into the kitchen.

"That's highly unlikely. As far as I'm aware, there have been no major volcanic eruptions that could have caused a dramatic climate change." Martin gave his hands a final wipe on the towel, returning it to its proper place on the hook at the end of the counter before turning a straight face to her.

A smile teased at the corners of her mouth. "I wasn't serious, Martin." Stretching up to kiss him, she pressed a book into his hands. "I have a bit of schoolwork to do. Can you read James his bedtime story?"

"Of course," he said, placing the backs of his fingers against his son's forehead. "He looks flushed."

"Oh, Martin. He's just rosy from his bath."

Palpating the toddler's neck for swollen lymph nodes, he conceded to his wife. "Mm, yes."

"Daddy's going to read to you tonight, James." Louisa carried the boy into the lounge and set him on the sofa. "Come sit down, Martin." She glanced up to find him staring at her, absently. "*Martin*."

"Mm, yes." Shaking himself from his daze, he limped from the kitchen and dropped heavily on to the sofa before James scrambled into his lap.

Louisa plopped a pillow on the coffee table and lifted her husband's legs on to it. "I'll get the ice," she said, giving his foot a pat.

"Thank you."

"*The Mousehole Cat*," he began. "*Once, at the far end of England, there lived in the village of Mousehole, a magical cat whose name was Mowzer.*"

James pulled his fingers from his mouth and tapped them against the page. "Mouw, mouw," he said, his voice artificially high in imitation of his mother.

"Mm, yes." Martin continued with the Cornish tale, and James sat, rapt, as the old cat and her owner Tom braved a bitter winter storm, heading out to sea to collect fish for a hungry village.

"There you go," Louisa said, returning with the ice packs. She leaned down to place a kiss on her husband's cheek before nuzzling her face into her son's neck. The boy pulled his chin into his shoulder and giggled.

"You're tickling him, Louisa," Martin said.

"I know I am. We're just having a bit of fun, aren't we, James?"

Martin threw his head back and waited impatiently for the moment of silliness to pass.

The sound of footsteps grew louder before Evan bounded into the room, making a final leap on to the sofa. "Did I miss anything?" he asked, tugging at the book to look at the cover.

"The first four pages." Martin huffed as he flipped through, searching to find where he had left off.

"Can you start over, Dr. Ellig-am?"

"Oh, for God's sake. At this rate, you and James will have outgrown the story by the time we finish it," he grumbled.

"Pleeease, Dr. Ellig-am."

Martin screwed up his face at the seven-year-old's pleading eyes. Flipping back to the first page, he began anew.

"Mouw, mouw," James squeaked, his fingers leaving a second juicy trail across the page.

Martin shifted him on his lap and reached into his back pocket for his handkerchief, drying the glossy paper before continuing on.

"*Mowzer was very partial to a plate of fresh fish. In fact, she never ate anything else.*"

"Huh! That's like you, Dr. Ellig-am!"

Martin bristled. "I don't just eat fish."

"But you like 'em a lot. And your favourite meals all have fish in 'em."

Martin grunted before continuing with the story, detailing a week's worth of traditional Cornish fish dishes. "*On Mondays, they made morgy-broth, Mowser's favourite fish stew. On Tuesday's they baked hake and topped it with golden mashed potatoes. On Wednesday's they*—you get the idea. The other days they had kedgeree, grilled fair maids, fried launces with a knob of butter—"

"What's launces?" Evan asked.

"They're eels."

"What's a knob?"

"The word has a number of meanings. In this case, it means a lump of butter, and butter is an unnecessary addition of saturat—"

Evan's finger tapped against the page. "Dr. Ellig-am, you're s'posed to just read it. You don't gots ta worry about it."

"I'm not worried about it, Evan. I'm merely trying to point out—" He shook his head at the boy's vacant expression before turning back to the story. "*On Saturdays, they soused scad with vinegar and onions. And on Sundays, they made star-gazy pie.*"

"I love star-gazy pie!" Evan said, "'Cause Miss Babcock let me stay for supper once, and she made star-gazy pie. And we even gots ta have sticky toffee pudding after!"

The boy pulled his knees up, wrapping his arms around them as he nestled into his guardian's side.

Louisa's attention was pulled away from her work by the sound of her husband's voice, and she sat at the table listening to his recitation.

"*...Mowzer purred as if she would burst, to tell him that she loved him more than any of these things.*" Martin turned his wrist, looking down at his watch before wagging a finger at the book. "Then they went to sleep. And so should you; it's getting late. We'll have to finish this tomorrow night."

"Ohhh, can't we do just a little more?" Evan whined.

Getting up from the table, Louisa pointed a finger towards the stairs. "You have school in the morning, young man."

She lifted her son from her husband's lap and the toddler buried his sleepy face in her shoulder. "Come on," she said, giving the seven-year-old a jerk of her head. "Martin, you stay put. I'll tuck them in."

Evan pulled his knees under him and wrapped his arms around his guardian's neck before kissing him on the cheek. "G'night, Dr. El-lig-am."

"Goodnight, Evan."

Breathy words were whispered into Martin's ear. "I love you even more than star-gazy pie."

Martin swallowed hard and pulled in his chin. Then, he whispered back, "I love you, too, Evan." He glanced up at his wife, who stood watching with a small smile on her face, and he cleared his throat. "Mm, sleep well."

He lay in bed a while later, listening to another round of rain tapping against the windows, weighing the pros and cons of bringing up the issue of the possible nerve entrapment problem in his leg. He would prefer to sweep it under the rug for the time being, addressing it if and when it was required.

But for Louisa, forewarned is forearmed. And if he withheld the information, she would feel he was shutting her out again. He breathed a hiss of air from his nose and smoothed the covers over him.

Louisa stepped out of the bathroom and took a seat on the bed. "How are you feeling?"

He raised an eyebrow. "Why?"

"It was just a general question, Martin."

"Ah. I'm fine."

She picked a bottle up from her bedside table and lotion bubbled from it into her hand. "I don't know why I keep asking you that, expecting a different answer." Turning, she leaned over and kissed him. "I'm happy for you—for us. Having two of those bloody fixators off will be quite a milestone, hmm."

"Mm."

"Well, *I* think it will be. Maybe cause for a celebration, even."

"Ohhh, Louisa. Can we please not—"

"Martin, we've had months of this two-steps-forward-one-step-back improvement. On Friday, we take two steps forward—one big leap, really. I'm bloody ready for something to celebrate; please don't spoil it."

"But, Louisa, we're far from having this nightmare behind us. In fact, there may be a—"

Leaning over, she silenced him with a kiss. "I don't want to think about what's to come right now. I just want to enjoy the good news you received today. Hmm?"

He ducked his head. "Yes."

"So, are you going to share with me what it was you and Evan were conspiring about tonight?" she asked, sitting back up to rub lotion on to her arms.

Martin pulled a hand under his head and furrowed his brow. "When were we conspiring?"

"When Evan was saying goodnight. He whispered something to you, and you whispered back."

"Well, I can assure you, there was no conspiring involved. That would suggest ill intent and neither Evan nor I were plotting anything."

"Okay. Let me rephrase the question. What did the two of you whisper to each other?"

"If we'd wanted it to be common knowledge, we wouldn't have been whispering, Louisa."

"Oh, for goodness' sake, Martin. *I'm* not common knowledge; I'm your wife." Her rubbing of lotion stopped, and she turned a taut face to him. "Does it have something to do with the mysterious visit to the vet's today?"

"Of course not! It was just ... man talk. And there *was* no mysterious visit. It was, as I said before, an opportune time to schedule Buddy's appointments."

Her face softened. "You called him Buddy."

"That is it's name, isn't it?"

"Yes. It's *his* name. It was just very nice to hear you use it."

"Mm, I see." His eyes locked on hers and he reached out to stroke her arm. "Ask Evan about what we said. I don't want to betray a confidence."

"Fair enough." She leaned down to give him a final kiss before turning out the light. "Goodnight, Martin."

"Goodnight."

Chapter 6

Martin sat at his desk the next morning, staring at the second hand on his watch as it inched around the dial, trying to ignore the pungent aroma of Marianne Walker's decades-old perfume. He rubbed at his forehead, too tired to care that he had no idea what the woman had been prattling on about for the past five minutes.

Hissing out a breath, he asked, "Mrs. Walker, do you have a medical problem I can help you with?"

The woman tugged at the scarf around her neck. "No, not really. I was just wondering if you could recommend someone."

Her gaze settled on the antique barograph decorating the fireplace mantel, and she got up to inspect it.

"Recommend someone?" Martin asked.

"That's right." She leaned forward, peering closely at the instrument whose brass parts had been fastidiously cleaned, repaired, and polished before being encased safely in a glass box. "This is lovely. What is it exactly?"

"It's a barometer."

"Did you do this? Like with all the clocks around here?"

"Yes. Mrs. Walker, you didn't answer my question. What do you mean, recommend someone?"

"For my son ... and his wife." She looked back at him, waving her gloves towards the mantel. "I don't suppose you'd consider selling it?"

"No." The doctor shook his head, grimacing when the movement triggered a throbbing behind his eyes.

"Oh." She pushed the strap on her handbag up to her elbow. "Well, if you can't recommend someone, perhaps you could see them?"

"I have absolutely no idea what you're talking about."

"Their difficulties—differences, if you will. I think if they could talk them through with a professional, they might be able to work things out."

Martin sat for a moment with his eyes closed before breathing out a heavy sigh. "Mrs. Walker, I'm a general practitioner, not a couples' therapist."

"Oh, I realise that. I just thought you might be able to make an exception."

He reached for his notepad, slapping it down in front of him before scratching out a note to himself. "Let me do some checking. I'll see if I can locate someone." He peered up at her. "Is there anything else?"

"No, I think that's all."

"Good. I'll call you as soon as I have any information."

"Thank you, Dr. Ellingham."

The woman walked across the room, stopping with her hand on the doorknob. "You look rather tired. Have you tried Gingko biloba? A few drops in my tea in the morning works wonders for me."

"I'm fine." Martin pushed himself up from his chair, herding the woman into the reception room and out the front door.

"That was your last patient, Doc," Morwenna said as he approached the desk.

"What about that cat woman ... Mrs. DeLaney.

"Mrs. *Dingley*. She didn't show."

"Typical!" He shoved Marianne's patient notes into the file cabinet, muttering, "I don't know why I bother."

Jeremy came in from the lounge and handed the receptionist several collection tubes and a lab request form. "Can you get those sent over to Truro, Morwenna?"

"Yeah, sure." Her chair squeaked as she turned to Martin, batting her eyes at him. "Is that a new tie, Doc?"

He glanced down. "No."

"Oh. Just never noticed how it brings out the blue in your eyes before."

"My eyes are green. What do you want, Morwenna?"

She dug around in her tote on the floor, pulling out a purple sheet of paper before handing it to him.

"What's this?" he asked.

"It's a notice from the paper. The Portwenn Musical Players are puttin' on a play—*Annie Get Your Gun*."

The doctor threw his head back, muttering, "Gawd."

"I wanna audition. Thing is see, the auditions are Saturday morning." She gave him an ingratiating smile. "Don't s'pose there's any chance of me getting some time off, is there?"

He handed it back to her. "No. I need you here."

"I could fill in for her," Jeremy said.

"You're my assistant, not my receptionist, Jeremy." The file drawer rumbled before slamming shut with a metallic bang. "The answer is no, Morwenna," he grumbled before limping off towards the hall.

The young woman slapped the piece of paper down on her lap as her shoulders slumped. "I really thought he'd say yes this time. He's not been as ... I don't know ... as difficult lately."

"Don't give up hope just yet. Let me talk to him," Jeremy said, as he headed back towards the lounge.

"Gee, thanks, Jeremy!"

The espresso machine was humming when the aide stepped into the kitchen. Martin glanced over his shoulder and gave him a grunt. "Would you like a cup?"

"Yeah. Thanks, mate." The aide took a sleeve of chocolate digestives from his backpack and pulled the packaging open. "So, I was thinking. About Morwenna and this audition she—"

"I said no, Jeremy." Setting two cups down on the table, the doctor limped to the refrigerator for the milk. He tucked the small bottle of semi-skimmed milk, meant for use in tea and coffee, under his arm before picking up one of his shakes.

He dropped heavily into the chair across from his aide, setting the bottle down in front of him.

Metal clinked softly against ceramic as Jeremy stirred sugar into his cup and eyed his boss. "So, here's what I was thinking. Morwenna works hard, she's a reliable employee—trustworthy and all that. If there was someone who could fill in for her, just for a few hours Saturday morning, would it be that disruptive to the practice if she had the time off to go do her theatre gig?"

"If you're talking about Louisa, no. We tried that before and it wasn't ... practicable."

"No, I wasn't talking about Louisa. I haven't asked her yet, but I was thinking maybe Poppy could help out. She's demonstrated an awareness of the need to control your exposure to communicable diseases. And she did a good job when she filled in before. Right?"

Martin took a sip from his cup. "She was adequate, yes." He bit at his lower lip staring out the window for a few moments. Then, he popped the top on his shake and took a swig. "If she's agreeable, we can give it a try."

"Great! I'll talk to her this evening." The young man reached for the milk bottle and sloshed some into his coffee. "So, how did your powwow with Mr. Christianson go yesterday?"

Martin screwed up his face. "My *powwow*?"

Jeremy shrugged his shoulders and pulled a digestive from the package. "I don't mean to pry, mate. I'm just interested in how things seem to be progressing."

The aide averted his gaze from the doctor's deadpan stare, and he hesitated, his finger drawing circles around the rim of his cup. "It's just that—well, I *am* part of your care team, so I'd appreciate being kept in the loop on these things."

Martin swallowed down more of his shake before glancing up at him, but he said nothing.

Jeremy's fingers drummed against the table. "What? You don't consider me a part of your care team?"

"I didn't say that, Jeremy," the doctor said, snapping open the morning paper.

The young man screwed up his mouth. "Oh, I get it. I'm just here to ride shotgun. In the event you need help and Parsons and Christianson aren't available, that it?"

Martin put a palm up. "Jeremy, I didn't say that."

"Then what? I know I'm low man on the totem pole, but I'm your first line of defence. I hope you're not expecting me to wait for the smoke signals from Truro to arrive!"

"You sound like you're *fixin'* to audition for that production with Morwenna," Martin said, peering at him over the latest international news.

"What?" The aide threw his head back. "Oh, very funny. You do realise my blood pressure goes up about twenty points when you do that, don't you?"

Martin stared back at him for a moment before pulling in his chin. "Mm, sorry."

"No, no, no. You don't need to apologise. It's just—I mean, I have no problem with you being ... well, you being you. But I don't expect it when you mess with me like that. And you do it *really* well."

"Mm, yes." Martin pushed himself up from the table, tossing his bottle into the bin before rinsing his cup out and putting it in the dishwasher. "The fixators come off the right tib/fib fractures on Friday. He'll also remove a few more pins from the femur."

Jeremy spun around. "Wow! That's great news, Martin! How did you keep from blurting it out when I came in this morning?"

Picking up the young man's now-empty cup, the doctor shook his head. "It's not all good news. The pain I've been having in the left leg may be due to a nerve entrapment issue. Ed consulted with Will Simpson, one of my surgeons up in London. The pictures were ambiguous, but callus may have formed around the peroneal nerve."

"Seriously? I didn't know that was possible."

"Mm. It's uncommon."

"So, what's the plan?"

Jeremy pulled his arms out of the way as Martin sprayed down the table with disinfectant and wiped it off.

"I'll carry on with the physical therapy. If the pain continues or worsens, Simpson will go in, free the nerve, fix the fractures internally and, I would presume, take care of the reconstruction at that time."

"That would be a bit of a setback."

"Mm."

"How did Louisa react to the news?"

"She didn't. I haven't told her."

"Oh, mate. You have to tell her. How long ago was it that you were lecturing me about truth in a relationship."

"Yes, I realise that!" Martin slapped the dishcloth down on to the counter. "I *tried* to tell her, but she shushed me." He shrugged. "She was happy about the fixators coming off; I didn't want to spoil it for her."

"Yeah, sure. Whatever you say," the aide replied with a grin as he picked another biscuit from the sleeve.

"Oh, wipe that smug look off your face. I'll talk to her about it tonight." Martin glanced at his watch. "I need to pick up some supplies from Mrs. Tishell. If you're not doing anything I could use an extra pair of hands."

The young man's grin broadened. "Need some help fending off her amorous advances, eh?"

"Nooo. It's a large order and I've been a bit ... unsteady lately."

"Yep. Let me finish this chocolate digestive, and I'll get my coat."

Martin looked him up and down, raising an eyebrow. "Do yourself a favour and bin the rest of that. The rest of the package, too, for that matter."

"Why? It gives me a mental boost about this time of the day."

"No, it's sugar, starch, and saturated fats that you can't afford."

"You saying I'm overweight?"

"Not necessarily. But you could easily lose a couple of pounds."

Jeremy gave him a roll of his eyes. "You'll appreciate those extra pounds if you need me to protect you from Mrs. Tishell."

He brushed the crumbs from his hands and shoved the biscuits into his backpack, getting to his feet. "Just a word of warning, mate ... I wouldn't try the you-could-easily-lose-a-couple-of-pounds line on Louisa. Women can be super sensitive about their weight."

Martin ducked his head and gave a tug on his ear. "Mm, I'm aware of that."

"You ready?"

"Yes," the doctor said, taking his coat from the peg behind the door.

The sun was warm on his face as Martin stepped out on to the terrace, but the cold caused him to cough as it hit his lungs.

"Watch your step," Jeremy said, wagging a finger at the crystal-clear ice that had formed on a puddle left from the morning mizzle. He reached over, getting a precautionary safety hold on his patient's good arm.

Martin sidestepped the hazard and glanced over at the aide, still hobbled by the recent injury he'd sustained in a "domestic incident" with his girlfriend. "Thank you. How's your knee doing?" he asked. "Are you still having pain or swelling?"

"Nope." The young man stiff-legged his way down the ramp to the tarmac, keeping a guarded eye on the doctor. "Another week with the brace and I should be as good as new."

"Good. Keep up with the exercises they gave you over in Wadebridge. You don't want it to tighten up on you."

"Yep, I am."

"What are you doing for lunch? Louisa and Evan aren't coming home today. We could go to the Crab."

"Erm, yeah. Yeah, that sounds good, Martin."

The smell of fish grew stronger as they neared the bottom of Roscarrock Hill. The fishermen had just returned with their catch, and Eric Collins, the fishmonger, called out, "Just got some nice cod in, Doc! You interested?"

Martin stopped. "Erm, yes. I'll pick it up a bit later."

"Right then. I'll set it aside for you," he said, stooping to hoist up another plastic crate laden with fish.

Martin grunted and turned on to Church Hill, towards the chemist. He took several steps before his toe caught on a triangular manhole cover, sitting slightly askew after the work done by the North Cornwall Water Company earlier in the week.

Jeremy grabbed hold of his coat, softening the impact as he fell into a pile of lobster pots stashed against the front of Mrs. Tishell's shop.

"You okay?" the aide asked.

Martin leaned back against the centuries-old building, waiting for his racing heart to slow. "I'm—I'm fine, I think."

He glanced around him, relieved to see that his less-than-graceful side trip had gone unnoticed by anyone other than a disgruntled gull, frightened from its perch. It dipped its head, chastising him with its shrill choking call. Martin straightened himself and gave it a curl of his lip. "Come on, Jeremy," he said before continuing on.

Mrs. Tishell was restocking shelves when the two men came through the door. "Be with you in a tick," she said before glancing back over her shoulder.

Whirling around, she tugged at the hem of her cardigan. "Dr. Ellingham! What can I do for you?"

"I need to pick up the supplies I ordered."

"Oh, I have those ready for you," she said, prancing towards the counter, slowing momentarily to give him an understated curtsy.

"Now, where did I put that? I know it's here somewhere." She rummaged around under the cash register, humming softly.

The intense burning sensation that had prevented Martin from getting any sleep the night before intensified, and he shifted his weight off his left leg reflexively. A sharp stream of air hissed from his nose. "Mrs. Tishell!"

"Yes, yes. It's here somewhere." Her brow furrowed before her hands flew up in front of her. "Of course. Where *is* my head!" She turned and removed a box from a cabinet behind her, setting it down in front of him. "Isn't that how it always is? You put something in a place you're sure to remember, and then when you need it"—her fingers tapped twice on the top of the box—"you can't remember where you put it." She gave him a coy smile, brushing at her fringe. "There you go, Dr. Ellingham."

"Mm, yes." Martin reached for it and the chemist gasped. "Oh, dear! You should have that tended to!"

Martin looked at her quizzically, following her gaze to the trickle of blood that ran from his right hand. "Oh, gawd," he said, closing his eyes to the now-spinning room.

Jeremy stepped forward and took hold of his arm. "You must have caught it on something sharp when you fell against those lobster pots."

"Well"—he sputtered—"obviously!"

The chemist leaned forward to inspect the wound. "You should have that treated directly. Those pots are bound to be teeming with bacteria, and saltwater infections can be particularly aggressive. Given your immunocompromised state, you would be particularly susceptible."

"Yes, I'm aware of that, Mrs. Tishell," Martin said, his eyes snapping at her. The pain in his leg was intensifying as he stood there discussing the situation, and a desperation to get off his feet came over him. "Just get me an antiseptic swab and a couple of plasters. I'll give it a thorough cleaning when I get back to the surgery."

"Oh, I think you should take care of that properly, straight away, Dr. Ellingham!" Mrs. Tishell said, her head swinging side to side.

Jeremy took hold of his patient's arm and pulled him aside, speaking softly. "I have to agree with her, Martin. We either take care of it here or walk back up to the surgery."

A pain and frustration-induced warmth spread through Martin. "I *can't* walk back to the surgery! I need a—a break first!" he hissed as his eyes darted to the woman behind the counter.

"Ah, the leg?"

"Yes, the leg, you idiot!"

"Okay, okay!" The aide glanced about the shop. "Mrs. Tishell, if you could gather some things together for me, I can take care of this here. Maybe we could use your stock room?"

"My stock roo—oh, of course. A bit of privacy—certainly. What do you need?"

"A chair for Dr. Ellingham for starters."

"Yes, right away."

The woman hurried off, and Jeremy began to pull supplies from the shelves—antiseptic, a bottle of saline, bandages, and a syringe.

Martin watched him incredulously. "You do know it's just a scratch, not a severed limb, don't you?"

"It's a deep scratch. And I'm not taking any chances."

"Here you are, Mr. Portman!" the chemist sing-songed as she reentered the room with a folding chair. "Where would you like it?"

"Anywhere in your stockroom is fine. And then if you could get me a basin of some sort and some paper towelling."

"Oh, for heaven's sake," Martin muttered.

"Come on," the aide said, giving him a jerk of his head.

The doctor rolled his eyes and sighed before following him towards the back room, the chemist's heels clicking against the floor behind him.

Mrs. Tishell waved a hand towards the chair sitting between the shelves lining the walls of the narrow room. "Let me help you, Dr. Ellingham," she said, taking him by the arm.

"Oh, for God's sake! Get off!" he snapped, yanking his arm away. "It's a scratch; I'm not dying!"

"Mrs. Tishell," Jeremy said, raising his eyebrows at her. "Could you please get that basin I asked for? I want to irrigate the wound."

"Certainly, Mr. Portman."

Sally hurried off, and the aide turned back to his patient. Martin stared at him, his expression thunderous.

"I'm sorry, Martin," Jeremy said, "but there's no way I'm going to stick a plaster on that and call it good." He took hold of the doctor's hand, inspecting it. "Is it just Mrs. Tishell that has you on edge, or is it something else?"

Martin glanced up, swallowing hard. "I didn't feel it, Jeremy. It's been four months and I still don't—"

"Here you go, Mr. Portman," the chemist said as she came back into the room, thrusting a plastic dishpan at the aide.

Jeremy gave Martin an understanding nod before wagging a finger at his wounded hand. "Okay, Dr. Ellingham, let's get this taken care of."

By the time Martin and Jeremy had finished at the chemist and were leaving the pub after lunch, a cold, heavy fog had settled in over the village. Hoar frost was forming on the hedge lining Roscarrock Hill, creating a feathery appearance to the winter-bare branches.

"I was, er ... wondering if you might be able to help me out with that massage you do, Jeremy," Martin said.

The aide gave him a roguish grin. "You mean the kind I give to Poppy?"

Martin screwed up his face. "Of course not!"

Jeremy pushed the kitchen door open and stepped aside to let his patient through. "Then you'll have to clarify."

Shaking his coat from his shoulders, Martin hung it on a peg. "I've been having some trouble with the ice pick headaches."

"When did this start?"

"A while ago."

"I assume they're pretty bad, or I doubt you'd be fessing up." The aide set the box of supplies down on the table and removed his jacket, slinging it over the back of a chair.

"I'm not *fessing* up. I'm keeping you apprised of the situation."

"Ah. Let's go upstairs. I'll take care of the massage, and then you better have a lie down. God, you look awful today, mate."

Martin cocked his head at him. "Thank you."

"Sorry, but you do." The aide picked the box of supplies up from the table and gave a jerk of his head. "Come on," he said as he headed down the hall.

Chapter 7

Martin rubbed at his eyes as the traffic slowed at the stoplight in Redruth, a picturesque old mining community an hour and a half south of Portwenn. He glanced at his watch—half twelve. Thirty minutes until the service for Jim Hanley would commence.

All was quiet and deserted when he turned right into the drive through Trewirgie Cemetery. Continuing to the end of the lane, he pulled the Lexus on to a no through road to await the arrival of the representative from the Cornwall County Council.

He tried to push aside the images from the night of Jim Hanley's death, closing his eyes and focusing his thoughts on his family. The gentle rocking of the vehicle, buffeted by the wind, combined with his fatigue to lull him into an uneasy sleep.

Voices could be heard from the other side of the door. Martin looked back at the still form on the floor and, with his pulse pounding in his ears, he reached for the knob. The sound of breaking glass sent a blinding jolt of adrenaline through him and he froze. He couldn't do it. He couldn't turn that knob.

He slowly backed away before racing to his grandfather's side. He wanted to flee—to run. But he had no place to run to. No secure arms to huddle in. No safe place to hide. He was trapped, forced to watch as Henry Ellingham exsanguinated.

The voices grew quiet now. He no longer heard his father's booming irate voice or his mother's scornful one. They'd stopped fighting.

His heart thrummed in his chest. It was his fault. It always was when bad things happened. And he knew this was an especially bad thing.

Footsteps grew louder, and light glinted off the glass knob as it began to turn. There would be consequences, as his father called them.

"Good God!" Christopher Ellingham said before hurrying over, grabbing his son by the arm and throwing him out of the way. He pressed his fingers to the old man's neck. "He's dead!"

He turned icy blue eyes to his son. "What—in God's name—is wrong with you?" he said through clenched teeth. "You should have gone for help. Why are you just sitting here?"

Holding his arm to his stomach, the boy shook his head and tried to speak, but the words wouldn't come.

"Well?" the eminent doctor barked.

Martin covered his face with his arm, trying to hide his tears, but it was too late.

Christopher looked at him with disgust. "Oh, stop snivelling! I have to deal with this first, but don't think there won't be consequences for what you've done," he said. His angry voice dropped—softer, but menacing. "And you won't have the old man to protect you anymore, will you, Martin?"

Martin's heart pounded as the room began to spin, and he ran, desperate to distance himself from the situation.

He stopped when he found himself at the top of an unfamiliar staircase. Teetering on the top step, he looked down in horror at the body of Jim Hanley. Evan looked up at him, his face tear-stained.

The whistling wind grew louder suddenly, and he whirled around. A dark form loomed in front of him again. He couldn't move, his feet seemingly glued to the floor as the lorry sped towards him.

The impact threw him back and he landed at the bottom of the steps, next to Jim Hanley's lifeless body.

A sudden gust of wind hit the car, waking Martin with a start. He tried to slow his breathing and rubbed a hand over his face. "Ten more minutes," he mumbled as he rechecked the time.

He sat, gazing out over the landscape, dotted here and there by the remains of long-since abandoned tin and copper mines. Some say that the town's name came from the blood red colour of the stream running along the bottom of Fore Street, turned red by iron oxide, a by-product of tinning.

A car door slammed and he craned his neck to look down the lane. Two men got out of a small silver vehicle, emblazoned with a Cornwall County logo, and stood pointing towards a recently opened cremation plot. Pulling in a deep breath, he pushed his door open against the winter wind.

Roger Delaney gave him a nod of his head as he approached. "Hello, Dr. Ellingham," he said.

Martin reached his left arm out and shook his hand. "Mr. Delaney."

"Dr. Ellingham, this is Tom Boyd. He's here representing the citizens of Cornwall."

"Dr. Ellingham," Mr. Boyd said. "I'm surprised to see someone bothered to show up for this bloke."

Martin gave the man's casual attire a critical once-over. "Mm. It seemed appropriate."

They stood awkwardly for several moments before Mr. Boyd gestured towards the plot. "All righty then. Let's get this fella in the ground before he takes up any more of my day."

The dense cloud cover lent a fitting funereal atmosphere to the moment, and as they approached what would be Jim Hanley's final resting place, a heaviness settled in Martin's chest. What a pitiful soul the man must have been. To have but two strangers and the family's physician show up to remember his existence on this earth.

"Well, these are pretty simple affairs," Tom Boyd said, unscrewing a plain brown plastic container and dumping the cremains into the hole. "That's about it."

"What do you mean, that's it?" Martin said, shaking his head in disbelief.

Mr. Boyd jabbed his thumb at the nearby pile of dirt. "Obviously, we'll cover it all up before we go."

"Well, can't you say a few words about the man?"

"What do you want me to say? That he was a worthless drunkard who died with unpaid bills and no one willing to bury him?"

"Noo. But surely the council has some standard sentimental claptrap that's read!"

"Sorry. We don't usually have anyone who shows up for these things. We just do the job and leave."

Martin swallowed back the lump in his throat as his thoughts turned to the deceased man's son. He felt sorrow, not for the drunken, abusive man they were burying, but for the boy who would never share a bond with his father. For the boy who had been deprived of the opportunity to say a proper goodbye to the man.

He had to say something. Someday, Evan would ask about this moment. And no matter what feelings the boy had for Jim Hanley, he would surely want to know that he came from stock worthy of better than this.

Clearing his throat, Martin gestured towards the cremains. "I knew Jim Hanley only as his doctor, so I won't speak directly to his character. What I've witnessed doesn't need to be said.

"But I do know his son. Jim Hanley was the father of an honourable young man. A boy who appreciates and values integrity. And I'd like to believe that at some point in his life, Jim Hanley appreciated integrity as well."

Mr. Boyd snorted softly, and Martin gave him a black look before continuing. "His life was far from perfect. But perhaps his experiences changed the way his brain functioned, leading to a failure to form normal neural connections and thereby weakening the structure of his brain."

His absent gaze settled for a moment on an old tin mine shaft projecting like a steeple above a distant hill, and his fingers twitched at his sides.

"But, I'm confident that, in his son, we'll see what could have been for Jim Hanley ... if he'd been given similar opportunities. And regardless of how his father's life ended, Evan Hanley should still take pride in who he is and in his genetic lineage."

Giving a grunt, Martin pulled in his chin. "That's all I have to say."

Mr. Delaney gave him a nod of his head. "Thank you, Dr. Ellingham. For being here in Evan's stead and for finding a bright spot in all of this."

Martin felt a hand settle on his shoulder, and he turned to see his aide standing behind him. "Jeremy?"

The young man shrugged. "I was in the neighbourhood."

Tom Boyd walked off to his car before returning with a shovel. He scooped the dirt that was piled next to the plot back into the hole, covering the cremains before tamping the soil down with his foot. "Well, we done here then? I'd just as soon not be late gettin' home tonight," he said.

Mr. Delaney glanced uncomfortably at the doctor and his aide before reaching down to brush his hand over the new gravesite, erasing the boot impression left behind by Mr. Boyd. "Yes. Yes, I suppose we are."

The four men walked back to the road together, and Mr. Boyd headed for his car.

"Thank you again for being here today, Dr. Ellingham," Roger Delaney said. "And I'm glad you chose to say a few words. I think they'll be reassuring, encouraging words for Evan if and when he should ask about what went on today."

"Mm, I hope so." Martin gestured towards his aide. "I'm not sure you've met my assistant, Jeremy Portman."

"We met briefly when you and Evan were in hospital," Roger said as he extended his hand. "It was good of you to drive all the way down here."

"I'm glad I came," the young man said.

A cold gust of wind rushed across the open expanse, and Mr. Delaney flipped his collar up around his neck. "Well, I won't take up any more of your time. I'll be in touch with you, Dr. Ellingham, as soon as I have further information regarding the"—he glanced at the aide—"the other matter."

"Mm. Jeremy's aware of the adoption."

"I see. Well, I'll be in touch. It was nice to see you again, Jeremy."

Roger started towards the county vehicle and the doctor called out to him. "Mr. Delaney! I'd, erm ... I'd like to provide a proper headstone for the grave. Can you make that happen?"

"I'd be happy to, Doctor."

Martin and Jeremy dipped their heads into the wind and made their way towards their cars.

Jeremy pulled his mobile from his pocket to check the time. "I passed a coffee house in the city centre. I thought I'd check it out on my way back through town. Care to join me?"

Fighting his natural inclination to automatically reject the young man's invitation, Martin gave him a nod. "Erm, yes. I have a bit of time before my physiotherapy appointment in Wadebridge. That would be fine—good."

The regional sheepdog trials were underway, and cars had filled Fore Street. Jeremy pulled into one of two vacant parking places and Martin turned in next to him.

"It's about two and a half blocks down," the young man said. "I'll drop you off then pick you up later."

"That's not necessary." The doctor fed coins into both meters and gave his aide a jerk of his head before moving off down the pavement.

By the time they reached the little restaurant, Martin's stomach had begun to rumble. He studied the menu, his attention focused on the food items on offer.

"What can I get you gents?" a stooped silver-haired gentleman asked as he pulled a pad from his apron pocket.

"I'll have a turkey sandwich and a bowl of the vegetable soup," Martin said, laying his menu aside. "And a cup of tea—white, no sugar."

The man scribbled on to the paper and turned to Jeremy. "And for you, sir?"

"I'll take a large mocha and a slice of your chocolate cake." He held out his menu, crinkling an eye at it. "On second thought, why don't you make that two slices of chocolate cake."

"Gawd," Martin muttered.

"Jolly good, sir." The waiter gathered up the menus and hurried off.

His fingers tapping against the edge of the table, Martin peered up. "So, what brought you down here, Jeremy?" he asked.

"Hmm?"

"You said you were in the neighbourhood."

"Oh, yeah." He picked up his water glass and took a sip. "I wasn't exactly in the neighbourhood. I had to make a trip to Wadebridge. It seemed like a nice day for a drive in the country, and I knew you had this thing on down here. Thought I'd join you." He took another sip and set his glass down with a clunk.

Martin scanned the dismal scene outside the large glass windows. "A nice day?"

Jeremy squirmed. "Okay, maybe I wasn't just out for a drive in the country. I suspected this could be difficult for you. I know what happened that night—well, that you feel some sense of responsibility for it. Which, as I've told you before, is misplaced. I thought it might help to have a friend by your side."

Blinking back at him, Martin hesitated before saying, "You drove all the way down here for me?"

"That's not so hard to believe, is it?"

The waiter returned, sliding plates and cups in front of them. "Can I get you gentlemen anything else?"

"No, I think we're good," Jeremy said, giving him a nod intended less as an affirmation than a signal to move on.

"Right. Just give me a shout if you need anything." The waiter laid a pile of napkins down on the table before heading back towards the kitchen.

Peering at his boss over the rim of his cup, the aide asked, "So? Is it that hard to believe?"

"No. No, it's not hard to believe. You're a capable driver."

"That's not what I was referring to, but thanks for the vote of confidence," the young man said, giving him a crooked grin.

"You're welcome." Martin picked up his sandwich and took a bite before turning his gaze to the window again. Then, laying his sandwich down, he dabbed at his mouth with his napkin. "It's just that—that we haven't known each other all that long."

"What does that have to do with anything?"

"Well, you don't really know me well enough to—to understand how I might be feeling about a situation. So, for you to drive the length and breadth of Cornwall just to stand by my side at a funeral—not even a funeral, really. Just a-a-a *duty* the County Council is required to perform in compliance with the Public Health Act of 1984."

Jeremy cocked his head at him. "What about it?"

"Well, for you to come all the way down here, just to keep me company could be perceived as—as—"

"As *what*?"

"Well, as—as potentially obsessive."

"*Obsessive?*"

"Mm. Work obsession—addiction has become an increasingly prevalent problem in the UK. Often referred to as the silent killer, its physical effects on the body can be catastrophic."

"Work addiction?" The aide shook his head, jabbing his fork at him. "I'm going to pretend you didn't say that—chalk it up to pain and fatigue."

Martin eyed him warily before pulling in his chin. "Yes."

The waiter returned, refilling Martin's cup with tea before hurrying off again. The two men sat quietly eating their lunch before the doctor broke the silence.

He tipped his head down and scratched at his brow. "Erm, you were correct—about it being difficult."

"Yeah?"

"Mm. I didn't have an opportunity to go to my father's funeral. Today was a reminder of that."

Jeremy pushed one empty plate aside and pulled his second piece of cake in front of him, prompting a grimace from Martin.

"That was a bloody bollocks thing for your mum to do," he said before filling his mouth with another bite. "It'll be different for Evan, though. You'll be able to tell him about today if he should ask."

"Mm, yes."

"I liked what you said by the way—about Jim Hanley. And that Delaney fellow seems like a good bloke. Not so sure about the other guy."

Martin grunted. "*That* man's an egotistical, ill-mannered moron."

"Yeah, I kinda picked up on that. So, what about Jim Hanley's death? Have you got your head around it?"

"In what way?"

The young man's fork circled in the air. "The whole feeling responsible thing."

"Ah." Martin picked up the pitcher on the table and dumped milk into his cup, staring down as the white clouds sank into his tea. "I worry about how Evan will remember that night. If he'll wonder at some point why I didn't wait for help—if his father might still be alive if I had."

"Evan's going to *remember* what it feels like to be smacked around—to being terrified of what an out-of-control drunk is going to do next. I think he'll be bloody grateful you didn't wait for help, mate."

"Mm, possibly."

They finished their lunch, and after leaving several five pound notes on the table, the two men headed back towards their cars.

"Careful on the drive home," Jeremy said as he pulled his driver's side door open. "It's icy in spots."

"Yes." Martin stood, toying with his key fob for a moment, the wind riffling through his hair. "Thank you for coming today, Jeremy."

"You're welcome, mate. We'll see you in the morning."

It was getting dark by the time Martin left the Wadebridge Physiotherapy Centre, and the air that was settling into the River Camel Estuary could be considered bitterly cold by Cornish standards.

As he descended into Portwenn, dense fog closed in, limiting visibility and making it difficult to navigate the tight turn on to Roscarrock Hill.

When Martin came in the kitchen door, Evan scrambled up from the puzzle he was assembling on the floor in the lounge and ran to him.

Clenching his jaws, Martin muffled a groan as the boy's arms constricted around his legs. He cast a bewildered look towards his wife.

The child loosened his grip and tipped his head back. "Where were you, Dr. Ellig-am? You should've been home by now."

"I had a physical therapy appointment." Martin's hand settled on the seven-year-old's head for a moment before he bounced back to the lounge to continue his play. He eyed his wife. "Mm. I may have forgotten to mention it to you."

Louisa wiped roughly at the moisture on her hands before dropping the towel on to the counter. "*Yes*, you did, Martin."

"I'm sorry. I was focused on the memor—the earlier appointment."

Her stern gaze softened, and she stepped over to slip her arms around his waist. "I'm glad you're safe. I was worried ... with the fog." She glanced at the seven-year-old. "And I think someone picked up on it."

"Ah, I see. The weather was fine until I came into the village." Wriggling free from her grasp, Martin went over to the high chair to brush his fingers across James's head.

"Well, we're ready to eat," she said. "Why don't you hang up your coat and wash up for dinner, hmm?"

"Yes." His palm settled for a moment on his son's silky, blonde locks before he limped off under the stairs.

Chapter 8

When Martin came back through under the stairs, his family was gathered at the table. His plate was filled to the brim with the hotpot Louisa had made, and his young charge was chattering excitedly about his school day.

The subject soon turned to the mouse that had taken up residence in the year two's classroom. The boy flopped back in his chair, giggling as he recounted his teacher's reaction when she reached for a pencil, and the little rodent leapt from the cup of writing implements on her desk.

"She jumped up on Caroline Robert's desk and—*she* was in the loo, see. Anyway, she started screamin'. And she didn't stop screamin' until Mr. Townsend—he's the guy that empties the waste bins—he came in and caught it in a can.

"She wanted him to kill it, but Mr. Townsend told her"—Evan artificially lowered his voice— "'I don't wanna 'ave that creature's blood on me 'ands!'"

Martin wrinkled up his nose and pushed his half-eaten dinner to the centre of the table. "What *did* he do with the mouse, then? I hope he didn't release the pestilence ridden creature in the school."

"Uh-uh. He named him Harry."

"Oh, it was a boy mouse?" Louisa said, nodding as she refilled James's bowl with meat and vegetables.

Evan snorted. "*Ohhh,* yeah! It was a boy all right!" He patted his guardian on the arm. "Dr. Ellig-am, did you know mouses gots big geni—" He glanced at his head teacher before whispering, "You know ... bits?"

Martin dipped his head and cleared his throat. "Yes. Yes, I'm aware of that. Now eat your dinner."

"But I have ta tell you about Harry."

"Eat your potato; then tell us about Harry."

The boy's fork tapped against his guardian's plate. "You gots ta finish your dinner too, don't you?"

Louisa raised her eyebrows and nudged her husband's plate back across the table. "Yes, you do gots ta finish your dinner, Martin."

He tipped his head down, peering up at her. "I will."

Washing his potato down with a gulp of milk, Evan continued with his story. "So, Mr. Townsend said he was gonna take Harry to his house. He gots a snake, and he said the snake would take care of him. That's a pretty nice snake, don't you think, Dr. Ellig-am?"

"I highly doubt that snake has anything nice planned—"

"Martin. Eat your dinner," Louisa said, pinching her lips together and shaking her head.

"Mm, yes."

As they began to tidy the kitchen after the meal, Martin broached the subject that he had, up to this point, failed to address with his wife.

"Erm, we should discuss something before tomorrow's procedure, Louisa," he said, rinsing another plate and setting it in the dish rack.

"Now's maybe not the best time, Martin." She gave a nod towards the seven-year-old, hunched over an exercise book at the table. "We'll get the boys off to bed, then talk about it." She lowered her voice. "We don't want to cause any worries right before bed, hmm?"

"Yes," he said, ducking his head before reaching for another plate.

It was almost nine o'clock by the time Martin had closed the book he and Evan were reading and turned out the lights.

Louisa looked up from her work at the kitchen table when his weight creaked on the bottom step.

"All safely off to the land of Nod?" she asked, her mouth stretching into a restrained smile at the sight of his rather dishevelled appearance.

"Mm. Bathed, Sudocremed where necessary, and teeth brushed as well."

"Thank you, Martin. Sorry I left you on your own with everything, but I really needed to finish up these reports before the staff meeting in the morning." She tipped her head down. "You manage okay with James? You look a bit the worse for wear."

Air hissed from his nose as he went to the sink, filling a glass with water. "I did fine. It's just more of a challenge than it used to be."

"Yeah? Well, if it makes you feel any less disabled, it's more of a challenge than it used to be for me, too."

"I *don't* feel disabled, Louisa. I had to fish him out from under our bed before I could put his pyjamas on him."

"What was he doing under our bed, for goodness' sake?"

"Following the example set by that godawful animal of Evan's."

Her lips quirked as the restrained smile returned to her face. "I see."

Downing the last of his water, he set the glass down with a thud. "Can we talk about tomorrow, now?"

"Yeah. Yeah, I need just a couple minutes more. I'm almost done with this last report, then we can."

Huffing out a breath, Martin headed for the hall. "Come and get me when you're available," he grumbled.

He was about to close the consulting room door behind him when the doorbell rang, and he hurried towards the front entryway to put a stop to the knocking that would, no doubt, wake the two little boys.

He yanked the door open, his ire primed and ready to deliver the rightful tongue-lashing to whomever stood on the other side. "For God's sake! What do you wa—*Danny*?" he said, his face contorting as if he'd suddenly been afflicted with a severe case of the lurgy.

The slightly built figure on the terrace gave him a grin that projected a misplaced confidence in the friendship between them. "Martin, mate, I'm glad you're home. It's my mother. I need you to take a quick look at her."

The doctor's upper lip curled in disdain at his old romantic rival, Danny Steel.

"She's in the car. I'll just go get her."

"No, you won't! The surgery's closed. Unless it's an actual emergency, make an appointment in the morning with my receptionist."

Danny flipped up the collar on his navy blue pea coat and pulled his hands into his armpits before stepping back to the doorway. "Thing is, Martin, I'll be gone. I'm heading back to London at the crack of dawn."

Martin grimaced and shook his head. "What's the problem?"

"Oh, there's no problem. I just have a big project on in Kensington—opportunity of a lifetime, really. I couldn't believe it when I got the call a month ago saying they'd picked yours truly to head it up. I don't dare stay away too long, though. My project superintendent is top of the range, but only if I can keep him sober," he said with a chuckle.

Martin stared back at him, steely-eyed. "I *meant*, what is your mother's medical problem?"

"Oh, right. Well, she seemed perfectly fine before we left home. Aside from the dizzy spell she had earlier. She hadn't eaten much for lunch, so I thought she might need some food in her stomach. You know—low glucose levels. I thought I'd take her over to Truro for a nice dinner out."

"Good for you. Enjoy your meal, then," Martin said, reaching for the door to swing it shut.

Danny put a hand up, stopping the door's momentum. "No. We've already had dinner. But she vomited in the lavatory before we left the restaurant and again at the service station when I stopped for petrol. And she's been complaining about indigestion. All the way back to Portwenn, as a matter of fact. I think she ate something that didn't agree with her. Can you just take a quick look?"

"Is she febrile?"

Danny stared back with a bemused expression on his face, and Martin threw his head back. "Is her temperature elevated?"

"Oh. No, I don't think so." He said before adding with a smirk that set the doctor's teeth on edge. "But then I don't run around with a thermometer in my breast pocket, do I?"

Martin stared at him, deadpan, and the younger Steel rubbed his hands together. "Sorry. So, what do you say? Can you take a quick look?"

A breath hissed from Martin's nose. "Bring her in."

"Thanks, mate. You're a godsend," Danny said before hurrying down the steps.

Martin grunted and turned, bumping into his wife as she tried to peer past him and out the door.

"That sounded like Danny Steel!"

"Did it?" he grumbled as he lumbered towards his consulting room.

She followed after him. "Was that Danny?"

"Unfortunately, yes."

"What was he doing here?"

"He says his mother's ill."

"Oh, dear. Poor Muriel. He's taking her down to Newquay, then?"

"No, he's gone to get the vile old bat from his car."

"Martin!" she hissed.

"What? She is a vile old bat, isn't she?"

Louisa cocked her head. "Well, yes. Yes, she is."

"He wants me to have a look at her."

"But, you're not supposed to be—"

"He says she's afebrile, and I believe the exposure risk is low."

"Yes, but you—"

"I need to see her, Louisa." Turning in the doorway, he gestured down the hall, keeping an anxious eye on the entryway. "I can take care of this," he said, keen to control any interaction between his wife and her former love interest. "You should go back to the kitchen—finish up with your reports."

"Oh, sure ... patient confidentiality."

"Mm, right." He held a hand out, waving her through under the stairs and watched until she disappeared around the corner before taking a seat behind his desk.

Danny entered the room a minute later, accompanied by his whey-faced, elderly mother. "It's going to be okay now, Mum," he said, leading her towards a chair. "Dr. Ellingham's going to have you feeling as right as rain in no time."

Martin shot him a dark look and got to his feet, picking up his stethoscope as he came around the desk. "What seems to be the problem, Mrs. Steel? Your son said you've been feeling ill." He inserted a thermometer into her ear. "Tell me about your symptoms. You've had some nausea and vomiting?"

Danny folded his arms across his chest. "Twice. Once before we left the restaurant and again at the petrol station. Like I said, I think it's something she ate."

Trying to tune him out, the doctor reached inside his patient's blouse with his stethoscope. "Mrs. Steel, are you having any chest pain?"

Muriel narrowed her eyes at him. "I'm not having a heart attack, if that's what you're suggesting."

"I'm not suggesting anything. I just asked you a question."

"No. It's my back," she said.

Danny rubbed a hand over her shoulders. "Maybe she's dehydrated again, Martin."

"She's not dehydrated." Taking hold of the woman's arm, the doctor palpated her wrist for a pulse, his brow furrowing. "I'm going to check your blood pressure," he said, pulling the sphygmomanometer from his medical cart. "Are there any other symptoms you need to tell me about?"

Muriel dropped her elbow to the armrest and let her chin fall into her hand. "My back hurts. I need some paracetamol."

"I know about your back. I'm asking if you're having any symptoms apart from the back pain.

"She had trouble getting her dinner down earlier," Danny said.

"What does that mean?"

"Well, you know ... like she didn't care for it. She actually gagged on a bite of her salmon. I kept telling her if it was that bad I could order her something else. She was just being contrary; she gets like that at times."

The doctor gave him a concurring grunt before directing his question to the elderly woman. "Are you having trouble swallowing, Mrs. Steel?"

Danny again injected himself into the conversation. "Her appetite isn't what it used to be, and she's prone to indigestion. I'm sure that's all it is."

"If you're so sure, then why did you bring her to see me?" Martin growled.

Danny put his hands up. "I didn't mean to tread on your toes. I just know my mother better than you do."

Giving him a sneer, Martin turned back to his patient. "Mrs. Steel, are you having any difficulty swallowing?"

"My back hurts!" she whined.

Danny leaned in, speaking softly. "She needs an antacid. I think you'll find that if you just—"

"Mr. Steel, I'd appreciate it if you'd be quiet and allow me to examine your mother before you make your diagnosis," Martin snapped.

Danny put his hands up again. "Forgive me. I'm only trying to help. I just think we could have her feeling better a whole lot faster if you'd just give her something for her upset stomach."

"Oh, do you?" The blood pressure cuff was wrapped around the old woman's arm, and Martin squeezed the bulb, listening to the whooshing of blood before repeating the procedure with the opposite arm.

"Is it high?" Danny asked.

"It's within the acceptable range." Pulling a cart over, the doctor uncoiled the leads to his electrocardiograph machine. "Mrs. Steel, I'm going to check to see how your heart is functioning," he said. "I need to unbutton your blouse."

She batted his hand away and pulled back in the chair. "I've been undressing myself for more than seventy years. I think I can manage a few buttons without you getting involved, little Marty."

Danny sighed loudly. "Mum, just cooperate with Dr. Ellingham. He's trying to help."

He turned to Martin. "Look, I realise I don't have your medical expertise, but I do know that high blood pressure is a major risk factor for heart disease. You just said her blood pressure is fine. I really think that if you'd just listen to me, we—"

Martin glared at him. "Mr. Steel—a word," he said, giving a jerk of his head towards the door.

The two men stepped into the reception room and the doctor stared at him pointedly. "I believe your mother may be experiencing an aortic dissection. If she is, the condition requires immediate medical intervention, or she may very well die. So, if you'd really like to be of help, then shut up and quit wasting precious time. Wait out here. When I've finished examining her, I'll discuss my findings with you."

Danny stood speechless as the doctor returned to the exam room, closing the door behind him.

Emerging a short time later, the doctor looked strained and sombre. "Louisa," he called down the hall.

Chair legs scraped against the floor in the kitchen before she appeared in the doorway. "What is it, Martin?"

"Would you stay with Mrs. Steel whilst I have a word with Danny. Get me immediately if you see any changes."

"Oh? Sure—sure." She gave him a puzzled glance before going to Muriel's side, and Martin went into the reception room, taking a seat next to the woman's son.

"You really think this is serious?" Danny said.

"I do. She's exhibiting a number of symptoms that would suggest she's suffered an aortic dissection—a tear in the wall of the aorta. There's a wide blood pressure difference between the right and left arm, her pulse is rapid and weak, her skin is pale and clammy, and you said she vomited earlier and may have been having difficulty swallowing. And back pain is a classic indicator of aortic dissection."

"And the ECG—was that abnormal?"

"No, it was fine. Which isn't unusual with this condition. I've called for an air ambulance. It should be arriving shortly. She'll have a CT angiography over in Truro to confirm my diagnosis."

"And then what? They confirm it and then what?"

"The tear will be repaired in an emergency operation."

"And she'll be okay then?"

"Yes. But you should be aware that there is a very real risk the aorta could rupture before we can get her to theatre. If that should happen, her chances of survival would be very low."

"Wow. I didn't expect this." Danny brushed his fingers through his wavy head of hair and blew out a breath. "Martin, I know we haven't always seen eye to eye, but ... well, could you do the surgery?"

"Nooo, Danny. That's not possible. I don't have hospital privileges, and if you hadn't noticed, I don't have full use of my hand at the moment."

"Yeah, Mum told me about your accident. Thank the Lord you survived it."

"Rrright." Martin got to his feet. "Well, I'll ride in the helicopter with her. You can follow in your car and meet us at the hospital."

"Shouldn't I go with you?"

Martin cringed at the very thought of his patient's sanctimonious, smart-arsed son praying over his shoulder and questioning his every move if things went south on the way to Truro.

"That's just not possible," he said. "It'll be crowded, and we need room to work. I'll stay with her, and you can drive over there."

"Sure, that makes sense. Bless you, Martin."

"Mm. Come back to the consulting room with me for now. You can stay with your mother until the ambulance arrives."

Danny followed after him, breaking into a broad grin when Louisa looked up from her perch next to his mother. "Lou! You look fabulous! How have you been?"

She got up, surrendering her chair to him. "I'm fine, Danny. I'm so sorry your mum isn't well."

"Yeah, well ..." The smile on his face fell into one of affected worry at the mention of the old woman's condition.

"Have a seat, Danny," Louisa said. She headed towards the door. "I'll be out here if you need me, Martin."

"Mm, yes." He gave her a nod as he removed a blue package from a drawer in his medical cabinet. "Mrs. Steel, we're going to take you to hospital. They'll run some tests in Truro to determine the cause of your symptoms. But for now, I'd like to get an IV started—save time and make things easier for the ambulance crew."

The woman watched her son as his eyes tracked Louisa into the reception room. "Forget the Glasson girl," she mumbled. "You need to find a proper girl."

"What are you talking about, Mum?" Danny said.

"I may be old, but I'm not blind."

Casting a furtive glance towards Martin, the younger Steel took a seat next to his mother. "Lou and I ... that was a long time ago, Mum. You know that. Besides, she's married."

"There's nothing wrong with my eyes, Daniel. I saw the way you looked at her just now."

Martin pulled his wheeled stool over next to his patient, dropping on to it heavily. Then, snapping on a pair of gloves, he pulled the IV set packaging open before swabbing the back of his patient's hand with alcohol. "Just a little prick now, Mrs. Steel," he said, giving his rival a smouldering glance before returning his attention to the task in front of him. The needle was slipped adeptly into the woman's hand and secured with tape. Martin dabbed at a drop of blood that oozed out, swallowing hard and clearing his throat.

Danny patted his mother's arm. "That will make you feel a lot better, Mum."

"Pfftt, I haven't given her anything yet," Martin scoffed. "I've just started the IV."

Pulling her free hand up, Muriel wagged a limp hand at her son. "It's not the way we do things. She's underclass, you know."

"Mum, you shouldn't talk that way about Lou. It's very unkind."

"I'll talk however I want to; I'm your mother. You need to marry a proper girl."

"Mum! Now's not the time—or the place," Danny said, his eyes flitting towards the doctor. He donned a contrite expression. "I hope you'll forgive her, Martin. She's not herself right now."

"Of course, she isn't. It's doubtful she's receiving an adequate amount of blood to her brain. She's lost the ability to filter out information that could be considered offensive."

Paper and plastic crackled as Martin gathered together the empty IV wrapping, crumpling it into a tight ball before tossing it into the bin. "I'll go see about that helicopter," he growled.

He left, returning a few minutes later with the ambulance crew. They situated the old woman on a gurney and wheeled her towards the front door.

Danny took her hand and held it to his cheek. "I'm saying a prayer for you, Mum."

"Ohhh, God. Zip it with the Bible bashing, Danny."

"Mum, please don't use His name in vain."

"I'll use it however I want. You're the last in the line, you know," she said. "Don't scotch the family name. Get married, and do it properly."

"I will, Mum. He's given me a whole new lease on life. You don't need to worry."

She rolled her eyes and then patted his cheek.

Martin tugged Danny away, giving a nod to the paramedics. "Get her down to the helicopter. We need to get a move on."

Five minutes later, the air ambulance lifted off from the Platt. Louisa and Danny watched from the surgery terrace as it disappeared behind the rooftops.

Danny turned to Louisa. "I hate to impose, but do you think I could sit down for a bit—have a cup of tea before I leave?"

She cocked her head at him. "Don't you want to get over to Truro to be with your mum?"

"Yeah. Yeah, of course. It's just that this has me pretty rattled. I need to steady my nerves before I hit the road."

"Of course, come on in," she said, stepping back into the house.

Louisa could feel Danny's eyes on her as she moved about the kitchen preparing the tea. He peered up as she set a steaming cup of brew and the sugar bowl down in front of him.

He gave her a feeble smile. "God bless you, Lou."

Hesitating, she pulled out the chair across from him and sat down.

"I was sorry to hear about Martin's accident, Lou," he said.

"Yeah, well it's been a difficult year to say the least."

"I'm sure. It couldn't have been easy playing nursemaid to Martin."

"It's not like that, Danny. Martin nearly died, so I'm thankful that I *can* be, as you put it, *nursemaid* to him."

"Oh, sure—sure. But he's not the easiest person to get along with, on a good day. The burden must be overwhelming at times. I'm just expressing my concern for you is all."

Her fingers tapped against the table and her lips drew tight. "Let's change the subject, Danny. Your mum's the one you should be worrying about at the moment."

"Of course, you're right." He stared morosely into his cup of tea. "Martin said she might not make it, Lou. The thought of losing her—"

"Martin will do his best for her, Danny. You know he will."

"Yeah. Yeah, you're right. It's just that ... well, I've been living up in London, not seeing her except for the occasional trip back to the village. But I've always known she's here if I ever needed her. The thought of her not—" He shook his head and put a hand over his eyes.

Louisa reached across the table and put her hand on his. "Let's think positive thoughts, hmm?"

Danny's fingers tightened around hers, and she sat, uncomfortably, while they finished their tea.

"Are you feeling a bit steadier, now?" she asked, pulling free from him before getting to her feet and putting the now-empty cups into the dishwasher.

"Yes, thanks to you. You've always had a way of calming me down."

"Well, I'm sure you're wanting to get going—be there for your mum."

"Yeah, of course." He took his coat from the back of his chair and pulled it on, staring absently.

Louisa gave him an understanding smile. Danny Steele had grown up an only child and the apple of his parents' eye. He was accustomed to being his mother's darling boy who could do no wrong. *If he loses her, it'll hit him hard*, she thought. "Try not to worry too much, Danny. Things could turn out just fine."

He stepped towards her and opened his arms. "I could really use a hug right now, Lou."

Hanging back a moment, she worked her wedding band around her finger. "Sure, Danny," she said before stepping forward to embrace him.

Her purely chaste gesture was returned in earnest, his grasp tightening before his hand slipped up her back, his fingers twining in her hair.

She stiffened as he leaned in for a kiss. "Danny, stop it!" she said, pulling away from him. Working her arms in between them, she pushed back. "That's really inappropriate!"

"You're right," he said, looking away. "It was uncalled for; I apologise." He donned an overripe expression of contrition and folded his hands in front of him. "Please don't tell Martin about this, Lou. I don't know what came over me."

Her arms hugged her body as she took a step back and struggled to meet his gaze. "I'll let it go, Danny ... blame it on the stress you're under at the moment. But don't let it happen again."

"Right. Of course." Rubbing his palms together, he nodded towards the front entryway. "Well, I better be going. It was really nice to see you again, Lou."

She followed him out on to the terrace, roughly wiping the last vestiges of his kiss from her lips as his tail lamps faded into the fog. Then, she went back inside, locking the door behind her.

Chapter 9

Louisa lay the next morning, her head rising and falling with her husband's slow breaths. It was nearly 3:00 a.m. by the time the taxi had dropped him off and he had finished with Muriel Steel's patient notes.

His ungainly movements, as he attempted to ready himself for bed in the dark, had awakened her, and in his very unvarnished manner, he had explained that Muriel Steel had suffered an aortic dissection that led to a fatal rupture before the air ambulance had even arrived at the hospital.

But what he kept well hidden behind his dispassionate tone and especially taciturn manner was obvious in his pounding heart when she rested her hand on his chest.

Though there was no love lost between Martin and either Muriel or Danny Steel, Louisa had come to understand that her husband grieved the loss of every patient, especially if he could have saved them given a different set of circumstances.

She had nestled in against him, with her head on his shoulder as he fell asleep.

Waking in the same position, she lay for a while against his warmth before slipping quietly from the bed to ready herself for her early staff meeting.

When Martin opened his eyes to the tepid rays of the reluctant winter sun, pots and pans were clanking downstairs in the kitchen.

The rich, smoky aroma of coffee enticed him from the bed, and he hurried through his morning bathroom ritual before getting dressed.

Dropping on to the bed he began to work his trousers over the hardware on his legs. He hesitated before pushing his foot into the right leg—the hardware that was due to come off that afternoon had served its purpose.

It had held his fractured bones in place while nature knitted them back together. But an illogical sense of vulnerability washed over him at the thought of putting weight on his soon-to-be-unsupported bones. He pushed his leg on through and reached for the tie he had laid out.

Louisa breezed into the room, pausing long enough to lean down and kiss his cheek. "I scrambled some eggs."

"Mm, thank you."

"I put them in the cooker to keep them warm," she said before disappearing into the bathroom.

She hurried back moments later, rubbing lotion on her arms.

"Louisa, can we discuss something before you leave for the school?"

Glancing at her watch, she huffed out a breath. "Martin, I have a staff meeting in twenty minutes, and I still need to get James dressed."

A dresser drawer squeaked open and she dug frantically through the stacks of clothing. "I know I had a scarf laid out. Have you seen it?"

"What colour is it?" he asked as he got to his feet and hoisted up his trousers.

"The *blue* one with the pink daisies. I just had it a minute ago!"

He pulled his belt through the belt loops and fastened it into place.

"It's in your hand, Louisa."

She looked down before rolling her eyes at him. "That's green, not blue. And those aren't daisies. They're roses, for goodness' sake."

"It looks like blue. And I'm not sure those are roses. They're gardenias."

Louisa pressed her palm to her forehead. "*Pink* gardenias?"

"He cocked his head and raised an eyebrow. "Problem?"

"Not a problem, Martin. But there isn't such a thing as a pink gardenia."

"Well, technically speaking, no. But there are ways—"

"Martin, I don't have time! Just help me find my bloody scarf!"

Plucking her pillow from the bed, she huffed out a breath. "Oh, there it is!" she said snatching it from the mattress.

"Mm. Louisa, there's something I really need to discuss with you be—"

"Martin, it's going to have to wait. I'm late the way it is."

"Yes, but we really need to talk about this. I can get James dressed and make sure Evan's ready for school if it will—"

"Oh, thank you," she said before starting for the hall. "You'll pick me up at half twelve for your procedure, right?"

"Yes, but Louisa—"

"Good." Giving him a passing peck on the cheek, she raced out the door and down the steps. "Have a good morning!" she called over her shoulder.

A long breath hissed from Martin's nose. The subject of the potential nerve entrapment issue was sure to come up in conversation with Ed Christianson. The issue would have to be addressed on the drive to the hospital later.

A soft *"mummy"* emanated from the nursery, and Martin crossed the landing to tend to his son.

James Henry stood in his cot with his arms dangling over the rail, watching as the stream of spittle he had produced dropped to the floor.

"No, no, no, no, no," Martin whispered stridently, clapping his hands softly so as to not startle the still-sleeping seven-year-old.

The toddler pointed a chubby finger at the puddle that had accumulated and gave his father a triumphant smile. "Funny," he said.

"No, it's *not* funny. It's an unnecessary mess that someone's going to have to clean up." Martin tried to give his son a no-nonsense look, but it softened into a subtle tightening of his left cheek when the child reached out to him.

"Good morning, James," he said, hooking his left arm around him and pulling him from the cot. He proceeded to change the boy's nappy and get him dressed for the day, a laborious task given his current limitations.

By the time a fully clothed James was set on the floor, Evan had woken up.

"Dr. Ellig-am, how long till I'm adopted?" the seven-year-old asked as he unbuttoned his pyjama top.

Martin pressed his fingers to the bridge of his nose and dropped a burp cloth on to the puddle of saliva next to the cot, wiping it around with his foot. "We go over this every morning, Evan. Why do you keep asking?"

Kicking off his pyjama bottoms, the child gathered them up, along with the previously-shed top, and shoved them under his pillow. "I dunno," he said with a shrug of his shoulders. "I guess 'cause I keep wantin' an answer."

"And I keep giving you an answer—the same as every other time you've asked. One day le—"

"I know, I know. One day less than the last time I asked."

"Mm, right. Hurry up now. Get dressed and make that bed."

Martin looked around the room, chock full of toys and dressers, their drawers packed with the usual accoutrements necessary for little boys, and bookshelves filled with books. It reminded him a bit of Mr. Moysey's home.

Evan wriggled as he tried to get his white polo shirt, part of his school uniform, over his head. He yelped when his hair tangled around a button.

"What on earth are you trying to do?" Martin asked.

"I'm *tryin'* to get dressed, but the buttons won't let my head through the hole. Can you help me, Dr. Ellig-am?"

The doctor looked across the hall into their bedroom and saw James toddle out of the bathroom with the tube of toothpaste in his hand. "You stay put; I'll be right back."

Evan stood with his shirt over his head and his arms sticking out of the sleeves in mummy fashion. "You mean me, Dr. Ellig-am?"

"Yes!" Prying the tube from his son's fist, Martin muttered under his breath, "If your mother would pick up after herself you wouldn't be constantly getting hold of things, would you James?"

"Dr. Ellig-am! I think I'm starting to suffacape!"

"*Yes, I know*. I'm coming." Taking the toddler by the hand, Martin limped across the hall, shortening his stride by two-thirds to allow the boy to keep up.

He closed the nursery door behind them and returned to assist his young charge.

"You need to unbutton the shirt *before* you put it on, Evan," he said as he freed the child.

"How come they gots ta be buttoned in the first place? I just gots ta *un*button 'em again."

"Because it results in a more orderly stack in your drawer. And you don't get as many wrinkles in the shirts."

The seven-year-old rubbed at the tender spot left by the pulling of his hair. "Mrs. Ellig-am doesn't button 'em before she folds 'em."

"Mm, yes. I'm aware of that. Finish getting dressed, and we'll go have breakfast."

Between the literal hang-ups with Evan's wardrobe, a glass of spilt milk at the table, the misplacement of the seven-year-old's homework assignment, and the short night the night before, Martin was more irritable than usual with his patients.

Fortunately, half of them had cancelled their appointments because of illness. He stepped out on to the terrace shortly before eleven o'clock and took in a breath. The sharpness of the air and the bright sunshine was both calming and invigorating.

He closed his eyes and let the warm rays relax him before taking in another deep breath. Then, he went back in to retrieve his key fob from the kitchen.

Poppy and James were on the floor in the lounge, playing with the toddler's train set. He stopped in the doorway and watched them, unnoticed.

Poppy *chug-chugged* an engine along the rails as James stood behind her watching, one arm wrapped around her neck and his chin resting on her shoulder.

The toddler leaned over spontaneously and placed a juicy kiss on the childminder's cheek.

"Well, thank you James Henry!" She reached back and pulled him into her lap, cuddling him as he giggled at the unexpected attention.

Martin stepped into the room, and James wriggled free to scramble over to him.

"Hi, Da-ee!" The boy pulled at Martin's trousers and he put a hand on the little blonde head.

"Hello, James."

"Da-ee, take up!"

"I can't right now, James. We'll do that later." He guided him back to the toys on the floor.

"I'm leaving now, Poppy. Is there anything you need before I go?"

"No. We're fine," she said, glancing up before her gaze raced back to the miniature train.

"Good. I'm, er ... I just wanted to say ..." He hissed a breath from his nose and gave a jab of his thumb. "I'll just get the key and be off, then."

Stroking his son's head a final time, he lumbered towards the kitchen, snatched up the fob for the Lexus, and hurried out the door.

Dropping into the seat behind the wheel, he slammed the driver's side door shut, a bit harder than necessary, mentally berating himself as he drove down Roscarrock Hill. *You only had to tell the girl you're grateful she's taking care of James.*

His fingers drummed against the steering wheel as he waited for a delivery van blocking the intersection on the Platt. *It shouldn't have been that bloody difficult.*

A lorry pulled up behind the stationary van. The driver got out and looked around for the van's owner. Spotting him coming out of The Mote, the man stomped off towards him, his arms gesticulating.

Louisa would have had no trouble with it. Even Ruth could have mustered the intestinal fortitude to thank the girl. Idiot!

His self-castigation was interrupted by shouted obscenities, and he craned his neck to peer around the lorry at the two men. The argument appeared to be escalating, and it didn't look as if either man would back down anytime soon.

"Ohhh! No, no, no, no, no!" Martin groaned, looking down at his watch. This would almost certainly make him late for his surgical appointment.

He pulled his mobile from his pocket and dialled Joe Penhale's number. As soon as he began to explain the situation, the constable interrupted.

"Stay in your vehicle, Doc, and keep the doors locked! I'm on it!"

Martin had no sooner pocketed his phone when Joe barrelled down Church Hill, sirens blaring and lights flashing.

The dispute was quickly resolved, and the two men got back into their respective vehicles before driving off.

The policeman came to the side of the car and rapped a knuckle against the driver's side window.

"Oh, for God's sake," Martin groaned again. The window slid down and he asked impatiently, "What is it, Penhale? I'm in a hurry."

"Seems like you're always in a hurry, Do-*c*. That's not good for you, you know—hard on the heart."

The doctor screwed up his face and shook his head. "What is it, Penhale?"

"Oh, just wanted to say the situation's under control now."

"Yes, I can see that," Martin said as the two vehicles disappeared over the hill.

"Good thinkin' that—callin' me and all. Hate ta think what could've happened if you'd ended up in the middle of *that* punch-up. You needed someone with the training and expertise to *de*-fuse the situation."

"Right. Now if you don't mind." Martin checked the time again. "I'm ten minutes late already."

The policeman snapped his fingers and gave him a grin. "Gotcha, Doc. I'll give you a police escort," he said, racing back to his Land Rover before Martin could get a word out.

"Idiot doesn't even know where I'm going," the doctor grumbled.

Joe drove off up Fore Street, his siren blaring, and pedestrians hugged the stone shop walls to avoid being knocked down. The doctor turned into the school parking lot, and the Land Rover continued on up the hill before turning right on to New Road.

Louisa, who had been watching from the playground, hurried over and got into the car. "My goodness! What's going on?"

"Penhale thought I needed a police escort. He didn't even think to ask where I was going. There's no telling where he'll end up."

Her head tipped to the side. "Oh, poor Joe."

"Mm. Let's hope this village never needs a real policeman."

"Oh, Martin. He does try hard, though, doesn't he?"

"Well, that's all right, then."

Louisa put a hand on his thigh. "And remember, he was very helpful the night of your accident. And he did find you and Evan out on the moor."

"Technically, Buddy found us." Martin cocked his head. "Although, I suppose Penhale did have the wherewithal to follow him."

"I like it when you talk like that," Louisa said, stretching across the seat to kiss his cheek.

Martin pulled in his chin and gave her a shy, sideways glance. "Like what?"

"Admitting Joe has a redeeming quality or two—using Buddy's name. I guess maybe I just like to hear you talk, period."

He raised an eyebrow. "I see." Working his hands around the steering wheel for the next mile, he stole the occasional look at her before finally saying, "There *is* something we need to discuss, Louisa."

"Oh?"

"Mm. I mentioned to Ed that I've been having some pain in my left leg."

"More than some, Martin. I hope you didn't downplay the severity of it."

"Of course, I didn't!"

"Well, you can understand why I'm sceptical—given your history with these things."

His brow lowered as air hissed from his nose. "May I continue, now?"

"Yeah. Sorry."

"The CT pictures may indicate a potential problem."

She shifted in her seat, turning towards him. "Problem? What kind of problem?"

"The pain in that leg may be resulting from a nerve entrapment issue."

"What's that?"

"Some of the callus that forms at the fracture site may have grown around the peroneal nerve. That could be keeping the nerve from moving the way it should. It could be pinching the nerve, thereby causing pain."

"Well, how do they fix it? They *can* fix it, can't they?"

"Yes. In all likelihood surgery could be done to free the nerve, which would hopefully stop the pain. They'd use internal fixation at that time to repair the fractures and would likely do some reconstruction as well."

Her ponytail flicked. "And you just now thought to tell me this—a half hour before we get to the hospital?"

"They're not going to do the surgery today, Louisa."

"Still, why didn't you talk to me about it before? I *am* your wife, you know."

"I'm aware of that." He gave her a glance and swallowed hard. "I'm reminded of it every night when I crawl into bed with you."

"*Mar-tin,* you know what I mean."

"Mm." He tugged at his ear as he sneaked another peek at her taut face. "I did try to tell you."

"When? When did you try to tell me, Martin?"

"Every time you told me it wasn't the time to discuss it—you had reports you needed to finish, you had to get to the school, or Evan was there and you didn't want him to hear."

"Well, you should have told me how important it was! How was I to know it was something that could be life-changing!"

"Ohhh, now you're exaggerating. I'd hardly classify it as life-changing." He bit at his lip and gave her another wary glance. "And ... well, I think you're being unfair."

The ponytail flicked again, and she turned towards the window. "Oh, do you?"

"Yes, I do. Why do you always find fault?"

She whirled to face him. "Ha! *I* always find fault?"

"Yes! You do!" His voice rose in pitch and volume as his face reddened. "You criticise me for not talking, but when I do try to discuss something, you hush me! You're too busy to listen! How am I to know if something's important enough to warrant your attention?"

He pulled up his chin and focused his scowl on the road ahead, mumbling, "Maybe I should make an appointment."

"Mar-tin." Louisa sat with her arms crossed in front of her as the moorland swept past them.

When they neared the park and ride on the outskirts of Truro, she wagged her finger. "Martin, pull in there and park."

"Louisa, we're going to be late as it—"

"I know. Just pull in and park."

"Oh, for heaven's sake," he muttered under his breath.

When the car had come to a stop, she unbuckled her seatbelt and leaned over, kissing him on the cheek. "I'll do that properly when we get home tonight."

"Ah. Does this mean you're no longer cross with me?"

"No, I'm not cross with you." She settled back into her seat and straightened her dress. "There was some ... er, a lot of truth in what you said. I'm sorry I let work come between us. I'll try to do better."

Martin fingered his watch. "Erm, it's a quarter past twelve. We should be going."

Giving him a self-conscious smile and nodded her head.

The check-in and pre-op procedure had become bog-standard, and Martin moved through the steps in relative silence.

Louisa put her hand over his as they sat, waiting to be summoned to an outpatient room. "You okay?"

"Yes, I'm fine."

"You're rather quiet."

He looked down at her anxious face and drew in a breath. "It's a bit ..." He shrugged. "It'll be a change."

"Yes, but a good change, right?"

"Mm, I hope so.

"You can't possibly mean you're going to miss it?"

He screwed up his face. "Nooo."

He stared at the television that hugged the ceiling, with the pretence of taking in the latest news and Louisa flipped absently through a travel magazine.

"I don't know, really," he said suddenly. "It'll take some getting used to, I'm sure."

Her attention drawn to his nervous habit of rubbing his thumb into his palm, Louisa stilled it with her hand. "It'll all go well, I'm sure."

A nurse stepped into the room, calling out his name, and he gave her fingers a squeeze before pulling himself to his feet.

Chapter 10

The removal of the fixators was a quick in-and-out procedure, and Martin was back in his outpatient room a half hour after they had taken him to theatre.

"Hello," Louisa said, brushing a hand across his head.

He blinked and squinted, trying to clear the haze from his eyes. "Mm. It's done, then?"

"Mm-hmm. It's done."

Trying to sit up, he swayed before falling back against the pillow, and the attending nurse quickly stepped over to raise the head of the bed. "Is that better, Dr. Ellingham?" she asked.

He tugged at the blankets in his semi-coherent state, attempting to uncover his leg.

"Here, let me get it, Martin." Louisa said before flipping them back.

Several white bandages covered the wounds left by the pins, but for the first time in almost five months, his lower leg was free of the mechanical devices that had held his fractured bones together.

Taking note of her husband's hard swallow, Louisa's smile faded quickly. "Martin? What's wrong?"

He shook his head. "I don't think they're strong enough."

"What, the bones? Of course, they are. Ed wouldn't have removed the fixators if he had any doubt." She caressed a hand across his shoulders and he shook her away.

"No. It was too soon."

The nurse pulled the blankets back up and lowered the head of the bed. "I'm going to dim the lights and let you rest a bit, Doctor. You'll feel much better after you sleep off the anaesthesia."

Louisa held his hand, and his eyes quickly drifted shut again.

"Is that normal?" she asked the nurse. "I thought he'd be happy."

"I think it's quite understandable, given the extent of your husband's injuries, Mrs. Ellingham. The external fixation was all that was holding those bones of his together for quite a long while. He's bound to feel vulnerable without them."

The door slid open, and Ed Christianson gave Louisa a jerk of his head before stepping back into the hall.

She followed after him, pulling the door shut behind her. "Did everything go okay?" she asked.

"Just fine. He's going to be pretty sore for a while until his bones adjust to taking the additional stress. I'll stop back in a bit and discuss the next step with both of you ... when he's thinking clearly."

"Sure. Thank you, Ed."

The surgeon headed down the hall, and Louisa gave a final peek in at her sleeping husband before making her way towards the canteen, unable to ignore the gnawing in her stomach any longer.

She bit at her lip as her heels clicked against the gleaming linoleum floors in the corridors. *Was it just the anaesthesia talking or is Martin really worried?* she wondered.

The canteen was relatively quiet when she arrived, as was typical for the post-lunchtime hour. She selected a sandwich, a fruit salad, a bottle of milk, and, on impulse, a bag of crisps. With any luck, Martin would still be sleeping, and she could enjoy them free of any lectures on the dangers of salt and saturated fat.

"That'll be seven pounds fifty, please," the girl said.

Louisa pulled a credit card from her notecase and held it out. "There you are," she said.

"Sorry." The clerk gestured to a small sign setting on the counter. "Our machine isn't workin' right now. Cash only, I'm afraid."

"Oh! Well, that's okay; I think I have the change."

Another customer came up behind her, and she glanced back at him before laying down a five pound note.

She pulled a plush puppet and a nappy, on hand in case of emergency, from her purse and dug deeper. *"Bugger,"* she muttered. "I'm sorry. I seem to be a bit short." Two pound coins clinked against the glass countertop, and she picked up the bag of salty contraband. "I'll just put these back."

A white coat-clad arm reached across in front of her and fifty pee joined her money on the counter.

"There you are," a voice said.

"Oh, thank you!" She turned to the tall man behind her. "That's kind of you."

"It's nothing."

"It's not nothing when you're just dying for a bag of crisps," she said with a chuckle.

"Well, I couldn't let such a beautiful woman go hungry, now could I?"

Louisa's brow furrowed. The man's face looked vaguely familiar. But then, she'd seen a lot of faces in the hospital in the last months.

"Mm. Thank you." She gathered up her things and gave him an awkward smile before leaving the canteen.

Martin was alert and sitting up in bed when she returned to his room. "Well, hello!" she said, giving him a kiss on the cheek. "I just ran out to get some lunch. I didn't think you'd wake up so soon."

"They just used light sedation for this procedure." He eyed the items in her hands. "Crisps? Erm, Louisa, you do know that—"

"Yes, they're full of salt, saturated fat, and God knows what. But it's what I fancy, Martin. And if you're going to spoil this rare treat for me, I'll go and eat in the waiting area."

He ducked his head. "That won't be necessary."

"Good. Because I'd really prefer to be here with you," she said.

"I actually found myself short of change in the canteen. Fortunately, there was a very kind gentleman who came to my rescue. Otherwise, I would have had to go crisp-less." She leaned down and kissed him again, this time more passionately on the lips.

The door rumbled open and Martin pulled back quickly, clearing his throat.

"Well, you're looking bright-eyed and bushy-tailed," Ed Christianson said. "How's the leg feeling?"

"It hurts, but nothing I can't handle," Martin said.

The surgeon suppressed a grin. "Of course not." He jabbed a thumb at the crutches leaning against the wall. "Those bones will need some babying for a bit," he said. "Use your friends over there as much as you can whenever you're up and about."

Martin swung his legs over the side of the bed. "Am I free to go, then?"

Ed put up his hand. "In a minute. A few instructions—I want you to keep weight off that leg most of the time for the first few days, and let me know if you notice any instability. Gradually wean yourself off the crutches over the following three weeks.

"Keep up with the ice and elevation, and for God's sake, use the pain meds. We'll get some more pictures in a month to see how those bones are holding up." He cocked his head. "Any questions?"

"No, I think I can figure things out on my own."

Louisa folded her arms across her chest and raised her eyebrows at her husband. "If I may ask a question?"

"Certainly," Ed said.

"What do you mean by, see how the bones are holding up?"

"Holding up without the support of the fixators—that no stress fractures are developing."

"That could happen?"

"It's possible, but unlikely ... *if* Martin follows the instructions laid out."

She narrowed her eyes. "Oh, he *will* follow instructions. I'll see to it."

Ed took a step towards the door and turned. "If the pain you've been having *is* a nerve entrapment issue, the quicker we get on top of it the better, Martin. So, if you have any sudden intensification of pain or new symptoms, I want you to notify me immediately," the surgeon said. "And I mean that literally—*immediately*."

Martin tugged at an ear and gave the man a look of mild annoyance. "Yes."

"Okay. I guess you're free to go, then." He held out his hand. "This is one giant hurdle crossed, Martin. Congratulations."

"Mm, thank you, Ed."

Louisa waited for the door to roll shut before lacing her fingers around her husband's neck. "Well, does it feel any different?"

"A bit of pain, but not bad."

"No. I mean does it feel a bit ... I don't know ... liberating?"

"I haven't even been out of bed yet, Louisa. And I am still rather encumbered."

"Fair point. Shall I get your clothes?"

"That would be preferable to walking out dressed like this," he said, glancing down at the less-than-generous hospital gown.

She pressed her forehead to his. "I rather like the look."

He pulled up his chin and averted his gaze. "Mm. Thank you."

They were running a good fifteen minutes early when they arrived at Dr. Newell's office for Martin's appointment. Louisa thumbed through a women's magazine, glancing over and smiling at her husband several times as she caught him studying her.

"I'm almost done with this, and then you can have it," she said, giving him an impish smile. "I'm assuming you're wanting to catch up on the latest fashion trends in women's clothing?"

"No." His fingers tapped on the armrest of his chair and his brow furrowed. "It, er ... took your friend Danny a while to get himself over to Truro last night."

Louisa kept her eyes fixed on the article in front of her. "Did it?"

"Mm. He apologised for not having been there sooner."

"Did he?" She licked her finger and turned the page. "Did he, erm ... did he say what kept him?"

"He *claimed* he had to stop for petrol."

She brushed at her fringe and gave him a nervous smile. "That would make sense."

"No, it wouldn't. Because he told me his mother had vomited in the lavatory when he stopped for petrol on their way back to Portwenn. Either the idiot forgot to fill up his tank the first time, or he was lying to me about the second stop."

Louisa flipped the magazine shut and glanced over at the receptionist's desk before lowering her voice. "Danny said he was feeling shaky—rattled. And he asked if he could have a cup of tea before he left, just to calm his nerves."

"Why didn't he say that then instead of telling me a barefaced lie?"

She glanced again towards the desk. "I don't think this is the place to discuss it, Martin."

The door at the end of the hall opened, ending the conversation. Martin sighed before pulling himself to his feet and working his crutches under his arms. "I'll be back in a while."

She gave him a sheepish smile. "I'll be waiting."

Louisa worried her lip as she listened to Dr. Newell's fading voice. Danny Steel's presence in Portwenn could once again strain her relationship with Martin.

The door clicked shut behind the two men, and Dr. Newell wagged a finger at his patient's leg. "This is new."

"Mm. The external fixation came off the lower leg today." An involuntary grunt escaped as Martin dropped heavily into the chair in front of the desk.

"That's fantastic, Martin. How does it feel to be free of a bit of the hardware?"

Martin stared back at the man, straight-faced. "Like I'm free of a bit of the hardware."

"Of course." He eyed the sheen of moisture on his patient's upper lip. "You sure you're up to this?"

"I'm fine."

Pulling himself forward, the doctor flipped open his patient's file. "I asked you the last time we met to work on the two lists of adjectives that you made before your accident. The list describing the man you would like to be and the list describing the man your wife and son—er, sons would like you to be. How did that go?"

Martin pulled a folded sheet of paper from his shirt pocket and handed it to him. "I've added some notes, as you asked. And, to expedite the process, I've put them in descending order of importance."

The therapist raised an eyebrow as he scanned it for a moment. "Okay. Let's talk about the list describing the man *you* would like to be. I see that being liked has overtaken social confidence on your list of adjectives. Let's start with that. Why did you give being liked a higher ranking now than you gave it before?"

"I believe I've seen improvement in my social confidence."

"And you're happy—comfortable with the gains that you've made?"

"Well, it would be difficult to quantify, but Louisa seems satisfied now with the amount of time we spend with friends."

"And you?"

Martin's thumb rubbed away at his palm. "There are people who I consider to be friends, now. I have lunch with Jeremy Portman on occasion, and I make an effort to stop and see Chris Parsons when I'm in Truro. Louisa would probably say my conversational skills have improved."

"Do you feel they've improved?"

He stared absently for a moment. "Yes. Yes, I believe so. Louisa and I certainly talk more. And I do with Chris and Jeremy as well."

"And other than Chris, Jeremy, and Louisa?"

"Well, James and Evan, obviously. And my aunt. It's difficult to carry on a conversation with James at this point; he's a toddler. But Evan and I do have what I would call conversations. And, of course, I talk with Ruth."

"So, you dropped social confidence to second in order of importance because you feel a sense of progress in that area, thereby raising being liked to the top of your list?"

Martin's brow furrowed, and he shook his head. "As I said before, Louisa seems to be more content now with the amount of socialising that we do. But I'm not sure she's happy with the tendency I have to put people off. So, that's now of primary importance."

"I see. But this list reflects what's important to *you*, Martin. Is it important to you that you don't, as you say, put people off—that the villagers, at the very least, find you approachable? Or that your professional colleagues find you to be a genial person?"

"God, no! I couldn't care less what the people in Portwenn think of me. And it doesn't matter if my colleagues"—he sneered—"*like* me or not. My concern is whether or not they respect my skills as a surgeon—erm, GP."

He squirmed in his chair and hissed out a breath. "Look, I did as you asked. But obviously, you're not happy with it. Why don't you just tell me what your expectations are, and I'll do the pointless assignment again."

Dr. Newell's fingernail clicked against the sheet of paper. "Martin, you've done just fine here. I'm just suggesting that perhaps being liked should be lower on *your* list. Or perhaps not on it at all if it's not really important to *you*?"

Martin, trying to tamp back his rapidly growing annoyance with the direction the man's questions had taken, answered slowly, with an air of exaggerated patience. "Nooo. I want Louisa to be happy, and it would make her happy if I were liked by the people in the village. Therefore, it *does* belong on my list."

"All right. Let's work with that. You want Louisa to be happy—why?"

"Why?"

"Yes, why? For me, life is much easier when my wife is happy. It may mean that I'll be sitting down to a lovely home-made pot roast as opposed to having a bag of takeaway dropped down in front of me."

"Louisa doesn't do a lot of the cooking. When she does, I try not to set my expectations too high."

The psychiatrist tipped his head down and rubbed at his temple. "Okay. When you take her for a nice meal out, to a concert, or buy her flowers—you must have some motivation for doing that. Perhaps to soften her up before you tell her something she's apt to be angry with you about? Maybe to set the stage for what you hope will be a romantic end to the day. Or maybe you're hoping she'll agree to—"

"Definitely not! I want to be a proper husband! Not to wheedle favours from wife! I'm not my father!"

He cleared his throat and gave the man a sheepish glance. "I, erm ... I want my wife to be happy."

Rocking in his chair, the therapist nodded. "Being a good and caring husband is important to you?"

"Yes." Martin pulled in his chin and stared back at the man for a moment. "I see. That should be what I put at the top of my list?"

"Correct. Bear in mind, however, that there are certain things that you can do to perhaps ease the relationships you have with the people in the village, if that would make Louisa happy. That motivation comes from your desire to be a good husband who cares about his wife's happiness—a quality that you want to see when you look in the mirror.

"I'd like you to talk with Louisa about this. It's fine to try to soften your approach with your patients—the villagers. But there is a limit to the changes you can make without it—"

"Coming off as smarmy," Martin interjected as a grimace tweaked his face.

"I'm sure that's true. But I was actually going to say that at your essence, you're a very straightforward and honest man. So, protect that quality if it matters to you."

"Mm, yes."

"When you talk with Louisa, make sure she appreciates your need to be who you are. And while you're at it, it would be good to clarify what it is that she's wanting from you. Are you sure that having the villagers like you is important to Louisa? Have you discussed it with her?"

Sharp pain raced through his freshly-abused leg, and Martin flinched before erupting. "It doesn't *need* to be discussed! It's been obvious since the day I arrived in that godforsaken backwater!"

"I would still like for you to discuss it. If there's been any sort of misunderstanding, now is the time to clear things up. Louisa's attitude may have changed as you've both grown in the relationship. And it's very easy for one partner to misunderstand what the other is asking. Hurt feelings can result"

Martin's brow furrowed. "I don't follow."

The therapist hesitated, staring at a paperclip as he tapped it against the armrest. "A long time ago, before I became the enlightened man that you see before you today, I admitted to a girlfriend that I didn't find her to be pretty.

"Nothing more was said until years later—more than thirty years of marriage later. My now dear wife was experiencing what I suppose could be considered a midlife crisis. It came out, in the midst of a disagreement, that the evaluation I'd made years before about her physical appearance had been interpreted by her in a very different way than it was intended. And, for thirty-plus years, it had coloured the way she thought I looked at her."

He squirmed in his chair. "Well, I don't have to tell you, we've all found ourselves flipping through a college flatmate's skin mag ... if we didn't have one stashed under our own mattress."

Martin gave him a vacant stare. "I'm sorry?"

"Pornography, Martin. We've all seen the airbrushed examples of perfection in those magazines."

"Ah, I see."

A soft breath of relief eased from Dr. Newell's mouth. "Good. Well, the point is, the artificially flawless beings that I'd seen in the magazines are what came to mind when she asked me, way back then, if I thought she was pretty.

"I didn't realise she needed to hear that I found—or find her to be beautiful. I didn't and still don't desire pretty. I want more than someone who fits that superficial description. We understand each other now, but I wish it hadn't taken us thirty years to get there."

Martin picked up his crutches and, grimacing, he got to his feet. "I'm sorry; I need to move," he said, hobbling towards the window.

"Yes, of course." The doctor rolled his chair forward, resting his elbows on his desktop. "Talk with Louisa, Martin. Make sure you're both on the same page about what it is that she wants. And make sure that you both understand that if there are changes she'd like you to make, there are limits to how much you can change."

Martin nodded before his eyes drifted shut and he listed back against the closed window. Hurrying over, the psychiatrist took hold of his patient's arm and led him back to the chair before perching himself on the edge of his desk.

"I think you've had more than enough for one day, so we'll wrap this up."

A flush spread up Martin's neck, and he tugged at an ear. "Mm, I'm fine. You were saying that there are limits to the changes that I can make. And yes ... I'll erm, talk with Louisa."

"Good. Before our next visit, I'd like you to think about the personal qualities that you feel are essential to your character," the doctor said as he slid to the floor. "You don't want to throw out the baby with the bathwater. You have many positive qualities, Martin, and it's important to identify and safeguard those that are the essence of who you are."

The psychiatrist slipped a hand under his good arm and helped Martin hoist himself to his feet. "Do you feel steady enough to get to the car on your own?" he asked.

Shaking the psychiatrist from his arm, Martin gave him an annoyed glance. "Of course."

"Excellent." The man tugged at his sleeves and adjusted his cufflinks. "Make sure you're keeping a record of those nightmares that have been troubling you. Hopefully, we'll have time to address them next week."

"Mm, yes; I have been."

"All done?" Louisa asked brightly when her husband returned to the reception room.

"Mm, yes." He fished the key fob from his pocket and handed it to her. "You'll need to drive."

Looking at his drawn face, she patted his cheek. "Obviously."

They drove home in silence with Martin sleeping off some of the residual effects of the anaesthesia and stress to his body. He only stirred when his wife opened her car door after parking next to the surgery.

Louisa pulled her handbag higher over her shoulder and stood at the ready, lest he lose his balance as he pulled himself from his seat. "Looks like Jeremy's come to help. That was nice of him," she said, giving a nod to the car in the extra parking space. Reaching down, she took hold of his arm. "Here, let me help you to—"

"I'm—fine, Louisa. And please don't hover," he grumbled. "Go on inside. I'll be along in a minute."

She hesitated before heading around the side of the house towards the back.

Martin was just starting up the slope to the slate terrace when his aide emerged from the front door. The young man silently guided him in through the front before steering him back to the consulting room. "Let's get some Toradol into you, then get that leg on ice, eh?"

Sliding back on to the examination couch, Martin gave him no argument, just a lethargic nod and a grunt.

Water hissed from the tap at the sink, and soon wisps of vapor began to rise into the air. "You know, these procedures over in Truro would be a helluva lot easier if you skipped the excursions afterwards," the young man said as he ran a small towel under the hot water before ringing it out. Then, drawing the Toradol up into a syringe, he jabbed the needle into his patient's thigh and slapped the still-steaming towel down on to his leg.

His jaw clenching, Martin waited for the residual burn to ease. "I'm just trying to make efficient use of my time."

Jeremy gave him a roll of his eyes. "Gawd. *I'd* go home and crawl into bed."

"Yes, I'm sure you would." Martin gave him a half sneer, brushing the towel away and working his trousers back up. He glanced up at his friend with a contrite expression. "Sorry. I appreciate you coming to help."

"No problem, mate."

Martin slid to the floor. The two men had just turned into the hallway when the doorbell rang.

"I gots it!" Evan called out. The muffled thud of his stocking-clad feet preceded the creak of the front door as it opened.

Louisa's voice joined the conversation in the entryway and, hesitating, Martin strained to hear what was being said. He groaned internally when he caught the words, *Martin should take a quick look at that.*

Heading back into the reception room, he gave the female visitor and her son a peevish stare.

"This is Amanda Crandall, Martin. It seems Michael here fell through the ice on their pond," Louisa said, tipping the boy's head back and giving him a disapproving look. "He's okay, thankfully, but he cut his hand on a screw on the dock. I told Amanda you—"

"—would take a look at it. Yes. Come through," he said, giving the woman a jerk of his head.

Fifteen minutes later, Martin had sent the Crandall woman and her son on their way. The boy with a fresh tetanus jab, his wound disinfected and butterfly-stitched shut, and a harsh reprimand about the dangers of venturing out on to an ice-covered pond.

Jeremy met him in the lounge with a bottle of one of his high-protein shakes. "Drink that down, then go on up to bed. I'll bring some ice packs up in a few minutes."

With no argument, the doctor drank down the contents and handed the bottle back to the young man. "Goodnight," he grunted before turning and heading for the stairs.

When Louisa came into the bedroom several hours later, he was standing in front of the bathroom sink brushing his teeth.

"Feeling better?" she asked.

He spit before wiping his face on the hand towel. "I'm still tired, but it's less painful." Leaning down, he kissed her. "Sorry. I left you on your own with the boys."

"We managed. Although Evan wasn't too sure you should be going to bed without eating your vegetables first."

"The shakes supply the daily recommended dietary allowance of any vitamins the vegetables would have contained. He needn't have worried."

Louisa tipped her head down and peered up at him. "I think he missed you at dinner, Martin."

"Ah."

He returned to the bed and watched as she readied herself for the night. His rather ravenous look did not go unnoticed.

Hesitating, she cast her pyjama top aside and nestled, half-naked, under the covers with him. "Long day, hmm?" she said.

"Yes." His hand came to rest on her hip before sliding down the inward curve of her waist. "Jeremy could be right. It might be best to avoid the scheduling of sessions with Dr. Newell on the same days as these procedures."

"I think *that* would be a very good idea." She stroked her thumb across his cheek. "How did things go with Dr. Newell today?"

"Fine."

"I'm not saying you have to talk about it, but if you want to ..."

"No, that's fine. We discussed expectations ... and motivation, I suppose. What I think you expect of me and what I expect of myself."

"Oh?"

"Mm. If I understand correctly, he thinks it's important that any changes I make are made for the right reasons."

"What do you mean?"

He studied her face before warily stepping into territory he feared could pose hidden dangers. "Do you remember when I attempted to be congenial to ... what's-her-name?"

Louisa's fingers brushed impatiently at her fringe. "If by what's-her-name you're referring to my friend, Holly, then yes, I remember."

"It seems you were correct. You have to want to."

"Really?"

"Yes. I believe the point he was trying to make was that my motivation for doing things needs to be internal. I suppose at the time, I was just trying to do what I thought you wanted me to do—to avoid losing you. And it came off as—well, as smarmy, as you put it. I was just pretending to be what you wanted me to be."

"And that's not who you are, is it?" she said, propping herself up on an elbow and peering down at him.

"No. It's not. He wants us to discuss some things—make sure we understand one another."

"Such as?"

Martin raised up, levelling the playing field. "My making an effort to be more likeable. That's something you've mentioned in the past, and Dr. Newell thinks it's important that you clarify what it is that you want from me. And that I think about how much of a change I can make for you without ... well, without becoming smarmy."

"I see."

"Yes. He shared a story about a misunderstanding that he had with his—" He stopped, not wanting to betray what may have been said in confidence. "Are you familiar with the works of William Shakespeare?"

She narrowed her eyes at him. "As difficult as it may be for you to believe, Martin, even here in the back of beyond, we did cover literature in comprehensive school."

"Yes, of course. Well, Dr. Newell's story reminded me of a Shakespeare sonnet that I'm particularly fond of. And it reminded me of us—erm, you."

Louisa lay back on her pillow, and he brushed a wisp of hair from her cheek before he began to recite.

"My mistress' eyes are nothing like the sun;
Coral is far more red than her lips' red;
If snow be white, why then her breasts are dun;
If hairs be wires, black wires grow on her head."

His seductive and sonorous tone went unnoticed by Louisa, even as his face softened and his eyes locked on hers. Her ears heard only the words.

"I have seen roses damask'd, red and white,
But no such roses see I in her cheeks;
And in some perfumes is there more delight
Than in the breath that from my mistress reeks."

She grew increasingly affronted as her insecure nature immediately presumed the literary master's words to be personal slurs from her husband. And old hurts were quickly resurrected.

"I love to hear her speak, yet well I know
That music hath a far more pleasing sound;
I grant I never saw a goddess go;
My mistress, when she walks, treads on the ground:
And yet, by heaven, I think my love as rare
As any she belied with false compare."

He gave her a shyly smug smile. "Shakespeare's Sonnet 130—I memorised it in my last year of prep school," he said in his still-silky voice. "It was compulsory."

He leaned down to kiss her, but she quickly rolled away from him, pulling her dressing gown around her before her footsteps faded away down the stairs.

Staring after her, a hiss of air rushed from his nose. He once again knew that he had upset her with his words, but he was clueless as to why.

Sighing, he forced himself from the bed, wedging his crutches under his arms before following after her.

He found her in the kitchen, staring out the darkened window.

"Louisa," he said softly. "Are you upset?"

Her mane swished across her shoulders. "I don't understand why you keep doing this."

"I thought you'd appreciate it. I'm sorry."

She whirled around, her eyes snapping. "Seriously? You thought I'd appreciate a poem that finds fault with every one of my physical features, Martin? Hmm?"

"Erm, it's a sonnet—a poem in a particular form. And to be fair, Shakespeare didn't find fault with *every* one of her features."

"Not *her* features, Martin! *My* features! You said you think of me when you hear that bloody poem."

"Yes, I do think of you. But if you'd let me explain, I think—"

"In some perfumes there's more delight than in my mistress' reeking breath?"

"No. It's, *'And in some perfumes is there more delight, than in the breath that from my mistress reeks.'*"

"Oh, well that's all right, then!"

His eyes darted as he searched for the words to defuse the situation. "The man wrote this sonnet more than four hundred years ago, Louisa. He couldn't possibly have been referencing you personally."

She slapped a hand over her eyes. "I don't care about William Shakespeare, Martin. This is about what *you* think of me."

Martin blinked back at her for a moment before his brow drew down. "You *did* hear the last lines, didn't you?"

Her hand slowly dropped to her side and she shook her head. "What do you mean?"

"*'And yet, by heaven, I think my love as rare, as any she belied with false compare.'* Shakespeare was saying that the love he has for his mistress is a far richer love than that being written about by other poets of his time—the shallow love of the perfect images depicted in their sonnets. He loves his mistress for the essence of who she is, not for some superficial, ideal qualities."

He tugged at an ear and mumbled. "Although, I must admit, I do appreciate your ideal qualities."

Louisa's eyes welled with tears as she considered his words, and his head dropped to the side. "I'm sorry; I haven't helped matters."

"Oh, Martin. Yes, you have. Very much so."

He pulled back his shoulders as his eyes rolled to the side. "Oh? *Good*."

She stepped towards him and her fingers brushed his arm. "Can we go to bed now?"

"Mm. Yes, of course."

Her hand rested on his hip as she followed him up the stairs, watching that he didn't lose his balance. They cuddled close together under the covers, warming each other after their excursion to the chilly kitchen.

Louisa's shivering quieted, and Martin sat up, pulling his tee shirt over his head, dropping it on to the chair next to the bed before turning decidedly hungry eyes on her.

"You sure you feel up to it?" she asked.

"Mm." He rolled her on to her back, exposing her breasts before placing gentle kisses on each one. Peering up shyly, he searched for and found the desirous expression that encouraged him to carry on.

His lips lingered at her cleavage where he found her scent to be the most intense, and drawing in a slow, silent breath, he whispered, "Oh, Louisa."

Her fingers, still cool from the chill air, slipped down his sides, searching for his waistband, before she rose up slightly and tugged his boxers from his hips. This signalled a brief intermission in their love-making while he manipulated them over his healing legs.

When he turned back, she had divested herself of the last of her clothing and now lay on the bed in front of him, completely exposed. The sight of her took his breath away. He studied her, committing to memory every one of her features.

"Martin? Everything okay there?" she asked as she tipped her head, trying to make eye contact.

He looked at her sheepishly. "Mm, sorry. I just ..." Air hissed through his teeth as he gave her a slow shake of his head. "You are a feast for the eyes, Louisa."

Her lips twitched. "Why, thank you, Martin. But come here now. Your," she cleared her throat, "dinner's getting cold."

"Oh, sorry ... sorry." Reaching over, he flipped the switch on the lamp and pulled up the duvet before burrowing under it with her. Then, in the darkness, without the visual distraction of her beauty, he made love to her—the intelligent, impulsive, feisty, emotional, and nurturing essence of her that he so adored.

They lay later, entwined and satisfied. Louisa cupped his cheek in her hand and pressed her forehead to his. "Martin."

"Hmm?"

"Say it again."

"Say what again?"

"The poem."

He hesitated. "Mm, best not."

"Please. I want to hear it again. All of it this time."

His arms tightened around her as he rested his chin on her head. *"My mistress' eyes are nothing like the sun ..."*

Chapter 11

Martin was roused Saturday morning by cold feet, shoved under his back as small fingers prised open his eyelid.

"Hi, Da-ee," James Henry whispered, giving him a juicy kiss on the forehead as Evan burrowed his feet a bit deeper under him.

"We didn't think you were ever gonna wake up," the seven-year-old said. "You must'a been really knackered!"

The doctor glanced over at him before breathing out a heavy sigh and closing his eyes again, waiting for his brain to clear. "What time is it?"

The feet were yanked out from under him and he yelped. "Ow! Be careful, Evan!"

The boy leaned over, peering down with an expression of concern on his face. "Sorry. Was I too rough on you?"

"No. You need to trim your toenails."

"I don't know how. But, hey! Maybe you could teach me this morning! We don't gots anything else fun to do."

Rolling James from his chest, Martin sat up. "I have surgery, so our fun is going to have to wait." He turned bleary eyes to the clock before hurriedly shoving himself from the bed. "Gawd, I'm late. Evan, go tell Morwenna I'll be down in fifteen minutes," he grumbled, grabbing his crutches and dressing gown and disappearing into the bathroom.

"Come on, James," the older boy said, dragging the toddler to the floor. "We can make Dr. Ellig-am something special for his breakfast."

James giggled and toddled after him, grasping tightly to his hand until they came to the stairs where he dropped to the floor and slowly slid down the steps on his bum.

When Martin came through the lounge a short time later, his breakfast sat steaming in a bowl on the table.

"We're having porridge this morning, Martin. Take a seat," Louisa said as she set another bowl down in front of Morwenna.

He pulled out a chair, eyeing the young woman and grumbling, "Why aren't you at your desk?"

"It's my audition this mornin', remember?"

He gave her a blank stare.

"For Annie Get Your Gun!" She huffed out a breath and waved a hand at him impatiently. "You know, over at the Village Hall."

"Mm, yes. That doesn't explain why you're sitting at my table, eating the food I paid for, though."

"Martin!" Louisa hissed. "Morwenna was gracious enough to stop by and get Poppy settled before she left her on her own. The least we can do is offer her a bit of breakfast, don't you think?"

"Mm. I see." He picked up a bowl of blueberries from the centre of the table and scooped some into his porridge before peering up at his wife. "You turned my alarm off again."

"Yes, I'm aware of that." Taking a seat next to Morwenna, Louisa drizzled her cereal with golden syrup. "You needed your rest, so I had Poppy reschedule your first two appointments so that you could sleep in."

Martin looked over at his young charge, busy with something at the counter. The boy turned slowly, balancing a mug on a saucer as he crept towards the table. Its contents sloshed over the side as he set it down next to his guardian. "It's hot chocolate. But it's not done yet, so don't drink any of it," he said.

He raced back to the counter and picked up a gold tin, tugging the lid off. "Okay, James. Now you can do your part of it," he said before the toddler scrambled over and reached a chubby fist into the container.

The first handful was quickly shoved into the eager little boy's mouth before he reached for another, this time holding tight to his precious load until he got to the table.

Evan wrapped his arms around James's chest and, grunting, hoisted him up so that the marshmallows could be deposited into his father's mug.

"There! Now you can drink it," the seven-year-old said.

Martin stared down at the sweet beverage, now adorned with sugary pink pillows. "Mm. I really don't—"

"Mar-tin." He glanced up at his wife's steely eyes and tight lips before air hissed from his nose.

James slapped a hand against the table and gave his father a broad smile. "Fo yo, Daddy!"

"Yeah, Dr. Ellig-am. Me and James made it to make you feel better. Those pink things are medicine to make you not so shirty. Aren't you gonna drink it?"

He turned pleading eyes to his wife. "Louisa, I would prefer not to be—"

"It's a gesture of love, Martin. Chin-chin!"

"Oh, this day is off to a brilliant start," he grumbled as he picked up the mug and took a sip.

Louisa suppressed a smile as she gestured with a finger to her lips, and Martin wiped away the pink foam on his mouth with his napkin.

The little boys watched in anticipation. "Do you like it?" Evan asked.

The doctor hesitated before giving him a soft grunt. "Mm. I feel better already."

Fortunately for Martin, the less-than-perfect start to his day led to a rather mundane schedule of rechecks and preventive care appointments.

He emerged from his consulting room shortly after noon. "Poppy, I left a stack of patient notes on my desk. Would you get them and file them away for me?" he asked as he balanced on his crutches. "I'm, er, somewhat encumbered."

"Oh, sure! Sure!" she said, hurrying off to retrieve them.

Jeremy came in from the lounge, tugging at his coat sleeve to check his watch. "That was the last of them, Martin. I need to get going or I'm going to be late for that class at Truro that I signed up for. Anything you need before I go? More Toradol?"

"Mm, I'm fine. You go ahead. I'll see you on Monday."

The aide eyed him momentarily. "Don't overdo it this weekend, okay?"

"Yes, I know." Martin waved him away. "Go on."

The door clicked behind the young man and the doctor turned for the kitchen. Whatever Louisa was cooking smelled of rosemary and garlic, ingredients that could be considered exotic for her culinary repertoire.

He turned as he passed his fill-in receptionist. "Erm, Poppy … would you like to join us for lunch?"

"Er, yeah. That'd be nice." She stared at him, goggled-eyed, before hurrying to the file cabinet.

When Martin came through under the stairs, he found his wife flitting about in the kitchen and the table set—for two. A flowered linen tablecloth had been laid out, and Auntie Joan's finest china had been pulled from the buffet.

He glanced around. "Where are the boys?"

"Al offered to take Evan over to Wadebridge to see that new animated movie showing in the theatre. And James just went down for a nap. I've been waiting for weeks for the opportunity to have a romantic lunch together." She turned and stretched up to kiss him.

"Oh."

Her shoulders dropped. "Oh, no. You had other plans, didn't you?"

"No, no, no, no, no. It's just," he sucked in a breath, "I'm sorry. I invited Poppy to join us."

Louisa tipped her head down and peered up at him with dubious eyes. "You invited Poppy to join us?"

"Well, I wouldn't have if I'd known you'd made special plans." He jutted out his chin. "And she was gracious enough to help out today. I assumed you'd think it appropriate to offer her a bit of lunch."

"No, it's fine, Martin," she said, putting a hand on his chest. "More than fine, really. It's nice that you did. I'll just set another place at the table." After pulling a casserole dish from the cooker, she tugged the oven gloves from her hands and tossed them on to the counter before giving him a tepid smile. "We'll still have some time to ourselves after she leaves, hmm?"

Poppy entered the kitchen and Martin quickly stepped aside, clearing his throat as he gave his wife a furtive glance.

Louisa kept up a polite natter with their childminder-turned-practice receptionist while her husband tucked into his meal. He cast more than one inquisitive look at her as he puzzled over her sudden foray into finer cuisine.

With both taste buds and stomach now satisfied by the Greek Chicken and the Pasta with Roasted Romanesco and Capers, he dabbed at his mouth with his napkin.

Louisa got up and began to clear the plates from the table and Poppy hurriedly joined in. "Let me do the washing up, Mrs. Ellingham."

"No, no, no, Poppy. You were our guest; I'll get this later." She turned to her husband and raised an eyebrow. "You must be exhausted, Martin. And Ed did say you should get plenty of rest this weekend."

"I don't remember him say—"

"That's probably because of the anaesthesia." She gave him a raise of her eyebrows, pre-empting any further discussion.

"Yes."

"Poppy, I hate to be a rude host, but I really need to get Martin up to bed," she said, lifting the young woman's coat from the peg behind the door.

"Oh, sure, Mrs. Ellingham; I understand."

Martin's mobile rang and he reached into his pocket, grimacing when the answering service icon flashed on the screen.

"Well, thanks for lunch. It was delicious." Poppy slipped on her coat and pulled her cap over her head, and Louisa followed her through the lounge, towards the front door. "Well, I know Martin appreciates you helping out this morning. It was the least we could—"

"Poppy, don't go yet," Martin called out after her. He limped towards the hallway. "I need your help."

"What's going on, Martin?" Louisa asked.

"That woman who was in with her son yesterday—the boy who tried to drown himself in the family pond. Her five-year-old's having an asthma attack, and he isn't responding to the inhaler. I need Poppy to drive me out there."

The girl stood motionless as her face blanched. "You mean drive your car?"

"Yes."

Louisa followed him under the stairs and into the consulting room. "Can't Amanda bring him in?"

He raised an eyebrow and cocked his head. "Amanda who?"

"Amanda Crandall, Martin—the mum, for goodness' sake."

"Ah. Her husband's gone and she doesn't have transportation." Drawers on his medical bag rattled as the doctor took a hurried inventory, pulling several vials and a package of tubing from his cabinet. He snapped the bag shut. "Can you carry that?"

"Sure," Louisa said.

"Poppy," Martin barked. "Get this oxygen tank and the nebuliser."

The childminder hurried over to pick up the items. "I need the keys," she said before dashing back to the kitchen.

Poppy's fingers gripped tightly to the steering wheel of the Lexus as they drove out of the village and turned towards Delabole. Martin's mobile rang again, and he yanked it from his pocket. "Yes?"

The young woman glanced over at him, her anxiety building as worry etched her boss's face.

"Acting funny, how?" he asked impatiently.

"Irritability would be expected if he's struggling to breathe."

His fingers began to drum against his arm rest. "What do you mean, his chest hurts?"

Shaking his head, he huffed out a breath. "We'll be there in five minutes. Try to keep him calm until we arrive."

He screwed up his face. "Well, I don't know. Can't you read him a story or something?"

Poppy leaned towards him and said in an undertone, "She could try singin' to him."

The doctor glanced over, giving her a nod of his head. "Mrs. Crandall! Mrs. Crandall, you need to calm down. It won't help your son if you get yourself all worked up. Try singing to the boy. We'll be there in just a few minutes."

He pocketed the phone again and wagged a finger at the childminder. "That was a good idea. Even if singing doesn't calm the child, it may keep that high-strung mother together until we arrive."

They turned off the tarmac roadway and on to the long, gravelled drive leading to the Crandall farm. The child whom Martin had treated the day before was waiting on the porch, and he ran to the car. "Hurry! Somethin's really wrong. He can't hardly breathe or nothin'."

Martin headed for the house and Poppy had the Crandall boy help her collect the doctor's bag and the other items from the back seat.

The ill child was lying on the sofa when they entered the family's living room. Martin cocked his head at the absence of the expected asthmatic wheeze before he snapped his fingers. "Poppy, bring me a chair."

The young woman grabbed one from the dining room table and quickly set it next to the sofa.

Falling into it heavily, the doctor dropped his crutches to the floor and removed an inhaler from a drawer in his medical bag.

"What's his name?" Martin asked.

The mother's hands worked around her elbows as she hugged herself. "Robbie."

The inhaler was inserted into the child's mouth. "Big breath in now, Robbie," the doctor said.

The boy's chest barely rose as he inhaled.

"And again."

He pulled his stethoscope from his bag. "Unbutton his shirt," he told Mrs. Crandall, pressing his fingers to the boy's forehead.

Palpating his neck, Martin tried not to allow the child's desperate gaze to affect his focus and professional objectivity.

"Has he been ill recently?" he asked as the mother hovered over him, wringing her hands.

"No. No, he's been fit as a fiddle this year ... till now. Hasn't even needed his inhaler in months. He was runnin' around outside with his brother just yesterday, in fact. What do you think it is? He's never been anywhere near this bad, Doc."

Pulling a tongue depressor and a torch from his shirt pocket, Martin noted the accumulation of foam in the child's throat and mouth. His eyes darted as the pieces of the puzzle began to come together.

He turned to the eight-year-old, Michael. "Did he fall through the ice, too, yesterday?"

The boy glanced up at his mother. "Well, yeah. He fell in first. I was tryin' ta get him out when I fell through. But I got him out right away, didn't I, Mum?"

"I wasn't there, Doc," the mother said. "But he didn't seem none the worse for wear. Not a mark on him. It was just this one." She caressed the older child's head.

"Robbie though, he was like a bear with a sore head this mornin'. I figured he was comin' down with something. Then he started rubbin' at his chest, sayin' it hurt, and havin' trouble getting air. It's just the asthma, right?"

Martin looked down at the cherubic features and deepening blue tinge to the Crandall boy's lips before pulling out his mobile. He handed it to the childminder. "Call for an air ambulance, Poppy. Tell them it's acute respiratory distress following a near drowning incident yesterday."

The young woman stepped from the room to make the call and Martin returned his attention to the five-year-old. Removing an oxygen mask from his bag, he connected it to the canister that Poppy had leaned against the sofa and opened the valve.

"What's wrong with him, Doc?" Mrs. Crandall asked as the gravity of the situation began to sink in.

"I believe your son aspirated ... er, inhaled water when he fell through the ice yesterday. In rare instances, near drowning can begin a cascade of events that inhibit normal lung function. I strongly suspect this is what's going on with ... erm, Robbie."

Poppy re-entered the room, handing the mobile back to her boss. "It's on the way. They said about fifteen minutes."

"Mm, thank you." The boy's eyes drifted shut and Martin pressed his stethoscope to his chest again, his features tightening as he listened intently.

"Anything else I can do, Dr. Ellingham?" Poppy asked.

Martin breathed out a heavy sigh and glanced back at her. "Yeah. Take Mrs. Crandall out to the kitchen and make her a cup of tea ... the boy, too. Then come back in here. I'll need you."

"Sure." The young woman took the eight-year-old by the hand, giving him a smile. "Come on. You can help me."

The anxious mother followed reluctantly.

When Poppy returned to the living room a few minutes later, Martin had instruments laid out on a surgical drape on the floor.

He looked up. "I need to intubate him. He's not pulling in enough air on his own. Can you move him to the coffee table?"

"Yeah. He gonna be okay, Dr. Ellingham?"

Martin glanced towards the kitchen and shook his head. "He's deteriorating quickly."

Working her hands under the small, limp body, Poppy laid him gently on the table top before heading towards the kitchen.

Martin waved her back. "Stay here. I need your help."

Aligning the child's head to give him a straight passageway for the breathing tube, the doctor gave her a nod. "Okay, Poppy, hold him in that position."

Reaching back to the floor, Martin picked up his laryngoscope blade. Then, prising his patient's jaws open, he inserted it over the child's tongue before passing the plastic tubing down his airway.

"Good. Now come around here," he said as he attached the bag-valve ventilator to the endotracheal tubing. Air hissed into the child's lungs as he squeezed the bag. "I want you to take over here whilst I go talk to the mother. Give the bag a squeeze once every three seconds."

Poppy shook her head. "I don't think I should. What if something goes wrong while you're gone?"

"Nothing can go more wrong than it already has. And there's no more that we can do." He gave her a nod, picked up his crutches and headed for the kitchen.

When he returned, an ashen-faced Mrs. Crandall was with him. She sat down on the sofa and held her son's head in her hands, pressing her forehead to his. Poppy couldn't understand the woman's whispered words, but she knew they were the prayerful pleas of a desperate mother.

Martin pressed his fingers to the child's neck, searching for the hoped-for carotid pulse. Then, he put a hand over Poppy's to quiet the hiss of the ventilator as he listened for a heartbeat.

"Mrs. Crandall," he said softly. "I need to examine your son's eyes."

Pulling her head away, she wiped the tears from her face, giving him a reluctant nod.

The doctor removed the torch from his pocket and shone it at the child's face. The absence of a pupillary response confirmed the little boy's death.

Poppy stared down, the doctor's trembling hands revealing more to her than his stoic expression.

"I'm sorry, Mrs. Crandall. Your son has died," he said.

"No!" the woman wailed. "You gotta keep tryin', Doc!"

"I'm sorry; he's gone."

"No, no, no, no, no, no. This can't be happening!"

He averted his gaze from the agonised expression on Amanda Crandall's face and looked up at the childminder. "Poppy, can you lift Robbie on to his mother's lap?"

The young woman bit fiercely at her bottom lip before nodding her head and shifting the lifeless form from the table.

"Is there a family member or friend ... neighbour who we can call to contact your husband?" Martin asked as he dropped his stethoscope into his bag and snapped it shut. "Someone who can stay with you until he arrives?"

Mrs. Crandall rocked back and forth, clutching her youngest child to her breast as she stared vacantly. "My sister. My sister, Mary. Mary Pemberton. She lives just down the road."

The doctor turned to the younger woman. "Call and cancel the air ambulance, Poppy. Ask them to send a ground ambulance instead. Then, see if you can reach Mrs. Crandall's sister."

Poppy took the mobile from Martin's hand and headed towards the kitchen before he stopped her. "Go out to the porch to make your calls. I need to talk with the older boy ... explain what's happened."

"Yeah. Right."

The sun had fallen below the kitchen windowsill by the time Martin had completed the required paperwork, Mary Pemberton and the little boy's father had arrived, and the body had been taken away.

The crunch of the gravel under his crutches seemed irreverently loud as the doctor negotiated his way through the bikes and toy dump trucks strewn around the driveway.

Poppy went to cross in front of him, heading for the driver's side of the Lexus, and Martin reached out, taking hold of her sleeve. "You're in no condition to drive," he told her.

"But your leg?"

"I can manage."

"They rode in silence for the first few miles. When they made the turn towards Portwenn, Martin cleared his throat. "Erm, do you have any questions about what happened today?"

Poppy squeezed her eyes shut against the tears that she'd been struggling to hold back for the last hour and a half and turned her face towards the window. "I felt so bad for the mum, Dr. Ellingham."

"Yes."

His fingers tapped against the steering wheel. "You did everything correctly. I'm glad you were there. I couldn't have managed the intubation without you."

"Because of your arm?"

"Mm."

He heard a sniffle and he pointed to the glovebox. "I believe there are tissues in there ... if you need them."

She glanced over at him and popped the latch. "It didn't help that little boy much, though, did it—my bein' there?"

Martin's mouth opened and closed before he pressed his lips together, sitting silent until they had passed Pendoggett. "You know, Poppy, sometimes we can't help the patients, but we can help their families. You did that today."

"That doesn't feel nearly as good, though, does it?"

"Mm, no. It doesn't." He pulled in his chin and slowed the car as they started down the hill into Portwenn.

"Could you drop me at Jeremy's?" she asked.

Martin turned on to Castle Rock and pulled into the carpark. "I don't see his car. He might not be home from his course yet."

"Yeah, I know. I just don't wanna have to talk to my mum and dad about this right now. I've got a key; I'll just wait for him to get home."

"Right."

He stopped in front of the neat, two-storey cottages, and the childminder pushed the door open.

"Poppy, I'm sorry that I asked you to come with me today, Martin said. "If I'd had any idea it would—"

"It's okay." She gave him a shy smile. "I know now why Jeremy can't quit talkin' about you sometimes."

The Lexus pulled away and Poppy let herself into her boyfriend's home. Turning into his bedroom, she crawled into the bed, pulling the covers up over her head before allowing her emotions to pour out in unrestrained sobs.

She woke a half hour later to the jingle of keys in the door. "Jeremy?" she called out softly.

He appeared in the doorway. "Poppy? What are you doing here?" he asked, going quickly to her side. "Are you sick?" His fingers pressed against her forehead.

"No. Something awful happened while you were in Truro. I just ... I needed you."

Jeremy looked down at her, perplexed, as she buried her head in his chest and began to shudder. "Poppy, what is it?"

"I went with Dr. Ellingham ... to see a sick little boy and—"

Another shudder went through her and Jeremy's arms tightened around her. "Poppy—what—happened?" he said softly.

"The little boy died, Jeremy. It was awful! I've never seen anyone die before. And he was just a little boy. His mum—watching her with him was so hard! And I couldn't let it show that I was upset.

"He was just a little, little boy, Jeremy. Five years old! He fell through the ice yesterday, and his mum thought he was fine. Then this morning, he started actin' sick. The mum thought it was his asthma, but it wasn't. Dr. Ellingham tried, but he just got worse and worse. It happened so fast!"

Jeremy kissed her head. "Oh, Poppy; I'm so sorry you had to see something like that. These things happen in medicine, though. More often than you'd think."

She tipped her head back to look at him and he brushed the tears from her cheeks. "What can I do to help?"

"Just hold me ... kiss me."

Jeremy pressed his lips to hers. "It'll be all right. Things will look much brighter in the morning, and the memories you have of this will fade."

She gave him a nod as she willed herself to believe him.

"What can I do? Do you want me to make you some hot chocolate?"

"Maybe ... just kiss me again?"

"I think I can manage that," he said, giving her a small smile. He pulled her closer and kissed her again, his lips lingering longer this time.

The more welcome emotion of the love she felt for the young man alleviated the overwhelming sadness she'd been feeling, and Poppy deepened the kiss. "Jeremy, make love to me," she whispered. "Please."

He hesitated before pulling away and cupping her face in his hands. "Poppy, I love you too much to do that. To allow our first time to be associated with such bad memories. We will, but now's not the time."

He got to his feet and held out his hand. "Come on. I'll get you a glass of wine and we'll cuddle on the sofa for a while. Then I can take you out for dinner, okay?"

"Yeah. Okay."

They had just arrived at one of Jeremy's favourite haunts in Wadebridge when Poppy's mobile rang. "Huh, it's Louisa," she said.

"She's probably checking up on you. I'll go get the drinks ... be right back." Jeremy gave her a wink before heading towards the bar.

When he returned to their table a short time later, Poppy turned a worried face to him. "Louisa wanted to know if I knew where Dr. Ellingham was. He didn't come home after dropping me off at your flat."

Chapter 12

Louisa huffed out a breath and swiped at the fringe on her forehead before jabbing at her mobile screen, dialling Ruth's number.

"Ruth, hi. Is Martin there by any chance? He's not answering his phone, and I'd just like to make sure everything's okay."

Ruth tossed her newspaper on to the sofa and glanced at her watch. "Why on earth is he traipsing about the village at this hour? He should be at home—with that leg of his iced and elevated."

"He's not *traipsing* about. He went to see a patient shortly after lunch. Poppy went with him because Morwenna had taken the day off. Martin didn't think he should drive—with his leg. It was a five-year-old, and things ended badly, Ruth. The little boy died.

"Poppy was rattled so he didn't think she should drive the car back to the village. He dropped her off at Jeremy's an hour and a half ago."

"And he hasn't come home?"

"No. I can't reach him on his mobile, either. I don't know if he had another patient to see or where he's at, Ruth. I was hoping you might know."

"No, I don't." There was a pause in the conversation before the elderly woman spoke again. "I have an idea. Give me fifteen minutes, and I'll get back to you. Try not to worry," she said before the call was ended.

Ruth slipped on her coat, grabbed her car keys, and headed out into the night. As she travelled the winding Cornish lanes, her thoughts turned to her own professional experiences. As a forensic psychiatrist, she had lost very few patients over the course of her career, but those few had all been to suicide.

There was one case in particular that had haunted her—a teenager who was a gifted musician with a potentially bright future. But the young man also struggled with schizophrenia. When she heard of his death, she felt sure that if she had taken a different tack with his treatment, the outcome would have been different.

She startled as she turned into the lane leading to the B&B. A fox was flushed from behind a gorse bush, and it darted through her headlight beams.

Breathing a sigh of relief at the sight of her nephew's Lexus parked on the side of the drive, she pulled up behind his car and dialled Louisa.

Louisa hurried over and snatched her phone from the kitchen table. "Ruth! Did you find him?"

"Yes. He's at the farm."

She dropped into a chair as the breath she'd been holding rushed from her chest. "Thank goodness! I want to talk with him, Ruth."

"Why don't you give me some time with him, Louisa. I'll make sure he gets home safely, and you can talk with him there."

"I just want to—"

"Give us some time, dear."

Louisa glowered at the mobile when her husband's aunt abruptly ended the conversation. "Bugger!" she muttered.

Evan looked up from his exercise book. "Are you cross at Dr. Ellig-am again?" he asked as his fingers picked at the corner of the pages.

She gave him a forced smile. "Of course, not. I just wasn't sure where he was. But Aunt Ruth is with him, so all's just fine, now."

"I can talk if ya want someone to talk to. Just till Dr. Ellig-am gets home." The child's eyes fixed on his book as his pencil tapped against the page of maths problems he'd been working on. "And I could even give you a hug. But ... if you don't want one, you don't gots ta' have one."

Her mind distracted, a rejection of the little boy's offer sat perched on her lips for a moment before she fully grasped his words.

She turned and held her arms open to him. "I think a hug from you right now would be lovely, Evan."

The seven-year-old slipped from his chair and hesitantly wrapped his arms around her neck. "Do you like it okay?"

Louisa tightened her grip as she nuzzled the child's neck. "Very much so; you give lovely hugs."

A smile crept on to his face as his hand patted her back. "You wanna talk about sharks?"

While Evan consoled Louisa, Ruth made her way towards the back door of the farmhouse. As she stepped into the enclosed porch, the haunting strains of Beethoven's Moonlight Sonata could just be heard above the creek of the door as it closed behind her.

She slipped quietly inside and stood by the dining room table until the final notes hung in the air. Then, she cleared her throat, revealing herself.

Martin whirled around on the bench, a hand clasped to his chest. "*Gawd!* Ruth!" He flipped the book on the music rack shut and struggled to his feet as he wagged a finger at the piano. "I was just—Mm."

She gave him a crooked smile. "Yes, I heard. It was lovely."

He pulled up his bottom lip and tipped his head to the side. "What are you doing here?"

"Well, it is my B&B, Martin."

"Ah, yes. Sorry. Sorry. I was passing and I just thought I'd ..." His voice trailed off as his gaze settled on his shoes.

"There's no need to apologise. I'm glad to see that you're making use of the instrument. What do you think? Do you like the sound?"

"Yes. Yes, I do."

"I must give full credit to Carole Parsons for that. I don't know the first thing about what one should look for in a piano."

She pulled her purse from her shoulder and took a seat on the sofa. "Louisa called me. She wanted to know if I knew of your whereabouts. Really, Martin, you should keep her informed so that she doesn't worry."

His brow furrowed before he pulled up his arm, turning his watch into the light. "Oh, *gawd*. I wasn't aware it was so late."

"You lost track of time?"

"Mm. Obviously."

"Good. I'm sure it was therapeutic, then."

He fidgeted before huffing out a breath. "I should be going," he said taking several steps towards the kitchen.

"Come and sit down, Martin. It won't be healthy for you to keep this to yourself."

"I'm fine."

"That *wasn't* a request. Sit down and tell me what happened."

He wandered back, reluctantly, and took a seat in a nearby chair. "If you're referring to what happened this afternoon, it's nothing I haven't seen before."

Ruth's head shook slowly. "Oh, Martin. Don't let things start to pile up on you again. You know that no good comes of it."

"I don't know what you expect me to say, Ruth."

"You could start by telling me what happened exactly."

A rush of air hissed from his nose. "Some mother was too busy to watch her children—probably drinking tea and passing gossip back and forth with a neighbour," he spat. They fell through the ice on the family pond. One of them succumbed to acute respiratory distress after the near drowning. What more do you want to know?"

Ruth stared back at his defiant gaze, undaunted. "That's a nice, tidy summation. And deftly told without getting unwieldy emotions involved, too. I do hope you dealt with the mother in a more sensitive manner."

"Of course, I did."

"What about Poppy?"

He threw her a dark look before rubbing a hand over the back of his neck.

"I never should have taken her with me."

"But you were correct with your assessment of your own ability to be driving. It really would be best if you weren't putting that kind of stress on your leg just yet."

"I could have managed. She needn't have seen it."

"Firstly, you had know idea what was going to transpire. And she's not a child, Martin."

"I'm aware of that. But she's ... sensitive."

"Yes, she is. But a sensitive adult being witness to a person's death is a far cry from a sensitive seven-year-old witnessing the gruesome way your grandfather died. And *she* has people to turn to—Jeremy and her parents."

He shrugged a shoulder. "Yes."

"She'll be fine, Martin. And in all likelihood, this won't be the only time in her life that she experiences death. It's a part of life."

"Don't you think I know that, Ruth?" He got up and walked over to the montage of old black and white photos on the wall, his eyes settling on a picture of Auntie Joan holding a very young Martin on her lap. "I should have warned the woman to watch for the symptoms," he said softly. "It never occurred to me."

"Are you saying you'd examined the child earlier?"

"No ... the brother. I treated a cut on his hand after the incident occurred yesterday. I wasn't aware of the five-year-old's involvement until today."

"I see. You think that if you had cautioned the mother yesterday to watch for symptoms with the older child, she would have been quicker to call you when the younger child began exhibiting them today?"

"I'm sure of it." Martin began a slow pacing from one side of the room to the other. "She wouldn't have put it down to his asthma. This could have been prevented."

"Martin, you were tired and in pain yesterday."

He spun towards her. "I *know* I was, Ruth! That's my point exactly! How many more mistakes am I going to make because I'm tired and in pain—my thinking is clouded by pain medication?

"If I'd been on top of my game I would have thought to mention the possibility of respiratory distress. Or if I'd just sent the woman on to Newquay, maybe they would ..." He pressed his fingers to the bridge of his nose. "I don't know."

Ruth sat quietly for several moments. "Martin, any doctor in Newquay would have almost certainly handled this case just as you did. Unfortunately, you're not just any doctor. You're an exceptionally good doctor with very high standards. Unreasonably high standards at times, in my opinion.

"You simply must not beat yourself up over this. It will be of no benefit to anyone to obsess about the what-ifs. You did the best you could under the given circumstances, and no one could question your competency here."

She gestured towards the piano. "How did it feel to tickle the ivories again?"

"Mm. The action's a bit tight on a few of the keys but nothing that can't be adjusted."

The left side of Ruth's mouth inched up into a restrained smile. "Duly noted. But I was actually inquiring as to whether you enjoyed it—whether the lack of practice and your arm injury have had any effect on your proficiency."

"I don't know that I was ever proficient," he mumbled.

"Martin."

"It was fine."

She narrowed her eyes at him and he tugged at an ear. "*Yes.* It was a bit painful. But I can see that there could be some benefit to it."

"So, you'll continue?"

He hesitated. "Yes."

"Good." Ruth got to her feet and put a hand on his arm. "Come on, I think Louisa is anxious to see you."

"Right."

He followed her back to the village before they went their separate ways at the bottom of Church Hill.

Louisa glanced up from the cup of tea she was making when the latch on the kitchen door rattled. She turned to him, and her hands dropped to her sides. "Oh, Martin; I'm so sorry."

He set his medical bag down on the floor and took a step back. "I need to get a few more things from the car."

"No, you need to go and sit down—put your leg up. I'll get your things." She stepped towards him and stretched up, pressing her lips to his. Her hand lingered on his cheek for a moment before she headed out of the house.

When she returned a minute later, he was standing at the sink with a glass of water in his hand. Setting the oxygen canister and nebuliser machine down, she wrapped her arms around him from behind. "*You* were supposed to go sit down."

"Mm. I was thirsty." He turned in her arms and looked down at her. "I'm sorry I worried you. I lost track of time."

"It's all right. I understand; you needed time to think, hmm?"

His eyes rolled to the side as he took in a breath, hesitating before saying, "I wasn't thinking. I was—er, I noticed Ruth's piano sitting there, and I was assessing the limits of my dexterity."

"I see."

"I started playing and didn't notice the passage of time until Ruth showed up. I'm sure I worried you, and I'm sorry."

"It's all right now. And Evan kept me from worrying too much really. He taught me everything there is to know about the life cycle of sharks."

"Ah."

She went to the freezer and pulled out a number of ice packs. "Did you know that the spiny dogfish can live to be over one hundred years old? That's almost as old as the other Dr. Ellig-am!" she said, her eyes sparkling.

"You did point out to him that the comparison might not be appreciated by Ruth, didn't you?"

"Yes, Martin; I did." She patted his chest and gave him a jerk of her head. "Now, go sit down."

The physically and emotionally demanding day had taken its toll, and Martin took a tentative step towards the lounge before stopping as he waited for the pain the movement caused in his leg to abate.

"You okay?" Louisa asked, eyeing him suspiciously.

He glanced back and gave her a grunt before his stiff movements propelled him forward again.

A soft knock on the kitchen door brought him to a stop. "Jeremy? What is it?" he asked when Louisa pulled the door open. "Is Poppy all right?"

"She's fine. I just thought I'd check in—see how the leg's doing. Do you need any Toradol tonight?"

"No." Martin took several more steps forward, balancing on his crutches as he stared at the step down into the lounge. His head began to spin and he listed to the side before his aide rushed over to steady him.

"When did you last eat something?" Jeremy asked.

The doctor huffed. "Lunch."

"For God's sake, Martin. It's no wonder you're about to fall down, then." The young man settled him on the sofa and returned to the kitchen, taking two of his protein-rich shakes from the refrigerator.

Louisa looked on as the aide thrust one of them at her husband, giving him a scowl before hoisting his leg on to the coffee table.

"Martin, you need to make sure you're—"

"Don't lecture me, Jeremy!" he snapped back. His face was etched with pain as pillows and ice were wedged in around his leg.

The aide gave him a no-nonsense look and aimed a finger at him. "Sit there and be quiet. I'll be right back."

He returned a minute later with a syringe in his hand. "Louisa, could you get a hot facecloth for me, please?"

"Sure," she said before hurrying towards the stairs.

Martin snarled. "I said I don't need the Toradol!"

"And I said to sit there and be quiet. Undo your trousers."

Martin eyed the young man's unyielding face and then pulled at the buckle on his belt.

By the time Martin and Louisa crawled into bed that night, the Toradol had worked its magic. His pain-induced irritability had eased, and Louisa broached what she knew would be a delicate subject.

"Martin."

"Hmm?"

"What happened at the Crandall's today?"

He pulled his hand behind his head as a scowl settled on his face. "You obviously know; you told Ruth."

"I got Poppy's version. I'd really like to hear your version. Please."

He brought his bad hand up and rubbed at his eyes with tremoring fingers. "It's something that can happen after a child aspirates water into their lungs. The water irritates the lining of the lungs and washes away surfactants that allow the lungs to inflate properly. This leads to acute respiratory distress. It's very rare, but it happens."

"That's scary. And there's nothing that can be done?"

"Yes, in hospital. But the Cramden boy was already in severe distress when we arrived. By the time I was able to work out exactly what was going on ... no, there was nothing that could be done."

"Oh, Martin. That's terrible."

He blinked hard and turned his gaze towards the window. "I'm tired. If you don't have any more questions, could we go to sleep now?"

She leaned over and kissed his cheek. "I'm sorry about Robbie Crandall. I have no doubt you did everything in your power to save him, though."

"Mm. Goodnight."

"Goodnight, Martin."

Reaching out, Louisa turned off the light and lay for a few moments before saying, "Muriel Steele's funeral is on Monday morning."

Her husband grunted.

"I really have to go, Martin ... for Danny."

There was a long period of silence before she heard a breath hiss from his nose. "I'll have Morwenna reschedule my appointments."

"Oh, that's not necessary. You hate that kind of thing ... all the people, emotions, and ... you know."

"Mm. Danny."

Louisa didn't need to see his curled lip to hear the sneer in his voice. "I'm just saying, I can pass your condolences on to Danny for you."

Martin's jaw clenched. "No, I'm going with you." With that, he rolled away from her, giving his statement an air of finality.

Chapter 13

Martin stood in the open doorway to the terrace looking out over the village. The high tide had filled the harbour with a choppy sea that blended into the Cornish granite skies made famous by Daphne du Maurier.

A curtain of mizzle was blown into the entryway, and he jumped back, sloshing hot espresso on to his hand. "Bugger," he hissed. He pulled his handkerchief from his pocket and wiped it dry. Then, he gave the dismal scene a last glance before slamming the door shut.

His thoughts returned once again to the looming funeral for Muriel Steele. He dreaded it; it would be ghastly to be sure.

He had no choice but to go though. The deceased woman's son had found his way into the proverbial hen house once already. Louisa had managed to evade his questions about what exactly had gone on that night, but he suspected something had occurred, and he wouldn't make it so easy for the weasel this time around. If Danny Steele made any advances on his wife, du Maurier's depiction of the area as a Gothic symbol of murder and madness could turn out to be quite apt.

He pulled up his chin, adjusted the knot of fabric at his throat, and headed towards the kitchen.

Evan gave a tug on his sleeve, and he set his coffee cup down on the table before leaning forward for what had become a morning ritual. The boy wrapped his arms around his neck and planted a kiss on his cheek.

"Have fun at your party," the seven-year-old said before racing out the door.

Martin's head whipped around, and he stared, wide-eyed, at his wife. "What party?"

Louisa glanced towards the door before lowering her voice. "The funeral and everything, Martin. I didn't think we needed to resurrect the subject of death right before school."

Martin gave a snort. "But a party?"

She huffed out a breath. "Okay, maybe that was a bit of a stretch."

He poked at the bits of cereal on James Henry's high chair tray, and the child latched on to his finger. "Erm, the subject's already been raised by the way—this morning before breakfast," he said. "I thought it best to explain things to Evan before he heard about the Cramden boy at school."

"The *Crandall* boy, Martin."

"Mm. The people around here will, no doubt, be spinning ridiculous tales, blaming that child's death on piskies or knockers."

"Oh, Martin," she said, giving him a roll of her eyes before setting her son's refilled sippy cup on the high chair tray. "You do like to exaggerate."

"I'm not exaggerating! The subject needs to be addressed with all the children at the school before the circumstances are perverted into some sort of-of *fairy tale*."

She sighed. "I've already spoken to Pippa about it. She's going to let the teachers know that there'll be an assembly for the students this afternoon. I'll talk to them about it then and send an email out to the parents."

He rinsed his cup and put it in the dishwasher before turning to her. "Are you sure it's wise to wait until this afternoon? Can't Pippa speak to them about it this morning?"

"I'm headmistress; it's my responsibility."

"Well, then perhaps you should be at the school this morning instead of going to—"

She narrowed her eyes and wagged a finger at him. "No. Don't go there, Martin. Danny's an old friend. I'd feel terrible if I didn't go to support him at a time like this."

"Yes." Glancing up at her, he whisked his breakfast dishes from the table and limped towards the sink.

Louisa bit at her lip and worried the tea towel in her hands. "I'm not entirely sure what to say though."

"I believe one of the customary platitudes would suffice; I'm sorry for your loss, she's gone to a better place, time heals all wounds." He hesitated before saying with a sneer, "Or, God's called her home."

Her ponytail flicked. "Not Danny. I meant the students, Martin."

"Ah, yes. Direct and to the point is usually best. Tell them what I told you. A few of them may be able to grasp the concept. Perhaps those who can will be able to put it into terms the others can understand."

She shot him an ineffectual black look. "That's very helpful, Martin."

"Mm, you're welcome. And while you're at it, a mention of the need to stay clear of iced-over farm ponds wouldn't go amiss."

"Thank you, but I think I can manage without your help."

Giving her a wary glance, he ducked his head. "Yes."

She nudged him aside and rinsed the milk from her cereal bowl. "I need to finish getting ready. Can you handle James all right, what with your ...?" She waved a hand at his leg.

"I'll be fine." He watched her walk off and then wiped his son's face before removing his bib. Slipping an arm around the boy, he set him on the floor.

The latch on the door rattled a short time later, and Poppy stepped into the house. James toddled over, presenting her with his fire engine.

"Good morning, James," the young woman said.

The scent of the perfume Jeremy had been examining on one of their last expeditions to the chemist drifted past Martin as she removed her coat. "Good morning, Dr. Ellingham."

He gave the table a final swipe with the dishcloth. "Mm, yes. How are you doing?"

"I'm fine, thanks. Perfectly healthy." She handed the toy back to the toddler and hoisted him to her hip.

He studied her with doctor's eyes. "I meant about what happened the other day."

"Oh. Well, I didn't sleep much that night, but Jeremy was right, things did look a lot brighter in the morning."

"Ah. Good."

Louisa rounded the corner into the lounge, breathless. "Hello, Poppy." She turned to her husband. "Sorry to keep you waiting, Martin. I couldn't find the scarf I was looking for."

"Again?" he said with raised eyebrows. "I could help you to get organised, if you like."

Her ponytail flicked. "Thank you, but that won't be necessary."

"We should be going," he said glancing at his watch.

"Yes, I know." She laid a sheet of paper on the table and jotted down a few more instructions for the childminder. "I'm not sure how long this will last, Poppy. Don't fix anything for us for lunch. If we get home in time, we can fend for ourselves."

Martin wagged a finger at his wrist. "Louisa!" he said as he headed out the door.

"Yes! I'm coming!" Her hand brushed over her son's head, and she kissed his cheek before racing off to catch up to her husband.

When she came around the house, he stood by the Lexus, fiddling with his watch, a disapproving look wrinkling his brow.

"I know, I know," she said, her heels clicking against the tarmac. "We have plenty of time, you know. What's the rush?"

"I want to be sure we get a rear pew. I'd rather not have half the village gawping at me from behind." He dropped his crutches into the back and settled into the passenger's seat with a soft groan.

Snapping her seat belt into place, Louisa backed out on to Roscarrock Hill. "I hope that's the only reason you're wanting to sit in the back. Because if you're considering sneaking out as soon as the funeral's over, there's the burial and the reception following the service."

"Oh, *gawd.*"

"If you're going to be miserable, Martin, I can go on my own," she said with a huff.

He gave her a sideways look and clamped his lips shut. "I'll manage."

"I'm sure you will," she said, smiling stiffly.

Sally Tishell sat perched on the organist's bench when they entered St. Endellion church ten minutes later. Martin grimaced at the cliched dirge being hammered out on the keyboard. It was reminiscent of the old horror movies he had been forced to endure in the name of weekend entertainment at boarding school.

He guided Louisa into a back pew and forced his stiffened limbs in next to her.

"Does Mrs. Tishell look her normal self to you?" she asked.

Martin glanced over at the woman. "There's a range of normality with Mrs. Tishell. You'll need to be more specific."

"She looks—" She waved her hand dismissively. "Oh, never mind." Glancing towards the entryway, she leaned over and murmured, "You sure you want to sit here?

He threw his head back. "*Yes*. I realise there's more of this nonsense to come. But I'd prefer to not be on display up in front."

"I understand that, but you know you're sitting right in the path of everyone who comes in the door, don't you?"

Martin jumped as a hand slapped his shoulder. "Mornin', Doc," Chippy Miller said. "No patients to see today?"

"No, I've closed the surgery for the morning."

"Oh, sure. You probably gotta do that for all your dead patients, eh? Professional etiquette and all."

He gave the fisherman a scowl. "Don't be ridiculous."

Agnes Cook, a woman Martin knew only as one of the village's chief busybodies, sidled up. "Hello, Louisa. Dr. Ellingham. Good of you ta come, Doc—support your wife and all. A *lot* of history between you and our Danny, isn't there, Louiser?"

Louisa ran a hand over her head as she leaned forward, attempting to avoid her husband's intense gaze. "Well, a lot is a bit of an exaggeration, but Danny and I *were* friends."

"Oh? Is that what they call it nowadays?" The woman's hand settled on Martin's arm. "It takes a big man to step up and support 'is wife at a time like this, regardless of the past. Especially with you bein' all crippled up now." She leaned down. "Don't mean ta pry, but is this as good as you're gonna get, or are—"

Martin brushed her hand away. "For God's sake, woman! That's none of your business!"

Putting her hand on his leg, Louisa gave Agnes a nervous smile. "We do appreciate your concern for Martin's health, but we're here to support Danny Steele today."

The woman flicked her scarf around her neck and moved on.

A steady stream of mourners filed into the old church, each of them stopping to greet the healing doctor and his wife while enquiring about his health.

The traffic into the building finally slowed. "What is it with these people?" Martin whispered stridently. "They have no sense of personal boundaries whatsoever!"

Louisa dug a packet of tissues from her handbag, peering up at him. "Good thing you aren't on display up front, then. Hmm?"

The dirge transitioned into a subdued arrangement of "Amazing Grace", and the congregation rose as the pall-bearers carried the casket into the sanctuary.

A sneer tugged at Martin's lips when Danny Steele, accompanied by several others who he presumed to be family members, filed past. *Tosser.*

He glanced down at his wife's cautionary stare, and his head tipped to the side in an expression of perplexion and naivety. She huffed out a breath as the congregation sat back down.

"What? I didn't say anything," he whispered.

"I know what you were thinking, so just shush!"

He pulled in his chin, and the pew creaked loudly as he shifted his heavy mass.

Louisa's disapproving eyes darted up. "Martin, shh!"

By the time the selected Bible verses had been read, the vicar had preached his homily, and Danny Steele had begun to deliver his tribute to his beloved mother, Martin could no longer fight off the effects of the tiring weekend and the additional pain medication.

His chin dropped to his chest as his body listed, his sudden weight against his wife earning him an elbow to the side.

Rubbing a hand roughly over his face, he drew in a long, oxygenating breath and straightened himself before the drone of his adversary's voice lulled him back to sleep.

He was awakened abruptly by a loud, hollow bang and the collective gasps of parishioners.

"Martin, it's Mrs. Tishell!" Louisa said as she sprang to her feet. "Something's wrong!"

The chemist had fallen backwards off the organ bench and on to the hollow wooden platform that supported it, the sound reverberating through the stone structure like an exploding boiler.

"Get my bag from the car," Martin said. He picked up his crutches and pulled himself to his feet.

Louisa dashed off out the door, and the doctor hurried towards his patient. "Don't touch her!" he yelled as Mike Chubb tried to sit her up. "She may have suffered a further neck injury."

Mike, aided by Chippy Miller, helped him to the floor.

"All right, everyone," Joe Penhale said, stepping forward and waving the crowd back. "Give the doc some room to work."

"Mrs. Tishell, can you hear me?" Martin asked. His hand slapped against her cheek. "Mrs. Tishell, wake up!"

The woman's eyelids fluttered, and she stared up at him, wide-eyed. "Dr. Ellingham?"

He pulled out his ever-present pocket torch and shone it in her face. "You passed out, Mrs. Tishell. Are you in any pain?"

"No. No, I don't think so." Her chest rose and fell heavily when he leaned forward to peer into her eyes.

"I just fell asleep is all."

"You fell *asleep*? On the organ bench?"

She batted her eyes and gave him a sheepish smile. "It was Clive."

"What does your husband have to do with this?"

Louisa pushed through the crowd, setting his bag down next to him. "Should I get her a glass of water?" she asked.

Martin reached for his stethoscope and blood pressure cuff, glancing back at her. "Mm, yes."

Danny Steele's face appeared over the doctor's shoulder. "I'm saying a prayer for you, Mrs. T."

Martin gave him a dark look and batted him away. "What do you mean, it was Clive, Mrs. Tishell?" he asked.

She glanced around at the eyes glued on her before wrapping her hands around the doctor's neck and pulling him down. "It's personal, Doc," she whispered.

"Mm, I see." He wagged a finger at the policeman. "Penhale, get these people out of here."

"But I haven't finished my eulogy," Danny said, looking to Louisa for support.

"You can finish it at the burial, Danny. Mrs. Tishell's health is more important at the moment," she said, setting the glass of water on the organ bench.

Martin gave him a look of restrained satisfaction before refocusing on his patient.

Joe held his arms out, herding the mass towards the exit. "Come on, everybody. Let's move the fes-*ti*vities outside."

The echoed murmurings quieted as air hissed through the blood pressure cuff wrapped around the chemist's arm.

"All right, Mrs. Tishell. Explain what you meant," Martin said. "What does your husband have to do with your collapse?"

"I didn't collapse, Dr. Ellingham! I just ... well, it's just that Clive left this morning to go back to work, you see." She glanced over at Louisa, giving her a smug smile. "He wanted to make the most of our last hours together."

"Erm, right," Martin said, grimacing. She tried to sit up, and he put a hand behind her back.

Her lashes fluttering, Sally peered up at him. "Clive has difficulty controlling himself around me."

"Gawd," he groaned softly, ripping the cuff from his patient's arm and shoving his equipment back into his bag. "Well, you don't appear to be concussed. Be sure to call me immediately if you should notice any symptoms. Otherwise, just go home and—"he tugged at an ear—"erm, go back to bed."

He turned to Louisa. "Mrs. Tishell really shouldn't drive herself; we should take her back to the village. I'm afraid we'll have to give the reception a miss."

"No need, Do-*c*." Joe Penhale's nasal voice echoed through the now-empty church. "Your local constabulary's here. I'll take care of Mrs. T. for you."

Martin gave him a dark look. The man had an unerring knack for offering up his assistance when it was least appreciated.

Louisa broke into a broad smile. "Why, thank you, Joe!" she said. "That's kind of you."

"Just part of the job, Louiser."

Martin grabbed on to a crutch, and Joe took hold of his arm, helping him to his feet, before picking up a long black feather and the hat lying next to it. "Not sure where this goes, I'm afraid, Mrs. T.," he said, trying to thread the feather through the headband before giving up and sticking it into her hair. Handing her the hat, he hoisted her up.

The mourners had moved on from the cemetery by the time Martin and Louisa left the church.

"I guess everyone's at Muriel's," Louisa said, pulling the car door open and giving him a smile. "We'll just head on over there, hmm?"

He dropped his crutches on to the back seat as air hissed from his nose. "Yes."

The lane leading to the Steele residence was lined with cars, vans, and pickups, representative of the diverse nature of those in attendance. Louisa pulled the Lexus up behind the local butcher's refrigeration vehicle and got out.

"Seems like ages since I was last out here," she said as she scanned the area. "It must be at least three years, I bet. Not since I helped Danny ..." She glanced over at her husband's stormy face and shrugged her shoulders. "Not since before the McLynns moved in here."

Martin grunted, working his way across the gravelled drive, stopping next to her.

Louisa sighed. "Muriel was absolutely heartbroken when Mrs. McLynn had her stroke. They'd become such fast friends."

"Fast friends?" he scoffed. "That would suggest some degree of loyalty between them. I'm not sure that loyalty and narcissism are compatible qualities."

"Oh, Martin. Let's just get inside; it's cold out here."

Navigating his way down the rocky drive was a slow and frustrating process. Martin caught himself as a crutch slipped on a stone, throwing him off balance.

"Oh, oh, oh! Be careful, Martin!" Louisa said, latching on to his good arm.

"I'm trying, Louisa!"

"Sorry. It just makes me nervous." She gave him a wary smile.

"Mm."

Guiding them around a pothole, she said, "You know, I'm surprised Muriel never sold this place."

"I'm not. I suspect she was receiving a substantial amount in rent from the McLynns."

"True." She quirked her mouth. "But now with Muriel gone, wouldn't you think Danny will want to get rid of it?"

Martin stopped and screwed up his face. "I haven't the foggiest idea what Danny wants, Louisa. And I really don't care."

"You don't need to use that tone with me, Mar-tin. I'm simply trying to make polite conversation. A concept that you'll never understand, I know." She huffed and gave a jerk of her head. "Let's just get in there before everyone starts to leave."

Martin clamped his lips shut and said no more.

Catering staff bustled about, offering them cider and hot coffee as they came in the door.

"Just water for me," Martin grumbled.

"I'd like some coffee," Louisa said, lifting a cup from the tray.

"A canape?" a woman asked, thrusting a silver platter towards her.

"Thank you! They look delicious, don't they, Martin?" she said turning to her husband.

He opened his mouth to speak, but his retort was cut short by the second sharp jab of her elbow that morning. Rubbing at the now-tender spot on his side, he gave the waitress a scowl. "Just the water."

An unctuous voice rose above the buzz of conversation in the room. "Martin! Louisa! I'm so glad you could make it," Danny Steele said as he zeroed in on them. "Didn't know, what with Mrs. Tishell and all."

"No, no. Martin got that all sorted, and Joe Penhale drove her home," Louisa said, giving him what Martin thought to be an unnecessarily bright smile.

"Oh, praise the Lord. Has she been ill? I mean, people don't usually just pass out like that."

"I can't divulge that kind of information about a patient!" Martin snapped. "Nor is it any of your business!"

Louisa put her hand on her husband's arm. "I'm sure Danny's just concerned."

"Thank you, Louisa. But no, Martin's right, it was inappropriate," Danny said. "I apologise."

The doctor's lip curled slightly as a soft growl rumbled in his throat.

Her eyes darting between the two men, Louisa pulled in a deep breath. "Erm, we were wondering, Danny, what's to become of the house now? We're assuming you'll sell?"

"I hadn't given it a lot of thought, really. Maybe I'll keep it. Come back on holidays. Although, if I received an attractive enough offer, I might be persuaded to sell," he said, giving Martin a simpering smile. "If you're interested, that is."

"No, I'm not." Taking his wife by the elbow, Martin led her away, weaving through the small crowd towards the farthest corner of the room.

"Was that really necessary?" Louisa said, swiping at the fringe on her forehead.

"He was asking me to divulge highly confidential information, Louisa. It was entirely necessary."

"Oh, Mar-tin! Not that! Couldn't you have made some effort to be sociable?"

He looked down at her with an aggrieved expression. "I thought I *was* being sociable."

"Ugh. This was a really bad idea. I think we better just go," she said, her ponytail flicking. "I'll go make our apologies to Danny."

Martin's brow furrowed at her retreating form before he followed after her. "I'm coming with you."

He tried to keep up as she wound her way through the people clustered in conversation. "Out of my way," he grumbled as the crowd grew denser.

He was stopped abruptly by a tug on his sleeve. "Oi, Doc. Got a picture ta show ya." Chippy Miller pulled his wallet from his back pocket. Flipping it open, he thrust it under the doctor's nose. "Look at 'em. Aren't they beautiful?"

"They're walking petri dishes of pestilence," Martin said, wrinkling his nose. "Not to mention the God-knows-what kind of parasites they could be infested with."

The fisherman pulled his head back. "There's no call for that, Doc. Irene gives 'em a bath every night before bed. And they're not even three months old; you can hardly expect 'em to be walking yet!"

Martin gave him a blank stare, and the fisherman glanced down at his wallet, his face reddening as he gave the doctor a sheepish grin. "Whoops, those are my spaniels. Sorry about that."

He flipped the plastic sleeve over and thrust out the new photos proudly. "There they are—my little lad and little lass. Whaddya think?"

"Very nice," Martin said. "I need to, er ... go." He had lost sight of his wife, and he quickly scanned the room for her.

Pushing forward, he approached Bert Large. "Bert. Have you seen Louisa?"

The portly man held his glass of cider up in the air. "Just havin' the one, Doc. So don't be givin' me none of your disapproving looks."

Martin shook his head. "Have you or have you not seen Louisa, Bert?"

"Oh, sure, sure, Doc. She was lookin' for Danny."

"Which way did she go?"

"You know, you probably don't know this, but there was a time when everyone in the village thought they'd end up together for sure."

"Do you or do you not know where she is, Bert?"

"Can't say with any certainty, but I'd keep an eye on her, if I were you."

He put his hand on the doctor's shoulder and leaned in. "I'm not suggesting our Louiser would do anything—shall we say *maritally* improper. But that Danny Steele's another matter altogether. A bit of a *smooth* operator, if you know what I mean. And there's a history."

Martin pulled his head away. "You smell like a still." He looked around, spotting Al Large standing twenty feet away. "Al! Come here!" he shouted over the drone of voices.

"What is it, Doc?" the young man asked as he walked towards them.

Martin snatched the glass of cider from Bert before taking hold of his arm, thrusting his wrist into his son's hand. "Take that, and don't let him have any more to drink," he told Al. "He's already exceeded the recommended guidelines."

"You got things all wrong there, Doc. Like I said—"

"Be quiet, Bert."

Martin moved away from them, ignoring the ex-plumber's continued pleas of innocence. Making his way down a long hall, he peered into the side rooms until his ears picked up the sound of hushed voices.

He stopped just short of an office doorway, listening.

"About the other night, Lou. I was under a lot of stress at the time, what with Mum and everything, so I didn't handle things well. But I've been giving it a lot of thought since then."

Martin cocked his head to hear his wife's soft reply.

"You've been drinking."

"Just a little liquid courage to say what needs to be said. The way things are now ... with you and Martin. It's not right. It's not how it was meant to be."

"This isn't appropriate, Danny."

"Yeah. Well, maybe I'm tired of being appropriate. You told me once that you don't think I know what I want. I *do* know what I want. I want you to be happy."

"Danny, stop this."

"No! We were meant to be together, and this may be our last chance. Things don't *have* to stay the same, Lou. You can't possibly be happy with him."

"You don't know anything about me then, Danny."

His voice dropped. "I know who you used to be. He's taken away your spirit. You're-you're—"

"What ... more responsible ... more committed?"

"Oh, Lou. Think back to the way things were. Things can change. You *can* be happy again. *We* can be happy again. *Together.*"

Louisa's voice rose as her previously understanding tone took on an edge. "You just buried your mother, so I'll pretend you didn't say all that. I just came to tell you that Martin and I are leaving. I wish you all the best in London, but nothing is going to—"

"Lou, don't say it. We've always had something special ... a bond. Martin's never going to make you happy. *Admit it.* Come back to London with me. You can even bring Jack if you like."

"James? Are you referring to *James*, Danny? My son?"

"I misspoke is all, Lou. Of course, it's James. Just give it some thought; that's all I'm asking." He reached out, caressing her arms.

"Don't touch me, Danny. I warned you when you-you-tried to *kiss* me the other night that—"

The image of his wife, locked in Danny Steele's embrace, ignited the same primal response that had commandeered Martin's actions in the past.

He stepped into the room, dropping his crutches to the floor and latching on to the smaller man's collar with his good hand. "You predacious prat! Take your hands off her!"

"Martin, leave it!" Louisa yelled. "You're going to hurt yourself!"

Danny pulled his hands up to his shoulders. "Hey, mate, just calm—down."

"Martin, please," Louisa pleaded.

With one hand still firmly attached to his adversary's collar, his bad hand began to work its way up his tie. Martin squeezed his eyes shut as he struggled to name his emotions. *Anger ... anger and-and ...*

Louisa's eyes widened in disbelief. This was a side to her husband that she had never witnessed.

The air felt hot as it hissed through his nostrils, and Martin focused on his physical responses to the situation. *Pounding heart, throbbing head, a hiss in the ears, tears stinging the eyes.*

Breathe in through your nose, out through your mouth. Okay, now relax the muscles in your hands, he told himself. He felt his wife's soft touch on his shoulder.

"It's fine now, Martin. You need to let go," she said.

His arms slowly dropped to his sides and his vision began to clear as the blinding rage eased.

Danny backed up quickly and adjusted his tie. "You have a problem, Martin. You need to get some help—seriously."

Martin swallowed hard as his jaw clenched. "Stay away from my wife," he said hoarsely.

Inching his way towards the doorway, and the safety of the visiting mourners, Danny shook his head. "Lou, surely you must be able to see it now—after *that* display."

"I've seen it all along, Danny." Louisa said, clasping on to her husband's arm. "All those times we were together, I wanted to be with Martin. I have absolutely no interest in you. I—*love*—Martin."

She bent down and picked up the crutches from the floor, handing them to her husband before whirling and wagging a finger. "And if anyone has a problem, Danny, it's you!"

She moved over, seeking the reassurance of her husband's touch. "You need to talk to someone when you get back to London. And if you really do care about me, you'll sell this house and never come back here. Have I made myself clear?"

Danny's eyes darted between the woman he'd spent the better part of a lifetime pining for and the much larger man in the room. "Yes."

"Good." Turning, Louisa gave her husband a tense smile. "Let's go home, hmm?"

Martin stared blindly ahead of him, unresponsive to her voice.

She took his hand and squeezed it. "Martin, did you hear me? I said I want to go home."

Licking his lips, he blinked his eyes hard before looking down and nodding. "Yes."

Louisa gave Danny a final glance before they brushed past him.

Chapter 14

Martin tapped at the screen on the car's console and adjusted the vents, directing a flow of fresh air to the passenger seat. He sat with his eyes closed, drawing in deep breaths.

Rubbing a hand over his face, he looked over at his wife. "Why didn't you tell me about what happened with—" he gave a jerk of his head towards the Steele house— "what's-his-name?"

"Martin." Louisa sighed and shifted the car into gear. "I didn't want to add to your stress. You had your surgery on Friday, and then on Saturday there was the awful incident with the Crandall boy."

"And yesterday when I asked you?"

She turned on to the tarmac road and glanced over at him. "I s'pose maybe I should've told you then."

"Well, of course you should have told me then!" he snapped.

"I'm sorry." She tucked a wisp of hair behind her ear, giving him a furtive glance. "I guess I was just hoping to get this funeral over with and that it would all go away."

"Well, that plan backfired, didn't it?"

"I said, I'm sorry."

The car slowed suddenly as they approached the rear of a farm tractor towing a rack of hay bales. A gust of wind buffeted the car, and a blizzard of fine chaff blew from the bales, pelting the windscreen.

"For heaven's sake, Louisa! Don't follow so close!" Martin barked. "We'll either plough into the back end of that wagon, or we'll end up off on the verge."

Her lips drew into a thin line as her ponytail flicked. "Don't tell me how to drive, Martin. I've been navigating these roads longer than you have."

"Mm." He looked furtively her way. "You don't have a lot of recent experience, though. Aside from the trips between the village and the hospital. You could use some practice."

"Martin, be quiet."

The farmer turned off the tarmac and Louisa relaxed back into her seat. Her freshly-manicured nails began to tap against the steering wheel. "I would think you could understand ... me not telling you about what happened the other night. What with all your study sessions with *Edith* during my pregnancy."

Martin's head whipped around. "What does Edith have to do with this?"

"Well, you can't honestly expect me to believe that a woman like Edith Montgomery never made advances."

He pressed a palm to his eyes and hissed out a breath. "You and I weren't married at the time, Louisa, so what Edith did isn't comparable to what Danny did."

"Oh? So, she *did* make advances, then?"

Her narrowed eyes fixed on him, and he wagged a finger at the windscreen. "You should keep your eyes on the road."

She gave him a petulant flick of her ponytail, and her frustration came out in a groan. "Look, I had no way of knowing that Danny would do what he did today."

"But you weren't keen to have me come with you."

"No, I really wasn't."

"I see."

"Oh, Martin. Don't say I *see* like that."

He pulled his head back. "Like what?"

"Like I was-was-I don't know."

"Hoping for time alone with him?"

"Aha!" She wagged a finger. "I knew that's what you were thinking!"

"And I was correct!" He gave a sharp nod of his head and then sat in a sulk until they reached the surgery. Louisa turned into the parking space next to the house and shifted the gearbox into park.

"All right, maybe it was a mistake to keep this from you," she said.

"Mm, not maybe—it was. He kissed you, Louisa."

"I'm quite aware of that," she said, wiping unconsciously at her mouth. "But as I said before, I didn't want to add to the stress you've been under." Her ponytail flicked again. "And I apologised already for not telling you."

"But you didn't want me there today, either."

She huffed. "Okay, I'll admit to hoping for some time alone with Danny. But only to set him straight on how I feel about him."

"Surely you knew that I wasn't going to let you go to that funeral alone. To be vulnerable to that-that *Tartuffian narcissist*. What did you expect me to do?"

"I expected you to trust me." She swiped at her fringe. "Although, maybe you wouldn't have come charging in at half-cock if I'd discussed it with you ahead of time."

He turned his head away quickly before his door handle clicked. Then, pulling himself from the car, he retrieved his crutches from the back seat and headed around the house.

Neither James nor Poppy were around when he came through the kitchen door. The ceiling creaked overhead, and he quickly surmised that the childminder was putting the boy down for his nap.

Louisa entered the house and stood watching him shrug his coat from his shoulders. She bit at her cheek as he avoided her gaze. "Can we talk about this tonight? I need to get to the school," she said.

"That's fine."

Her hand brushed his as he dropped his coat over a peg behind the door, and she lifted her satchel from the peg next to it. "I'll see you later, then?"

"Mm." He wedged his crutches under his arms and limped off towards the stairs.

Dinner that evening was a quiet affair. Only James seemed to be enjoying Martin's meticulously prepared baked mackerel and steamed vegetables.

Louisa forced a smile to her face as she asked Evan, "So, how was school today? Did you learn anything new?"

He flopped back in his chair and rolled his eyes at her. "Learning's how come I *go* to school, Mrs. Ellig-am."

Martin shot him a disapproving look. "Don't get cheeky. Just answer the question politely."

The boy blew out a breath and poked his fork into a potato, inspecting it before nibbling a bit from the edge. "I learned Gareth's a dunderhead."

Louisa pulled her head back and raised her eyebrows at him. "Evan, name-calling isn't allowed."

"But he was tellin' everybody at the school that Dr. Ellig-am *scared* Michael Crandall's brother to death. I tried to 'splain to him what really happened but he was too dumb to understand. So, he *is* a dunderhead!"

Martin looked up from his plate. "Well, there you are, then," he mumbled before taking another bite of his fish.

"No! Not, there you are, then, Martin." She gave her husband a huff and turned back to the boy. "Evan, people are going to say things that are untrue. You know that what Gareth said is untrue, and Gareth knows it. And after our assembly this afternoon, every student at the school knows it. The best thing to do would be to ignore him. This will all quiet down with time."

Her admonishing stare drove the little boy's gaze back to his plate. "Yes, miss."

Louisa got up and hoisted her son from his high chair. "I'm going to take this one up for his bath. Can I trust you to not encourage any more disparaging remarks while I'm gone?"

Air hissed from Martin's nose, and he gave her a resentful look. "Of course, you can."

"Hmm. See you two upstairs, then."

His wife had just laid James Henry down for the night when Martin entered the nursery, and a freshly-washed Evan jumped on to his bed.

"Goodnight, Evan," Louisa said, placing a kiss on the child's forehead. She turned to her husband. "See you downstairs?"

"Yes." Martin lowered himself to the mattress and the seven-year-old scrambled out of his way.

"Dr. Ellig-am, when are you gonna find the supstitution for my problem?"

"I'm sorry, what problem?"

"You know, my vegetable problem."

"You mean a solution."

"Yeah, that."

"First of all, su*b*stitution, with a *B*, means replacing one thing with another. A solution is the same thing as an answer—solving a problem. And to answer your question, yes, I've come up with a few ideas that might prove useful.

"That vet over in Wadebridge called last week. We can take that dog of yours over for obedience cla—"

A small hand was slapped over Martin's mouth before Evan jumped from the bed and peered out the door.

Assuring himself that the coast was clear of listening ears, he darted back to the bed. "Okay, you can tell me now."

Martin cleared his throat. "Yes. As I was saying, we can take it over to Wadebridge on Wednesday to start its training. I thought we could do a bit of shopping afterwards. See if we can come up with something you can stomach for dinner."

"Just you and me, right? 'Cause it gots ta be a surprise for Mrs. Ellig-am, remember?"

"Mm, I remember."

"Kay." The boy gave his guardian a broad grin and shoved his feet under the covers.

"Goodnight, Evan."

"Goodnight, Dr. Ellig-am."

Martin switched off the light and headed towards the door.

"Dr. Ellig-am."

A hiss of air streamed from Martin's nose. "What is it?"

"Is it dishonest to not tell the truth?"

"Of course, it is."

"But Gareth *is* a dunderhead. So, I can't say he's *not* a dunderhead or I'm being dishonest. What am I supposed ta say, then?"

"You keep it to yourself."

"You mean I don't say *nothin'*?"

"You don't say *anything*."

"That means the same thing, Dr. Ellig-am."

"Yes, I realise that. But anything is proper English, nothin' is not."

"Oh." The boy crossed his arms over his chest and huffed out a breath. "But if I don't say *anything*, then he'll just keep thinkin' he's clever when he's not."

Martin hesitated. "Yes. It's difficult at times, I know. But it's been my experience that life has a way of making the point in the end."

The child stared at him as he worked through what his guardian had said. "Oh, you mean Gareth probably felt like a right plonker when he found out how come Michael's brother *really* died?"

"Mm, yes. Goodnight, Evan."

"Goodnight, Dr. Ellig-am."

Louisa looked up from her magazine when she heard her husband's footsteps on the stairs. "Have a seat," she said, patting the sofa beside her.

"I'll just make a cup of tea first."

"Martin, just come and have a seat ... please."

A soft sigh whispered from his chest, and he dropped down next to her.

"Are you still on the morphine?" she asked.

"Mm, just paracetamol and naproxen."

"Really? And that's enough?"

"I have patients tomorrow. I want to be able to think clearly."

"Ed did tell you to take your pain meds, though."

"Which I did. I'm fine now, however, and I would prefer to have my wits about me tomorrow."

She laid her magazine down on the coffee table and pulled in a deep breath. "Okay, let's talk about Danny."

"Gawd," Martin mumbled through a curled lip.

Reaching behind her to the end table, she picked up a glass of Grenache and a tumbler full of her husband's single malt.

"Louisa, do you think you can ply me with whiskey, and I'll forget about what went on between you and him?"

"Don't be silly, Martin. I have other plans for the whiskey."

He tugged at an ear as a flush of pink warmed it. "I see. But I told Evan I don't drink."

"Evan's sound asleep in bed."

"Yes, but I don't like being dishonest." He held the glass up in front of him, raising an eyebrow. "And that's a lot of whiskey."

"You don't have to drink it all," she said. "And as far as Evan is concerned, you're not really drinking for the sake of drinking." She peered up at him warily. "It's sort of medicinal."

"*Medicinal?* If your other plans involve what I think they do, then I'd hardly call it medicinal."

"Mar-tin, shush. It's no worse than all the pain medication you've had to use."

His eyes flitted back and forth for a moment. "No, I suppose that's correct. Although the pain medication is a controlled substance and is taken according to a calculated dosage rate."

"Oh, Martin, just drink it and try to relax a bit."

He pulled in his chin. "Mm, yes," he mumbled before bringing the glass to his lips.

Louisa gave him a satisfied smile, and her ponytail bounced with a nod of her head. "Now, first of all, we do need to get the Danny matter sorted."

She nestled up against him. "Martin, what will allow you to let my past relationship with Danny go?"

"I don't think I'm the one having difficulty letting your *relationship* with him go. He hasn't given up."

"Well, I must say, I was quite surprised by his behaviour today."

"I don't know why, after the other night. He thinks you're unhappy with me. And until it's been made perfectly clear to him to the contrary, he'll continue to think so. *And* to be a risk to our marriage."

"I can assure you, Martin, Danny Steele will never be a risk to our marriage." Louisa quirked her head. "And I thought I *was* clear with him. I don't know how I could have been much clearer, do you?"

Martin stiffened, and she pulled back to look at him. "What? You didn't think I was direct enough?"

He shifted and rubbed at his forehead. "I may not have caught the entire conversation."

"You were standing right next to me when I said it, Martin. How could you have missed it, for goodness' sake?"

"I was distracted," he said, taking another swig from his glass. "I don't remember much of what happened after I—I grabbed him by the collar."

She nodded slowly before her hand settled on his. "You're saying that you weren't aware of your actions?"

"No. I was fully aware of my actions. I was just ..." Air hissed from his nose and he drew in another swig from his glass. "I was trying to get my actions under control."

"I see."

"I'm sorry about that. He was threatening you, and I reacted without thinking."

"Well, he wasn't really threatening me, Martin. I just didn't like him touching me, after what he tried the other night."

Martin's brow pulled down as his eyes rolled to the side. Then, squirming away from her he got to his feet and limped unsteadily towards the kitchen.

"I was very clear with him, Martin. I told him that it's you I love and that if he cared about me, he'd sell his mother's house and never come back to Portwenn."

Swallowing down the last of the whiskey, Martin filled his glass with water, falling back heavily against the counter as he breathed out a sigh.

Louisa got up from the sofa and joined him in the kitchen, slipping her hands around his waist. "I also told him that all those times I was with him here in the village, I really wanted to be with you."

She stretched up to kiss him. "I really don't think he'll be coming around again. And if he does, it might be me throttling him the next time," she said, giving him an impish smile.

Groaning, Martin turned his head away. "It's not a joking matter to me, Loui-Louissa," he said, his speech beginning to slur.

She took a step back and peered up at him. "Oh, Martin, you never would have really hurt Danny, if that's what you're thinking. I didn't worry about that for a moment. I was just worried that you were going to hurt yourself. That Danny might do something stupid and you'd end up hurt."

Tugging at his ear, Martin dipped his head and looked at her sheepishly. "I'm sorry I didn't handle things better."

"It's okay. History gave you good reason to be distrustful of Danny." She shrugged. "And your instincts were spot on, hmm?"

He screwed up his face, muttering, "Smarmy arse. Always hanging on you the way he did." Glass clinked sharply against the countertop as he set his tumbler down, swaying slightly. "With hiss sancto-mini-minious attitude and those ridiculous trousers he wore."

Louisa eyed him worriedly. "I think we better get you up to bed before you end up on the kitchen floor ... and I miss my opportunity."

They lay in bed a while later, Martin studying her face as she rested her eyes. "I don't need whiskey to want to"—he cleared his throat—"you know, with you."

Her eyelids opened slowly, and she turned to him. "On a good day, no. But this hasn't been an especially good day, has it?"

He reached out, his finger tracing languidly around her ear. "Mm, no. But the day got better."

She rolled towards him, pressing her forehead to his. "Very much better. Goodnight, Martin. I love you."

"Yes. I love you, too."

Chapter 15

It's been said that in Cornwall, one can experience all four seasons over the course of a day. Though the change in their weather wasn't quite so dramatic as that, Portwenn woke Tuesday to bright sunshine, gentle breezes, and the spring-like smell of warming earth in the air.

When Martin picked Evan up at the school for his appointment with Abby Peterson, the boy skipped towards the car, the sleeve of his jacket clutched in his hand as the rest of it dragged along the tarmac behind him.

"Hi, Dr. Ellig-am!" he said, throwing his backpack across the rear seat and scrambling in before fastening his seat belt into place.

"Evan, your coat's going to be filthy if you keep dragging it around like that."

Lifting it up, the boy examined it closely. "How *should* I drag it around, then?"

"You don't drag it around at all! You either wear it, or you put it in your backpack."

"Oh. When we get done at Dr. Peterson's, can we go see Old Doc?"

"Yes, that would be fine."

"Good! I like surprisin' him."

Martin rubbed at his gritty-feeling eyes. The seven-year-old had woken them several times the previous two nights, with nightmares similar to those that plagued him immediately following his father's death. These disruptions, in addition to his own less-than-pleasant dreams and the continuous pain in his left leg, had kept Martin up most of the night.

Louisa seemed not to have noticed his increasing weariness as of yet. He hoped that Dr. Peterson might be able to determine the cause of the child's nightmares and nip the problem in the bud before his weariness developed into a full-on fatigue, obvious to his wife.

Dr. Peterson was behind the reception desk when Martin and Evan entered her office. The boy jumped up to see over the counter.

"Where's Mrs. Teague?" he asked.

"She's out with the flu, I'm afraid," the therapist said.

"Mm," Martin grunted. "I'm glad she had the sense to keep it at home. Not bring it to work with her, thereby infecting every child who walks through the door."

"I'm afraid this is likely where she picked it up. We've had a steady stream of children in here with persistent coughs this week. It's a wonder I'm still standing, actually," Abby said with a chuckle that Martin made immediately clear he did not appreciate.

"Influenza outbreaks are no laughing matter," he said. He waved a finger about. "Have all of these toys been properly disinfected since the last sick child was here?"

"Well, we do our best, of course, but—"

"Right then; let's get started. I'd like to limit the boy's exposure as much as possible." Putting his hand on his young charge's head, Martin guided him towards the hall.

A slightly flustered and taken aback Dr. Peterson hurried after them. She hesitated at the doorway. "You can wait in the reception area, Doctor."

Martin held up a finger. "Could I have a word with you first?"

"Certainly."

Leaning around her, he called into the therapy room to the boy. "Keep your hands clear of your face until we can wash off any possible pathogens, Evan."

Abby shook her head. "Dr. Ellingham, what is it?" she asked, her impatience with the doctor's interference growing.

"Yes. I need to mention that Evan's been having difficulty with nightmares recently. It could correlate with the death of one of the children from the Portwenn area—a five-year-old who suffered complications after a near drowning on a frozen pond this last weekend."

"Oh, how awful. Was the boy someone you knew?"

"A patient. Evan didn't know him."

"I'm so sorry, Dr. Ellingham."

He pulled in his chin and averted his eyes from her sympathetic gaze. "Mm. I just wanted to bring it to your attention."

"It's good that you did. Has he talked with you about the dreams?"

"Just that there's a black man who's chasing him. He seems to think that this man is going to take him away from us."

"I see. I'm assuming you and your wife have discussed the five-year-old's death with him?"

"Yes. He's aware of the medical facts of the case. And my wife held an assembly at the school to explain it all to the children. In intellectually undemanding terms, I would imagine."

"I'll try to introduce the subject into our play today. See if I can tease out what might be bothering him. Thank you, Dr. Ellingham."

"Yes." Martin tugged at an ear, limping back towards the reception room.

Evan was crouched down, examining the miniature figurines lining the wall, when Dr. Peterson entered the room.

"Why don't you come and sit at the table, Evan. We're going to do some drawing today," she said as she gathered together several sheets of paper and the box of crayons.

The boy galloped across the room and dropped into one of the diminutive chairs. "What do ya wanna draw?"

"I'm curious as to what your room is like at home. Do you think you could draw me a picture?"

"You mean at my new house or my old house?"

"Let's start with your new house." The psychologist slid a piece of paper in front of the child and took a seat next to him.

He dropped his head to the side as his eyes rolled towards her. "James and me gots a lot of stuff in our room. It could take a while."

"Well, how 'bout if we start with the things that are most important to you. Then, if there's time, you can add more detail."

She pulled a sheet of paper in front of her and picked up a cornflower blue crayon before sketching in walls and two windows.

Evan leaned over and watched her. "Huh, we gots that colour on our walls, too. 'Cept it's in the flowers."

"Oh, you have wallpaper in your room?"

Staring at her absently for a moment, the boy held his hand out. "Here, I'll show you. But you gotta let me use that crayon."

Abby gave the boy a smile and held it out to him. She watched as he covered the walls in his room with blue dots.

He handed the crayon back to her, and then dug around in the box for a new colour before adding the gold dots representing the other flowers on the wallpaper.

"Oh, it's dotted wallpaper?"

"Those are s'posed ta be flowers. But they take too long so I just made spots. And these are James's cot and my bed," he said as he scrawled them in. "James is still a baby, so he gets ta have these side things to protect him." Evan drew the vertical lines representing the rails on the cot.

"Yes. I'm sure Dr. and Mrs. Ellingham want him to be safe when he's asleep." Abby returned to her picture and drew in a window.

His fingers picking at the paper wrapper on a navy blue crayon, Evan eyed her drawing. "How come we can't have those side things unless we're babies?"

"The rails ... like are on James's cot, you mean?"

"Yeah. 'Cause then we wouldn't have ta worry about the scary stuff. James never worries about the scary stuff. He just sleeps."

"Well, when we get older, we don't need the rails to keep us from falling out of the bed and getting hurt."

"But what about the scary stuff? Dr. Ellig-am gets the scary stuff, so you can even be all grown up and still get it."

"Do you mean like bad dreams?"

"Mm." A thin strip of blue paper spiralled from the seven-year-old's crayon before dropping to the floor. "James never gets it. He just sleeps," he said, shrugging his shoulders.

"Well, James is just a bit too young to be experiencing bad dreams."

"Is that 'cause his brain isn't developed enough yet?"

Abby pulled her head back and raised her eyebrows at him. "That's exactly right, Evan. You're a clever boy!"

"That's how come Dr. Ellig-am says James doesn't do lots of stuff. But I think he doesn't get the scary stuff 'cause he gots the sides on his bed."

"I'm sure he feels very safe in his bed." The therapist watched as the child drew a small human form inside the sides of the cot and held his picture up in front of him. "Very well done, Evan. That's a lovely looking room."

"Yeah, I know. But I'm not done yet." He drew in a bookshelf, quickly adding another next to it. "These are all my books here on the top. And these are James's books."

"My, that's a lot of books! You must enjoy reading."

"Yeah. These ones on the bottom are for little kids, but when Dr. Ellig-am reads 'em to James, I listen anyway."

"That's nice. We don't have to stop enjoying things just because we grow up, do we?"

"I like sittin' on Dr. Ellig-am's lap, even if I am almost growed up."

Dr. Peterson rested her elbow on the table and dropped her chin into her hand. "You know, I still have one of my very first books. And it's still one of my favourites. It's called *The Velveteen Rabbit*."

The seven-year-old jumped from his chair. "Hey! Dr. Ellig-am gots that one in his drawer by his bed!"

"Really? It's a wonderful story. It's the book my son chooses most often when we read at bedtime."

Evan started to giggle. “I asked Dr. Ellig-am to read it to me once, and he made a funny face and stuck it back in the drawer.

“Mrs. Ellig-am told him,” he gave his head a flick and said in an artificially high voice, “ohh, Martin, don’t be silly. I never told ya you were praphetic and full of pits.” The crayons rattled together as he began another search through the box. “Dr. Ellig-am’s silly a lot.”

Abby’s brows furrowed as she puzzled over the boy’s words. “Do you think she may have said pathetic, not praphetic?”

“Something like that. But I don’t know how come she said he’s full of pits.” He shook the crayon at her. “He does like cherries a lot. Maybe that’s how come.”

A smile tugged at the therapist’s lips when she deduced the more likely explanation—that the word pitiful had been used in the exchange between the Ellinghams.

They worked in silence for a while until Abby glanced over to see the child laying down the black outline of a human figure.

“Oh, that’s interesting,” she said, her fingernail clicking against the paper. “Can you tell me about that person?”

Evan pulled the sheet of paper away and quickly covered the figure with his hand. He looked up at her warily. “It’s just the black man. But I changed my mind about him,” he said before covering the figure in black scribbles.

“Does the black man have a name?” she asked, returning her gaze to her own drawing.

“Jim.”

“Can you tell me about Jim?”

The boy picked at a fingernail. “He’s just the black man.” The seven-year-old crumpled up his picture, and then walked to the bin and tossed it in. “I don’t wanna do this anymore.”

Glancing at her watch, Abby got to her feet. “Well, it’s a good time to finish up. I really enjoyed colouring with you today, Evan, and thank you for showing me what your room looks like. It's a very fine room."

"You're welcome. Your room looks pretty good, too, even if you don't gots any toys."

She put her hand on the boy's head and guided him out the door. "You won't have Mrs. Teague's company today, but you may still have some milk and a biscuit if you like. Are you hungry?"

"Yeah!" Evan raced on ahead to the little kitchenette behind the reception area.

"I'll be right with you," Abby said as she passed Martin.

She returned a minute later and took a seat next to him.

"Well, I didn't find out a lot, I'm afraid. We did some colouring today ... of our bedrooms. Evan did draw what looked to be a black silhouette—or a shadow."

"Do you think that's what the nightmares have been about?"

"I suspect so. He just called it the black man. But I'm afraid that, aside from the fact that the black man's name is Jim, he didn't say any more."

A breath hissed from Martin's nose. "His father's name was Jim. I guess we haven't made as much progress with him as we'd hoped."

"Not necessarily, Doctor. If the black man is his father, his referring to him as Jim rather than Dad could show that he's feeling a more diminished relationship with his father. This may allow his relationship with you to develop into one more typical of a healthy father and son relationship."

"And in the meantime, how do we deal with the nightmares?"

"Continue to reassure him that his father is gone. The death of the child from the village is a good opportunity to reinforce the idea that death is irreversible. That his father will never be alive again."

Abby leaned forward, resting her elbows on her knees. "The bed he's been sleeping in ... was it purchased for Evan, or is it a bed that you had before he arrived?"

"No, it's not new. It was in the room before the boy came to live with us. It needs replacing."

"Well, I'm just wondering if a shopping trip might be in order. Evan seems to feel that James gets some protection from the rails on his cot. If you already had future plans to purchase a new bed, perhaps now's the time to do it. Evan could choose a bed where he feels he has the sort of security that James has."

Martin pulled in his chin. "Mm, I see. I'll discuss it with Louisa."

"Good."

The psychologist got to her feet and smoothed out her skirt. "If you do decide to proceed with the new bed, I'd recommend you encourage Evan to choose a bed that he'll be *comfortable* sleeping in. Try to avoid suggesting that he might feel safer in one bed than another. He could interpret that to mean that there's something he needs to be protected from."

The seven-year-old came running in from the back room and bounced up and down in front of his guardian.

"Dr. Ellig-am, can we go surprise Old Doc Parsons now?"

Martin pulled up his arm, glancing at his watch. "Mm, yes. But what do you say to Dr. Peterson?"

The boy turned to her, scratching at an eyebrow. "See you later?"

"How 'bout thank you?" Martin said, giving him a stern look.

"Oh, yeah. Thanks!" he said before bolting for the door.

"Evan, wait!" Wincing, Martin struggled to keep up, finally losing sight of the boy when he turned into the wing housing the administrative offices. When he reached the door, emblazoned with the words Chief Executive Officer, he glowered through the glass at the child, and Evan squirmed on the sofa in the outer office.

Martin pushed the door open, glancing at the receptionist before giving his young charge a jerk of his head. Evan stepped out into the large hallway, keeping his head lowered.

"What have I told you about running off like that, Evan?" Martin said through clenched teeth.

"Sorry, Dr. Ellig-am. I forgot again."

"That's *not* an acceptable excuse. I called to you, and you ignored me. It's not safe for you, and it forces me to take risks that I shouldn't take right now."

The boy's gaze shifted up slowly. "How come you gots ta take risks?"

"Because I don't want to lose track of you, Evan!" Martin hissed out a breath when he noticed the curious passers-by gawping at them, and he leaned down, lowering his voice. "When I go faster than I should, I risk tripping—falling."

"That could hurt you."

"*Yes*. I'm well aware of that."

The seven-year-old looked down, kicking a trainer against the floor. "I don't want you ta fall, Dr. Ellig-am. I'll go slow the next time. I promise."

Martin cleared his throat and straightened himself. "Good. And just as importantly, you need to listen when I call to you."

"I only kind'a heard you. I didn't hear your words. But I'll stop next time I hear ya, just in case you got something important to tell me."

"Well, I'm glad we got that sorted. Let's go see Old Doc Parsons."

Chris laid his biro down when his friend stepped through the door, hurrying over to assist him with a chair. "Mart, this is a surprise," he said, his bald head wrinkling as he raised his eyebrows at Evan.

"Mm, we had an appointment and thought we'd stop and say hello."

Chris returned to his seat and the boy stepped on to the base of his chair, wrapping his arms around his shoulders.

"How are things, Evan? Are you keeping my friend here out of trouble?" Chris asked.

The child dropped back to the floor and was drawn to the pendulum toy on the desk. "Yeah, 'cause I'm gonna slow down from now on."

Old Doc raised an eyebrow and Martin shook his head. "Just a discussion we had in the hall."

"I see. I, er ... understand you got an invite," Chris said tossing an embossed card across the desk.

Martin picked it up, looking at it for a moment before flicking it back with a grunt. "Mm, that overpitched meet-and-greet for the new editor-in-chief at the Lancet. I'm busy that day."

"That's not what Louisa said. I should warn you, Carole is fully expecting that we'll be attending with the two of you."

"Why?"

"Oh, come on, Martin. She and Louisa have grown quite close since your accident. You should have known they'd be looking for any excuse to get together."

Martin pulled up his bottom lip and blinked back at him. "Fine. Then let's go out for dinner."

"I don't think that's what Carole had in mind. And I believe it's already been discussed with Louisa."

"She hasn't said anything to me about it."

"Sorry, mate, but I think the plans have been made."

"Oh, *gawdd.*"

Evan put his hand out, stopping the rhythmic clicking of the little silver pendulum balls. "Whatcha gotta do, Dr. Ellig-am? Something bad?"

Chris's chair creaked as he leaned back and crossed his ankles. "It's just a party, Evan. And I'm sure Dr. Ellingham just needs a little time to warm up to the idea."

"Are there gonna be girls there?"

"Yes. There'll be girls. Should be fun, eh, Mart?" Chris gave his friend a roguish grin, and Martin blew out a breath through tight lips.

Evan's head shook slowly. "I dunno, Old Doc. Girls usually just mess up parties. They gots ta have all the sparkly stuff and dance around looking stupid. And everything gots ta be pink and purple. And the boys just gotta sit and be quiet."

"Sounds pretty rough. But it's one of those things men have to do."

"You mean 'cause it's gentlemanly, right?"

"Right."

"Yeah, I had ta be gentlemanly at Lydia Bigelow's. But it wasn't so bad. She even smelled better than usual."

Chris's hand slapped down on his desktop. "Well, there you go, Mart. Maybe Louisa will smell better than usual. How can you turn down an evening like that?" He gave his friend a wink before noting his thunderous expression.

"Come on, it won't be that bad, Mart. And you'd be doing me a favour by being there. You'll be a reminder to the man that we may be in the back of beyond, but we have highly skilled surgeons and some cutting-edge research going on down here."

"Need I remind you that I'm no longer a surgeon?"

"Yes, I realise that. But you're still regarded as a giant amongst vascular specialists. And Ed Christianson could get some much-deserved recognition for his surgical skills.

Martin's lips pursed. "I see. You plan to use me as some sort of object lesson, don't you?"

"Of course not," Chris said. "But if this new editor's inspired by your story and he decides to call attention to the work going on down here, all the better."

A breath hissed from Martin's nose. "Come on, Evan. We'd better be getting home."

Martin tried to mentally absorb a bit of the tranquillity as he and Evan entered the village. There were things that needed to be discussed, and he hoped he and his wife would not be at daggers drawn over the upcoming event at the Royal Cornwall.

He and Louisa worked around one another in the kitchen preparing dinner that evening.

"Well, when *were* you going to tell me?" Martin asked, his voice rising to a level that got the attention of his son and young charge.

Louisa glanced over at the little boys assembling puzzles on the floor in the lounge. "Keep your voice down," she said, giving a jerk of her head.

He pulled open a door below the counter and removed a colander, dropping it into the sink.

"Martin, I was going to tell you last week, and then the whole thing with Danny's mum happened. I just thought you might be more receptive to the idea when—"

"What? When he wasn't leering at you over his mother's coffin?"

"Okay, now you're just being horrible. I'm not sure that Danny would have behaved as he did if he hadn't been distraught at the time."

Martin rolled his eyes and tugged on a pair of oven gloves before reaching for a pot on the hob. "The man wasn't distraught, Louisa. It was all theatrics."

A cloud of steam burst from the pot of pasta as he dumped it into the colander, and he pulled his head back. "The only thing missing from his repertoire were the glycerine tears," he grumbled.

"That was uncalled for and unkind, Martin."

She pointed a ladle at him before dropping it into the pot of marinara sauce on the table. "I could understand at first, but this jealousy of yours is quickly getting tiresome."

"It's not jealousy!" he hissed in an undertone. "It's-it's-it's—"

"It's what?" She stared him down, her fist wedged into her hip.

"I'm defending my territory."

"Your territory!" she hissed back. "I'm not some sort of land acquisition, Mar-tin."

"I didn't mean it that way." He huffed out a breath and pulled in his chin. "Maybe we should eat ... discuss this later."

She nodded, her eyebrows rising as she said through taut lips, "Oh, we'll discuss it later, all right." Then, donning a contrived smile, she called to the boys. "Evan and James, time to eat!"

There was no further mention of either the upcoming event at the Royal Cornwall or of the lingering emotions associated with Louisa's former admirer until they crawled into bed that night.

Louisa dropped on to the mattress and sat, vigorously rubbing lotion into her hands and arms before punching at her pillow to fluff it.

"You're still upset," Martin said phlegmatically.

She flopped back and gave the covers a jerk, pulling them from him. "That's very intuitive of you."

"Mm, yes."

Flipping on to her side, she propped herself up on an elbow. "Martin, I don't know what else I can say or do to get you to forget about Danny Steele. But you need to let it go, or we're going to continue to have these rows because of him. Is that what you want? To let him come between us?"

"I'm not the one who brought it up."

"I made a reference to his mother's death, that's all."

"You used his name, though."

"Fine. I'll do my best to not use it again." Her tight features softened and she cupped his cheek in her palm. "There's no need to be jealous of Da—of him."

"As I said before, I'm not jealous."

"Yes. You're just defending your turf."

His eyelids drifted shut for a moment. “I really didn’t mean it that way.” Looking over at her, he swallowed hard. “You’re so very beautiful, and I’m not ...”

A breath hissed softly from his chest, and he shook his head. “I’m sorry. In future, I’ll try not to get angry about what’s-his-name. But I would *really* appreciate it if you wouldn’t mention him again.”

She leaned forward and kissed his chest. “I’ll do my best.”

Her eyes fixed on his, and she gave him a wary smile. “Now, about the party Friday night. I realise that I should have brought it up with you before. But Carole called last week, all excited about it. I got caught up in the moment, I suppose, and I said we’d go. And then everything happened with Da—with his mother and—”

“Yes, yes, yes, yes, yes. We don’t need to cover that ground again.”

“Right. So anyway, after all that Chris and Carole have done for us over the last five months, I figured you’d be happy for the opportunity to reciprocate. It would help Chris out, and Carole’s so excited about it.”

“Louisa, I’d be happy to take them out for dinner every week for the rest of my life if I didn’t have to humiliate myself in front of those people at RCH.”

“Humiliate yourself? Martin, the accident wasn’t your fault. And I think you should be proud of the way you’ve fought back from all of this.”

He lay staring at the ceiling for some time before turning to her. “I’ll be surrounded by surgeons, Louisa.”

She watched him for a moment. “Oh. And you don’t know if you’ll ever be able to be a surgeon again.”

“Mm.”

“I think I understand now.” She sighed. “Well, you have to be over there for your appointment with Dr. Newell anyway. And, unfortunately, I’ve committed us to being there. How ‘bout if we go, stay the first half hour or so, and then slip away? Go do that dinner out with the Parsons? I think Carole will understand our abbreviated stay at the hospital thing."

Turning slowly yielding eyes to her, he gave her a nod. "All right."

"Thank you, Martin," she said, pressing her lips to his, allowing her kiss to linger before pulling back again.

He cleared his throat. "Are you still upset?"

"No, Martin. I'm not."

"Then could I have some of the covers back, please. I'm getting cold."

Chapter 16

Martin quickly signed off on the last patient's notes and looked up when Morwenna stuck her head in the door late Wednesday morning.

"What is it?" he asked, shoving the notes back into the sleeve and holding them out to her.

"It's, er—it's Florence Dingley, Doc."

He screwed up his face. "God. All right, send her in."

"Yeah. It's just that I thought you might appreciate a bit of warning. You might not recognise her otherwise."

"Why? What's happened now?"

She batted her round eyes at him. "Nothing's happened. She's just not ... herself."

"Consider me warned. Now send her in, Morwenna."

"Right."

She hurried away before the door opened again, and a cloud of pungent perfume filled the room.

Martin wrinkled his nose and looked up. "What on earth?" he said, sitting transfixed.

Mrs. Dingley's trademark foetid attire had been replaced by a clean, albeit dated and slightly oversized, navy blue and white ensemble. And the disgusting old hat that had once perched on her head was gone, revealing her full head of not only curly but now coiffed hair which had been dyed a rich sable brown.

And Morwenna was correct that, without her heads-up and Mrs. Dingley's distinctive whiny, brittle voice, he would not have recognised the woman behind the heavily applied makeup.

"Don't look at me like that, Doctor!" she snapped. "A person can do a bit of smartenin' up, can't they?"

Martin cleared his throat and grabbed for the woman's patient notes. "Of course, Mrs. Dingley. I'm just surprised is all." He gestured towards his exam couch. "Take a seat."

The old woman took off her cardigan and folded it, laying it on the exam stool before climbing on to the table.

Giving her a furtive glance, Martin turned his back to her and removed his watch, dropping it into his trousers pocket as he prepared to test the woman's cognitive ability. Then, making a display of pulling up his arm and tugging back his sleeve, he said, "I seem to have forgotten my watch today. Do you happen to know what time it is?"

"Of course, I do. My appointment was for half eleven, so it's just past half eleven."

He pulled in his chin. "Mm, yes."

Reaching for his stethoscope, he slipped it into his ears and worked the diaphragm under her blouse. "Breathe in."

She wagged a finger. "You realise your surgery is full of clocks, don't you?"

"Shush, Mrs. Dingley. I need to listen to your lungs. Breathe in—and out—and again."

He moved the instrument up and to the left and studied the woman's heart sounds.

"What do you do with all these clocks if you don't use 'em to keep track of time?" she asked.

"I repair them." Martin coiled the stethoscope around his hand and deposited it on to his supply cart before snatching his ophthalmoscope from his desk.

"Do you know when the Second World War started?" he asked as he peered into her left eye.

She pushed his hand away. "Why all the questions? Maybe I should just go over to Wadebridge next time. I hear he's not much on talking—not that you'd ever talk the hind legs off a donkey, either. But *he* serves tea and biscuits while you wait."

"The Wadebridge surgery is closed until further notice."

"Figures."

"Have you done away with the rest of your cats?"

"There's not a single cat left in my house."

"Good." He leaned in to examine the right eye, then straightened, eyeing her, stony-faced. "What about outside the house? Do you still have that chicken coop full of vermin in the back?"

She pulled her chin up and stared at him. "I don't have *any* cats left on my property, Doctor."

Her mouth, coated generously in bright red lipstick, spread into a grotesque simulation of the clown faces that used to terrify him as a child, and Martin recoiled, slapping a hand to his pounding chest. "Jeesh!" he said under his breath.

"Are you all right? You look terrible," the old woman whined.

He tried to shake the image from his head as he collected himself. "Di-did Mr. Portman get a blood sample?"

"Yes. He's not very good at it, you know. Maybe you need to send him back for more training."

"Mr. Portman is perfectly capable."

Martin turned, blowing out a slow breath before dropping into the chair behind his desk. "Everything seems to be in order, Mrs. Dingley," he said, scratching notes into her file. "Make sure you get to all of your appointments in Truro. If transportation's a problem, contact Morwenna and she'll line something up for you with social services."

"I don't need any help from social services. Got my own chauffeur now."

"Really?"

"Yep." Florence pulled her jacket up over her shoulders, gave Martin another unnerving smile, and left the room.

Morwenna leaned back in her chair, crossing her arms over her chest when Martin emerged with Mrs. Dingley's patient notes. "Well, what did ya think?"

He glanced over at her as an involuntary shudder ran through him. "Gawd."

"Think she's gone off her head or somethin'?"

"I haven't the foggiest idea. She appears to be of sound mind, but let me know if you notice any more unusual behaviour." The file drawer slammed shut, and he returned to his consulting room.

The clattering of pots and pans in the kitchen woke Martin a half hour later. He sat himself up abruptly from his desktop, pulling a sticky note from his arm.

Didn't want to wake you, but I figured you'd be okay with me going home. See you in the morning—Morwenna. Oh, and don't forget your afternoon lie-down!

He screwed up his face, crumpled the piece of paper, and threw it in the bin before heading off under the stairs.

"Well, hello!" Louisa said as she turned from the coat rack.

"Hello." He brushed his fingers across his son's head and looked into the lounge. "Where's Evan?"

"He's having lunch at the school ... Lydia Bigelow."

Removing one of his shakes from the refrigerator, Martin pulled up his lower lip. "Mm. They must be dishing out fish fingers again today."

"Yes, as a matter of fact, I think they are." She turned to their childminder. "Can I help you with anything, Poppy?"

"Erm, you can put the salad on the table if you want," she said, gesturing towards a bowl on the counter before picking up a platter of sandwiches.

Martin pulled out a chair and dropped into it before leaning his crutch against the wall and popping the top on his shake. "I'll pick

Evan up from school today. That dog of his has an appointment with the vet."

Louisa took a seat across from him and filled her bowl with salad. "Poor Buddy, I hope they don't have to stick him with a needle every week."

Martin peered up at her. "I don't think that's likely."

"Well, that's good." She held a plate out to him. "Sandwich?"

"Mm, thank you."

"You know, I think this being involved with Buddy's medical care will be good for Evan," she said. "It may give him a better understanding of how a loving and responsible parent should behave."

Martin stopped chewing and furrowed his brow at her. "It's a dog, Louisa."

"I'm aware that Buddy's a dog, Martin. I'm just saying that this will help Evan learn to be a nurturing person."

"I didn't realise it was a learned skill."

"Oh, Martin, you know what I mean."

He gave her a dubious look and pulled in his chin. "Mm. I'm going to take him to the supermarket after we get done at the vet's. I've been doing a bit of research online regarding his aversion to vegetables. There were a few ideas worth trying."

"Oh? You do realise the internet is populated with self-professed experts, don't you?"

"They were NHS endorsed sites, not blogs for new mums."

She tried unsuccessfully to hold back the grin tugging at her mouth as his cheek twitched and his gaze shifted to his plate.

"Really, I think that's a wonderful idea, Martin," she said.

James Henry reached for his father and Martin held out his finger. The boy latched on to it and held tight until the meal was over.

Picking up her satchel, Louisa stepped over and kissed her husband's cheek. "You *will* get a lie-down in today, won't you? You're looking very tired."

"Yes. It's on the schedule." Martin eyed the childminder, now busy at the sink, before returning the kiss.

"Good. Drive carefully this afternoon." She bent down, nuzzling her son's neck before dashing out the door.

Martin climbed the stairs a while later, stopping to look in on his napping son before heading to his own room.

He ran his hand over the boy's head, and he stirred, pulling his knees under him as he turned his head to the other side. His cheek was pink and moist. With the backs of his fingers, the big man brushed away a bit of drool that had collected in the crease impressed into the child's soft skin.

First glancing towards the empty hallway, Martin used a finger to transfer a kiss from his lips to his son's head. Then, he made his way across the landing.

His was awakened an hour after his head hit the pillow by a pair of jackdaws, squabbling over a rotting fish head that had likely been salvaged from the bins outside the fish sellers.

He sat up and wiped a palm over his perspiring face as his gaze darted about the room. A rush of air left his chest as his familiar and friendly surroundings began to fade the upsetting images from his dream.

God! He dropped back to the pillow and pulled an arm up over his face, trying in vain to restrain the tears stinging his eyes. Choking back emotion, he collected himself before forcing his stiffened body from the bed.

He watched out the window as the jackdaws continued their bickering, tchak-ing back and forth while bandying the foetid remains between them. *Disgusting creatures.* Then, he pulled his notebook from his bedside table and recorded the latest variation to his recent nightmares.

Evan was playing with the latch on the school gate when Martin came to collect him shortly after three o'clock.

The boy pulled the rear door open and looked about the car. "Where's Buddy?" he asked.

"Who?"

"*Buddy.* Don't we gots ta bring him along?"

Martin huffed out a breath and waved him in. "We'll have to go back for him."

Evan slapped a hand to his forehead and rolled his eyes before crawling into the back seat.

The unscheduled trip back to the surgery led to an even further delay when Evan decided a snack and a toilet stop was needed before the trip to Wadebridge. When they entered the large metal building attached to the veterinary surgery, Barbara Collingsworth put down her armload of balls and squeaky toys and approached them.

"Dr. Ellingham, still have your shadow following you around I see," she said as she came over, crouching down to greet Buddy before standing up to shake Martin's hand.

He extended his left arm and her gaze was drawn to his injured right arm. "I ran into your aunt Ruth a while back. She mentioned you'd met with some misfortune. I was sorry to hear it."

"Mm. We've brought the dog to be trained."

She crossed her arms over her chest and gave him a knowing smile. "I believe Joanie used the words direct and straight to the point to describe you when you first came to Portwenn. She was bang on there."

Martin cringed at what he found to be an overly-familiar variation of his aunt's name. Although he had heard it used by a few others in the village, such nicknames were deemed common and wholly unacceptable amongst the Ellingham clan.

"How long will this take?" he huffed.

She pulled a dog lead from her pocket and glanced at her watch. "It depends on how long Buddy can concentrate. About an hour, I'd say."

"*An hour?* You do realise the animal has the attention span of a goldfish, don't you?"

"It's all a matter of makin' it interesting. Buddy might surprise you."

"I highly doubt it," Martin scoffed. "We don't have a lot of time. We have something we need to get done yet today, and the boy likely has homework to finish tonight."

"I s'pose we could dispense with the formalities—waive the formal induction and get straight to it."

"Mm, thank you."

Barbara leaned down, resting her hands on her knees. "And what's your name?" she asked the seven-year-old.

Slipping behind his guardian's leg and peering up, Evan kept a firm grip on his trousers. "Can you tell her who I am, Dr. Ellig-am?" he whispered loudly.

Martin put his hand on the child's head, and his grip relaxed.

"This is Evan. He's the animal's owner and will be responsible for the training."

Barbara stared up at him for a moment, poker-faced. "You *will* be required to attend all of the classes with Evan, Dr. Ellingham. And he'll need a lot of help from you to reinforce what Buddy learns here in his lessons. Don't mean to be contrary, but if you can't commit to that, this will all be a waste of my time *and* yours."

Air hissed from Martin's nose. "Yes, I'll help the boy."

"All right, let's get started then." She bent down and clipped the lead on to the little terrier's collar. "The first and most important thing that Buddy needs to learn, Evan, is to come when he's called."

Fastening a belt around the boy's waist, she snapped a small treat-filled pouch on to it before handing the lead to Martin.

"Dr. Ellingham, I want you to stand right here with Buddy. And Evan, I want you to come over here and crouch down," she said, guiding the boy to the middle of the room.

"You're going to say, 'Buddy, come'. And Dr. Ellingham's going to drop the lead as soon as he starts to run to you. You'll reward Buddy for coming by giving him one of those treats. But I also want you to big him up. Act excited, and tell him what a good boy he is—scratch his ears.

"I'll do it once, so you can see what I mean. And then I'll turn it over to you."

Barbara crouched down and called to the dog, clapping her hands enthusiastically before Buddy bolted towards her, pulling the lead from Martin's hand. Putting his front feet on her knees, he took a swipe at her nose with his tongue.

"Ohhh," Martin said with a grimace.

The trainer held out a treat and praised the little dog effusively. "He's a smart dog, Evan. Now you try it."

The game was repeated several times, with the seven-year-old in charge, before adding a bit of fun and challenge to the game.

"Dr. Ellingham, you hang on to Buddy over here, and Evan, I want you to go hide behind one of those boxes on the other side of the room. Then you're going to call Buddy, and he needs to come and find you. When he does, make a big fuss and give him one of those biscuits."

"Okay!" The seven-year-old darted off and crouched down behind a bright-red cardboard cube as Barbara led the trainee back to Martin.

He took the lead from her and gave her a scowl. "I think I've got the picture. We'll just practise this at home."

The petite woman gave him a blank stare. "I know you will. Every day." She turned and called out, "Okay, Evan. Give your command!"

The boy's soft voice cracked as he put all his energy in trying to sound authoritative. "Buddy, come!"

The terrier bolted, stopping in the middle of the floor and pricking up his ears.

"Keep calling, keep calling," the trainer said.

"Buddy, come! Come here, Buddy!"

The little dog trotted over and disappeared behind the red box before giggles were heard. "He found me, Dr. Ellig-am! He found me all by hisself!"

Evan stood up, giving his guardian a proud grin, and the big man's left cheek nudged up.

Martin grew increasingly uncomfortable as the game was repeated, over and over, and he leaned against the wall, trying to relieve his aching legs of some of the weight.

He heard a rustling behind him and turned.

"Here you go, Doctor," Tressa Brown said, opening up a folding chair next to him. Her finger wagged towards the nearby observation window. "I peeked in on you." She hurriedly added, "And your son. You looked uncomfortable."

"Ah." Martin gave her a sideways glance before taking a seat. "Thank you."

"How's Buddy doing with the training?"

"He could prove useful should we ever need him for coursing children."

She gave him an amused smile. "You may be surprised by how useful the simple *come* command can be."

She leaned back against the wall, sliding to the floor next to him and his head whipped to the side. He looked down at her with an expression of surprise tinged with panic.

"How long have you been a GP?" she asked.

"Why?"

She gave him a shrug. "I'm interested."

"Mm. Four and a half years."

Tressa's brow furrowed. "Four and a half years? What were you doing before that?"

"I was a surgeon—erm, a vascular specialist in London."

"Oh?"

"Mm."

They sat quietly for a few minutes, watching as Barbara Collingsworth took Evan through the steps required to teach Buddy to spin in a circle on command.

"Oh, that should prove useful as well," Martin grumbled.

"It actually is. I have my dogs spin on the rug when they first come into the house. It works a treat for getting their feet dry on a soggy day."

The doctor pulled up his bottom lip and quirked his head. "Possibly."

"So, you were a vascular specialist in London. That's impressive."

"Not really. It's what I was trained to do."

She leaned back and rolled her eyes at him. "It's still impressive, Dr. Ellingham."

"Mm."

"And what brought you to Portwenn?"

Martin threw his head back. "Oh, for God's sake! Why all the questions?"

"I'm sorry. As I said, I'm just curious."

Screwing up his face, he let the words patter from his mouth. "The former GP was incompetent and drank himself to death, the village needed a replacement, and I accepted the position. Does that satisfy your curiosity?"

"Sorry. I'm afraid I've overstepped the mark. I didn't mean to."

Martin cleared his throat and, after a slight hesitation, wagged a finger at his charge. "Evan's not my son. The adoption request has been submitted, but we won't get confirmation until next summer sometime."

"I see. Well, that explains his calling you Dr. Ellingham. I thought maybe you just preferred formalities."

"Of course not."

"Right. May I ask how you met Evan?"

"I should, er ... watch what they're doing." He gave a tug on his ear and pulled up his chin before feigning a rapt interest in the training session.

Pulling her knees up to her chest, the vet sat quietly until Martin asked, "When did you open your surgery?"

"Three years ago," she said. "I'd been working in a practice in Kensington for the first ten years after I received my licence."

Martin mentally estimated the woman's age. *Thirty-five? Forty?*

"I grew up there," she continued. "Went to Cambridge. I'd never ventured far from home, and I guess I finally heard the call of the wild. Cornwall took a bit of getting used to—the people down here. But I've grown to appreciate the place."

He startled when she reached up and tapped a finger against the outer fixator on his arm. "I saw Kirschner splints used on dogs and cats during my surgical rotation in school. I've always wondered what it's like for them. What has it been like for you?"

His brow drew down, and she put a hand up as she fumbled for the words to explain herself. "Obviously, a dog or a cat's not going to find it—what I mean is, for you the emotional aspects must be much worse than—or at least different—no, probably worse than—"

She closed her eyes and breathed out a heavy sigh. "Let me try this again. I realise that external fixation doesn't have the psychological impact on a dog or cat that it does on a person." Her eyes flitted up. "But is it painful? I'm sure it was initially, but how about now?"

Martin watched the woman out of the corner of his eye, intrigued by her intelligence but unsettled by her intimate questions. "Obviously, it was at its worst in the first days and weeks. It's still painful, to varying degrees."

"Is it muscular or skeletal pain?"

Turning slowly, he gave her a look of incredulity. "Both," he said through clenched teeth.

"Right." She got to her feet, brushing any possible dust from her pristine surgical scrubs. "I had an HBC come in this afternoon. I should check on him."

"An HBC?"

"Sorry. Hit by car—tractor actually. He's a lovely old bloodhound. The farmer didn't see him on the verge, and he ran out in front of him. The left hind leg was fractured. I could deal with that. It's been reduced and splinted, but I'm holding off on casting. His foot's gone cold, so I suspect a vascular injury. I'll probably need to amputate the leg in the end."

She shrugged. "I feel a bit of a fraud in cases like this."

"Well, it's my understanding that four-legged creatures get by just fine with the loss of a hind leg. What's the problem?" he asked.

"I'm worried about the owner. He feels terrible about hitting the dog, and he was adamant that I do everything I possibly can to save the leg. And from what his wife told me, he's just barely holding it together the way it is—mentally."

"It's a dog. It's a leg," Martin said, his lip curling. "I'm sure they'll all recover."

The vet shot him a black look. "That's a bit harsh. And it's not always that black and white. I didn't get many details, but I think the man's been quite depressed. His wife's worried about him. I'd like to be able to help the dog, but I'm no orthopaedist or vascular specialist. And there's no way the owners could afford the expense of one of the specialists in Truro or Exeter."

"Mm, I see," Martin mumbled. "Besides the cold foot, what other hard signs are there? Active haemorrhaging, absent distal pulse, pulsatile haematoma, paraesthesia?"

"Well, the patient hasn't complained of any tingling or pins and needles sensations," she said, giving him an impish grin.

"Mm," he grunted as a pink flush spread across his cheeks.

Her fingers stroked across her throat. "No, aside from a weak distal pulse, there aren't any other hard signs."

"Well, then it may not be a vascular injury," Martin said, getting to his feet. "It could be compartment syndrome. A fasciotomy would remedy the situation."

"This is a general small animal practice, Dr. Ellingham. I'm not a specialist." Her face brightened. "But you could do it!"

Recoiling, he put a hand up in front of him. "No, no, no, no, no. I'm a doctor, not a vet. Even if I were willing, which I'm not, I'm not licensed to practise."

Tressa bit at her lip. "What if you told me what to do?"

"As I said," Martin enunciated slowly, "I am not a vet."

Giving him a guarded smile, she threw her hands up. "Between the two of us, though? It's worth a shot. I'll have to amputate the leg for sure if we don't try. Please?"

"Oh, *gawwd*," Martin groaned.

As soon as the day's obedience lesson had come to an end, he collected Evan and Buddy, settling them in the reception area before following Dr. Brown back to the little surgical theatre.

By the time they emerged forty-five minutes later, the seven-year-old had fallen asleep on the floor, his furry companion curled up next to him.

Martin stood over them, wrinkling his nose at the thought of what manner of contaminants his charge might be lying in.

"I can't thank you enough for your help, Dr. Ellingham," the vet said, sidling up next to him. "Are you sure you're feeling all right now?"

"I'm fine."

She eyed him carefully. "You still look pretty peaky. You may be coming down with that ghastly influenza that's making the rounds. Best get home and off to bed."

He tugged at his ear and gave the woman an ambiguous grunt.

"You're an excellent tutor," she said. "Too bad you didn't stick it out up in London. Who knows, you might have even worked your way up to chief of surgery one day."

"Mm." He nudged the seven-year-old with his foot, and the boy rolled on to his back, staring up at him. "It's time to go, Evan. Get your coat on."

The child rubbed at his eyes and got to his feet, retrieving his coat from one of the reception room chairs.

"Tell that farmer to come and see me," Martin said to the vet. "His depression should be treatable."

"Thank you, I will."

The trip to the supermarket in Wadebridge took longer than Martin anticipated, but after much dithering by Evan in the produce department, they emerged with enough supplies for the doctor to thoroughly test the possible treatment options for the boy's vegetable-osis.

But their research would have to wait another day. When they came in the kitchen door, the house was already filled with the aroma of poached salmon and baked bread.

"For goodness' sake! What took you so long over in Wadebridge? I was really beginning to worry, Martin," Louisa said as she distributed plates around the table.

"Oh, you didn't need ta worry, Mrs. Ellig-am. Me and Buddy were just sleeping on the floor at Dr. Tressa's."

She cocked her head at her husband. "Wasn't this just a check-up for Buddy? What took so long?"

Evan flopped his coat over a peg and hurried to his guardian's defence. "Oh, we did check up on Buddy. But then Dr. Ellig-am and Dr. Tressa went off in another room, and me and Buddy got tired waiting, so we fell asleep. That's all."

"Martin?" Louisa said.

He screwed up his face and set his grocery bag down on the counter. "She had a patient she needed my help with. I talked her through a fasciotomy. It's a simple procedure, but it took a bit of time. She's not a surgeon. I'm sorry; I should have called."

Louisa raised her eyebrows and pulled in her chin. "What about your"—she glanced at the seven-year-old—"your problem?"

He sighed. "I was able to keep it under control until after the procedure was finished."

"Oh, I see. Well, that was nice of you to help ... I s'pose." She shoved the oven gloves on to her hands. "But yes, you should have called."

"Yes." Martin ducked his head and headed to the lounge to see his son.

"Look, Da-ee! Bok!" the toddler said, holding the red, wooden alphabet block up when his father approached.

"Mm, yes. Hello, James. How are you?" Dropping into the chair next to the fireplace, Martin closed his eyes and blew out a slow breath.

He looked up when the scent of his wife's perfume and the touch of her lips to his forehead stirred him from his doze a few minutes later.

She watched him worriedly. "You're overdoing it, Martin. You look absolutely shattered tonight."

"I'm fine."

"Of course, you are. You're always fine." She dragged the coffee table over in front of him and plopped a couple of pillows on to it before hoisting up his legs. "Let's get your leg icing. You can eat your dinner here."

"That isn't necessary, Louisa. I feel bet—"

"Martin, be quiet." She turned, returning to the kitchen for the ice packs. "Is this too much for you? Buddy's check-ups and all? Because I could run him over there every week if the appointments were a bit later in the afternoon."

Evan scrambled from his seat at the table and gave his guardian a vigorous shake of his head.

"No, no, no, no, no. That's not necessary, Louisa," Martin said. "I can handle this."

She nested the ice in between his leg and the pillows and gave him another scrutinising look. "I'm not sure you can. You really do look awful tonight."

His eyes were drawn to his young charge in the background, standing with his hands clasping his head as his angst was growing by the second.

"I really want to do this," he said. "I—I should—I should probably get to know the dog if it's going to be living with us." He cringed internally when he saw Evan slap a hand to his forehead, suspecting his words may have sounded a bit contrived.

She eyed him dubiously for a moment. "Hmm. I guess we can give it a couple more weeks ... see how you do."

She turned back for the kitchen and Evan jumped down into the lounge, giving his guardian a cheesy grin and a thumbs up.

Chapter 17

Martin looked up from his desk when his receptionist knocked on his door late Friday morning.

"Come!" He eyed the young woman's white cowboy boots and the red bandana hanging around her neck.

"Doc, Malcolm Raynor's here to see you," she said.

"Gawd. What is it this time?"

"I don't know."

"Morwenna, need I remind you that it is your job to get that information and pass it on to me—in *advance* of my seeing the patient?"

"No, you don't need ta remind me. I just can't tell ya on account of his bein' cagey about it and all. He says it's personal."

She held out the patient notes in front of him, and he snatched them from her hand. "All right, send him in."

The door began to close before the young woman stuck her head back in. "Erm, he's actin' kind'a suspicious about it all."

"And?"

"I dunno. I just thought you'd want that information—in *advance*."

"Just send him in, Morwenna," he growled.

"Okay. But could you try ta be a little less grumpy with poor Malcolm? He's kind'a the neurotic sort, you know."

"Morwenna!"

The plastic wagon wheels, dangling under her earlobes, swung back and forth, and she gave him a huff before leaving the room.

Malcolm came in a few moments later, closing the door behind him and taking a seat in the chair by the desk. "Mornin', Doc," he said in his sandpapery voice.

"I'm assuming you're here about your rhinitis? And your ... cats?" Martin said, his nose wrinkling as he scanned the man's notes.

"No problems there, Doc. That stuff you gave me took care of my bunged-up nose."

"What is it, then?"

The permanent furrows, caused by years of imagined impending doom, deepened in the man's craggy face. "It's my reputation, Doc."

Martin crinkled an eye and tipped his head to the side. "I beg your pardon?"

"My reputation for bein' a socially conscious citizen. I wanna do what's right. I wanna get tested for all of it. I don't wanna be responsible for communicating any of them nasty diseases when we—you know."

His chair creaking, the doctor leaned back and screwed up his face. "I have absolutely no idea what you're talking about. Before you *what*?"

Malcolm cast a furtive glance towards the door and lowered his voice. "I didn't think I'd hafta spell it out for you, Doc." He put his arm on the desk and leaned forward. "Partake in a bit of the other. I want all of them tests—HIV, crabs, syphilis, The Clap, chlamid—"

"*Yes*, I think I get the picture," Martin said, grimacing before removing a form from his drawer. "I'll need a history of your past and current—activity. From that I'll make a determination as to which tests are necessary." He slid the sheet of paper and a biro across his desk.

Malcolm scanned the questions on the form and rubbed a hand over his stubbly throat. "This gets awful personal."

"It's strictly confidential."

"I'm a private man, Doc. How 'bout you just do all of 'em. Then we don't have ta worry about bein' confidential."

"I'm not in the habit of running tests willy-nilly, Mr. Raynor. Once I have a general accounting of your sexual habits, I can assess your risk for infection and decide which tests are needed.

"The form and the results of the tests will be assigned a unique identification number separate from your general medical records. Neither your identity nor your test results will be disclosed to anyone other than the two of us. If a test does detect the presence of disease, I can advise you on how to go about notifying your partner ... or partners."

Malcolm gave the doctor a blank stare. "Well, I don't think I got a disease. I just don't wanna be takin' any chances—flirtin' with disaster, if you know what I mean."

Biting back his temptation for sarcasm, Martin cleared his throat. "Your concern for your partner's health is commendable. But I should remind you that it's equally important that she—erm, or he, be tested as well."

"*He?*" Malcolm wagged a finger at him. "I'm not the judgy sort, Doc, so I won't say nothin' about your open-minded principles. But it's like they say, if you keep an open mind, too much can fall into it. I prefer to play it safe—keep mine closed up nice and tight. Course she's a she."

The doctor's jaw clenched. "Then *she* can either make an appointment to see me, or she can go to the clinic in Truro to have the necessary tests run."

"I can't tell 'er that! It'd go down like a lead balloon! I'd be safer takin' my chances with the diseases, Doc."

"I'd strongly advise against that approach," Martin said, working his biro between his fingers. "This is a serious health issue."

"I know it's serious. That's how come I'm here." Malcolm squirmed, his craggy face sagging. "Okay, I'll tell 'er."

"Good." The doctor pulled another form from his desk and began to fill it in.

Malcolm stared forlornly out the window. "I don't got much choice in the matter, do I? Once again, life's dealt me a bum hand. It don't really matter which way I play it," he said, his voice characteristically woebegone. “If one’a them diseases doesn’t get me, the sleep deprivation will. I need my sleep. I *gotta* tell her.”

“Right,” Martin said absently as his biro scratched away.

“And I’ll fill out the form.” Pooching out his lips, Malcolm gave a firm nod. “I trust you, Doc.”

“Good. If you’re in a monogamous heterosexual relationship and you aren’t exhibiting any symptoms, an HIV blood test and a simple urine test to check for chlamydia and gonorrhoea should be sufficient.”

Reaching across the desk, he set a clear plastic vial down in front of his patient. “Leave a urine sample with Morwenna on your way out. And I’ll have Mr. Portman collect a sample of your blood for the HIV test.”

He nudged the first form closer to the man before handing him a second form. “Give this to your partner. She’ll need to take that with her if she chooses to go over to Truro.”

Malcolm took it and then picked up the biro before scratching his answers on to the original sheet of paper.

When Martin emerged from his consulting room a half hour later, Malcolm Raynor had left and Jeremy was passing his blood sample off to Morwenna. She glanced down at the label on the tube.

“HIV? You sure this is Malcolm’s?”

The doctor pulled the file drawer open and tucked the man’s notes into it. “Don’t ask questions, Morwenna. Just get it sent off to the lab.”

“Yeah, right.” She batted her eyes before crossing her legs and wiggling a boot-clad foot in front of him. “Did ya notice anything different about me today, Doc?”

The file drawer rumbled shut, and he furrowed his brow at her. “You look a bit pale,” he said, reaching out to press his hand to her forehead.

"No!" She batted him away. "My new look! You're impossible, you know that?" She reached under her desk and pulled out a hat, setting it on top if her head. "Does that make it any clearer?"

"Mm, I see—Hopalong Cassidy."

"*Seriously?* Did Hopalong Cassidy wear a skirt?"

"Well, I don't know, Morwenna! What do you want me to say?"

"I'm s'posed ta be Annie Oakley! Jeremy got it right away."

"Well, good for Jeremy," Martin said, giving his assistant a half sneer.

"She got the lead in the play, Martin. That's great, eh?"

The doctor huffed out a breath. "I suppose that means you're going to be wanting time off for all this folderol?"

Morwenna got to her feet and folded her hands in front of her. "Seeings how you brought it up, yeah. I'll have rehearsals on Saturday mornings."

"Great."

"Not to worry. Poppy said she could fill in for me."

Tipping his head back, Martin jutted out his jaw and gave a nod of his head. "Fine." He limped back towards his consulting room before stopping. "Erm, congratulations, Morwenna."

She glanced at Jeremy, opened-mouthed, before blinking her eyes at her boss. "Thanks, Doc."

Grunting, he closed his exam room door behind him.

Martin dropped into his chair, rubbing at his throbbing leg before pulling open his drawer and removing the small notebook he'd been using to record his frequent nightmares. He scratched in what details he could recall from the most recent intrusion into his attempts at sleep, hissing out a breath before slipping the book into his shirt pocket and heading off down the hall.

The kitchen was empty when he came through under the stairs. Louisa was working through her lunch break so that she could leave the school early that afternoon to prepare for the hospital event in Truro.

Distant toddler chatter could be heard upstairs as Poppy readied James Henry for his nap. Martin glanced around, scowling at the empty room before pulling the makings for a plain turkey sandwich from the refrigerator and taking a seat at the table.

He laid down a thick layer of breast meat slices on a piece of bread, slapping the lid on his lunch, then stared abstractedly at the prismatic images being cast by the Christmassy crystal snowflakes that still hung in front of the window.

There was a time when he relished his midday solitude before the barrage of whingers descended on the little surgery once again. But today, he found it left him feeling empty.

It had been but a fleeting eighteen months since he was living contentedly here on his own. Auntie Joan had said he was lonely and miserable. He grunted. Even as a child, she presumed to know him better than he knew himself.

His attention was drawn to the sloppy sounds of Buddy, lapping up the bits of turkey that had escaped his master's sandwich unnoticed. Martin's hand slapped down on the table before he struggled to his feet.

"What are you doing in here?" He snapped his fingers as he limped towards the door. "Get out!"

Buddy sat back on his haunches, blinking at him from under the fringe of hair half covering his eyes and whined softly.

The emptiness Martin felt moments before intensified, and a wave of nausea hit him. A melancholia fell over him like a sudden weight, and he went to the sink, splashing cold water on his face. Drawing in deep breaths, the queasiness and the vise-like grip on his chest began to ease. He reached for the tea towel, drying his face. Then, giving the terrier a glance, he headed off up the stairs.

When Louisa returned later that afternoon, Poppy and James were just heading out the door for a walk before collecting Evan after school.

"We'll probably be gone by the time you get home," she told the childminder. "Evan and James have their hearts set on pizza tonight. It's going to be a nice evening so I thought you might enjoy the walk to get some." She lifted up the bowl of fruit on the table and wedged a twenty pound note underneath. "That should cover it. I'm not sure what time we'll be home."

"We'll be fine, Mrs. Ellingham," Poppy said, pulling James's hood over his head.

"Well, be sure to call if you need anything." Louisa crouched down and kissed her son's cheek. "You be a good boy for Poppy. Bye, bye."

"Bye, bye, Mummy," the toddler said, waving a hand as they moved out the door.

Louisa watched them from the lounge until they disappeared down Roscarrock Hill. Then she climbed the stairs.

Taking a seat on the bed next to her napping husband, she watched him for a minute, his brow furrowing as his fingers twitched involuntarily in his sleep.

She leaned over and kissed his forehead. "Martin. It's time to get ready to go," she whispered. He brought an arm up abruptly, and she pulled back as his fingers closed on her sleeve. "Martin, it's almost time to go."

"I don't want to go!" he said, his eyes popping open. He drew in a slow, ragged breath as he glanced about the room. His gaze settled on hers momentarily before flitting away.

Louisa tipped her head down, studying him with a furrowed brow. "I thought we'd come to an understanding about this. And the Parsons are expecting us. We can't very well back out now, can we?"

A large hand covered his face, and he shook his head. "No. No, just give me a minute."

"Okay. I'm going to freshen up a bit—do my hair. Then you can have a turn in the bathroom, hmm?" she said, brushing a hand over his head.

"Mm, yes."

She screwed up one side of her mouth. "You feel all right? You're sweaty."

Taking hold of her wrist, he moved her hand away. "I'm fine; go get ready."

"Right." She eyed him questioningly before heading into the bathroom.

He waited until he heard the latch click behind her before swinging his legs over the side of the bed and getting to his feet.

Though winter had shown them a reprieve recently, and a softness and warmth had returned to the air, the sun still hovered low over the Atlantic horizon.

Martin's lip curled as he watched at the window for a moment. The notorious pack of female delinquents flipped their vacuous heads side to side, giggling their way down the hill.

Looking over the options in his wardrobe, he hissed a breath from his nose. The bathroom door opened, and he turned to his wife. "Just what am I supposed to wear to this hoo-ha?"

She pulled out a drawer on the dresser and dug around in her lingerie. "I don't care, Martin. You always look very smart. Carole said cocktail attire, so maybe one of your darker suits?"

He stood in his tee shirt and boxers, blinking at her. "Perhaps you're forgetting, my choices are rather limited at the moment."

She turned. "Oh. Oh, dear. Well, maybe wear your dark gray trousers and a white shirt?"

"Louisa, why didn't you tell me this was formal? I don't want to be the only one in the room who's not in a suit!"

"Oh, they'll understand, Martin." She eyed him suggestively before slipping her arms around his waist. "I quite like what you have on at the moment."

"You're being dismissive." He squirmed away and the bathroom door slammed shut behind him.

Martin barely said two words on the drive between Portwenn and the hospital campus. Louisa bit at her lip as they entered the carpark.

"Martin, I'm sorry about earlier—being dismissive. I don't know why it didn't occur to me that you might feel a bit underdressed for this."

"*Underdressed?* That's a bit of a trivialisation."

"I really doubt anyone will even notice."

"Right. I'll just blend in with all the other haemophobic ex-surgical department chiefs hobnobbing in their casual wear and external fixators." He gave her a sideways glance and shifted the gearbox into park. "And why did you have to wear *that*?"

She pulled back her shoulders as her eyes snapped. "What's wrong with what I'm wearing?"

"Nothing's *wrong*. But every licensed debauchee from Devon and Cornwall will be ogling you!"

A wisp of a smile flitted across her lips. "I see."

"Well, there's nothing to be done for it now. We'll just have to make the best of it. Get out of there as fast as we can," he said as his door handle clicked.

"Sounds absolutely lovely, Martin." She sighed, following him into Dr. Newell's office.

Louisa took a seat in one of the chairs in the reception area, sneaking furtive glances at her husband over the top of the latest issue of a women's magazine in which she had no real interest.

He paced around the room, stopping to look through the handouts in the display rack on the wall by the reception desk. He flipped through several, returning each one to its respective slot.

The door opened down the hall, and a young woman came through the room, giving Louisa a smile before exiting the building.

"Martin ... Louisa, hello," the psychiatrist said when he followed shortly after.

"You okay, Dr. Newell?" Louisa said.

"Yes. Lovely weather for a change, isn't it?"

"It is. Did you stay healthy through our cold spell?"

"Mm. I seem to have managed to evade the virus making the rounds, despite the best efforts of several of my patients."

Martin slipped another pamphlet back in the rack and turned to the man. "What sort of virus?"

"Influenza. But that's a purely symptomatic diagnosis." He waved a hand. "Come on back, Martin."

Martin felt at his shirt pocket, reassuring himself that he hadn't forgotten his notebook, then trailed the psychiatrist down the hall.

The door clicked shut behind them, and Dr. Newell settled into his chair. "Your gait's a bit more tentative today. Everything okay?" he asked.

Hesitating, Martin shook his head. "I'm fine." He couldn't contain a soft groan as he dropped into the chair in front of the desk, and he quickly waved off the therapist's disturbed expression. "I'm just having some muscle stiffness, which is to be expected."

"Yes, I would imagine it is." The man flipped open the file on his desktop. "How are you doing with your sleep? Still having the nightmares?"

"Mm. I've been recording them as you asked." He pulled the notebook from his pocket and passed it across the desk.

The psychiatrist scanned through his patient's notes, nodding his head occasionally. "Has this written accounting of your dreams proved useful to you in any way?"

"I think I remember more details, but is that useful?"

"I guess we'll find out." Dr. Newell's eyes panned down a few more pages. "Have you noticed any recurrent themes to your nightmares?"

Martin stared at the man, deadpan. "I would think that would be obvious."

"I'd like to hear your interpretation."

"Gawd. Are we playing at dream theory?"

Rolling away from his desk, the man leaned back, setting off a shrill protest from his chair and Martin winced.

"I'm not a Freudian, so no, we're not. I do, however, think that there's some validity to Freud's conclusions. Chiefly, the idea of thought suppression and how it can manifest itself in dreams. I see looking at these nightmares that have been plaguing you only as a tool."

Air hissed from Martin's nose as his eyes drifted shut momentarily. "As I noted for you on the last page, they, for the most part, seem to end with the accident—or the suggestion of it."

"Yes. That's the only notation I see here. Any other similarities that you can see with these dreams?" he asked, sliding the book towards his patient.

Martin huffed and snatched it up, thumbing through it quickly. "They're unpleasant."

"Can you be more specific?" the psychiatrist asked as he scratched at an ear.

His patient gave him a scowl before flipping, again, through the pages. Slapping it back down on the desk, Martin wagged a finger at the notebook. "Unpleasant incidents lead up to further unpleasant incidents. I don't understand what I'm supposed to be getting out of this nonsense."

Dr. Newell rolled forward and picked the little rubber ball up from the bowl on his desk. "Let's talk about that night," he said as he worked it in his hand. "What preceded the accident? Tell me about that day."

"There's not much to tell really." Martin tipped his head down, furrowing his brow. "Much of it's murky. I would imagine I'd had a full schedule of patients, but I would have closed early to make my appointment with you."

He got up and limped to the window. "I stopped to see Louisa at the school before I left the village. There was some sort of event that night, and I wanted to wish her well, I believe. We'd had a discussion the night before about a list I have of some of my—my less desirable qualities. Things I need to change."

"The crap list?"

Martin glanced back at him, tipping his head to the side before giving him a grunt. "She'd like for me to be more ... demonstrative. So, I'd stopped to wish her luck on her event."

His fingers worked around his crutch handle as he turned back towards the scene outside the window. "I told her—I told her how I feel about her, and then I left. I had my appointment with you, which you likely recollect more clearly than I do. Then I walked over for the meeting with the committee at the hospital. That's it."

"I would imagine Louisa was very pleased that you stopped at the school."

"Mm."

"Did she tell you as much?"

"Not in so many words. But it was made clear."

"So, you left the village on a high note? I can only imagine you were looking forward to getting home to her that night?"

Martin hesitated, tugging at his ear as the memory of her promised proper kiss and his plans for the rest of the evening replayed in his head. “Yes, I would say that I was looking forward to getting home.”

“Home to your family? To their love and affection? To *her* love and affection?”

“Mm.”

“And then life intervened and very nearly took you away from that love and affection.”

The psychiatrist took note of his patient’s suddenly rigid posture. “Martin, why do you think the accident happened?

Turning, he limped back to his chair. “Because some sleep-deprived idiot got behind the wheel of a lorry and crossed into my lane.”

“Yes. It’s regrettable that you didn’t leave the hospital thirty seconds earlier. Or been delayed by thirty seconds. That lorry never would have collided with you.”

Martin’s head snapped up. “Are you suggesting my timing was bad?”

“Certainly not.”

“Good. Because it *wasn’t* my fault.”

Dr. Newell reached out with his biro and nudged the notebook towards his patient. “I’d like you to look through your notes. Focus on what leads up to the inevitable catastrophic endings to your dreams. Tell me what you see.”

Screwing up the side of his mouth, Martin reluctantly picked the book back up, scanning the pages yet again. “As I said before, unpleasant incidents.”

“Yes. More specifically”—the therapist’s finger searched out the notes as he leaned forward, peering at his patient’s file—“a failure to follow your father’s rules, a failure to act decisively as your grandfather died in front of you, a failure to get a little boy out of a dangerous situation without people being hurt in the process, and a failure to control your tongue. In other words, you fall short of someone's expectations in some way."

Martin gave the man a black look and, grimacing, forced himself to his feet, turning his back to him again. "I'm aware of my shortcomings! There's nothing suppressed! They don't need ferreting out! And they most certainly don't need to be explained through some unproven and—and borderline nonsensical pseudoscience!"

Relaxing back in his chair, Dr. Newell tapped his steepled fingers together in front of him. "No, your perceived shortcomings are quite apparent in your notes. As are the punishments that immediately follow those shortcomings. Be it through a jolly good belting or the withholding of love and affection. Or ... through the horrendous physical injuries caused by an accident."

His fist worked at his side, and Martin spat out through clenched teeth, "You think that accident was some sort of—of *retribution*?" He turned slowly and stared the man down, his chin trembling. "That was *not—my—fault*!"

Tears welled in his eyes, and his teeth drew blood as he bit down on his lip in an effort to stay in control. "It's not *always* my fault." A hand settled on his arm, and he turned his head.

"Martin?" Dr. Newell's muffled voice grew louder. "Let's go sit down—get the weight off those legs."

Martin nodded and shook himself free of the man. Then, he limped back to his chair and dropped heavily into it. He gave his therapist a quizzical look before averting his eyes. "Erm, did you ask me a question?"

"We were just discussing." The psychiatrist pulled a chair up next to him. "Martin, the accident was in no way your fault."

"Mm." He pressed his hand to his forehead as a throbbing behind his eyes set in.

"And to be clear, I was not suggesting that you were in the wrong in any way whatsoever."

"What were you suggesting?"

"That knowing and accepting that you did nothing to precipitate the accident does not necessarily mean you don't, on some level, feel deserving of the pain you've endured as a result of it. Or even, had you not survived it, that you would have been deserving of being taken away from a family who loves you."

Martin looked at him askance and shook his head. "No. I've *never* felt deserving of all this."

"Maybe not consciously, no. But take that notebook home and look it over, keeping in mind what we've just discussed." Dr. Newell got up and returned to the chair behind his desk. "Now, I wanted to talk a bit about your most recent dream."

"Gawd. I don't think that's necessary," Martin muttered.

"Well, humour me. This one seems to have been different from the others you've recorded, and it relates to a subject that I find quite interesting."

The psychiatrist reached behind him and pulled a magazine from a shelf. He thumbed through it before marking a page and passing it across his desk. "There's an article in here you might like to read. I'm done with that, so take it home with you and have a look at it later." He gave him a roguish look. "Just maybe not after dark."

Flipping it open, his patient rolled his eyes. "You do realise I've outgrown the clown phobia, don't you?"

"Yes, Martin." The man stretched out his feet and pulled his hands behind his head. "It's really beyond me why adults persist in *entertaining* children with clowns. The majority of kids find them to be disturbing at best."

"I certainly did."

The man reached for Martin's notebook and flipped to the last entry, scanning it over. "The dream you had earlier this afternoon, where you say your mother was made up like a clown ... I think it's worthy of discussion before we wrap things up today.

"It's not surprising that most people find clowns to be unsettling. We've evolved to rely on facial expressions when judging another person's feelings or intentions. The painted-on, artificial smile or frown on a clown's face inhibits our ability to do that. It puts us at a disadvantage and, quite naturally, can make us feel vulnerable. Especially children, who are already vulnerable to potentially malevolent adults."

His brow furrowing, Martin stared off distractedly.

Dr. Newell let his patient sit with the information for a few moments before saying, "You say in your notes that you were being sent away to boarding school—that you were pleading with your mother to not make you go. When you looked up at her, a clown was smiling at you. Do you have any thoughts as to how the two elements in your dream—being sent off to boarding school and the clown—might relate?"

Martin blinked back at him. "I'm not sure. I told her that I didn't want to go and she smiled at me." His thumb dug away at his palm. "I didn't trust her smile. I watched her eyes instead."

"Her eyes?"

"Mm. Her smile meant nothing. I learned to watch her eyes. They almost always looked cold."

"So, as with clowns, it was hard for you to read your mother's facial expressions?"

The creases deepened in Martin's forehead.

The psychiatrist jotted notes into his patient's file before getting to his feet. "I'd like you to give some thought this week to how the hollow smiles you received from your mother may have affected your ability to read facial expressions, both as a child and as an adult. We'll talk about it at our next session."

When Martin and Louisa got into the car a short time later, he laid his head back on the headrest and closed his eyes.

She gave him a worried look. "You okay?"

"Mm, just tired," he said before starting the engine.

Chapter 18

The Knowledge Spa, the Royal Cornwall's continuing education and events centre, was located just minutes from Dr. Newell's office.

They walked in silence from the carpark to the main doors, Martin's pace slowing as the pain in his legs intensified. He reached out to open the door for her and Louisa slipped around him, grabbing hold of the handle.

"I've got it, Martin. You go first."

Glancing back over his shoulder, he saw several other couples coming along behind them. "I can get it, Louisa," he hissed.

"It's easier for me. You've got your crutch and you're—"

"Louisa! Please!"

She reluctantly relinquished the door handle to him before hurrying inside.

Carole greeted them when they entered the large conference room overlooking the city. "Well, hello you two! I'm happy to see you here."

Martin grunted his salutation before mumbling to his wife, "I'll go and get you a glass of wine."

Louisa watched him as he limped off, then she turned to her friend. "What do you mean, you're happy to see us here? You knew we were coming."

Carole took another sip from her glass and waved a hand dismissively. "Oh, it's Chris. He was just sure Martin was going to back out of this. I told him he wouldn't. If Martin says he'll do something, he'll do it—come hell or high water."

The conversation shifted briefly to the spell of above-average temperatures before Martin returned, handing Louisa a glass of Chardonnay.

Chris sidled up next to him, nudging him with his elbow. "Glad to see you made it, mate."

Martin pulled his head back. "I told you I was coming."

"Yeah. Yeah, you did." Shoving his hands into his pockets, Chris gave a jerk of his head. "Come on. I'll introduce you to the new editor-in-chief."

"Jolly good," Martin grumbled, his lip curling as he followed after.

Carole watched the two men walk away before turning to Louisa. "Poor Martin, I didn't give any thought to how uncomfortable this would be for him."

"Hmm, yes, I'm a bit worried. I don't think he's feeling his best today. I shouldn't have pushed him into this."

"I was actually referring to the awkwardness of the situation. What are *you* talking about?"

Louisa raised her glass towards their husbands. "Well, look at him, Carole. You can tell he's hurting. Help me keep an eye on him, will you? He's likely to bite my head off if *I* try to get him to sit down." She drank down another sip of wine before turning a furrowed brow to her friend. "And what, specifically, are *you* referring to?"

"The awkwardness? Isn't it obvious? Every pair of eyes in the room is on him, for one reason or another."

Louisa scanned the crowd, divided into clusters of men appearing to be bringing their companions up to speed on what they no doubt were describing as the ex-surgeon's rather tragic history.

"You don't want to humiliate him in front of his peers, do you?" Carole continued. "The last thing Martin wants is pity."

"Of course, I don't want to *humiliate* him. But I can't just ignore it if I think he's overdoing it."

"I'm just saying, be discreet."

The crowd began to close in around them, and Carole and Louisa made a move towards the buffet table before seeking out a quiet corner near the bar.

Across the room, Chris was making introductions. "Martin, this is Rupert Newcombe, the new man at the helm of the Lancet."

He gestured towards his friend. "Mr. Newcombe, this is Martin Ellingham, our GP over in Portwenn."

"Yes! Yes! And not an unfamiliar name at the Lancet. It's a pleasure to meet you, Dr. Ellingham." He held out his hand and Martin reached for it. But the man glanced down and pulled back, patting him on the shoulder instead.

Shifting awkwardly, Martin gave him a grunt. "Congratulations on your appointment."

"Thank you. I'm honoured to be reviewing the works of such esteemed surgeons as yourself. It's a shame about what happened."

"It's been an inconvenience, but I'm recovering. We've been able to open the surgery back up on a limited basis," he said, his fingers working around his crutch handle.

"Good. I was actually referring to the loss of our top vascular surgeon. But yes, your accident must have been a horrible blow."

"Mm." Martin looked across the crowd to his wife who was involved in an animated conversation with Carole. The soft pink in her dress accentuated the wine-induced flush in her face, and her chestnut mane, freed for the evening from its usual constraints, brushed her cheeks. She caught his eye, giving him a smile, and his chest filled with air.

Chris's voice refocused his attention.

"... the research being done here, isn't that right, Mart?"

He gave him a vacant stare. "I'm sorry?"

"Your support for the cutting-edge research being done here at the Royal Cornwall," Chris said, raising his brow as he gave him an exaggerated dip of his head.

"Ah, yes. Yes, definitely cutting edge."

Mr. Newcombe's eyes flitted between the two men.

"And Martin can certainly attest to the skill of our trauma centre and surgical staff, can't you, Martin?"

Making a more concerted effort to focus on the matter at hand, Martin turned away from their wives. "Yes, Ed Christianson and his team are top notch. I owe them my life. Some recognition in your publication would be well-deserved."

A familiar voice drew his attention away yet again, and Martin groaned inwardly.

"Hey there, Chief. Didn't expect you to be here," Adrian Pitts said, sidling up with a pint in his hand.

"And you must be the new liege lord of the Lancet." He held his hand out to the editor. "Adrian Pitts. I'm on the surgical team here at the Royal Cornwall."

"Ah!" Mr. Newcombe shook his hand. "I presume you're one of the surgeons I can thank for Dr. Ellingham's presence with us tonight, then?"

"I'm afraid I wasn't on call when the unfortunate accident occurred."

Chris tipped his head and raised his eyebrows at his friend.

Wedging his free hand into his pocket, Pitts gulped down a swig of his ale. "I, er ... couldn't help overhearing Martin mentioning the possibility of RCH getting some press in your periodical," he said. "I have a couple of ideas I'd like to bounce off you, if you have a few minutes."

Chris gave him a dark look and held up a finger. "Excuse me, Mr. Pitts. But I'm afraid we're in the middle of a conversation at the moment."

The younger man cleared his throat and took a step back. "Sure, sure. Sorry to interrupt. Just wanted to say hello to Martin really." He raised his glass and wiggled his eyebrows. "I see a new face or two here tonight. Better check 'em out—see where it leads, if you know what I mean," he said, moving off across the room.

Martin and Chris gave him a simultaneous sneer before returning their attention to the editor.

"Mr. Pitts is a capable surgeon. He trained under Martin's excellent guidance, in fact," Chris said, putting a hand on his friend's shoulder. "But perhaps he's not the best spokesman for our team, Mr. Newcombe."

The medical dignitary waved a hand. "Don't worry about it. It seems there's one in every hospital. We had our own proverbial surgical department prat both at St. Mary's and up in Liverpool." He took a sip from his glass. "Now, let's talk about that recognition you'd mentioned, Dr. Ellingham."

Martin scanned the room for Carole as Adrian appeared to be zeroing in on Louisa. "Yes, erm ... well I can certainly speak to the Royal Cornwall's exemplary trauma team, but I believe Dr. Parsons is more conversant with the research be— "

Martin was suddenly on alert as the younger surgeon now appeared to be engaging in conversation with his wife. "I have to go," he said abruptly.

His elbow knocked against Rupert Newcombe's arm as he pushed past him, sloshing the man's red wine down the front of his shirt. Limping across the room, he was oblivious to the small-scale disaster being left in his wake as he ploughed through the clusters of people enjoying refreshments and friendly conversation.

Chris grabbed a stack of napkins from a nearby table and handed several to the editor. "Here, let me help you with that," he said, dabbing at the man's front.

Mr. Newcombe put a hand up. "I've got it, Dr. Parsons."

A metal serving tray clattered behind Martin's retreating form, and a member of the catering staff scrambled about, gathering up the smoked-salmon canapes that had been strewn across the floor.

Chris sighed softly as he gave the guest of honour a sheepish smile before stammering out an excuse for his friend's rather sudden and bumbling departure.

"Sorry about that," he said. "He, erm—his balance is still a bit off. And he has a lot of pain. Pro—probably needs to put his feet up. Or—or he may have needed the lavatory. These things come up on him without warning sometimes."

As Martin closed in on his wife and Adrian Pitts, a hand grasped on to his arm.

"Slow down there, Martin!" Ed Christianson said. "You're supposed to be *easing* those bones back into full service."

"Ah, Ed. How are you?" He looked down, nonplussed, and pulled his shirt sleeve from the surgeon's grasp.

"I'm fine. But seriously, you're putting too much strain on that leg of yours. And if you're not careful, Parsons and I'll be hoisting you off the ground again. You're going to fall. What's the rush?"

He watched as Louisa flashed Pitts a warm smile. She nodded and brushed a wisp of hair from her eyes in what Martin found to be an all-too-seductive gesture.

He screwed up his face before turning to look at his surgeon. "I was just—just. Yes, fine, I'll slow down."

"Good. How's the leg feeling? Are you sensing any instability when you put weight on it?"

"No."

Martin's jaw clenched when Adrian threw his head back and a loud chuckle could be heard.

"What about pain?" Mr. Christianson asked.

"Pain?"

"In the leg, Martin."

"Ah. A bit more than there was, but nothing I can't handle."

"Of course not." Ed gave him a lopsided grin and crossed his arms over his chest. "So, you met Rupert Newcombe?"

The surgeon shifted, and Martin leaned to the left slightly to see past him.

"Well? What did you think?" Mr. Christianson said.

"About?"

"The new editor, Martin. Are you all right tonight?" Ed pressed his fingers to his patient's forehead before his hand was batted away.

"I already told you, I'm fine!" Seeing Mr. Pitts's hand settle on Louisa's arm, Martin moved forward, his crutch coming down on the surgeon's toes.

"Martin, for God's sake! Watch where you're going!" Ed pulled up his foot and rubbed ineffectually at it through his shiny black dress shoes.

"Mm. I have to go." Martin hurried off towards the corner of the room.

Louisa's brow furrowed, and she brushed Adrian's hand away before looking up to see her husband approaching. She gave him a relieved smile and took his arm. "Martin, remember me telling you how I was caught short of change in the canteen last week? This is the man who settled my bill for me."

He gave Adrian a curl of his lip. "Oh, is he?"

"This is my husband, Martin," Louisa said, gesturing. "He's the GP over in Portwenn."

Adrian burst out laughing. "You're kidding me, right?" His former tutor glowered, and he clamped his lips together.

Louisa looked quizzically between the two men. "Oh, you thought Martin was still a surgeon?" She pulled her arms up across her chest and moved closer to her husband. "He's a very fine GP. The best the village has ever had, as a matter of fact."

"No, it's not that," the younger man said. "It's just—well, I just didn't know the two of you were together is all."

She eyed him uncertainly before her posture relaxed. "Oh, I see."

Martin gave him the dismissive stare a surgical department head would give a lowly registrar. "Louisa, this is Adrian Pitts. He's the surgeon who performed that take-away boy's splenectomy a few years back."

"Peter Cronk?"

"Mm."

"Oh!" Her affect grew suddenly chilly again. "I didn't recognise him; he looks so much older."

Martin's brow furrowed. "Well, it has been a number of years, Louisa; it's to be expected. There's no stopping the ageing process."

She leaned towards him, hissing, "*I realise that, Martin. It was meant as a jibe.*"

"Why?"

"*Because! He was being intentionally rude to you!*" She leaned in. "*You've gone off the subject.*"

Giving her a grunt, he turned back to the surgeon. "What do you want, Adrian?"

"I just recognised Louisa and came over to say hello."

The doctor's jaw clenched as he watched his former pupil's gaze slither over his wife.

A smirk spread across Adrian's face as he looked around at the more elegantly attired men in the room. "You must have missed the memo, Chief. Dress-down Friday's been cancelled."

Louisa blinked at him in disbelief before her head flicked to the side. "Excuse me?"

"I was joking."

She stepped forward and jabbed a fingernail into his chest. "Don't you *dare* joke about what my husband's been through."

Martin tugged at her arm. "Louisa, don't."

She pulled away. "No, Martin. What kind of person makes light of something like this? Very few men could have survived injuries like yours, let alone with the grace and dignity that you've shown. And *he's* certainly not one of them!"

Glancing around the room at the attention they were attracting, Martin said softly, "Louisa, you're make a scene."

"Sorry, Chief. I didn't mean to start a row. She's the nervy type, is she?"

The GP stared back at him for a moment, his nostrils flaring before he moved in front of his wife. "You're on thin ice, Adrian. You'd better start spending more time honing your barely-passable surgical skills and less time chasing skirts down the hospital corridors. If it was up to me, you'd have been out on your ear by now."

Pitts swallowed hard and gave a nervous laugh. "Good thing for me it's not up to you then, eh, Chief?"

Martin took hold of the impertinent surgeon's sleeve, pulling him aside. "Don't get flip with me."

Stepping closer, he murmured forbiddingly, "If I ever find you *touching* my wife, *speaking* to my wife, or even *looking* at my wife again, I'll personally see to it that no medical facility within a thousand miles allows you to mop piss and shit off the floors, let alone set foot inside a surgical theatre."

He gave Pitts a penetrating stare. "Have I made myself clear?"

Adrian nodded silently and Martin took a step back.

"Everything okay over here?"

Martin turned at the sound of Chris Parsons' voice. Chris, Carole and Ed eyed Adrian, who stood tugging at his collar.

"Yeah, fine," Martin said before heading out of the room.

His hands began to tremble as he made his way towards the lavatory. The room was empty when he pushed through the door, and he hurriedly splashed cold water on his face, drawing in deep breaths. Pulling a towel from the dispenser, he dried his face and stared back at himself in the mirror for a moment before heading for the door.

Louisa and the Parsons were waiting for him when he returned to the hall.

"You ready to go get some real food?" Chris asked.

"Erm, yes. Yes, I am." He gave his wife a small smile and she returned it before taking his arm.

Martin had kept a nervous eye on Louisa as they ate their dinner. He couldn't make head nor tail of her behaviour. She was distracted, poking at her salad, but not really eating any of it.

And she further perplexed him with her coy smiles accompanied by what felt like ominous silence as they left the restaurant. He cast frequent glances her way as they walked across the carpark, but shadows and the glaring light from the streetlamps overhead made reading her facial expressions nearly impossible.

He pulled the passenger-side door of the Lexus open, and she slipped past him, her fingers intentionally brushing his before she dropped into her seat.

A light rain began to fall by the time they reached the outskirts of town, and he turned on the windscreen wipers. Their soft, persistent whooshing, the ticking of water droplets as they impacted the car, and his inability to read her mood, all merged to recreate the agonising emotions he felt the night she first rejected him.

Unable to take her silence and the uncertainty any longer, he blurted out, "I realise I disappointed you tonight, Louisa, but what would you have had me do?"

She pulled back, cocking her head at him. "What do you mean?"

"Adrian Pitts! Do you realise you didn't speak a word to me at dinner?"

"Oh, that."

Martin released a bit of nervous tension in a hiss from his nose. "I warned Chris about him before they hired him. But the powers that be overruled him in the decision. They ended up with a mediocre surgeon, and they got an arse into the bargain as well."

"Oh, dear. Poor Chris."

"*Poor Chris?*"

"Well, he's stuck with him now, right?"

"Chris can take care of himself, Louisa. It's those who are at the mercy of the smarmy womaniser that I worry about."

With her knee-jerk defensiveness triggered, Louisa's head flicked. "If I'm one of the '*those*' to whom you're referring, Martin, you needn't have worried. I can hold my own with the likes of Adrian Pitts, thank you very much."

"Yes." He gave her a sideways glance before ducking his head. "Are you still upset?"

"I was never upset."

The silence returned to the Lexus before she reached for his hand. "Yes, I could have handled him myself. But I was a bit relieved, actually, when I saw you storming my way."

"I hardly think I'm capable of *storming* anywhere at the moment," he said, tugging at an ear. "And I think my handling of the matter was perfectly reasonable."

Her hand shifted to his thigh. "It wasn't meant as a criticism. And I wasn't quiet at dinner because I was upset. I just had ... *other* things on my mind."

"What other things?"

"Well, your behaviour was rather, shall we say," she brushed her hair back from her face and turned her gaze to the passing darkened landscape, "*provocative*."

He wagged his nose in the air. "I wasn't trying to *provoke* Adrian. He was out of line, and I needed to make it clear, in no uncertain terms, that I won't tolerate any of his adolescent antics where you're concerned."

"That's not what I meant by provocative," she said. "I quite like how you were protective of me."

She returned her hand to his thigh before allowing it to creep up his leg, and his eyes darted down before the penny dropped. "Ah, I see."

"Hmm, probably not the half of it, Martin. I guarantee you, Adrian Pitts was the farthest thing from my mind at dinner."

Her hand crept up a bit farther and his breath caught in his throat.

"Mm, yes," he croaked.

They continued on to the village in relative silence, Louisa's eyes lingering on him occasionally in what Martin found to be an almost vulturine manner.

After dropping his wife off, he drove Poppy home. When he returned to the surgery, she had already gone upstairs. He found her in the nursery, and he stood in the doorway, watching as she placed light kisses on each of the two little boys' heads.

Her eyes sparkled in the bit of moonlight coming through the window, matching the happy, loving emotion he saw in her smile.

This was a moment he had dreamed of when he'd admired her from afar, during those days when the possibility of their ever being together seemed remote at best.

His own mother had never—*would* never feel anything but animosity towards him. But Louisa loved James, despite the fact that his own genetic material was so much a part of the boy. And she loved Evan, despite the fact that he had been deemed unlovable by *his* own mother.

She tousled Buddy's head and straightened before she noticed him watching her. Tiptoeing from the room, she took his hand, and they crossed the landing to their bedroom. Stopping in front of the dresser, she turned her back to him.

"Can you help me with my zip?" she asked.

"Mm, yes." He ran his fingers through her hair before pushing it aside and kissing each shoulder. "You looked beautiful tonight."

Her gaze met his in the mirror, and she gave him a demure smile. “Thank you, Martin.”

Quickly averting his eyes, he slid the pull down on her dress. The seam fell open, exposing the gentle arch low on her back, and his hand was drawn to it. “Louisa,” he whispered, burying his face in the crook of her neck.

His breaths brushing against her skin aroused her, and he watched, mesmerised, as her nipples responded under the delicate fabric of her dress.

Cupping her waist in his hands, his thumbs traced the small prominences of her spine. Then, his good hand slid forward, caressing its way up to seek out her breasts.

Her weight settled against him, and she let her head drop back against his shoulder. Watching in the mirror, he studied her responses to his sexual ministrations, wanting to please.

Her eyes drifted shut, and she drew in breath when his thumb flicked across a nipple. “Oh, Martin,” she murmured as she pressed against him.

Slipping the straps from her shoulders, his gaze fixed on the splendid image in front of him as he let the dress drop to the floor, exposing her form.

Lest she bring a premature end to a most enjoyable moment, Louisa forced her eyes to remain closed, allowing his tender sensibilities the privacy to fully appreciate her in his own way. Resting against him, she thought of nothing but the sensations that he was stirring in her.

The hand of his injured arm kept a secure grip on her waist as his left hand caressed its way down her front before slipping under the lace band of her panties, coming to rest between her thighs. He adjusted the pressure of his touch, searching for the sweet spot that would bring the moment to a climax. She moaned softly, and the hint of a satisfied smile crossed his lips.

Tears began to sting at his eyes, a wash of emotions overwhelming him with the awareness that she was allowing him this level of intimacy, welcoming it from him.

He watched as her body responded to his touch, as her chin quivered slightly and she arched back. "I've got you," he whispered softly into her ear. "I've got you."

Her breaths slowed, the intense expression of ecstasy on her face easing, and he shifted his arm up to encircle her as she relaxed into him. Only then did she open her eyes, her reflected tender gaze fixing on his.

She turned and tugged at his tie, pulling it from his neck before her fingers lithely slipped the buttons of his shirt through the buttonholes. He shook it from his shoulders, and she tossed it on to a nearby chair.

Stopping for a moment, she stretched up and pressed her lips to his as her hands cupped his cheeks. Then, reaching down, she unbuckled his belt and pushed his trousers over his hips and fixators. He kicked them from his feet, and his boxers quickly followed.

"There, that's much better," she purred.

She pressed up against him and a low moan rumbled from his lips. "Louisa?"

"Hmm?" she said, trailing kisses down his chest and belly.

"I'm—I'm not sure how much longer I can hold out here."

She peered up at him mischievously. "You're my extraordinary man, Martin. You can hold out as long as necessary."

He tugged at an ear. "That's not—not what I was referring to. I'm not sure how much longer my legs can hold out. I don't want to end up on top of you."

"Oh, right." Wedging herself under his arm, they walked to the bed, and he fell back heavily on to it.

"Everything okay?" she asked as she scrutinised him with a worried brow.

"Mm, thank you."

Her fingers brushed over his dewy forehead and the right side of her mouth began to tug up.

"What?" he asked, giving her a scowl.

"It's just—well, I'm afraid you're likely to end up on top of me regardless, aren't you?"

He screwed up his face before his annoyed expression softened into one more decidedly lustful. "Quite possibly." Tugging her to him, he slid her panties down.

"Better now?" she asked as her head tipped to the side.

Swallowing, he gave her a throaty grunt. "God, yes."

"Good." She crawled in and pulled him down next to her. There was a chill in the room, but his body was luxuriously warm, and she stretched out against the length of him.

His very apparent growing readiness throbbed against her thigh, fanning a vestigial flicker from her earlier arousal, and she pulled his hips to hers, eliciting a soft moan from him.

When he could take the stimulation of her movements no longer, he pushed himself up with his good arm, positioning himself between her legs. She waited breathlessly as he was poised to make love to her.

His eyes glinted as he watched her intently for a moment. "Is this what you want?"

Wincing at his residual feelings of unworthiness, she took his face in her hands. "Very, *very* much. I want you to make love to me, Martin."

He lowered himself, pressing his lips to hers. As the kiss deepened, he entered her.

His slow and purposeful movements rekindled, even more intensely, the sensations from before, and she rose up to capture all of him.

He stopped, staring at her before his eyes drifted shut, and he dropped down, resting his body lightly against hers.

"Martin? Everything okay?" she asked softly.

"Mm. I just ... I want to think about you ... feel you."

Her arms tightened around him and they lay quietly for a moment before he kissed her and his movements began anew.

The pleasurable sensations built in him in waves, like the tides that twice daily pushed into the harbour—ebbing and flowing, but each wave more intense than the last. His thrusts slowed as he tried to stave off the inevitable high tide.

Looking up at him, her eyes dark with lust, she nodded her readiness.

His lips tugged at her ear before whispering the words, "I love you."

The final surges hit him like a tidal swell and, his mind now fully engaged in the physical sensations, he allowed them to rush out, exquisitely uncontrolled.

His movements slowed with the easing of his urgency. He hesitated, reluctant for it to end, before moving from her.

"Thank you, Martin," she said as she brushed the hair back from her still-flushed face.

His thumb stroked her cheek. "The pleasure was all mine." His eyes closed and he released a soft sigh.

Louisa was awakened shortly before midnight by the backfire from a pickup making its way up the hill. She ran her hand over her husband's still-damp hair, and he stirred, rolling on to his back with a groan before falling back to sleep.

Their protracted lovemaking after a long and stressful day had left him spent but sated, and fatigue had claimed him before he could carry out his usual bedtime routine. Louisa hesitated before jostling him awake.

"Martin. Martin, you need to take your pain medication."

He prised his eyes open and sighed. "Mm, yes."

"Need some help getting out of bed?"

"No, I've got it." He pushed himself upright and swung his feet to the floor, then disappeared into the bathroom.

Louisa pulled the blankets back when he returned to the bed. She wedged pillows under his legs and tucked the covers in under his chin before placing a kiss on his lips. "I enjoyed our evening very much." Fluffing her pillow, she fell back on to it. "And just to be clear, I wasn't at all disappointed in you."

"Good." He turned his head and gave her a shyly smug smile. "I put forth my best effort."

Her brow furrowed. "Are we both talking about what happened with that Pitts fellow?"

He gave her a sideways glance. "No. I thought you were referring to our ... *activities*."

"I see. Well, just so you know, I was quite proud of you tonight."

He pulled up his chin. "Thank you."

Louisa propped herself up on an elbow, giving him an amused smile. "Granted, your sexual performance was exemplary, but again I'm referring to how you handled the situation at the party. I think your don't-mess-with-me side is growing on me."

"Ah, I see."

Rolling forward, she kissed him. "Goodnight, Martin. I love you."

"Goodnight. I love you, too, Louisa."

Chapter 19

"It's going to be a lovely day!" Louisa said as she returned to the kitchen after putting out the rubbish. "Martin, I was thinking we could take the boys on a picnic. Maybe even invite Ruth to join us."

He cringed behind the cover of his newspaper. "Mm. Cheese and fruit in the gazebo at the farm. Yes."

"Actually, I was thinking of doing something a bit more adventurous. The boys would love Boscawen Park, don't you think?"

He gave her a blank stare and she huffed.

"Overlooking the Truro River."

His mouth opened and closed silently as he blinked his eyes at her.

"You *know* which one I'm talking about, Martin. The one with the walking path and all the play equipment ... along the river." Her hand circled in the air. "In *Truro*."

She shook her head. "It doesn't matter. We have this rare warm day, and I think it'd be nice to get out and enjoy it before it turns cold and wet again."

He snapped the paper shut and laid it down on the table. "Maybe you and Ruth should take the boys. I'd likely slow you down."

"You seemed able to keep up the pace just fine last night," she said, giving him an impish smile.

The tips of his ears reddened and he cleared his throat.

"And you know very well Ruth won't be able to keep up with the boys either," Louisa continued. "So, I was thinking the two of you could find a bench—sit down and enjoy the sunshine while the boys play. Getting out in the fresh air would be good for all of us."

He sighed heavily and gave her a grunt. "I suppose we could do some shopping for Evan's bed whilst we're there."

"Yes, we could." She kissed his cheek before glancing at her watch. "Speaking of Evan, I wonder when he's going to get up. Maybe I should wake him."

"Best not. He didn't get a lot of sleep last night."

"Hmm, neither did you." Louisa sprinkled a few more bits of dry cereal on to James's high chair tray. "Poor Evan. Do you really think the little Crandall boy's death is what's triggering these recent nightmares?"

"I haven't the foggiest idea. And I highly doubt a new bed is going to be the solution to the problem. But we need to try something, and his bed does need replacing."

"So, should I call Ruth?"

Martin rubbed a hand over his eyes. "Mm."

The park was abuzz with activity when they arrived, and Martin quickly pointed out a picnic table off in a remote corner where they could eat in relative seclusion.

Though the sky was a clear azure blue, the sun was still low in the sky, and its winter rays were weak, lending a slight chill to the breeze, gentle as it was. Martin snugged up his son's hood before doing the same with his charge.

"Dr. Ellig-am, that's too tight! I can't see," the seven-year-old said, tipping his head back to peer under the elasticised edge that was now pinching his eyelids shut.

"Mm, yes." He adjusted the toggles, and the child coughed, tugging at the top of his jacket.

Louisa and Ruth spread a plastic cover over the top of the table, weighing it down with containers of sandwiches, carrot sticks, and cheese and apple slices.

Evan ate hurriedly as he surveyed the play equipment. His gaze landed on the climbing net at the far end of the park. "I'm all done eating. I'm gonna go play now."

"No, you're not," Martin said. "You need to finish your sandwich and drink down your milk first. Then you're going to ask to be excused from the table."

"It's just a picnic table, not a *real* table, Dr. Ellig-am. And the other kids are gonna get all the good stuff if I don't hurry."

He stared pointedly at the boy. "Finish your lunch and excuse yourself properly."

Louisa looked at her husband disapprovingly. "Maybe he could just have one more bite, and then—"

Giving the younger woman a furtive shake of her head Ruth interjected, "Your *father's* right, Evan. You're going to need those calories. Your muscles need to be well fed if you intend to climb to the top of that net you're drooling over. So, eat up."

The seven-year-old looked across the table to Louisa who glanced at Ruth before pointing a finger at the remnants of his lunch. "Yes, finish up, Evan. Then you may go play."

The parenting contretemps having been successfully mediated by Aunt Ruth, the family finished the meal, and Evan set off for the climbing net while Louisa took James to the swings.

Martin and Ruth gathered together the picnic supplies, packing them away in the basket before searching out a bench overlooking the river.

"You called me his father," Martin said as he sat down next to her. "I'm sure you must have had a reason for that."

"A slip of the tongue."

He tipped his head down and eyed her from the side. "Is anything else slipping? You're not normally prone to solecisms."

She gave him a black look. "No." Digging around in her handbag, she removed a pair of thin leather gloves. "It was meant as a reminder to the both of you that you are soon to be the parents of that little boy. You need to at least appear to be on the same page when it comes to discipline. Evan, more than most children, will need consistency."

"I see." He pulled up his chin. "I've been wanting to line up a competent contractor to do the work on your porch."

"I do appreciate the offer, Martin, but really, it's not necessary. I'm perfectly capable of navigating those cobblestones." Ruth flipped the collar up on her coat and worked her hands into the gloves.

"The haematoma you sustained recently would suggest otherwise. I've been wanting to have some work done at the surgery. I'll have them do the work on your porch steps first, though."

"Oh? Are you finally breaking down and replacing that old boiler?"

"It's on the list, yes."

She raised her eyebrows at him. "You have a list?"

"Well, obviously, we're going to need more space. I have in mind to extend the first floor on the back of the house. Expand the kitchen and dining area. Add a bathroom and master bedroom. But the house is a Grade II listed building, so I need to find a contractor who has experience working with the local council."

"Right. You *will* want to protect its historical integrity. And you certainly don't want to end up in a legal battle with the authorities."

"Mm, no."

"If you'd like a recommendation, Duane O'Dubhan is the contractor who drew up the architectural plans for me at the farm. I understand he's quite well-respected for the work he's done on a number of historic buildings in the area. And he knows how to grease palms, so to speak."

"Can you provide me with his contact information?"

"I'll get it to you tomorrow." She watched as several kayakers paddled past. "And Louisa? I assume she's in agreement on all this?"

"She will be, I'm sure."

"You haven't discussed it with her? Oh, Martin, you're playing with fire there."

"I'll get around to it!"

Ruth put a hand up. "All right, I'll say no more."

A small group of boisterous boys raced past and Martin quickly pulled his legs out of the way to avoid a painful impact. "Watch it!" he barked.

"How have things been going with your therapy lately?" A shiver went through the elderly woman, and she pulled her arms around her.

He struggled to his feet. "You're cold," he said, removing his jacket. He wrapped it around her slender frame and sat back down.

"Thank you, Martin. That's much better." She eyed him for a moment. "Should I persist in getting an answer to my question, or would I be wasting my breath?"

He screwed up his face and turned away. "It's going fine."

She rolled her eyes before sighing softly. "Martin, I'm not asking you to divulge anything said in confidence. I'm just worried about you."

"Why? Did Louisa say something?"

"Nooo. But you do have a lot to overcome, and it would give me some peace of mind to know that you're still moving forward with it all."

He grunted. "The pain in the left leg hasn't improved as I'd hoped it would. Ed Christianson will consult with Will Simpson after my next appointment if needs be—decide how to deal with it."

"And the arm? Are you keeping up with the piano playing? That could prove to be of great benefit."

"This week has been busy."

"I see. I thought that would be the case. Unless you make it a priority, it will never happen. So, I was thinking we could have a standing lunch date.

"I'll do my best to cook something you'll find marginally palatable out at the farm. We can partake in delightful conversation while we eat, and then you can retire to the sanctuary of the living room ...

and the *piano*. I'll go upstairs and work on whatever I have a mind to work on."

"Mm, that wouldn't be possible. I'm to be getting a lie-down in every afternoon."

"And I happen to know that you already let that one slide on a regular basis."

Martin's head dropped to the side. "Oh, Ruth, I realise you're just—"

"Good. How does Monday work for you?"

He glanced over at her resolute face and groaned. "Fine."

She crossed her legs and her fingers laced together over a knee. "And now back to my original question—your appointments with Dr. Newell," she said.

"Mm. I don't seem to be making much progress lately. I seem to be stuck."

"Stuck?"

"There are things that just don't seem to change."

"Well, there will be plateaus with therapy. Give it time."

Giving him a sideways look, she asked, "Things don't change? Are you referring to feeling undeserving?"

"No." He stared off, his palms rubbing together.

"Martin, is it Louisa? Do you still feel undeserving of her?"

"No, of course not." He gave the elderly a woman a furtive glance. "I'm not sure. But it's not about feeling *un*-deserving. It's about feeling deserving."

"Well, it's a two-stage process, really, isn't it? First you must understand that you're not *un*-deserving of Louisa's love. Then, you must accept that you do indeed *deserve* her love. It may take time."

He huffed out a breath and grimaced. "It has to do with the accident—nightmares regarding that night. Dr. Newell believes that on some level I feel I deserved it."

"And what do you believe? *Do* you think you deserved it?"

"I'm not sure." He pulled his shoulders back and turned his head away. "Possibly."

"Oh, Martin." She put a hand on his arm. "My natural inclination is to argue the point with you, but I'm afraid that would be of no use to you whatsoever. Your lovely parents endowed you with an overdeveloped sense of personal responsibility. Try not to worry; Barrett Newell will help you get it resolved."

Rocks skittered against the walking path, and Evan walked up, the air wheezing in and out of his lungs.

"Mrs. Ellig-am said—ta tell ya my inhaler's not—doin' the job."

"Mm, no it's not," Martin said, unzipping the boy's jacket and putting his ear to his chest. "Take a big breath in for me. And out." His brow furrowed. "Where's Mrs. Ellingham?"

"James had a stinky nappy. She took him to the toilet ta change it."

"Mm." He glanced at his watch and turned to Ruth. "We should be going if we're going to get our shopping done." Pulling himself to his feet, he wedged his crutch under his arm before holding his hand out to her.

"Oh no, Martin. I don't want to be responsible for you hurting yourself. I can manage on my own."

"I can help ya, Dr. Ellig-am," the seven-year-old said, taking hold of her arm and grunting as he pushed against her. "You're pretty heavy for bein' so skinny."

Ruth raised an eyebrow at her nephew. "Well, I'm not sure if I should be flattered or insulted by that remark."

By the time they arrived at the furniture store, the seven-year-old's breathing had improved. He skipped alongside his guardian before hurrying ahead of everyone to pull the door open.

"Thank you, Evan. That's very helpful," Louisa said, manoeuvring the pushchair over the threshold.

"What are we gonna do at this place?" he asked.

"*We* are going to see if we can find a new bed for you." She patted his cheek and gave him a smile.

He stopped in his tracks. "But the bed I gots still works. And I like it."

James began to fuss and fight against his restraints, and Louisa hurriedly dug through the nappy bag to find the container of Melba toast, handing a piece to the boy.

"Well, let's just take a look around, hmm?" she said distractedly, returning the container to the bag.

Martin had tracked down a salesperson and was explaining what they were searching for when his charge came up and tugged on his sleeve.

"Dr. Ellig-am, I gots ta tell you something."

He bent down and the boy whispered in his ear. "I don't *want* a new bed! I like the one I gots now!"

"It needs replacing, Evan. It doesn't provide you with the support you'll need as you grow." Martin winced as he straightened. "Come on." He limped off towards the children's beds on display in individual bedroom mock-ups.

Ruth approached the boy as he dropped on to a leather sofa, burying his face in his hands. She took a seat next to him. "For a young man who's about to pick out a smart new bed, you don't look very happy."

"That's 'cause I don't want a new bed. Even if it is smart." He looked up at her with teary, red-rimmed eyes. "How come I can't stay where I am now, Dr. Ellig-am? I don't *wanna* sleep somewhere else."

"Not even in a comfortable new bed?"

"The one I gots now *is* comfortable! It's the most comfortable bed I ever had! I don't *want* a new one!"

Ruth's fingers tapped against her knee. "Well, it sounds as if the bed you have is very special. What is it that you like about it?"

The child shrugged his shoulders. "It's warm."

"Warm is a very important quality in a bed."

"And it smells good." He slid to the floor, growing more animated as he listed the other positive attributes of his current sleeping situation. "It gots a fuzzy sheet that feels nice. And it even gots aeroplanes on it! And the duvet is all puffy. And it doesn't gots any spots on it either. And Dr. Ellig-am reads to me and I get hugs and ki—"

His cheeks flushed and he pulled his hands behind him, scuffing a trainer against the floor. "I just don't want a different bed."

"Well, first of all Evan, you must understand that you won't be sleeping *somewhere else* when you get your new bed. It will be in your very same room in Dr. and Mrs. Ellingham's house.

"And I can certainly appreciate why you wouldn't want to part with all those lovely things. I wouldn't want to either. And thank goodness you don't have to if you get a new bed. You get to keep all those lovely things."

"Really?"

"I'm almost certain of it. But you'd be wise to ask my nephew, just to be sure."

"I will!" The boy ran towards the bedroom displays before darting back. "Do you want me ta push you up again, Dr. Ellig-am?"

Ruth leaned forward and gave him a crooked smile. "Just between you and me, my poor old feet are a little tired. So, I think I'll stay right where I am for now."

"Okay." The seven-year-old wrapped his arms around the elderly woman's neck, kissing her on the cheek. "Thanks Dr. Ellig-am. I feel lots better now."

Staring after the boy as he gambolled over to her nephew, Ruth's fingers touched the slightly damp spot left behind by his expression of affection, and a sparkle came to her eyes.

Evan slipped in between Martin and Louisa, latching on to his guardian's wrist. Martin glanced down at his touch.

"Mm, there you are."

"Yeah, here I am. I was just talkin' to the other Dr. Ellig-am."

"I gathered as much. This woman here," he said, giving the salesperson a jerk of his head, "will show us the beds they have on offer. We're going to try to find one that you'll be comfortable in."

"But can I keep my other stuff, Dr. Ellig-am?"

"What other stuff."

"The lovely stuff that my old bed has."

James struggled to extricate himself from the pushchair, and Louisa leaned down, hoisting him from the seat and setting him on the floor. "What's the lovely stuff you're referring to, Evan?"

"The smellin' good, the fuzzy sheet with the aeroplanes, the readin' and—"the saleswoman approached and he pulled at Louisa's sleeve before whispering into her ear—"the hugs and stuff!"

She kissed the boy's forehead. "All of those things come with Dr. Ellingham and me, not your old bed. So, yes, you may keep all of it. You needn't worry about that."

A broad grin spread across his face, and he scanned around the room. "Which one are you gettin'?"

Martin held out his hand, and the boy took hold of it. "We're going to decide together. But you better hurry up, or they'll be closing up shop before you see the half of it."

The possible options were quickly whittled down. Evan's first choice, a child-sized bed with a large plastic shark's head perched on the headboard, ready to devour any trespasser, was deemed too small and impractical at best by Martin—flimflam intended to extract money from weak-kneed parents by capitalising on a child's active imagination.

His second choice, a castle complete with a moat and a keep where one could lock up their most treasured possessions or annoying siblings, was quickly ruled out for its sheer size, an impracticality in a small cottage.

"How 'bout bunk beds, Evan?" Louisa said as she admired a set off in one corner of the room. You'd have a place for a friend to sleep if you had a sleepover, and James could sleep in one of the beds when he's older. It would make more space in your room."

"No, no, no, no, no," Martin said, shaking his head. Significant injuries can result from falls during sleep—lacerations, fractures, even concussions."

"Well, how about this one over here?" the saleswoman said. "It was designed with safety a priority. The top bunk is securely enclosed all the way around, aside from the entrance area."

Louisa ran her hand over the dark glossy finish. "I don't see how he could possibly roll out of bed in his sleep in this one, Martin. And see, no ladder. It has steps instead."

"Which a child could easily fall from in the middle of the night."

"That's not likely, Martin. They're enclosed on both sides. Oh, and look! There's storage under the steps and under the lower bunk!" she said, pulling out a drawer.

"Mm, yes."

"And we can get bed rails for the bottom bunk. James can sleep there. He's going to outgrow his cot soon."

Evan climbed to the top and laid back on the mattress. "And I can pretend I'm in a tree, Dr. Ellig-am!" He bounced up on his knees and peered over the protective side. "And nothing can get me up here, either!"

Martin scratched at an eyebrow as he struggled to come up with a legitimate argument to the potential purchase. "Do you feel comfortable up there?" he asked the boy.

"Really comfortable! And Buddy will be comfortable, too, 'cause it doesn't gots a ladder. It gots steps, so he can still come up and sleep with me."

"Yes." Huffing out a breath, he conceded defeat. "Fine."

Louisa reached out and took his hand, squeezing his fingers. "Thank you, Martin."

Though Evan left the store disgruntled that his guardian refused to haul his new bed home on top of the Lexus, they had a delivery date set for Monday morning. And two days can seem like an eternity when you're seven years old.

Chapter 20

Louisa set Martin's plate of eggs down, shaking her head and narrowing her eyes at him in warning.

He bit at his cheek and sighed before checking his watch. "They're due to deliver it in two hours, Evan. Now eat your breakfast."

"Maybe I should stay home from school and help 'em. What if they put it in the wrong spot?"

"Oh, for God's sake. You've clearly outlined the location with tape on your floor. If they can see well enough to get that bed over here without crashing on to the verge, they'll be able to work out where it goes in your room."

"Oh, no! If they crash, my bed might get broke!"

Louisa huffed out a breath. "I'm sure Dr. Ellingham's not suggesting they'll actually crash, Evan. But you do have the location clearly marked, so I'm sure all will be just fine. Your new bed will be all set up for you when we come home for lunch."

Martin carried his dishes to the sink, rinsing them and putting them in the dishwasher before refilling his coffee cup. "Well, I have patient notes to review. Remember, I'm supposed to have lunch with Ruth today."

"Yes. I'm glad you're spending some time with her," Louisa said.

"Mm." He leaned down, kissing her cheek from behind before brushing his fingers over his son's head. "Have a good morning, James."

The toddler held out his hand. "Hew, Daddy. Fo you."

Martin reached out and his son deposited several slimy bits of cereal into his palm. "Mm, thank you, James." He turned and washed it down the drain.

Slipping from his chair, Evan tugged his guardian down before leaving a kiss on his cheek. "See ya at lunch, Dr. Ellig-am."

"Mm, yes. Have a good morning, Evan."

Martin was engrossed in Malcolm Raynor's most recent chest images when Morwenna knocked on his consulting room door later that morning.

"Doc, you have a new patient," she said, laying the required NHS form on his desk. "Since when did you start takin' referrals from veterinarians?"

He grimaced at her. "What?"

"The guy says some vet in Wadebridge told him ta come see you."

"Oh, right. Send him in, Morwenna."

"Seriously?" She inched back in front of the desk. "I'm kinda worried about you now, Doc."

"Why would you be worried?"

"Well, I get that some folks might have a bit of a problem with you being shambly and all. I mean, who wants to go see a doctor who's worse off than they are, right?

"But you really don't need to resort to recruiting patients. Most folks around here know how messed up you are. It makes 'em worry a bit." She put a hand up. "Not about you as a doc. Just about *you*. But if you start recruiting patients from vets—well, they might start worrying about you as a doc. It seems a bit desperate."

"This is none of your business, Morwenna. Go tell"—he glanced down at the form—"Mr. Adwell to come through."

"Right." She looked at the doctor apprehensively and then headed for the door.

"Morwenna," Martin said as it began to swing shut behind her.

"Yeah, Doc?"

"You have nothing to worry about."

"If you say so."

The latch clicked before he heard her muffled voice. *"Mr. Adwell, the doctor can see you now."*

A burly, middle-aged man opened the door a few moments later. He hesitated in the doorway, pulling his herringbone flat cap from his head.

"Come in and sit down. I'll be right with you," Martin said. He signed off on a set of patient notes and looked up as the man lowered himself into the chair in front of the desk.

"My wife told me to come see ya, Dr. Ellingham. Well, Dr. Tressa told me, actually."

"Yes. Why don't you tell me about your symptoms, Mr. Adwell." He scrutinised the man's unkempt appearance and the bags under his eyes.

"Collywobbles. And, well, I never been the nervy type, but I'm like a cat on hot bricks lately. Darlene's worried." He grimaced. "Thinks I'm—I'm *depressed.*"

"Darlene's your wife?"

"Yeah. Married comin' up on nineteen years now. We'd been good, *really* good. But somethin's wrong. She says I'm not the man she married. I 'ad ta come see ya. I'm afraid if I don't get things put to rights, I'll wake up one day and she'll 'ave done a runner."

"Any other symptoms you need to tell me about? Difficulty remembering things—concentrating? Any sexual difficulties?"

Abel's face reddened and his fingers worked at his cap brim. "Darlene complains all the time about me forgettin' things, yeah."

He dropped his head. "And ... yeah, the other, too. I don't know what's wrong with me, Doc. I just can't ... don't even care about *it* anymore, if you know what I mean."

He screwed up his face. "'Course you don't know what I mean, cause it t'aint normal fer a fella ta not care about that."

Martin grunted ambiguously. "Have you been under any undue stress recently?"

The man squirmed in his seat. "Maybe. There's been somethin' weighing on me," he said, picking at a frayed fingernail.

"And then there's the economy and all, ya know. My girl wants ta go off to uni next fall." He shook his hat. "Smart as a whip, that one." A weak smile came to his face. "Even got a scholarship. I been tryin' ta pull the rest of the funds together so she can go, but ..."

"I see." Martin reached for his stethoscope. "All right. Get up on the table for me, please. I need to examine you."

Abel walked to the exam couch, and the doctor picked up his crutch, following along behind him.

"Undo the top buttons of your shirt for me," he said as he slipped the earpieces of the instrument into his ears.

His patient's overt stare began to unnerve Martin, and he reflexively pulled his injured arm behind him. "Breathe in—and out."

Coiling the stethoscope around his hand, he laid it down on his medical cart. He wagged a hand at him. "Untuck your shirt and lie back."

The man's gaze moved over the doctor, and he swallowed hard. Nodding, he pulled his shirttails out and dropped back on to the couch.

"What do you mean by collywobbles?"

"Stomach ache mostly," Abel said. "Bit'a the squits now and again."

"Does this hurt anywhere?" he asked as he palpated the man's belly.

"Not really. The stomach ache comes and goes though. It doesn't bother right now."

His eyes settling on his patient's hands, Martin noted his gnawed fingernails. "Okay, you can sit back up now. And button your shirt up."

Returning to his desk, he dropped into his chair, laying his crutch back down on the floor. "You can come and take a seat over here."

He reached into the cabinet behind him and removed a copy of Beck's Depression Inventory, sliding it across his desk before setting a biro next to it. "I'd like you to fill out this form, Mr. Adwell."

The man did up the last buttons on his shirt and sank into his seat. Leaning forward, he glanced at the paper. "I'd just as soon not, Doc. I never been good at tests."

"It's not a test. They're just some general questions. Your answers will help me make a proper diagnosis." He picked up his crutch and got to his feet. "I'll step out for a few minutes. Take your time with that." He felt the man's eyes on him as he traversed the room.

Stopping into the hall, he huffed out a breath. There were days when the thoughtless gawping of patients seemed impossible to ignore.

When he returned to the consulting room a short time later, his coffee cup in hand, his patient sat, a knee bouncing up and down nervously.

He limped to his desk. Abel watched him intensely before Martin caught his eye, and he quickly averted his gaze.

Setting his cup down, Martin dropped into his chair with a soft groan, grimacing as a jolt shot through his left leg. He pulled in a deep breath before tallying up the numbers for each of the man's answers.

When he finished, he looked up at him. "Mr. Adwell, I strongly suspect that your wife was correct in her diagnosis. Your scores do suggest that you are depressed.

"Your depression is manifesting itself mainly through physical symptoms. I believe the best course of action would be to get you started on an antidepressant. I'd also like for you to consult with a mental health therapist."

"You sayin' I've gone mental?"

"I'm saying that something has triggered a change in your brain chemistry. A therapist will try to determine what triggered it and teach you coping mechanisms which may help to prevent it from happening again."

"What if I don't wanna talk to some head doc? Won't the drugs fix it?"

"The medication only addresses the physiological changes in the brain. Your answers on the depression inventory indicate you could benefit from the help of a competent therapist."

Abel stared absently before giving the GP a nod. "How do I go about findin' someone competent?"

"I can assist you with that. Give me a couple of days to do some checking. I'll have someone give you a call—set up an appointment." Martin pulled in his chin when he found his patient's gaze once again fixed on his injured arm. Then he reached for his prescription pad.

Abel sat as the doctor's pen scratched softly. Then he gave a jab of his thumb. "Mind if I ask—what, er ... what 'appened there?"

The top sheet of paper was ripped from the pad and slapped down in front of the man. "Accident," Martin grumbled. "Mrs. Tishell can fill that for you. Take one in the morning and one before bed. You won't see immediate improvement, but you should be feeling better in four to six weeks. And you should be getting a call from a therapist in the next few days."

Folding the prescription in half and sliding it into his pocket, Abel got to his feet before perching his cap back on his head. "Thank you, doctor." Giving him a nod, he hurried through the door.

A loud commotion emanated from the reception room shortly before half ten. Martin blew out a breath and laid his mobile back on his desktop. The call to the therapist, recommended by Barrett Newell, would have to wait. The proper positioning of Evan's bed was now the pressing matter at hand.

"Doc, these men are from the furniture store over in Truro," Morwenna said when he came out of the consulting room. "They're here to deliver a bed."

"Yes, I gathered that from the godawful racket being made."

One of the men dropped his clipboard to his side as his eyes tracked over him. "Blimey! What happened to you?"

Martin gave him a dark look. "None of your business. You're being paid to make a delivery, not to ask questions. The bedroom's upstairs," he said, pushing past him and making his way up the steps.

The deliveryman looked to Morwenna, and she waved him off. "You heard the man—go!"

By the time the delivery crew had completed their work and Martin had finished with the last of his patients, Louisa and Evan had arrived home for lunch. He heard the child's trainers thunder down the hall and past his door. He got up to follow after him.

Standing in the middle of the nursery, the seven-year-old admired the majestic new piece of furniture against the wall.

Louisa came up behind her husband, slipping her arms around his waist. "Well, are you going to try it out," she asked the boy.

He gave her a grin before scrambling up the steps. "Wow! It gots all my covers and my pillow already!"

"Mm, I asked Poppy to make it up for you," Martin said. The tension he'd been feeling all morning eased as he watched his young charge yank his shoes from his feet and set them, almost ceremonially, on the top step before entering his new inner sanctum.

After receiving a lecture from Martin about the rules to which he must strictly adhere, including no standing on or jumping from the top bunk, the seven-year-old was allowed to try out the bottom bunk and each of the storage drawers.

"It's the best bed ever!" Evan finally pronounced.

"Well, I'm glad you're happy with it," Louisa said. "But we need to eat our lunch now, or we'll both be late getting back to the school, hmm?"

"Kay." The boy darted past them and down the steps.

"I'll be off to the farm, then," Martin said.

"It's so nice that you'll have this time with Ruth. But we're going to miss you on Mondays," Louisa said, tightening her grasp on him.

"Mm, yes." He turned and kissed her. "I'll see you after school."

When he ducked through the low kitchen entryway at the farm ten minutes later, he was greeted by a nostalgic aroma. Ruth had just pulled Auntie Joan's hotpot from the cooker.

He raised his eyebrows. "It smells good."

"Yes, it does, doesn't it? I've even surprised myself," the elderly woman said as utensils clattered on to the table. "Joan always said, start with fresh, quality ingredients, and you get a quality meal. She may have been right. Wash your hands and sit down, Martin. We're almost ready to eat."

Giving her a grunt, he flipped on the tap. "Evan's new bed arrived."

"Oh, good. Is he happy with it?"

"I think you could say that." He shook the worst of the water from his hands and reached for the tea towel. "Louisa seems taken with it as well."

"And how was your morning?"

Martin groaned as he hung the towel over the hook. "The usual—jabs and exams for repeat prescriptions, mostly."

He helped his aunt with her chair before taking a seat across the table from her.

A cloud of steam rose from the casserole dish when he broke through the crust of thinly-sliced, golden potatoes on her painstakingly-prepared dish. Three chicken thighs, followed by several heaping spoonfuls of vegetables, landed on his plate.

She gave him a crooked smile. "I'm glad to see you're eating well."

"Did I leave you enough?" he asked, his eyes darting from his aunt to his plate and back again.

"I wasn't being glib, Martin. I'm very happy to see that you're taking care of yourself."

"Of course, I'm taking care of myself," he grumbled.

"Well, I can't help but be concerned. There are many people concerned for your health. It's not just me."

"Jolly good." He stabbed his fork into a chunk of turnip. "I suspect there are a few people who are only too happy to share their concern with everyone down at the pub as well."

Ruth filled his glass with milk, eyeing him over the pitcher. "So ... it was *that* kind of morning?"

Air hissed from his nose. "They watch me like they'd watch a trained seal at the zoo. Like they're waiting for me to stand up on my tail, clap my flippers, and bark for a sardine."

His knife screeched against his plate, and his utensils dropped to the table as he pressed the heels of his hands to his eyes.

"Martin?"

He put a hand up before drawing in a ragged breath. "I'm fine. It's just a headache. I'll have Jeremy do whatever it is he does when this happens."

"Hmm, yes," the elderly woman said, reluctantly returning her attention to her own meal. "You were comparing yourself to a trained seal, I believe. Go on."

He shook his head. "I'll just be glad to have this over with."

Ruth watched him for several seconds as he jabbed at his dinner, his face set in a scowl. Her eyes grew moist before she reached across the table and put her hand on his. "I'm sorry, Martin."

He looked up, grunting and quickly averting his eyes.

Several seconds of silence passed before he asked with feigned nonchalance, "Do you think my injuries are off-putting?"

"I hope you're speaking in generalities. Otherwise I'd be deeply offended by that question," she said. "*I* most certainly do not find them off-putting. What others think, I can't say."

She dabbed at her mouth with a napkin. "Martin, ignorance abounds in this world. That doesn't make it any easier to tolerate, but there are times when it's of no use to try to enlighten. In this particular situation, you're best off trying to ignore."

He screwed up his face and glanced over at her. "It's getting difficult."

"I would imagine it is." Her hand settled on his again. "It's much harder to suffer fools when you're tired and in pain. You will certainly owe no apologies if you need a break from everything."

His brow furrowed as he tipped his head to the side. "Are you suggesting I close the surgery?"

"Not at all. But perhaps you and Louisa should get away for a bit. Find someplace quiet, away from all the curious eyes. Poppy, Jeremy and I can manage the boys for a few days."

He stared back for a moment. "Thank you, but I'm fine," he said before turning back to his meal.

Ruth breathed out a silent sigh.

Her worried thoughts were still on her nephew as she retired to her office upstairs later. *Perhaps I should discuss this with Louisa. No doubt she'd be agreeable to her and Martin having some time away together.*

The sound of scales being played could be heard, and she smiled. Her nephew struggled with the concept of emotion. His feelings were rarely expressed, aside from his frequent uncontrolled, angry outbursts.

Though he'd made it through the most intense period of his physical recovery, he had months yet with the external fixators in place. And the reconstructive surgeries down the road would be no walk in the park.

The scale work transitioned to a piece she recognised from the radio. *Must be some of that music that Carole Parsons left here,* she thought. The repetitive left hand arpeggios were not typical of the music that her nephew favoured.

His playing was stilted, with frequent discordant notes in the right-hand melody. Trying to master the fine movements required to play the instrument might well prove impossible in the end.

The music came to a stop with a particularly jarring chord, and a loudly uttered expletive made its way upstairs.

Ruth bit at the end of her biro as she questioned the wisdom of forcing her nephew back to the bench. Perhaps she should have trusted him to return to the piano when he felt ready. But Martin found expressing his emotions through words to be terribly difficult. The keyboard might just be the platform he needed to do that.

She could hear his growing pain and fatigue as his fingers fell short of the keys with increasing frequency. Suddenly, it grew quiet and the fallboard slammed shut.

"Ruth!" he barked up the stairs a moment later. "I need to go!"

She shook her head and slipped her papers into her satchel, snapping it shut.

Chapter 21

Martin pulled Duane O'Dubhan's contact information from his pocket and sat down behind his desk. Ringing the contractor up, he made an appointment to meet with him. It was the off-season for construction work, but Martin was still caught unawares when the man asked to come by that evening to discuss possible changes to the cottage.

He glanced at his watch. *Bugger!* He was now in a precarious position with his wife. She was due home from the school in minutes. The matter would need to be raised immediately, and if he didn't choose his words carefully, she would almost certainly feel he was acting arbitrarily—something that had not gone down well with her in the past.

Ducking his head under the steps, he limped out to the kitchen to make himself a cup of coffee. Perhaps the caffeine would counter the mind-numbing effects of the morphine he had taken after returning from the farm.

The rich toasty aroma of the espresso powder wafted up when he removed the lid from the can. Holding it under his nose he inhaled the aroma. He found the scent to be almost as hypnotic as that of his wife, and his eyes closed involuntarily as he pulled in a slow breath.

A movement in the bushes outside the window caught his eye. A grey squirrel, rarely seen in the village, dug in the leaf litter on the ground. He grunted and returned to his coffee-making. Filling the filter basket, he tamped down the powder before locking the device into the machine.

Buddy began to bark furiously out on the back terrace, and the squirrel sought refuge in a small tree, just out of reach of the terrier. Giving the dog a curl of his lip, Martin slid a cup under the spout and pressed the power button.

The coffee maker began to whirr, and the dark brew dribbled into his cup. Drawing in that first satisfying sip, he turned when the latch on the kitchen door rattled and his charge's voice bubbled into the room.

"Can I, Mrs. Ellig-am?"

Louisa swung the door shut and glanced at her watch. "Yes, you may go practice your sleeping. But just for fifteen minutes. We should take Buddy for his walk before James and Poppy get back from the library. And we're supposed to have heavy rain moving in later today, so we don't want to dawdle."

"'Kay."

"And Evan, you have homework to do. You'll need to get right to it when we get back. I don't want you up past your bedtime working on it."

"Uh-uh! Me either. Not on the first night in my new bed."

The child pulled off his trainers before racing past his guardian without so much as a hello. Martin's head jostled back and forth as he blinked his eyes. "For heaven's sake, it's a bed."

"Yes, Martin, it's a bed," Louisa said as she came over to kiss him. "But it's likely the nicest thing he's ever been given. He's just a bit excited. There's nothing wrong with that."

He could have argued the point with her, but he decided it imprudent given the matter he was about to broach.

"Martin, we really need to get a larger area fenced in for Buddy," she said. "You know, I just don't think he's happy out there."

"Happy?"

"Yes, Martin. A dog needs to feel a part of the family. I don't know why he has to be banished to the back garden during the day."

"Because, Louisa, I simply can't allow that animal in the house when I'm holding surgery. He'd no doubt make a nuisance of himself, not to mention it's against the law."

He pulled in his chin and cleared his throat. "Would you like a cup of tea or coffee? Or a glass of wine?"

She cocked her head at him. "Erm, yes. Yes, a glass of wine would be wonderful actually. Pippa was gone, today of all days, so I was a bit overwhelmed."

Slipping her coat over a peg behind the door, she shook a finger. "She has an uncanny knack for calling in sick whenever there's an upcoming meeting with the Board of Governors."

Martin grunted before taking a glass from the shelf and filling it a third of the way with Merlot.

"I had all of *her* responsibilities in addition to *my* usual responsibilities," she continued, her voice rising.

A bit more wine was poured into the glass.

"*And,* I had to prepare the notes for the meeting!"

Her satchel landed with a thud on the table, and he added more Merlot.

"And to top it off, a number of the children became ill at school today."

He returned the cork to the bottle and handed her the glass.

"Thank you, Martin. That's very nice of you."

He tugged at his ear, and she stretched up, kissing him again.

"Mm. What are their symptoms?"

"Hmm?"

"The sick students—what are their symptoms?"

"The usual—fever, cough, headaches, vomiting."

His brow furrowed. "Chris mentioned the other night that the influenza virus that's been making the rounds has been moving west. And it appears to be a particularly virulent strain."

"Well, thank goodness *we* have a doctor who made sure we had the vaccine." She flashed him a smile before taking a seat at the table.

"Mm, this particular strain was missed by the vaccine. They do their best to predict which strains might be a problem in a given year, but it's common for some unexpected viruses to show up."

He drank down the rest of his espresso, refilled his cup, and sat down across from her. "Erm, Louisa, there's something we should discuss."

"Can it wait, Martin? I'd like to get an email written up to send out to the parents, just to let them know about this bug that's shown up at the school."

"Actually no, it can't wait. I, er ... I made an appointment with a contractor. He's coming over tonight to discuss some changes I'd—some changes we—*possible* changes we might consider making to the house."

She stared across at him. "Oh? May I ask why you waited until now to discuss it with me?"

"I just called the man today. I didn't realise he'd want to come over so soon. Now that we have Evan, the nursery seems a bit cramped."

"Yes, it is a bit cramped. But the bunk beds, and the storage they provide, will free up a lot of space once James is no longer in his cot. I don't see a rush."

"Well, there's also the matter of bathroom space. What we have is small to begin with. There's barely enough room for the bath toys, the boys' shampoo and soap, not to mention all of your things."

Her eyes narrowed. "And yours."

"Of course."

"Just what did you have in mind, if you don't mind my asking?"

"No. No, I don't mind at all. We'll need to be mindful of the regulations regarding listed buildings, so I would think the best course of action might be to add on some space to the first floor at the back of the house. Perhaps expand the kitchen and lounge area and add a master bedroom and *en suite* bath. Evan and James would then each have a bedroom upstairs."

Louisa took a long sip from her glass before eyeing him ominously. "You seem to have put a great deal of thought into this."

His head tipped to the side and his mouth opened and closed silently before he ducked his head, mumbling, "Yes."

"Well, perhaps you should have worked your physical condition into the equation when you planned this all out."

"I didn't plan anything out. These are just ideas—possibilities. And I don't know what my physical condition has to do with it. *I'm* not doing the work."

"Oh, Martin, you have enough to deal with already. This just is *not* the time to take on a construction project."

"I beg to differ! I'm only seeing patients in the morning. That gives me the afternoon to monitor the progress of the work crew.

"The cracks in the upstairs ceilings need to be addressed, and we need to replace the boiler. We'll be fortunate to get through the winter without a major breakdown. We should replace it as soon as possible, and it seems prudent to make the construction changes at the same time, don't you think?"

She huffed. "I s'pose you have a point. But Martin, the last thing you need is more stress."

"I'll be fine."

Her ponytail flicked. "I really wish you'd stop saying that. You're not fine. You saying you are just makes me worry."

He cocked his head. "I don't follow."

Emptying her glass, she set it on the table with a clunk. "There's no hiding what you're going through, Martin. Your constant assurances don't make this any easier for me. I'd much rather you admitted when you're in pain, and let me help."

He turned his head away as air hissed from his nose.

"Martin. Look at me." She leaned to the side, trying to make eye contact. "You remember when I broke my collarbone?"

He winced. "Of course."

"You remember how it felt when I wouldn't let you help me? When I wouldn't let you in the ambulance?"

Swallowing hard, he nodded. "I'm sorry. I shouldn't have walked off on you."

"That's *not* what I meant! That was more my fault than it was yours. I'm a grown woman. I certainly should have had the sense to not run out into the street like that."

Her thumb stroked over the back of his hand. "I'm just saying that it makes it less painful for me to see you going through this when you give me a way to help."

He hesitated. "It would help me if you allowed me to provide for you and the boys."

"Provide—as in roomier accommodation?"

"Yes."

She bit at her cheek. "Okay, then. But may I make a request?"

"Certainly."

"Our current bedroom is large enough for both of the boys. Maybe they could share our room, both have an *en suite* bathroom. And ... well, I could use the nursery as an office."

His eyebrows nudged up and he pulled up his bottom lip. "That's quite a good idea. You'd be less distracted—could get your work done more efficiently—and we'd be rid of some of the flotsam that's always strewn about the kitchen."

Her ponytail flicked. "Yes, Martin." Her fingernails clicked against the table top, and she peered up at him warily. "And then there's the matter of Buddy."

"Buddy?"

"That little brown and white terrier that lives with us, Mar-tin."

He screwed up his face. "I know who Buddy is. But what *matter* are you referring to?"

"Well, where is he going to go? There won't be very much space for him out in the back if we add on to the house."

"Ah. I see. Well, technically, Ruth's the dog's owner by succession, so it seems appropriate that he'd go back to her."

"Oh, really? By succession?" She leaned back and folded her arms over her chest. "Joan thought of you as her son. That, I would argue, makes *you* her successor."

"Nooo. If you recall, when King Edward abdicated the throne, his brother, King George, became his successor."

"We're keeping Buddy, Martin, so don't even go there again. If we're going to have all this work done, we can have them close off the private area of the house. Buddy can be inside during the day, hmm?"

Air hissed out from between his pursed lips, and he threw his head back.

Her defensive posture relaxing, Louisa said, "So, we've come to an agreement, then?"

He grunted. "This Duane O'Dunham fellow will have suggestions, I'm sure. So, we'll need to remain flexible."

"I can be flexible."

"Yes. Yes, you can."

She went to the pegs behind the door and pulled on her coat before picking up the dog leash and calling for the seven-year-old.

When Louisa, Evan, and Buddy returned from their walk a while later, Martin had soup simmering on the hob. He sat at the table engrossed in an article on his laptop. Giving them a grunt, he returned his attention to the latest news on the recent influenza outbreak.

James got up from his tower of blocks and toddled over, tugging at Evan's hand. "Pay, Ebby!"

"I gots ta do my homework, James," the seven-year-old said, hanging his coat up and pulling his maths book from his backpack.

Louisa hoisted her son to her hip. "Let's get you a snack, James," she said, reaching for a banana from the basket on the counter. "Martin, when is Duane coming?"

He scowled at the interruption, and air hissed from his nose. "I can't say *specifically*, Louisa."

His fingers clicked against his keyboard as he typed *Met Office* into the search bar. "There's a line extending from Swansea on to the southwest. Another hour, maybe." His hand reached for his mouse. "I can read you the latest forecast discussion if you like."

Giving him an amused smile, she slipped her son into the high chair. "That's very thoughtful, but I wasn't asking about the weather. In case you hadn't noticed, we came home wet. The *rain's* already here." Leaning over, she kissed his cheek. "I asked, when is *Duane* coming?"

He tugged at an ear and snapped his laptop shut. "Mm. Six-thirty. I made some soup, so we can eat if you like."

"Thank you, Martin. I'll just go dry my hair and be back down." She wiggled her fingers at the seven-year-old. "Come on, Evan. Let's get you into some dry clothes."

They had just finished with the dinner dishes later that evening when the doorbell rang. Martin lifted his arm. "Hmph. He's timely. Six-thirty, on the dot."

"Well, that's promising. I'll get it," Louisa said before hurrying off.

A fine mist was blown into the entryway when she opened the door, and the contractor quickly stepped inside. "Sorry about that," he said as he pulled the hood of his mackintosh back.

"That's quite all right, Mr. O'Dunham. It's just one of the drawbacks of living here on the cliff. I'm Louisa Ellingham," she said.

"It's O'Dubhan."

"I'm sorry?"

"The name's Duane O'Dubhan, Mrs. Ellingham, not O'Dunham. Not a problem. Just thought I'd get it sorted up front. It's probably easier if you just call me by my Christian name."

"I see. You can hang your coat on the rack," she said, gesturing towards the pegs by the door. "My husband's in the kitchen. Come on in."

They stepped around the two little boys, busy on the floor in the lounge.

"This is James," she said, brushing her hand over her son's head. "And this is Evan."

Giving him a glance, the seven-year-old picked up his exercise book and hurried out to the kitchen, latching on to his guardian's trousers.

Martin slipped the towel over the hook on the end of the counter as his wife came through the lounge with the contractor.

"Martin, this is Mr. O'Dubhan."

The contractor stepped up into the kitchen and held out his hand. "Dr. Ellingham. Pleased to meet you."

Ready with a sharp retort should the man comment on his obvious disability, his arm hovered in mid-air for a barely-perceptible moment before he took his hand. "Yes."

He gently prised his charge's fingers from his leg and gestured towards the lounge. "Go back and finish your homework, Evan."

The child sidestepped the stranger, watching him warily as he passed by.

"Mm. Have a seat." Martin hurriedly gathered together the miniature cars, trucks, and train engines that his son had lined up on the end of the table, transferring them to the counter.

"A cup of coffee, Duane? Or tea?" Louisa asked as she filled the kettle with water.

"A cuppa, please." He pulled out a chair and took a seat before removing a writing pad and a pencil from his satchel. "I'd like to start by making a list of your wants and needs. Then I'll take a look around—see what's structurally feasible."

By the time the contractor had gathered the needed information and left the house that evening, it was past the boys' usual bedtimes.

The new sleeping accommodation for Evan meant a slight alteration to their usual routine. The bedtime story was read on the bottom bunk. Then, stopping to check out the adhesive, motion-activated night lights that Martin had fastened to the front of each of the steps, Evan eagerly climbed up to his bed.

Buddy wasn't as keen on the new sleeping arrangements. Martin snapped his fingers. "Go on, get up there," he said. The little dog put his feet up on the first step before backing away and sitting down on his haunches.

Evan patted his hand on the top step, calling to him. "Buddy, come! Come on, Buddy!"

The little terrier blinked up at the doctor and whined softly.

"Oh, for goodness' sake," he muttered before picking him up and depositing him next to the boy.

"I'll practice with him tomorrow, Dr. Ellig-am. He just gots ta learn how ta do it."

"Mm, yes."

He turned to leave and Evan called out, "Dr. Ellig-am, I didn't get my hug and kiss!"

Glancing at his watch, Martin said gruffly, "All right. Hurry up and get back down here."

Evan slid down the steps on his bottom, wrapped his arms around his guardian, and the requisite affections were exchanged. "G'night, Dr. Ellig-am."

"Good night, Evan."

Martin stopped at his son's cot and laid a hand on the sleeping toddler's head before leaving the room.

Louisa looked up from her novel when her husband walked past her on his way to the kitchen.

"Off to the land of Nod?"

He flipped on the tap and waited for the hot water to flow before washing the canine contaminants from his hands. "James is asleep. Evan's in bed."

After drying his hands, he joined her on the sofa. A soft sigh eased from his chest as his eyes drifted shut.

"Maybe you should go to bed, too. You look exhausted," she said, caressing his knee.

"I will in a minute."

"How was your day?"

"Stressful."

"Oh? Difficult patients?"

"No, not really." He sat quietly, and she returned her attention to her book.

"Ruth suggested that you and I go away together," he said offhandedly.

"Really?"

"Mm. I may have let more slip than I intended."

Louisa slid her bookmark into place and set the novel on the coffee table. "Let what slip?"

The creases in his forehead deepened. "I may have given her the impression that the gawps and inappropriate questions are beginning to rub me up the wrong way."

"Beginning to? Haven't they always?"

He screwed up his face. "That's not the point!" Snatching up a journal, he snapped it open. "It's not important."

"I'm sorry." She caressed his thigh. "Martin, I'd like to help if I can. Please."

He huffed out a breath and rubbed a palm across his eyes. "I'm just tired of this, Louisa. All of it."

"Well, then maybe Ruth has a point. Maybe we *should* get away for a while. Go somewhere quiet where no one knows us, somewhere secluded maybe. How does that sound, hmm?"

He stared absently for a moment before shaking his head. "We'd best not. Something could happen. Jeremy's here if something should go amiss."

"Well, we wouldn't have to go that far afield."

"It's just not a good idea."

Louisa got up and went to the kitchen, filling the tea kettle. "Would you like a cup?" she asked.

"No, thank you."

Setting it back on its base, she flipped the switch and returned to the step-down into the lounge. "Is there something else, Martin? Some other reason you don't want to go away? Is it the boys? Because if it's the boys, I'm sure we could work something out with Poppy."

"It's not the boys."

"Your patients, then?"

He shook his head. "No."

"Are you sure? Because they can always go down to Newquay for treatment."

"I'm aware of that, Louisa. The only genuinely sick patients I've treated recently have died. This village would get on just fine without me."

He gave her a sideways glance and flipped to the next page in his journal. "You have school, you know."

She wedged her hands into her armpits. "I realise that, but I can get away for a few days. Pippa owes me."

The kettle began to hiss, and she returned to the kitchen to make her tea. Coming back to the lounge, she set her cup down and nestled in against him. "Please give some thought to Ruth's suggestion, Martin."

His magazine dropped to his lap. "I *have* given it thought, Louisa! I don't want to have something happen when I'm off alone with you somewhere."

"What do you mean?"

"Fall, get sick, develop sepsis. There are any number of things that could go wrong. Things could go south in a hurry right now, and I don't know that you could deal with that."

He mentally berated himself when he looked down and saw her wounded expression. "Louisa, I didn't mean that the way you think. To feel responsible when something goes wrong is an experience I would never wish on you."

Her husband hadn't discussed his feelings after the recent deaths of Muriel Steele and Robbie Crandall. It was now clear that he hadn't shaken it off as easily as she'd thought.

"I see."

Moving closer, she pulled his good arm around her and they relaxed quietly together until the mantel clock chimed ten o'clock.

She tipped her head back. "We should go to bed, hmm?"

"Yes."

Chapter 22

Whether it was the new bed or just the fatigue that came with the sheer excitement of it all, Evan had slept soundly, nightmare-free, for two straight nights.

And aside from a few middle-of-the-night excursions into the nursery to assure himself that all was well, Martin had slept better, too. Therefore, he barely grimaced when his receptionist handed him Florence Dingley's patient notes Wednesday morning.

"What's her problem this time?" he asked.

"Don't know, Doc. She got all twitchy when I asked, so I figured I'd better let you handle her."

Air hissed from his nose as he yanked the notes out of the sleeve. "Send her in."

Morwenna left the room, and the old woman shuffled in a minute later.

Signing off on a repeat prescription, Martin slid the pad to the side before looking up. "What seems to be the trouble, Mrs. Dingley?" he asked.

"There doesn't always have to be trouble, does there?" she replied testily. "Maybe I just came for a check-up. Or a bit of advice."

"You were just in for a check-up, so I have to assume you're in need of advice, then."

"Something like that." She pushed the sleeves back on her slightly oversized lime green and hot pink jumper. "I need ta get tested."

The doctor's brow furrowed before a scowl set in on his face. "For Bartonellosis? You've acquired more cats, haven't you, Mrs. Dingley?"

"No! I got rid of 'em, just like you said. Those other tests are the ones I need." She tipped her head back and glared at him defiantly. "And if you're fixin' to haul me over the coals for *that*, I'll have Malcolm drive me over to Truro to get 'em done."

His eyebrows pulling down into a vee, the doctor's head listed to the side. "Malcolm *Raynor*?"

"Know any other Malcolm's around here?"

"Erm, no." He cleared his throat and turned quickly, reaching behind his desk before handing a sheet of paper across to her. "I'll need you to fill out this form."

She pulled her glasses from her handbag, balancing them on her nose, and scanned it over.

"I'm not answering these questions! It's none of your business!"

"Mrs. Dingley, your answers will help me to determine which tests I need to run. If you don't fill out the form, I'll have no choice but to run them all. Is that what you want?"

She gave him a black look, and his tone softened. "Your anonymity is guaranteed, and the information will be held in the strictest confidence."

He held out a biro, and she snatched it from his hand.

"I'll leave you to finish that up," he said. "I'll be back in a few minutes."

Leaving the room, he returned a short time later with a steaming cup of coffee. The now filled-out form had been shoved across his desk.

"You better keep that to yourself," Mrs. Dingley said as she removed her glasses and deposited them into her bag.

Martin sat down and scanned her answers. "I'll, erm ... need a urine sample before you leave," he said, reaching behind him for a container. "And Mr. Portman will need to draw some blood."

"It was Malcolm's idea," she said suddenly.

"I beg your pardon?"

"It was all Malcolm's idea. We were both at the animal centre over in St. Columb. Him with his pigeons, me with my cats. I took *his* birds—keep 'em in the pen behind my house. He took *my* cats."

"Oh, for heaven's sake," Martin grumbled. "How long have the two of you been ... erm, together?"

"Couple of weeks. That's on account of what you said, too."

"What *I* said?"

"You told Malcolm to find himself a human companion, didn't you?"

"Well ... yes! But I didn't mean it literally!" A throbbing set in behind his eyes, and he rubbed at them. Getting to his feet, he yanked the door open. "Morwenna! Tell Jeremy to come in here."

He limped back to his desk. "Mr. Portman will draw a sample of your blood. It'll be sent for testing over in Truro. The results should be back in a week to ten days."

He dropped into his chair, and his biro tapped against his desk. "Until then, you should use protection whenever you ... mm." Pulling in his chin, he quickly signed off on the form.

Jeremy finished up with Mrs. Dingley fifteen minutes later, and Morwenna watched her leave as she set the phone back down in its cradle. "Marigold Marley just cancelled, Doc!" she yelled through the open consulting room door. "You're done for the day!"

Martin grumbled to himself. "Total waste of my time."

The cold, dank days of winter had returned and, as was typical during periods of heavy rain, only the hardiest of souls, or those with a genuine medical concern, actually showed up for their scheduled appointments.

He pulled up his arm—just past eleven o'clock. He hissed out a breath and tossed Mrs. Dingley's file on to the corner of his desk before getting to his feet.

"Jeremy!" he called out. Pulling open drawers on his medical cabinet, he took a quick visual inventory.

The young man appeared in the doorway moments later. "Did you need me for something?"

"Mm. We're going to make a trip to the chemist. Get your mac."

"It's really nasty out there. I can go on my own. Just make me a list."

Martin shook his head as he jotted notes on to a pad of paper. "I want to get some fresh air. Is there anything you need to pick up while we're there?"

"Yeah, Poppy mentioned she's getting low on toothpaste," the aide said, scratching at his jaw. "She has sensitive teeth, and the over-the-counter stuff just doesn't—"

"Not for your girlfriend! For the surgery! Syringes? Gloves?"

"Ah. I'm okay on gloves and syringes for a while, but I should pick up some twenty-three gauge needles."

Martin added the item to his list and tore off the sheet of paper. Folding it, he slipped it into his shirt pocket before giving his assistant a jerk of his head. "Let's go."

They donned their rain gear, then dipped their heads into the wind as they walked down Roscarrock Hill. Martin tuned out Jeremy's nattering as he focused on maintaining his balance in the gusty winds pushing in off the Atlantic.

A shouted greeting between fishermen drew his attention away for a moment, and his right foot came down on a deposit of gravel on the road. His foot slipped forward before hitting the tarmac and coming to a jarring stop.

"Bloody—hell!" he blurted out. He pulled his leg up reflexively and clenched his jaw, waiting for the searing pain to ease.

Taking hold of his arm, Jeremy glanced around, looking for someplace to sit him down. Wedging himself under Martin's left arm, he helped him to the low roof over the building housing the public toilets.

Martin dropped heavily on to the slate tiles, and his aide pulled open the Velcro closure on his trousers. "What's going on, Martin? Did the bones give?" he asked.

"I don't think so."

The younger man crouched down, and his hands felt gingerly for any sign of refracturing. He looked up, rain splattering his face. "Any better now?"

The sharp, electric pain that had knocked the wind from him moments earlier had eased into an intense ache. "It's fine," Martin said. "We can go."

Jeremy's hands examined further before he refastened the closure and helped him to his feet. "I want to check you over when we get back to the surgery."

The doctor took a tentative step on the leg and shook his head. "No, that's not necessary. It's fi—"

"No arguments!"

The aide's fixed stare gave the doctor pause, and he pulled in his chin. "Yes."

Jeremy glanced over as they eased their way downhill. "You didn't have much to say. I take it you disapprove?"

Coming to a stop, Martin cocked his head at him. "Disapprove of what?"

"Me—proposing to Poppy!"

"Mm, sorry. I wasn't lis— Mm."

The young man pulled in a long breath. "Well, *do* you disapprove?"

"What about medical school? Have you ruled it out?"

"No, of course not! But being engaged doesn't obligate us to rush into a wedding three or four weeks from now."

Martin shot him a quizzical look and cleared his throat. "No. No, it doesn't."

They rounded the corner on to Church Street, and Jeremy pushed open the door to Mrs. Tishell's shop.

"Poppy's okay with waiting until I get settled into med school to get married, but I know the ambiguity of our relationship, as it stands now, makes her uneasy," the young man said. "I want her to know, in no uncertain terms, that I'm committed to her."

Martin limped past him and pulled the hood of his mac back.

The aide went on. "I want to propose, but obviously, I need to get her a ring. Can you recommend a jeweller?"

Unzipping his coat, the doctor reached into his pocket for his list. Sally Tishell leaned to the side, giving him a coy smile as he stepped up behind a woman with long, dark hair, waiting at the counter.

"I'm not the one to ask. I'd never set foot in a jewellery store before Louisa dragged me into one when we bought our wedding bands. I'd recommend you get her advice. I suspect she'd be happy to help you out."

The dark-haired woman gathered up her purchases and turned to Jeremy. "I hope you don't think me a busybody, but I couldn't help but overhear." She pulled a card from her handbag and passed it to the young man.

Martin studied the woman, struggling to place her.

"Oh, I should introduce myself. I'm Carrie Wilson." She held out her hand.

"Jeremy Portman. I'm Dr. Ellingham's assistant."

"Oh! And so young, too!"

Her handshake lingered one and a half seconds beyond what was comfortable, and Jeremy pulled back.

That ghastly woman with the dog! Martin thought. Poorly chosen words slipped from his mouth. "Gawd, *you've* put on weight!"

"Oh!" the chemist squeaked, raising her eyebrows.

Mrs. Wilson whirled on him. "I don't believe I was speaking to you." She turned back to Jeremy. "As I was saying, I'm Carrie Wilson. I used to own the Wilson Hotel. I sold it a little over a year ago and opened a jewellery boutique in Wadebridge."

"Ah." The aide studied the card. "What about engagement rings? Do you have a good assortment?"

"Well, it's not De Beers, of course. But people say my shop has a selection and sophistication you won't find anywhere else in Cornwall. Make an appointment, or just stop in sometime," she said. "I'd be happy to help you find what you're looking for."

She flicked her hair back over her shoulder. "It was nice to meet you, Dr. Portman." She gave Martin a dark look and brushed past him before hurrying out the door.

Sally's mouth quirked at Martin before she waved a hand. "I wouldn't worry, Dr. Ellingham. I'm sure it will all be forgotten—eventually."

He pulled in his chin. "I'm not *worried*. I just didn't know she was still around," he said, handing her his list.

"Oh, *yes*! She lives in that fancy new-build on the top of the hill. Her prescriptions have been signed by that Dr. Lippolis over in Wadebridge ever since the *incident* though."

She picked up a box of exam gloves and stood, fingers tapping against the side of it, as she gazed sympathetically at him. "It must have been *very* difficult for you." Shaking her head, she spat out softly, "The whispers and all the finger pointing. *I* never gave any credence to those rumours. Just codswallop, I kept saying."

Martin rolled his eyes and breathed out a heavy sigh. She set the gloves into a box on the counter and turned, rummaging around on a low shelf along the wall. Martin averted his eyes from her now-upturned bum and glanced over at his aide, scowling at the smirk on the young man's face.

A box of needles joined the gloves, and Mrs. Tishell clicked her tongue as her head wagged back and forth. "Yes, nothing more than codswallop. You were so unfairly implicated in that death, Dr. Ellingham. And *murder?* Whoever started that rumour deserves locking up, if you ask me! To sully your fine reputation that way!"

Jeremy's head swung around, his eyes wide. His questions, however, would have to wait as the bell on the door signalled the arrival of another customer.

Joe Penhale stepped in out of the rain. "Afternoon, Doc ... Jeremy. Fancy meeting you here. What brings you out on a day like this?"

"Supplies," Martin grumbled, avoiding eye contact lest he encourage further conversation.

"That makes sense. You bein' in the medical pro*fess*ion and all."

The doctor caught sight of the blood-spotted white bandage on the constable's hand. "What happened to you?" he asked.

"Dog bite. I was trying to apprehend a repeat offender—vagrancy. She didn't take kindly to my dog grasper." He put up his uninjured hand. "Completely humane and police-issued dog grasper, of course."

"Let me see it," Martin said, steeling himself for his uncontrollable visceral response.

"I don't actually have it on my person. I'd look a bit silly with something like that hanging from my belt, don't you think?"

"Not the noose, you idiot! Your hand!"

The man snapped his fingers and gave him a suddenly-enlightened grin. "No need, Doc. My police training included an intensive course in first aid, so I'm prepared to deal with all crisis situations. I've taken care of it."

The doctor grunted. "Just make sure you come to see me at the first sign of infection." Then eyeing the officer uncertainly, he added, "You'd better just come see me."

Penhale gave him a vacuous grin. "We're kindred spirits, eh, Doc? Both of us always on the job."

"Hmph." Turning back to the counter, Martin found the chemist gazing abstractedly at him. His palm slapped against the glass countertop. "Mrs. Tishell! My supplies!"

She shook her head and blinked. "Oh, yes. Right away, Doctor."

Jeremy covered a snicker with a forced cough, and Martin gave him a threatening look.

There was a loud metallic clatter as Joe hoisted up his duty belt, and his handcuffs fell to the floor. He leaned down, unfazed, and picked them up. "So, I understand an in-*ves*-tigation is underway."

"An investigation of what?" Martin asked.

"Well, of Louiser I s'pose you could say. I had a visit from a fellow from Children's Services this morning. Friendly chap. *Suspiciously* friendly in my opinion."

Martin pulled up his chin and peered down at him. "What was he wanting?"

"Just askin' questions. I understand you and Louiser have decided to take in Jim Hanley's boy."

"We've already taken him in, Penhale. We're adopting him."

"Oh, that's nice."

"What sort of questions were being asked?"

Joe gave Mrs. Tishell and Jeremy a sideways glance. "Perhaps this isn't the *appropriate* place to be talking about sensitive matters, Doc. If you know what I mean."

"Mm, yes. Stop by the surgery at five o'clock, Penhale. We can discuss it, and I'll dress that wound properly."

"Right you are, Do-*c*."

"Here you are, Dr. Ellingham," the chemist's voice lilted. "I believe that's everything."

Martin gave her a grunt, and Jeremy picked up the box.

They were halfway up Roscarrock Hill before the aide mustered the courage to enquire about the doctor's history with Carrie Wilson.

"So, this death Mrs. Tishell referred to. Did you like, I dunno, get a dosage wrong or something?"

Martin stopped and stared at the young man indignantly. "Absolutely not!" He screwed up his face. "I ran over her dog."

"Ouch!" the aide said.

"No, it died instantly. I doubt it felt anything."

"I meant, that could put a crimp in a relationship."

"We didn't *have* a relationship, Jeremy. She came to me with imagined symptoms, and I ran over her dog—that's it."

"So, this murder allegation.... Well, I know there's no love lost between you and man's best friend, but I have a difficult time seeing you deliberately committing vehicular homicide to do one in."

"Of course, I didn't. It got under the wheel of my car, I backed up, and it was ... squashed. I don't know what the woman expected me to do. I even wrapped the disgusting animal up before returning it to her."

"What? You mean like a gift?"

"Nooo! In a newspaper!"

"Oh, I'm beginning to get the picture. Still, how was this your fault? She shouldn't have been letting the dog run loose."

"Exactly! And when I informed her that it was her responsibility to properly dispose of the body, she—she took offense."

"I see. Hmm, I guess I'll give her a call about the ring."

"Well, in that case, *Doctor*, you'd better make your proper title clear straight away." He gave him a sideways glance. "If it were me, though, I'd steer clear of that woman."

Jeremy grunted, scrutinising his patient's gait as they crossed the slate terrace to the front door of the surgery. "Go through," he said, waving him towards the consulting room.

Martin's head snapped to the side, and the aide gave him a grin. "I've been waiting for an opportunity to say that." He pointed a finger. "I need to have a look at that leg."

"It's not necessary, Jeremy. It's fine now."

"We had an agreement, Martin. If I was going to be your assistant, I'd call the shots regarding your health."

Air hissed from the doctor's nose, and he cast an annoyed look the young man's way.

"Get up on the couch," Jeremy said as he pulled open his backpack and removed a thermometer.

The metal hardware on Martin's leg clanged against the table, and he grimaced, slapping a hand to his forehead when he was hit by the resultant ice pick headache.

"Well, how long has *that* been going on for?" the younger man asked.

"A few days. I intended to mention it to you before you left today. Do you have time to do that—that thing you do to stop it?"

He doubled over, groaning as the pain intensified, and Jeremy pressed his thumbs to the base of his skull.

"Hang in there, mate. It should ease up soon."

Martin's gasps for air slowed as he straightened. "Thank you."

"You're welcome. Let me check you over," the aide said, running a thermometer over his forehead. His brow furrowed. "Ninety-nine point seven. How long have you been running a fever?"

"I haven't seen a need to check it lately. And technically, that's not a fever, you know."

"Don't argue semantics with me, Martin. Any elevation in your temperature warrants watching."

The doctor screwed up his face. "I'm getting hungry. Are we almost done here?"

"No." The aide gave him a no-nonsense look. Then, leaning down, he pulled open the closure on his patient's left trouser leg. "This feels a bit warm to me."

"Check the other one. I think you'll find I'm just hot."

Jeremy tugged at the Velcro on the opposite leg. "Hmm, yes. Well, I want to keep a close eye on things. You could be developing an infection or coming down with something."

Martin gave him a sideways glance. "Or, I'm just hot. We just walked up that damn hill, Jeremy."

"Take off your shirt."

Removing his stethoscope from his pack, the aide inserted the ends into his ears.

"This is ridiculous," Martin grumbled, fumbling with his buttons.

"Oh, stop your whinging and breath in. And out—and in—and out." The stethoscope was moved from his chest to his back.

"Have you heard me cough once, Jeremy? You're not going to hear anything."

"Not if you keeping talking, I'm not! So, shush!" He shook his head. "Breath in—and out—and in—and out."

Levelling the head end of the table, the aide gestured. "Lie down and I'll see what I can do about those headaches."

Jeremy had just finished with the massage technique when Evan charged down the hall and rounded the corner into the room.

"What are you doing?" he asked, eyeing his guardian's bare torso.

"I'm annoying Dr. Ellingham," the young man said, giving the boy a wink. He handed Martin his shirt. "I'll let Mr. Christianson know that everything seemed to check out all right. But I want to monitor your temperature."

"You mean you gots ta annoy him some more?" The seven-year-old grasped on to the door latch, swinging himself back and forth.

"Something like that," the aide said, zipping his backpack shut. He tousled the child's hair and gave his boss a grin before heading out the door. "I'll see you in the morning," he called over his shoulder.

"Mm, yes." Martin peered down as he buttoned up his shirt. "We have your dog's class today, so I'll be picking you up after school."

"Yeah, I know. Do ya think that Collingsworth woman'll be surprised 'cause Buddy's learned his tricks so good?"

"So *well*, Evan. And you should refer to her as Miss Collingsworth."

"Why come?"

"Because it's appropriate."

"What does 'propriate mean?"

"It means she's never been married so her proper title is miss. And her last name is Collingsworth, therefore, it stands to reason that you should refer to her as Miss Collingsworth."

"Oh, I get it! It's like I call Old Doc, '*Old Doc*', 'cause he's old *and* he's a doc. So, it's 'propriate."

"Mm. That's right. It's *a*-ppropriate."

"But you don't call Miss Collingsworth, '*Miss Collingsworth*'. You call her"—he lowered his voice—*"that Collingsworth woman."*

"I don't call Chris Parsons, '*Old Doc*', either."

The boy screwed up the right side of his face. "Sometimes you're really hard ta understand, Dr. Ellig-am."

"Yes. Let's go eat lunch."

Louisa was settling James into the high chair when Martin and Evan came through under the stairs. She looked up and gave him a taut smile. "Hello."

"Hello. How was your morning?" he asked as his fingers stroked his son's head.

"Gawd, don't ask."

"Mummy, hungee!" the little boy said, trying in vain to reach the bowl of food sitting just out of reach on the table.

Louisa hurriedly shifted it to the high chair tray before kissing his head. "And what do you say?"

"Onkoo."

The toddler toys parked on top of the refrigerator rattled together as Martin pulled the door open to retrieve two of his shakes. "Did you know what's-her-name, that Wilson Hotel woman, still lives around here?"

"Everyone knows that, Martin. She has the most expensive home in the area." She eyed him suspiciously. "And why are you asking about Carrie Wilson?"

"I ran into her at the chemist today."

"Not literally, I hope."

His brow furrowed. "No."

"How is she?" she asked, giving her ponytail a flick. "Still dallying with your affections?"

His head shot up. *"What?"*

"Oh, Martin, the woman couldn't have been any more obvious about her interest in you."

He pulled in his chin and slapped two slices of bread down on his plate. "Don't be ridiculous."

Louisa set the seven-year-old's lunch in front of him before taking a seat across from her husband.

"I don't think it's ridiculous, Dr. Ellig-am," the boy said. "Lots of people think you're interesting. You know lots of stuff." He picked a carrot stick up from his plate and waved it at him before snapping off a bite. "I bet you know more about mannered bacteria than anybody else in the world."

Martin gave him a grunt. "It's all manner of bacteria, Evan. Not mannered bacteria."

"Oh. Well, maybe she's interested 'cause you know about all the manners of bacteria. Do you think, Dr. Ellig-am?"

He grunted.

Louisa batted at her fringe before attempting to divert the subject. "Erm, I understand from some of the teachers that there's been a man nosing about the village. Some investigator who works for Chil—" She noted their soon-to-be son's rapt attention. "Well, you know."

"It's part of the process, Louisa. I wouldn't worry about it."

"It's not *your* father they're asking about, Martin. So, don't tell me I shouldn't be worried."

She glanced over at the seven-year-old and forced a smile before again changing the topic of conversation. "Well, you and Dr. Ellingham take Buddy to the vet today, don't you?"

"Yeah. We're gettin' his condition monitored again." He laid his sandwich down and wiped his hands on his shirt front, looking up at his guardian. "Dr. Tressa thinks you're interesting, Dr. Ellig-am."

Louisa's ponytail flicked again. "Oh? What makes you think that, Evan?"

He shrugged his shoulders. "I dunno. She just gots that same I-think-you're-interesting look that you gots. And the lady at the chemist gots."

Her head tipped to the side as she turned to her husband. "Just how many more of these appointments will be necessary, Martin?"

Averting his eyes, he bit at his cheek. "That will depend on Buddy's progress."

"Well, lets hope he progresses quickly, then, hmm?" She got up from the table and began to clear away the dishes. Giving a nod to the seven-year-old, she said, "Evan, we better be getting back to the school."

"But I gots ta use the loo first."

"Well, hurry up, then. We're going to be late."

Taking a large bite from his sandwich, the boy dashed off towards the steps.

Martin gathered together an assortment of jars and was returning them to the refrigerator when a shriek cut through the air, startling James into tears. Evan raced through the lounge to his guardian, latching on to him.

Grimacing, the doctor clenched his teeth and braced himself against the wall.

"For goodness' sake, Evan! What's the matter?" Louisa asked as she tried to comfort her son.

The boy buried his face against Martin. "It's the black man!" his muffled voice said. He waved an arm blindly towards the lounge windows. "He's out there!"

Peeling his young charge away, the doctor limped into the adjoining room, peering out the window and up and down the hill. "There's no one out there, Evan. You must have been imagining it."

"Uh-uh! He was out there! Evan said. "Don't let him take me to the dead people, Dr. Ellig-am!"

Air hissed from Martin's nose as he exchanged concerned looks with his wife. Returning to the kitchen, he took a seat at the table, waving his charge to him. "Evan, your father's dead. He can't take you anywhere."

"It's not *him*, Dr. Ellig-am! It's Jim Reaper! *He's* gonna take me away!"

Louisa set James on the floor and crouched down next to the seven-year-old. "Evan, did you hear the big boys at school talking about The Grim Reaper a while back? At recess?"

He blinked back tears and shook his head. "That's not his name. It's *Jim* Reaper. If he gets you, he takes you to live with all the dead people."

"Is this the person in your nightmares? The black man?"

"Uh-huh. But now he's here—for *real*. He was standin' out there watching for me."

Martin hooked his arm around the child and pulled him on to his thigh. "Evan, The *Grim* Reaper is fictitious. He's not real. It's just a story. That was probably just someone walking by."

The boy cast an anxious glance towards the window. "Can you come with me to the loo, Dr. Ellig-am. I really gots ta pee."

"Yes," the doctor said with a sigh.

The high drama of the lunch hour seemed to have been forgotten by the time Martin picked Evan up from school that afternoon.

A smile spread across the child's face when he opened the rear door of the Lexus. "Hey, you remembered him this time!" he said, giggling as Buddy greeted him enthusiastically with licks to his face.

"Yes. Hurry up and get in. And don't forget to buckle your seat-belt."

"I know, Dr. Ellig-am. I'm not a little kid."

The seven-year-old chattered excitedly between Portwenn and Wadebridge. A new child had moved to the village, and Miss Soames had seated him next to Evan.

"His name's Colin and he gots ginger hair. And he's about this much bigger than me," he said, holding his hands about ten inches apart.

"Mm."

"And he likes whales. And he likes sharks, too! So, we're gonna start our own club. It's gonna be all about the animals that live in the ocean."

"Interesting."

"And Colin's favourite food is tuna! Isn't that funny, Dr. Ellig-am—that we both like tuna?"

Martin sighed and rubbed at his forehead. "Yes. Erm, don't you have reading you need to do before school tomorrow? Maybe you should get that done in the car."

"Nope. I don't gots *any* homework. So, we can just talk and talk and talk."

By the time he turned the Lexus into the carpark in front of the Wadebridge Veterinary Surgery, the doctor's head was pounding. "You go on ahead with the dog," he told his charge. "I'll be right in."

"Okay. Come on, Buddy!"

The door slammed shut, and Martin was left alone with the residual ringing in his ears. He closed his eyes, luxuriating in the silence for several minutes before pulling himself from the car and heading into the building.

A row of chairs, left behind from a group class, was positioned against the far wall, and he limped towards them.

"Dr. Ellingham!"

He turned at the sound of Tressa Brown's voice. "Mm, yes. Hello."

The woman stepped quickly to catch up to him. "I wanted to give you an update on our patient."

He ducked his head and continued across the room.

"Things looked a bit precarious the day after his fasciotomy. He developed an infection," she said as she walked alongside him. "But that appears to be in hand now, and the leg appears to be healing well. I sent him home yesterday, in fact. "

"Mm, good."

Air rushed from his lungs as he dropped into a chair.

She took a seat next to him, and he turned a bemused face to her.

"I want to thank you again for your help last week," she said. "Mr. Adwell was so distraught, the poor man."

He mumbled hollowly, "Understandable."

"And I shared your advice with Mrs. Adwell," she went on. "Did he come to see you?"

Air hissed from his nose. "Dr. Brown, I understand that patient confidentiality wouldn't be of primary importance in your practice. *My* patients, however, demand a degree of privacy. If you're concerned for Mr. Adwell's welfare, you need to discuss it with Mr. Adwell—or his wife."

She quickly looked away, and Martin felt the briefest pang of remorse for the sharpness of his words. He softened his tone. "I'm sorry. I'm not at liberty to say."

"No. I'm the one who should apologise," she said, putting a hand up. "I should have known better."

They sat quietly for a moment, watching as Barbara Collingsworth took Evan and Buddy through the steps of the down command, before she said with feigned nonchalance, "I actually find your honesty refreshing. Attractive, really."

Martin froze, only his eyes moving in a furtive glance towards the woman as his ears reddened. She got to her feet, and his cautious gaze shifted up to meet hers.

"Well, I have a couple of patients to look in on before closing up shop for the day," she said. "I enjoyed working with you last week. I learned a lot. And it was a very nice thing you did—helping to save the Adwell dog's leg."

"Mm. I'm glad it's a happy outcome, then."

"Me, too. See you next week."

"Yes." His head tipped to the side as bewilderment wrinkled his brow.

Chapter 23

Evan scrabbled up the steps to the surgery as Joe Penhale stared down at him imperiously from the terrace, his feet spread wide and his fists wedged on his hips.

"Stop right there," he said with mock seriousness. "You're going mighty fast, you know."

The boy's eyes grew round, and his hands worked nervously around Buddy's leash. "Tha—that's just 'cause I'm in a hurry."

"We're all in a hurry, aren't we—life's too short and all that? In accordance with the Road Traffic Act of 1991, I *should* issue you with a fixed penalty notice."

"But I'm not on the road. And I'm not traffic. I'm just a kid."

"Well, in that case, I guess I can let it go ... *this* time. But I'll be watching you," the constable said, his first and second fingers drawing an imaginary line between his eyes and the boy.

Buddy bounced around on his hind legs, tugging at the leash, and the seven-year-old slowly sidestepped the officer before racing towards the back of the house.

"Was that really necessary, Penhale?" Martin asked as he came up the ramp to the terrace.

"Not necessary, *per se*. Just trying to instil a healthy respect for the law into him before he turns to a life of crime, Doc."

"He's seven!"

Joe shrugged. "Just havin' some fun, really— trying to encourage a bit of community engagemen-*t*."

"It wasn't very effective, was it? He just beat a hasty retreat into the house." He glanced at his watch. "You're early."

"Technically speaking ... no, I'm not. I've been conducting a surveillance operation."

"On the steps of my surgery?"

"The alert came across my scanner this afternoon. A gang of druggies has been breaking into medical facilities and chemists across Devon, stealing drugs and selling 'em on the street. They appear to be on the move, heading west from Exeter. The boys in Launceston are on the *qui vive* as we spea-*k*."

"I still don't understand why you're loitering on my front terrace—if they haven't been seen in Launceston yet."

"I need to familiarise myself with the normal foot and motor traffic up and down this hill—be better able to identify the nef-*arious* individuals if they try to move their operation into the village."

Martin grunted, dipping his head as the rain began to fall heavily again. "Very wise. Come in, and I'll check your wound."

Joe narrowed his eyes and took a final look up and down the hill before following the doctor into the house.

When Martin ducked under the stairs after tending to the constable's injured hand, Louisa was putting dinner on the table.

She gave him a tense smile. "We're just about ready to eat."

"Mm, yes." He went to the refrigerator for one of his shakes and leaned back against the counter, popping the top. "How was your day?"

She groaned. "It didn't get any better this afternoon."

"More sick children?"

"No. Well, yes, there were. But I expected that. What I *didn't* expect was to discover that while I was at home having lunch with you, that man from Children's Services was at the school, gathering information from *my* teachers!"

She set a pot of pasta on the table and pulled off the oven gloves, turning and slapping them down next to her husband. "Can they do that? Just come into someone's place of work and start asking personal questions?"

"Evidently, they can."

She gave him a quizzical look. "And just how would you know that?"

"Louisa, why did you ask me in the first place if you didn't think I'd have the answer?" A breath hissed from his nose. "I just had a conversation with PC Penhale. I asked him the same question."

"Oh."

"Mm. As long as they don't disrupt the work environment, they're free to ferret around all they like."

"Well, up until today, most of the teachers at Portwenn Primary never brought up the fact that my father was ... you know."

"A thief?"

"Thank you, Martin. I was going to say *away*."

"Mm, yes."

She brushed roughly at her forehead. "Just when I thought this village might be ready to let that go, the whole thing had to be resurrected."

Martin glanced towards the two little boys playing in the lounge as he thought over what he'd learned from the constable minutes earlier. He would need to wait for a more appropriate time to share that information with his wife.

He busied himself in his consulting room after dinner, fine tuning the workings of Ruth's grandfather clock. It was shortly after seven o'clock when there was a soft tapping at his open consulting room door.

"What is it, Evan?" he said when he looked up to see the boy peering around the door frame.

"Are you too busy for talkin' about snakes?"

He pushed the tray containing the clock parts forward and waved the boy in.

"What's your question," Martin asked as he approached.

Evan set a book down on the desk, flipped it open, and tapped a finger sharply against the exposed pages.

"*This* says snakes eat rodents."

Martin peered down at the picture of a boa constrictor, the first six inches of it made bulbous by a recently ingested rat.

"Mm, yes," he said, knowing instantly the conversation could be going down a rocky path.

"And mouses are rodents."

"Yes. Yes, they are."

"Harry's a mouse."

"Yes, I believe that's what you said."

"So, what I wanna know is, what kind'a snake does Mr. Townsend got at his house?"

"I have no idea, Evan. You'd have to ask Mr. Townsend. But is that really what you're wanting to know?"

"Yeah. 'Cause if he gots a kind'a snake that *doesn't* eat rodents, then I don't hafta ask my other question." He picked at his fingers. "And I don't wanna hafta ask my other question."

Martin tugged at an ear and sighed. "I'm afraid that almost all snakes do eat rodents, Evan. And I'm sorry, but I suspect Mr. Townsend's snake did likely eat Henry."

"Harry, Dr. Ellig-am." The seven-year-old's elbows landed on the desktop with a thud, and his head dropped into his hands.

Squirming in his seat, Martin patted the boy's back. "It's sad, I know. But that's the way that nature works. The bigger or more powerful creatures eat the smaller, weaker creatures. In most cases, anyway.

"There are exceptions, obviously. People—well, some people—eat beef. Beef cattle weigh much more than a human does. But we've become more powerful than even the largest animal because we've acquired tools and weapons."

Evan turned a teary face to his guardian. "I know that. But Harry *just* wanted someplace warm to live ... and for somebody to love him. And instead, Miss Soames sent him away. And she didn't even try to send him to a *nice* place. She didn't care what was gonna happen to him 'cause she didn't like him. *That's* what makes me sad."

Martin stared blankly at him for a moment before he nodded his head. "I see. Well, I think I can safely say that it didn't hurt Harry's feelings when Miss Soames didn't want him.

"And it didn't hurt Harry when she sent—when she sent him away to live with a snake." He cleared his throat. "Well, strictly speaking, it did, because in all likelihood he died. But animals don't have the same sense of death that people do. They don't think about it."

"But are you sure it didn't hurt his feelings?"

"Mm, I'm sure."

The boy wiped at his eyes. "Is it like when Potato catches rabbits?"

"Erm, yes, I suppose it is. An animal like Potato is a carnivore, or meat eater. That meat has to come from somewhere, and in Potato's case, it's the rabbits in Miss Wilcox's garden."

"You mean Miss Babcock's?"

"Mm."

"And for Mr. Townsend's snake, it's Harry?"

"That's right."

Martin studied the boy's face. "Did you find that useful?"

His brow furrowing, Evan finally nodded, and a faint smile crept on to his face. "I still feel *kind'a* sad 'cause Harry was really cute. But I feel better 'cause I know it didn't hurt his feelings, and it didn't bother him ta get eaten by a snake."

"Good."

Small feet pattered into the room, and Martin slipped an arm guardedly over the fixator in his thigh before his son flopped on to his lap. "Hello, James," he said softly.

The boy looked up, wrinkling his nose and giving him a grin. "Hi, Daddy."

"What's this for, Dr. Ellig-am?" Evan asked, tapping his finger against an instrument lying on the doctor's desk.

"That's called an ophthalmoscope. I use it to see into a patient's eyeball."

"Wow, that's like Superman!"

Martin stared blankly and Evan clarified, "You know—like how he can see through walls and stuff."

"Mm. You can't see through the walls, Evan." The doctor picked his son up and set him on his lap. "Give it to me. I'll show you how it works."

Evan slid it across the desk and Martin picked it up. "Now look at me."

The boy tipped his head back, and his guardian leaned forward to peer into his right eye.

"Can ya tell what word I'm thinkin' of?"

"I'm sorry?" Martin said, pulling back.

"I was thinkin' of a word really hard. Could ya see it?"

"I can't see into your brain, Evan," the doctor said, screwing up his face. "Just into your eyeball." He handed him the instrument. "Here, you examine James," he said, setting his son on the floor.

The older boy crouched down to the toddler's eye level, and his guardian held the younger boy's head still.

"Put the scope up close to your eye—nope, against your face. That's it. And make sure you're looking through the eyepiece." He took hold of the ophthalmoscope, shifting it down a bit. Then, he positioned the seven-year-old's head so that he was nearly touching the toddler.

"Wow! There's a bunch of red squiggly lines in there!"

"Mm. Those are blood vessels."

James pushed the older boy away and grabbed on to the instrument. "Dems do it!"

Evan pulled it back. "James, you're too little to do it. You might break it."

Letting out a wail, the toddler stomped his feet. "Dems *do* it, Daddy!"

"Shh, shh, shh, shh, shh." Martin wiggled his fingers. "Give it to me, Evan. Then come and stand by me. I'll help James."

He pulled his son back on to his lap and repeated the same procedure between the two boys, this time in reverse.

James's forehead banged into the older child's with a soft thud, and Evan pulled back. "Ow!" he said, rubbing at the now-tender spot.

Martin repositioned the instrument. "Let's try again."

No bruises were inflicted on the second try. However, each time the doctor got the scope properly positioned, his son squinted one eye and raised up to peer over the top of it.

"I'm not sure you're grasping the concept, James."

But, when one is eighteen months old, grasping the concept pales in comparison to the sheer thrill of imitation. The toddler turned and gave his father a triumphant grin. "Dems do it!" he said, clapping his hands together.

His father's head tipped to the side. "Well, sort of."

There was a movement in the doorway, and Martin looked up to see his wife watching.

A wisp of a smile crossed her face when his gaze met hers. "I hate to put a stop to your play, but it's getting late."

He gave her a scowl. "We weren't *playing,* Louisa. I was demonstrating how an ophthalmoscope is used."

"*Huh,*" Evan grunted. "It *felt* like we were playing, Dr. Ellig-am."

"Yes," Martin said, tugging at a reddening ear.

She held out her hand. "Come on, James—Evan. You can have a snack before brushing your teeth."

Martin waited as the two boys followed after his wife, and then he got up to pack his scope away in its box. He turned to clean up his clock repair operation, and his attention was drawn to the kaleidoscope on the dresser behind his desk.

He lifted it from its brass stand and let his fingers play along the glossy surface. The tan colour in the polished, burled wood swirled into the rich brown background like just-poured cream into coffee.

Sitting back down, he put the instrument to his eye. The designs created were crisp and brilliant. He watched as the seemingly endless variations slipped smoothly in the oil, from one to the next. Auntie Joan's kaleidoscope had been crude by comparison, and she would have taken great pride in being the owner of such a work of art.

He hesitated before pulling open a drawer on his desk, revealing the box of letters he had stashed away weeks before. Letters he had written to her in some of his most lonely and desperate days as a young boy. His fingers grazed the lid before he slid the drawer back shut, leaving the letters untouched.

He had just finished tidying away the clock parts when a scream set his heart racing. Limping towards the stairs, he heard the desperate pleas of his young charge and his wife trying in vain to soothe him.

"What's going on?" he asked when he reached the landing. Evan released his grip on Louisa and ran to him, pulling at his clothes as he tried to climb into his arms.

Louisa lifted the boy, and Martin leaned back against the wall before allowing him to latch on around his neck.

"I'll go see to James," she said before hurrying off to her whimpering son.

"All right, all right. Calm down, Evan, and tell me what's going on," Martin said.

"He was out there again, Dr. Ellig-am! The black man was out there again!"

A hiss of air eased from the doctor's nose. "We talked about this, Evan. There *is* no such thing as The Grim Reaper."

"There is so, 'cause I saw him! He was standing on the road, lookin' in the window. I saw him from your room."

"I'll go take a look around. But it was probably just someone walking by." He groaned as he leaned forward and let the boy slide to the floor.

"No! He might get you, Dr. Ellig-am! Then he'll take you where all the dead people are!"

"I'll—I'll just look around from inside the house, then."

He limped back downstairs, peering out the consulting room windows and then the lounge windows, before deeming the residents of the home safe from anyone with sinister motives.

When he returned to the landing, James had fallen back to sleep, and Louisa had managed to get Evan into bed.

"Did ya see him?" The seven-year-old whispered as he peered over the side of the bed.

"The street was empty, Evan. As I said, it was probably just someone walking by."

He shook his head vigorously. "I *saw* him, Dr. Ellig-am. And he wasn't walking. He was standin' there looking in the window."

"Evan, sometimes our brains can play tricks on us. It's getting late, so I think you should—"

"I think Dr. Ellingham is going to suggest that you try to think about your new friend at school," Louisa interjected. "Maybe he could come over for a playdate ... or a sleepover sometime! That would be fun, wouldn't it?"

The child huffed out a breath. "Yeah. But my brain's *not* playing any tricks." He flopped back and pulled the blankets up over his head.

Louisa lifted Buddy on to the top bunk. "How 'bout we leave the light on in our room so it's not so dark? We'll turn it off when we come up to bed."

"'Kay," came his hesitant, muffled reply. "G'night."

"Goodnight, Evan."

Louisa busied herself in the kitchen filling the tea kettle when they came back downstairs.

Getting himself a glass of water, Martin walked to the lounge window, staring out at the inky harbour. This newest development with his young charge was worrisome. The nightmares were understandable. But what had to be called hallucinations during the child's waking hours could not be explained away as easily. This was a far more concerning issue.

Louisa took a seat on the couch, setting her cup of tea on the coffee table. "Come and sit down, Martin."

"Mm, yes."

He dropped down next to her, and she studied his face. "Are you worried this could be a bad sign?"

"I thought we were making progress. I don't know how to handle this."

Louisa moved up against him and took hold of his hand. "*You* don't have to handle it. We're Evan and James's parents—*together*. And we have Dr. Peterson. Maybe you should call her tomorrow."

He grunted. "We were just over to see her yesterday. She said things were going well and that he seemed to be adjusting to his more secure environment. What's happened? Did something happen at school?"

"*No*. Not that I'm aware of anyway." She slid closer, and her hand caressed his thigh. "Look, I know you're worried. But this is probably just a phase. Children Evan's age have very active imaginations, and they're still learning to separate fantasy from reality."

"Mm." His hand worked over his knee. "PC Penhale stopped by today. He had some news regarding the adoption investigation."

"Oh?"

"Do you, erm, remember that smarmy fellow who was causing trouble for me a couple of years ago—that," his lip curled, "doctor's friend fellow, Garwin something-or-other?"

She turned a crestfallen gaze to him. "Yes. Why do you ask?"

"Well ... it seems he's no longer working under the direction of the NHS. When they made their recent restructuring changes, his position was eliminated. He was hired by Children's Services—to investigate pending adoptions."

"Oh, *gawwd,* Martin," she groaned. "Can't we catch a break? He's going to be digging up every bit of dirt on you that he can find!"

"Mm, yes. But, erm ... I'm afraid there's something else you should know." As he looked at her anxious face, a lump worked its way up his throat. "It's not your father he's been asking about. It's you."

"Me?"

"Yes. It seems there may have been some talk around the village about the occasion—occasions when you've left."

"Left?"

"Yes. Left, erm ... me."

"But that's in the past! And it's no one's business but our own."

Martin struggled to put together the words his wife needed to hear—the words that could spare her hurt. "Evan's mother rejected him—left him. They're concerned that if—well, about the effect it could have on Evan should it happen again."

"I would never go off and leave a child, Martin! I never went off and left James!"

"No. No, you didn't. But ..."

"But what?"

He pressed his fingers to his eyes. "The concern is that if you were to ever leave again, Evan would either be taken from me, or feel rejected by you—rejected by a second mother."

"Oh, Martin!"

"You're a wonderful mother, Louisa. We just need to make it clear that neither of us would ever do anything to harm Evan in any way."

She sank back in against him, and he wrapped his arm around her shoulders.

"Ugh, I can't think of a worse person to have investigating our case, can you?" she said softly.

"Mm, possibly."

"Who?"

"My mother." She tipped her head back, looking at him uncertainly, and the slightest suggestion of a smile on his face eased her tension. "Well, that's something to be grateful for, then."

"Yes."

He kissed her before pulling back. "Erm, there's something I've been needing to discuss with you."

"Oh, dear."

"You needn't worry. Dr. Newell just feels it necessary that I pin down exactly what it is that you need me to change—for you to be happy."

"I *am* happy, Martin."

"Well, in the broadest sense of the word, possibly."

She sat up, furrowing her brow at him. "What is it that you want to know?"

"Well, it's difficult to say because I'm not completely clear on this myself. I need to change; I understand that. But there are certain things about myself that I can't or shouldn't change."

"Such as?"

He huffed out a breath. "How important is it to you that people like me?"

She pulled in her chin. "Well, people do like you, Martin."

"Some, yes. But there are others who don't—the people in this village, my peers, your mother, *my* moth—"

"Your peers like you!"

"Mm, some."

"Martin, when you were in hospital, everyone was so concerned about how you—"

"Yes, because they respect my previous surgical skills. But we're getting off the subject. I believe Dr. Newell is asking us to discuss this so that I'm clear about what it is you want me to change—if you're to be happy. And that you're clear on what I *can* change without feeling as if I've compromised my principles or that it's all pretence."

"Martin, as I said, I *am* happy. There was a time when I did wish you were different. But I don't feel that way now."

"Really?"

"Mm-hmm. To be honest, I feel a bit smug at times that I'm the only woman clever enough to see beyond your rather unique and perhaps slightly difficult personality to the very fine man that you are."

She tipped back and gave him the smile that she reserved for him. "I quite like that, really. It's like I have a little secret. Everyone thinks I'm eating broccoli when in fact it's really a chocolate digestive in disguise."

"You do realise that broccoli is far better for you than a digestive, don't you?"

"You're overthinking it, Martin." She screwed up her mouth. "Or maybe it wasn't the best analogy ... considering."

His eyes rolled to the side. "Are you saying there's *nothing* you want me to change?"

"*Well* ... I appreciate your honesty, I really do. But sometimes you could be just a *little* less honest. Maybe?"

He shook his head. "That would be on my list of things I can't change."

"*Oh?*" she said, her eyebrows lifting. "You have *another* list?"

"Mm. What I feel are positive characteristics—things I'm ur ing to change."

"Oh, good! Good! Yes, that's good." Her fingers tapped together. "Well, you could try to be more, I don't know, considerate with your honesty."

He stared absently at the floor for a moment. "No, straight and to the point is best. It's been my experience that most people won't hear what they need to hear, otherwise."

He worked his thumb into his palm. "We don't seem to be getting anywhere. Perhaps we should refer back to the crap list."

She wedged her fists under her arms. "If it were up to me, we'd burn that bloody list, Martin. You don't need to change who you are for me.

"Maybe it's maturity. Maybe it was the experience of almost losing you, but those things that used to annoy me just aren't as important anymore."

"I see. But they do still annoy you?"

She bit at her lip. "Well of course, at times. But I can usually overlook it."

"Because you do things that annoy me, too?"

"Erm, yes. Yes, I suppose I do," she said, pulling in her chin.

"Good. We annoy each other, then."

"Yes, Martin. We annoy each other. I s'pose all couples do, don't they?"

"Mm."

She nestled in against him, and they sat in silence for several minutes before she said, "I would really like to see you happy."

"I'm happy."

"It might be more accurate to say that you're happ*ier*. I still see that sad little boy in you quite often."

"Mm, I'm sorry," he said, brushing a bit of lint from his trousers.

"You're working through it, Martin. Dr. Newell's helped you a lot, but the sad little boy might always be there to some degree."

Glancing at his pensive face, she reached up to undo the top buttons on his shirt. "You know, all this talking has you looking a bit like a chocolate digestive."

She smiled at his look of bewilderment before leaning over to coo into his ear. "And I'm feeling quite peckish."

"I see," he said, swallowing hard. "I'll just lock up, then."

She kissed him, and he watched as she swayed away. Then, setting his empty water glass on the counter, he flipped the latch on the back door before turning out the light and crossing the lounge.

As he passed the window, a movement caught his eye. He peered out at the road, and his heart skipped a beat as a figure, clad in a black, hooded mackintosh stared back at him.

Standing motionless for several seconds, he forced himself towards the front door. He stepped out on to the terrace as the shadowy form moved quickly down the hill. "Hey, you!" he called out.

Fettered by his injuries, he could only watch as the figure disappeared quickly into the mist.

Don't miss out!

Click the button below and you can sign up to receive emails whenever Kris Morris publishes a new book. There's no charge and no obligation.

https://books2read.com/r/B-A-PAJD-IKUQ

Also by Kris Morris

Battling Demons

Battling Demons

Fractured

Fragile

Headway

Insights

A Cornwall Christmas

Mis-Perceptions

Interactions

About the Author

Kris Morris was born and raised in a small Iowa town. She spent her childhood barely tolerating school, hand rearing orphaned animals, and squirrel taming. At Iowa State University she studied elementary education. But after discovering a loathing for traditional pedagogy and a love for a certain tall, handsome, Upstate New Yorker, she abandoned the academic life to marry, raise two sons, and become an unconventional piano teacher. When she's not writing, Kris builds boats and marimbas with her husband, who she has captivated for thirty years with her delightful personality, quick wit, and culinary masterpieces. They now reside in Iowa and have replaced their sons with ducks.